Doctor's Secret Match

Sharon Woods

*For Helen and all the memories of our time with your AF.
You're such a strong woman and won't let it get in your way.
I admire and love you. S xo*

Chapter 1

ADRIAN

I'M PARKED IN THE middle of the road after driving for hours, leaving my old life behind. It's a chilly Sunday afternoon, and I find myself under attack from an aggressive bunch of turkeys.

They're strutting across the road, completely unfazed by my presence, gobbling like they own the place. Looking straight at me, they stop right in front of the *Welcome to Pulse Point* sign. I sit in my car, trying to make sense of how ridiculous this is, questioning whether I should get the hell out of the road or try to scare them off. But there are too many to count, and one even starts pecking at my bumper.

No way am I going to sit here any longer and wait. The turkeys need to move so I can drive. This is me taking control and facing whatever comes next head-on.

I push the door open and step outside, the cold air hitting my face. I don't move at first, even as I stand there, staring them down. Just as I start to wonder how to handle this crazy situation, wings flap hard beside me and a blur of feathers flashes past.

"What the—" My pulse rises, and I turn just in time to see the damn thing hopping onto the driver's seat. I'm about to close the door, but it's too late… It's already made itself at home. And of course, I'm driving a Mercedes-Benz with doors that open like wings. *Fucking great.*

My hands rest on my hips as I switch my gaze between the turkey in my car and the others edging closer. If I lock the turkey in there, it's sure to make a mess, but if I leave the door open, I could end up with all his friends inside.

Waving my arms, I lunge forward. "Go on, move!" I shout, but the turkey in the driver's seat doesn't budge. Of course, I expected that to work… at least a little. But the damn bird just stares at me like I'm the idiot. As a last-ditch effort, I let out a weak gobble… Don't ask me why. The other turkeys respond with even louder gobbles and march toward me. A groan slips out of me as frustration bubbles to the surface. *This is absolutely absurd.*

My mind races through the possibilities. What the hell am I supposed to do? I press my palms against my temples, trying to think clearly over the gobbles.

Fucking hell.

I'm tired, cranky, and desperately want to sit down with a drink after an incredibly long day. Most of my stuff is in storage, but everything that actually matters is crammed into that car, and if that turkey makes a mess, I'll have nothing left.

Pulling out my phone, I check for service… Nothing. Not that I even know who I'd call. Animal control? AAA? Maybe Isaac, my friend, just so someone can laugh at this with me. I can't even Google *how to remove a turkey from a Mercedes.*

What the fuck is wrong with this place?

I shove my phone back into my pocket just as the sound of an engine revs. Hope fills me as a blue Toyota Corolla pulls over and out jumps a woman wearing a blue New York Yankees hat, matching leggings, and a fitted tank top.

Perhaps she's from around here. Which means she's probably dealt with turkey standoffs before. Maybe things are about to get better.

"Looks like you've got yourself a problem here." She glances at the turkeys.

A smartass. Great.

"You think?" I cross my arms.

She bursts out laughing, and for a second, my shoulders drop, the tension in my neck easing against my will. It's not funny, but her laugh is so damn infectious that even I can't help but crack a smile. Maybe the problem lies with my car. Perhaps they can sense I'm not a local.

"Do you know how to get rid of them?" I point to the one in my car.

"What kind of car is this?" she asks, raising an eyebrow, confusion flickering across her face.

Is she serious? It's a Mercedes-Benz SLS AMG... How does she not know that? I guess it's a sign of just how far I am from New York.

"A Mercedes." I glance at my sleek, high-tech car that's fetching compliments everywhere I go. But right now, I'm seriously regretting it. It's not built for these situations. I really wish I had something that I have zero pride in protecting instead.

"This one right here?" She points to the turkey in my car. "He's the king of the flock." She doesn't hesitate, her tone matter-of-fact. "You need to nudge him away for the rest to follow."

Nudge him? Right. I doubt it's that simple. He looks like he'll peck my face off.

I raise an eyebrow, wondering how she knows that, but it makes sense. The big guy's puffed up, while the others keep their distance, waiting for him to make the first move.

As I lock eyes with her, something sparks: a challenge in her gaze that draws me in and dares me not to back down. A smile lingers on her lips, as if the entire situation is a big joke to her. My attention drops to her athletic build, and for a split second, I wonder how she finds this so amusing while I'm stuck in this nightmare. I shake my head and draw my focus back to the turkey in the front seat, now preening its feathers like it's got all the time in the world. The rest of the flock stands by, watching, as if they're waiting for some kind of signal to move.

If that signal is *all aboard!* I'm screwed.

If it's *attack the new guy*, I'm really fucking screwed.

Still, I square my shoulders. I didn't pack up my entire life and move to a new town just to be outsmarted by a fucking turkey.

So, if the plan is to nudge him, then fine... I'm going in.

"Okay, so how do we get him and the rest to go? What do I need to do to make him leave?"

She bends into her car, and my eyes involuntarily glance down at her ass before I force myself to look away.

"Sorry, Russell, this is all I have today." She pulls something out of her car.

I snort. "The turkey has a fucking name?"

"Yeah, Russell's definitely the star around here."

"You'd be better off cooking him." As if he hears my words, Russell waddles out of my car and right up to her, flashing me a look that says he's more confident than I am... *Great*.

With a deliberate move, she tosses something to him, and he happily pecks at it before she dusts off her hands, a satisfied smile spreading across her face as the other turkeys scatter off the road. "I'm assuming you're heading into town?"

"Yeah."

"Get in quick!" she yells, hopping back into her car. I hesitate for a moment, glancing at the feathers scattered everywhere, and a strong, musky odor hanging in the air. With no time to clean my seat, I ignore it, grumbling under my breath as I jump back in, quickly slamming the door behind me.

She takes off, her car zipping down the road, and I follow, focusing on the way the turkeys disappear in the rearview mirror. Relieved to leave them behind, I lose sight of the Corolla but keep my attention on the directions I need to get to Keith's, my dad's best friend's, place.

I cruise through town, playing "More Than A Feeling," my father's favorite song, which brings me comfort, turning it up as I take in the wide sidewalks, the vibrant storefronts, and the bare trees lining the road with their autumn leaves falling. A few small businesses catch my eye… like an old-fashioned bakery with a hand-painted sign and a cozy café with tables spilling out onto the sidewalk. There are trucks and SUVs here, blending seamlessly with the charm of the town. Which makes me feel out of place.

Pulling into a long driveway, my mouth opens at the sight of Keith's white weatherboard house with its green tile roof. It looks like paradise compared to what I've left behind. It's surrounded by lush trees, and a big fountain in the front garden with flowers around it. You don't get that kind of welcome at a New York condo.

After I park, turn off the engine, and step out, I can't even be bothered to be concerned about the mess from the turkey or even gathering my bags because the front door swings open. All I want to do is say hello.

As I approach, a friendly smile greets me. It's a familiar face... with gray hair, black-rimmed glasses, and a gray beard. Something tightens in my chest. I hadn't realized how much I missed seeing someone who actually knows me.

"Adrian, so nice to see you. It's been too long." Keith wraps his arms around me. At first, I'm stiff with surprise, but as his warmth seeps in, I settle into the embrace. My muscles relax, and I return the hug with a firm grip. The last time I saw him was at my dad's funeral—a moment that now feels like a lifetime ago. When it's only been a year.

I step out of the hug and roll my shoulders, trying to release the stress of the last few weeks. Pretend I'm just tired from the road and not everything else.

"How was your drive?" Keith looks at me with fatherly concern.

"Long." I meet his gaze for a second, then look away, forcing a shrug. Because *long* is easier than *I don't know what the fuck I'm doing.*

"Where's all your stuff?" He gestures toward the trunk of my car.

"I left it in the car."

"Let's go grab it." He starts down the path, and I follow. He's acting like this is just another normal day, but I'm bracing for the comment of *is that it?*

I open the trunk and pull out a couple of cases and bags.

Keith's brow creases. "Where'd the rest of your stuff go?"

"In storage for now." *So is my old life.* I follow him back to the house and into my new life. "When I find a place here, I'll have it all moved."

"Good idea. There are a few places up for sale. I'll happily take you to check them out when you're ready."

"I'm in no rush. I just want to get settled here and work."

The heaviness of my past still eats at me.

"Of course. Just let me know when you're ready. Meanwhile, it'll be good having someone around." He pats me on the shoulder.

It hits me—the raw vulnerability in his words. He lost his wife, Sage, a few months before my dad passed, and I know that pain of loneliness all too well... being an only child and losing both my parents.

When he called one day to check in on me, I told him I'd lost my job. He listened quietly as I explained what happened, and then he mentioned his general practice was expanding and he was hiring. "You should come work for me," he said, almost casually. But I remember the way he paused, waiting for my answer, and how his voice cracked just slightly with relief when I said yes... as if he'd been hoping I'd ask for help but knew I never would.

I do have a couple of friends, but in terms of family, he's it. My father met him back in college. When I realized my reputation was in ruins after being dismissed for failing to follow orders, the idea of working at another big-city hospital made my stomach churn. I wanted a change, and his offer felt like a lifeline, a chance to start over.

We head into his house in silence; the only sounds are our footsteps on the hardwood floors. The place smells of coffee and clean linen.

I've never been here before. There was always an invitation, but I had excuses. Work or timing. I didn't think my dad or Sage would go so soon. Now it feels like I've arrived too late.

Keith leads me down a short hallway, then into a bedroom. He drops the bags on the floor with a grunt. I take a look around the bedroom, which has wooden floors and matching furniture. A gray rug sits beneath a bed with green and white sheets, and artwork brightens the wall.

His house is far bigger than I expected. The room is spacious, filled with light streaming from the large open windows. Keith points out the features, like the television and Wi-Fi.

His pride shines through as he continues his tour of the house. Wooden accents carry throughout, with subtle reminders of his wife scattered around the place.

Photos of the two of them laughing, hiking, and dancing. Little trinkets line the shelves. The living room has a fireplace, a gray sofa, and a coffee table piled with their books. It's like she's still here, just in another room.

"Do you want a drink?" he asks as he goes into the kitchen.

"I'd love one." I follow him.

My heart jumps as I notice a community newspaper that's open on the counter. I can't help myself and read the first two lines before Keith snatches it away. Bold letters scream: **New Doctor Due to Arrive in Town After Being Professionally Dismissed in New York City.**

"They make it sound worse than it was," I start as my stomach sinks, but the words come out weaker than I'd like.

"Don't read that bullshit." Flailing his hand, he gestures for me to dismiss the article.

I nod, though it still stings to see. It was to save someone's life, but the board didn't care about my motives... They only saw the breach of protocol.

Keith hands me a beer, and I take it without a word. He lifts his bottle, and I tap mine against it, the clink cutting through the silence. I take a long swig, letting the bitterness settle.

"To new beginnings," I murmur.

He discards the newspaper into the trash, and for a moment, I'm grateful for his distraction. "Oh, before I forget, there's a welcome party next week. The community wants to introduce you." He hesitates before adding, "I think it'll be good to counter the bad publicity. Show your face."

My gaze shifts from the trash back to him. "I don't think that's what they want."

With his expression serious, he leans forward slightly, like he's silently promising that one day, this will all be behind me. "You're a good man, Adrian. This town is lucky to have you."

I smile, or at least try to, even though my insides feel tight. It's been a rocky start. First, the turkeys don't like me, and already, the gossip is starting, but I just want a clean slate.

"How far off is the general practice from being ready?" I tap my fingers on the beer bottle, the rhythm helping to calm the nerves. I'm dreading heading back into a hospital while I wait for the practice renovations to finish, but I cling to the hope that the environment here will feel more welcoming.

"Twelve months. It's a lot slower here than in the city."

"Right," I mutter as my stomach twists once more with unease. "I hope the people are a little different here."

"They will be. You'll blend in. The doctors here are like you," he assures me, a glint of confidence in his eyes. "Smart, driven, and they get results, no matter what it takes."

"Do they know about my dismissal?"

"Yeah. There's a section of the weekly community newspaper that's called 'Dr. Whisperer.' Best to avoid that for a bit."

"Thanks for the tip." I take another sip, the refreshment hitting just right.

"I didn't know what you were thinking for dinner. Did you want to stay in or head to the bar?"

"I'm happy to grab some takeout. I want to hit the sack early tonight."

"That sounds like a plan." Keith's grin stretches wider before he takes another swig of his drink.

Needing to change the subject, I say with a shake of my head, "I met Russell on my way in."

"Oh, you did? Those nuisance turkeys."

I finish off my beer. "I literally got stuck trying to get here. They wouldn't get off the road. Russell even jumped into my car, took a shit on my seat... I couldn't get him out."

Keith nearly chokes on his beer, a laugh escaping him. "He's the worst."

I toss my bottle into the trash. "I'm going to clean my car and take a quick shower before we order dinner."

"Sounds good."

Turning away, I head outside, but something stirs in my gut. This is it. This is where I'll seek my redemption.

CHAPTER 2

AMELIA

"Amelia, do you mind coming into my office for a minute?" Luna's voice carries across the moderately spacious newsroom of The Pulse Bulletin.

Several heads pop up from behind their computer monitors. The newsroom is unusually full today. Hunter and Corey huddle by the coffee station, discussing the upcoming city council vote, and Olive furiously types at her desk, organized with color-coded folders and press releases. Even Detective Lawson has wandered in from the police station across the street, wanting to discuss the weekend crime report.

Everyone's staring as I grab my laptop and push back from my desk, my stomach churning with nerves as I walk through the office. I like the feature of cubicles in the newsroom, but not when I'm getting called to Luna's office.

Sunlight streams through the tall windows, and the glass walls with their black frames seem to close in around me.

I smooth my cream sweater, making sure it still looks neat against my black pants. Luna rarely calls anyone into her glass-walled office unless something significant is happening... good or bad. I've been knee-deep in an article about the upcoming welcome party, but this feels important.

"Looks like someone's in trouble," Hunter whispers to Corey, just loud enough for me to hear. "Maybe City Manager Ezra finally complained about that piece on the development project."

A few chuckles ripple through the newsroom.

"If Ezra had a problem with my reporting, he'd need to read it first."

Hunter lifts his hands in mock surrender. Corey grins.

Violet shoots Hunter a withering look before giving me an encouraging smile. *Ignore them*, she mouths.

Violet's always had my back, since most people here are disconnected from me. My quiet way of working and my relationship with Luna outside of work has pissed off pretty much everyone over the years. They respect my work because they have to, as my investigative pieces bring in the readers and boost our numbers, but they keep their distance. I rarely get invited to drinks at Pulse Point Tavern, and conversations die when I walk into the room.

Olive doesn't even bother looking up as I pass, but I notice how her typing becomes more aggressive, her fingers hitting the keyboard with unnecessary force.

As I make my way toward Luna's office with its clean 'EDITOR-IN-CHIEF' lettering on the glass door, I feel the eyes of everyone in our newsroom. I hold my head high despite the discomfort, my laptop clutched to my chest. Behind me, the whispers begin again with theories about why the boss wants to see me.

Inside Luna's office, I settle into the chair opposite her. As always, she looks impeccable. Long brown hair falling over a beige silk blouse, big gold hoops shining in the light. Her pink nails are flawless, makeup bold yet tasteful. She leans forward, hands clasped, a bright, genuine smile spreading across her face, which comforts me.

"So, I called you in to let you know I'm scaling back," she says, her eyes focused on me. "I need someone to help lighten the load. It's starting to feel like too much, especially now that I'm getting older."

I'm surprised. At fifty-one, she's not what I'd call old. But I get it, running a growing company isn't for the faint of heart.

"I've decided to hire someone for my role part-time," she continues. "I'm pulling people in individually to see if there's leadership potential. If you're interested, I'll be keeping a closer eye on your work moving forward."

The idea of being both a journalist and a part-time editor-in-chief makes my heart race in the best way. "I'd love that opportunity," I say, barely containing the excitement in my voice.

"I'm pleased. After twelve years, Amelia, you're practically the foundation of this place. I remember when you covered that shop fire your first month here. Look how far you've come. Your knowledge is irreplaceable, and that network of contacts you've built across Pulse Point to the surrounding towns takes years. The newer staff may not realize it, but half of our scoops come from relationships you've made."

My chest swells with pride. I sit a little straighter, feeling that rush of validation. Maybe this is it... my shot at something more. I've earned it.

I've always wanted to be a journalist. Luna is my mom's closest friend, and I've worked here since I was fourteen. Luna would let me come to work with her to sort the mail, restock the breakroom, and pretend I wasn't eavesdropping during story meetings. Those afternoons, surrounded by the noise of printers and the smell of fresh ink, planted the seed of desire in my heart.

But this isn't the life I imagined.

I thought I'd outgrow this town. Take what I learned and run with it. Maybe I'd land a bigger paper, in a city where people didn't know me as Luna's best friend's daughter. And follow my dream of reporting on more lifestyle topics like fashion, beauty, and trends, but that kind of coverage isn't exactly popular in a town like this. But then Mom got sick, and running wasn't an option anymore. So I stayed. And that meant working my way up here, in the same building where it all started.

"And congratulations on your latest article," she adds. "It was sharp, engaging, and stirred up just the right amount of buzz."

"Thank you."

"You're welcome." She smiles.

I wrote about the new doctor in town. The one who broke protocol by administering unauthorized medication and was dismissed from a major New York City hospital. I still don't understand why someone like that thinks they can just waltz in here, setting up shop as if nothing happened. Exposing him felt like doing the town a favor.

"Are you working on another piece about him?" she asks.

Ever since the article ran, locals have been calling and emailing the paper or stopping Luna in the street, asking for more.

"Yes, and one on the welcome party." The words feel bitter on my tongue.

"It'll be sensational," Luna says. "I want you covering it. Photos, articles, the works."

"Of course. I think it's great to welcome him," I manage, though I'm not convinced he deserves it. But I keep my opinions to myself. No way am I jeopardizing this promotion. Because this isn't just a title; it's a raise that means I can pay medical and daily bills with ease, and have more control over the stories I pitch, and finally get some respect in the newsroom.

Sure, the town's heard the rumors, people talk, but that's never stopped them from showing up with pie and chairs. That's just how they are. They'd rather be seen as warm and neighborly than risk looking judgmental or divided. Hosting a welcome party doesn't mean they're taking sides; it just means they're being polite.

Still, I can't help but wonder why he'd agree to come. Surely he knows someone will be there covering it. Then again, who knows... he might not even show up.

"I'm opening the position externally too," she adds casually, as if it's no big deal.

The words hit like a punch. My stomach sinks. I thought it would stay within the team. Most of us have been here for years, staying in this town, covering the usual local stories... Minor fires, car accidents, the mayor's latest drama about ducks, or more recently the Mercedes-Benz driver's turkey takeover. I remember how a few days ago, I saved Adrian when his car got overtaken by turkeys. And I'm not talking about a few birds. No, I'm talking about an entire flock, led by King Russell himself. I'll never forget the look on his face when I pulled up. I knew food would work. As soon as Russell started pecking, I warned Adrian to get in his car before the turkeys figured out they'd been tricked. Then I took off, heading home after picking up medication for Mom from the nearby town, Prescott Valley.

I force a smile. "Let me know if you need anything else for the weekend."

"I know you'll do great," she says warmly. "Better let you get back to it."

As I leave her office, determination flares within me. This isn't over. Not by a long shot.

I head back to my desk, my heart still racing from the meeting. My butt barely touches the chair before Violet leans over her laptop, whispering across the white desk.

"What was that about?"

I know she hasn't had her talk with Luna yet, but she will.

Violet and I are similar in style... Black pants, a camel coat draped over her chair, a sleek black top, and her straightened, glossy black hair falling perfectly into place. She only started here a couple of years ago when her family moved to town.

I'm about to tell Violet about the meeting, just as Luna calls her name.

Violet stands, smoothing her pants, and heads into Luna's office.

When she returns, she drops into her chair.

"Are you excited?" I ask, leaning forward.

"No," she replies flatly.

"You don't want it? You're not even going to apply?"

She shakes her head. "No, I'm happy where I am. You go for it."

I sit with that, the simplicity of her answer both shocking and enviable. Wouldn't it be easier if I could be content?

A flicker of dedication lights me up again. I dive back into my follow-up story, determined to impress Luna.

A new email from Luna hits my inbox. Subject line: *New Restaurant Opening. Pulse & Co, Soft Launch Tonight.*

Of course. Another food feature. My fourth this month.

It's not that the food isn't good. It's just... how many ways can I describe a tasting plate before I start to sound like a menu myself?

I close the email without reading the rest.

The office clears out at five, but I stay until five-thirty, as usual. That extra half-hour feels like a quiet promise to myself. A reminder that I'm willing to go the extra mile.

Before I head out, I look through my socials. I'm mid-scroll when a video auto-plays on my feed. It's my sister, Aurora, standing on a rooftop in LA, the skyline behind her. *First week as a junior buyer at Bloomingdale's. Still feels surreal,* her caption reads, followed by three champagne emojis and the hashtag *#PostGradDreams*.

A hollow ache settles in my chest. People always leave... for school, for jobs, for something bigger. *And I stay.* Even

Aurora, my little sister, she's twenty-three and already living the life I used to dream about.

I used to imagine myself in a city like that, going after stories that set my heart on fire. I even had the application saved for a job in New York.

But then Mom was diagnosed with atrial fibrillation a few years ago. The bills piled up. And here I am, watching someone else live the life I wanted, while I write about turkeys hijacking luxury vehicles.

Mom used to teach art at the elementary school. She loved it, always came home with glitter in her hair and paint on her sleeves. But since the flare-up a few months ago, the dizzy spells and the new meds, she's been on medical leave. She says it's just until things stabilize, but I've seen the way she touches her chest when she thinks no one's looking. She hasn't been back to the classroom yet, and I'm not sure when she will.

Fifteen minutes later, I pull into our large circular driveway, climb the three steps to the front door, and let myself in with my key. The noise hits me instantly. Home.

I'm the oldest of seven. A chaotic, wonderful mix of boys and girls. At twenty-seven, I carry the invisible badge of eldest child responsibilities. Ignoring the noise of the kids, I drop my bag in my room and head to the living room, where Mom's curled up on the sofa, her face a little paler than usual. I tell myself not to overthink it. She's just tired. Still, a twist curls in my stomach.

"Hey." I lean down to kiss her cheek. "Have you eaten?"

She blinks up at me, smiling. "Not yet. Just needed to rest a bit first."

"I'll get started. What would you like for dinner?"

"I'll help." She slowly rises. "I hadn't planned anything in particular."

I hold out my hand. "No, you rest. I've got it."

"I'm sick of resting. That's all I do." She waves me off.

I glance at her as she walks into the kitchen, noticing how carefully she moves, the way she pauses slightly when catching her breath.

"Mom," I say softly behind her.

Grabbing vegetables from the fridge, she lays them on the counter.

"How are you feeling today?" I grab a knife, cutting board, and pot.

I wait, expecting her usual answer while chopping broccoli. But stay hopeful for something different.

She smiles, but it doesn't reach her eyes. "I'm fine, sweetheart. Just a little tired."

I put the knife down gently. "You don't have to pretend with me."

With a sigh, she leans against the counter. "I know. But worrying about it won't change anything. I'm managing."

I watch her from the corner of my eye as we work. Her breathing is shallow again, the kind that barely reaches past her ribs and makes me worry. She used to glide through the kitchen, humming, wiping down counters, stirring sauce, or checking on the oven. Now she has to pause just to catch her breath.

A tightness builds in my chest as my mind races. *What if I don't get that promotion? What if something happens to her, and I can't afford the hospital bills? What if I'm not enough to hold all this together? Will I be forced to tell my siblings about our financial situation?*

I swallow hard, the words catching in my throat. *I'm scared, Mom. I keep thinking... what if something happens to you? I feel like I'm trying to hold everything together, and I don't know if I can.* But I don't say it. I can't. Because if I do, I'm sure tears and panic will come. Pretending is the only thing holding me together.

Opening the fridge, I try to decide between chicken or fish, like my world isn't shifting from underneath me.

When I return to the counter, she reaches for my hand, her fingers cool. "Amelia, you don't have to carry it all. I know you feel responsible, but I'm still your mom. I'm still here. And I'm proud of you... for everything. I don't want you to sacrifice your life for mine. You're young. You should be out with friends... or a nice man."

Of course, she knows.

I never said a word, but she saw it anyway... she always does. But that's the thing about her: she can see it even when I think I'm hiding it well.

"Luna said I'm being considered for a promotion. I'm trying not to get my hopes up."

Her face lights up, pride shining through the exhaustion as she squeezes my hand. "I'm so proud of you. You deserve this."

I nod, feeling both lighter and heavier at the same time. "Thanks, Mom."

I return to cooking, the clink of utensils and the low hiss of the stove bringing me back to the moment. Behind me, the familiar noise of my family fills the kitchen.

The table's nearly full now. Hazel, sixteen, lounges at the far end, one leg draped over the other, eyes glued to her phone. "Fifty-eight seconds flat," she says without looking up. "Coach nearly cried. Honestly, I should be scouted already."

Next to her, Atlas, fourteen, hunches over a napkin, tongue poking out the corner of his mouth as he adds scales to a dragon's tail he's drawing. "Hey, move your elbow," he mumbles when Sofia leans across him, holding out a piece of paper.

"Guys, can you read with me? Just this scene," Sofia, who's twelve, pleads. "It's for tomorrow's audition."

"Only if the dragon gets a voice too," Atlas mutters.

A blur dashes past the table—six-year-old Felix, wearing nothing but superhero undies. "Spiderman doesn't do broccoli!" he yells, leaping onto the sofa.

Jasper, fifteen and full of opinions, leans back in his chair. "Did you know, in Finland, they don't even give homework? And the kids there are super smart." He shrugs. "I'm just saying, maybe we're the ones doing it wrong."

One chair remains empty. No one ever sits there, even though we've long stopped setting a place for him.

Dad's seat.

The back left leg still wobbles. I keep meaning to fix it, but I never do.

The noise used to feel overwhelming when I was younger, each new sibling adding another layer to the chaos. But it wasn't the volume, it was the weight of helping, of stepping in, of becoming the one who holds it all together when no one else does.

Now, though... the noise feels like home.

After dinner, we clear the table, and Mom pulls out Monopoly. It's our weekly tradition... no phones, just us, rolling dice, laughing, and bonding.

It starts off innocently enough. Atlas grabs the race car before anyone else can. "I'm the car. It gets better mileage," he says seriously, like that has any effect on dice rolls.

"You never even play it right," Sofia mutters as she snatches the banker tray and tucks it close to her chest. "You can't buy utilities and skip paying. That's not how strategy works."

Atlas shrugs, already rolling. "Worked last time."

I land on Mayfair. And of course, there's a hotel.

"Fourteen hundred," Sofia says smugly, extending her hand.

"Seriously?" I groan as I toss her the bills.

Felix slaps a Chance card down and yells, "I win!"

"Felix," I say gently. "You're in jail."

He frowns, then grins. "Spiderman can do whatever he wants 'cause he's awesome."

Looking insulted, Jasper chimes in. "Is anyone listening? I was talking about other countries' school systems. No homework. Kids are happier." He picks this conversation back up from dinner.

"Jasper," I mutter. "We're playing Monopoly."

"Are you sure you're not cursed?" Hazel jokes from her spot next to me. She likes watching me suffer in board games.

"I'm not cursed," I grumble, handing over my last blue fifty-dollar bill. "It's a test of character."

"And how's that working out for you?"

"Not great."

By the end of the game, alliances have crumbled, fake bills are dramatically thrown across the room, and Felix is trying to convince us that "free parking" means that he owns the car now, not Atlas. We laugh until our stomachs hurt.

This is home. This is why I stay. *This promotion could help us.*

Chapter 3

Adrian

I step into the house after an eight-mile run, sweat clinging to my skin, still catching my breath from the last push. The cool morning air feels different in Pulse Point… crisper, like it cleans my lungs with every inhale. Being here for a week, this has become my new routine, and honestly, it's more peaceful than I expected.

With so little traffic, I can let my mind wander and work out any problems. Sure, the past lingers like a shadow, but I focus on what's right in front of me. Every day, I pick a new direction to run in. The best part? No crowds. No accidental shoulder bumps. Just me and my footsteps on the sidewalks.

I quietly close the door behind me, trying to stay quiet, but the rich scent of fresh coffee leads me straight to Keith. He's at the kitchen counter, pouring steaming coffee into a mug.

"Morning," I say, hands on my hips, lungs burning from the sprint finish.

Keith glances over with a smile. His plaid shirt is wrinkled, flat hair on one side like he rolled out of bed ten minutes ago. He holds up a mug in a silent offer.

I wipe the sweat from my brow. "I'd love some, but I'm gonna shower first."

"Go right ahead. I'll wait a few minutes, then brew a fresh cup just for you. Want me to make some eggs too?"

I shake my head, appreciating the offer, but feeling a pang of guilt. "Nah, don't worry about it, Keith. You're already doing more than enough for me."

Inside the bathroom, I peel off my damp clothes and step into the hot shower, letting the water wash away the tension in my muscles. Afterward, I towel off and pull on a pair of new blue jeans and a brown t-shirt, both a little softer and better fitting than the daily suit I'm used to. I run a hand through my still-damp hair and glance at my reflection. I look presentable. Almost like I belong.

It's been a week, and tomorrow, I start as a doctor at the hospital until Keith's practice is ready for me. This week has been about settling in, getting my bearings. But today, I've got one thing on my list: a haircut at the barber Keith pointed out the other day.

A few minutes later, I'm back in the kitchen, where my coffee waits for me on the counter. "Thanks." I take a long, satisfying sip. The bitterness is exactly what I need after another restless night.

"How'd you sleep?" he asks, clutching his own cup.

"All right," I lie, not ready to unpack the mess in my head. Thoughts of dismissal, feeling like I wasn't enough, echoes of my dad's words to "toughen up," still lurk in the background. But I'm here to start over, to move past all that. Sleep will come eventually. I just need time.

"So, what's the plan for today?" I ask, wanting to change topics.

"I thought we could stop by the practice after we head into town. Just check in. Then, later, there's the welcome party."

My stomach tightens at the reminder. A flicker of something like dread washes over me. I rub the back of my neck, suddenly too aware of the way the collar of my t-shirt sits against my skin. Parties aren't really my thing, not now, when everything already feels rocky. But maybe it'll work in my favor, especially with Keith there. "What time?" I ask.

"Five. We'll head back here around four to get ready. I'll drive since I'm bringing food and drinks."

"What are you bringing?"

"Mac and cheese. Everyone brings a dish. I'm not spoiling the surprise, though. You'll see why this place is special soon enough."

I nod, draining the last of my coffee.

At the very least, I can show up looking like I've got it together... even if I don't feel like it yet.

I push open the door to the barbershop, the bell chiming softly overhead. The place looks just like the ones back in the city with brick walls, chairs in a line, big windows letting in streams of natural light, and that familiar mix of wax, hairspray, and aftershave lingering in the air. Nothing fancy, but it has a charm, the kind that feels lived in.

A bearded guy in his mid-thirties, with a solid build like he spends serious time at the gym, greets me with a friendly smile. Tattoos snake up both arms, and his confident stance says he owns the place, or at least runs the show.

"Hey." He pauses mid-trim, clippers still in hand, and glances up to greet me.

"Hi. Do you have time for a haircut?" I ask, wiping sweat from my temple.

His eyes scan me briefly, not in a judgmental way, just a quick once-over. Normally, I don't overthink stuff, but here, in this unfamiliar place, even the smallest thing makes me feel like I stick out.

"Yeah. Take a seat here." He points to one of the black chairs. "I'll be a couple of minutes, then I'll be right with you."

I slide into the seat, noticing he's the only barber working. But it's nine a.m., so maybe it's just early.

There's a small TV in the corner, playing the morning news on low volume. I watch it for a few seconds, then glance at the barber, who finishes up with an older gentleman, their conversation drifting from sports to grandkids.

After a few friendly pats on the back and a chuckle, the man pulls out his wallet, hands over a bill, and waves off the change with a grin. There's something easy and familiar in the way the barber interacts with him, like he knows how to make people feel comfortable without trying too hard.

When he's done, the barber brushes off his hands and walks over to me.

"I'm Derek," he says, offering a hand. "I own the place."

"Adrian. I just moved here." I shake his hand.

He doesn't mention the article, doesn't give any sign he recognizes me from the picture, and maybe he doesn't. Or maybe he does and just wants to form his own impression. The thought makes my chest feel like it's opening up, just a little.

"So, what brings you to town?" He drapes a cape around me and snaps it in place.

"I'm joining Keith Montgomery's practice."

He raises an eyebrow, a flicker of recognition. "Keith Montgomery, huh?" He pauses. "So you're planning to stick around, then? Not just a couple of months kind of thing?"

"Yeah, I'm here for good. I'm staying with Keith while I look for something to purchase."

I'm staying because, truthfully, I have no other choice. No hospital's going to take me after the way things ended, and Keith gave me an opportunity when no one else would. I owe him.

"Smart move. All right, tell me what you want."

I run my fingers through the hair on the sides of my head. "Short on the sides, like a one or two, faded up. Keep the top a bit longer, you know, just clean it up."

"Got it." Derek grabs the clippers and starts working. A steady buzz of the clippers fills the space, mixed with faint music playing from a radio in the corner.

"You from here?" I ask.

"Born and raised. My dad owned this shop before me."

"Do you work alone?"

"Most mornings, yeah. I've got a guy who helps out in the afternoons. Regulars like their routines."

We fall into easy conversation. He tells me about the local bar, The Pulse Point Tavern, good for watching sports, with an awesome outdoor area.

"What about gyms? Cafes?" I ask.

Derek lists off a gym just down the road, a bakery with the best pastries, a coffee shop that knows how to make a decent cold brew, and a smoothie spot I'd probably never find on my own. Some of it overlaps with what Keith has shown me, but he adds his own personal twist.

We talk about where to buy a house, which spots are quiet, and which ones have character. He doesn't sugar-coat anything, which I appreciate.

When he finishes, he brushes off the stray hairs and adds a bit of gel.

"What do you think?"

I check it out, running my hand over the fresh fade. "Nailed it. Thanks."

Derek unclips the cape, gives it a shake, and grins. "Nice meeting you, Adrian. See you next time."

"Definitely. Thanks for the suggestions."

I pull out my wallet to pay, and as I turn to leave, he calls out, "Hey, take my number. A couple of buddies and I head out to the bar on Fridays. I could introduce you around if you want to tag along."

"Sounds good," I say, surprised at how natural the offer feels. After the mess at the last hospital, I'm wary of making new friends, especially at work. But maybe having a circle outside of that would be better.

I step outside, and for the first time in a while, I feel lighter. Like maybe starting over isn't just possible... it might actually be nice.

On my way back to Keith's truck, where he's waiting for me, my phone vibrates in my pocket. I pull it out, glancing at the screen. *Isaac.* Relief hits me as I answer.

"Hey, man," he says. "How's it going out there in the sticks?"

"So far, so good. Still finding my feet," I reply, relief settling into my chest at the familiar voice.

"You start work yet?"

Huffing out a breath, I kick a loose rock as I walk. "Nah, not yet. Checking out the practice later today. Haven't been inside the hospital yet. I start tomorrow."

"How you feeling about that?"

I reach the truck, leaning against the door as I rub the back of my neck. "Fucking scared, honestly. Like... the shit from the city will follow me."

Isaac sighs. "Try not to think about that, man. It's a fresh start."

I roll the words around in my head, knowing he's right.

"How is it back there?" If anyone knows, it's him. He's still in the thick of it at the hospital.

"They've moved on," he says. "You know how it is—one drama, then on to the next."

I scoff. "Yeah, well, I'm sure if I were still around, they'd be talking about it."

"Probably." He doesn't lie, and I appreciate that. "But you're not. And honestly? You're gonna be better off where you are."

A deep chuckle leaves my throat. "How the fuck would you know?"

"I don't," he admits. "I'm just trying to make you feel better. Is it working?"

I shake my head, smiling despite myself. "You know what? It kinda is."

"Good. My job here is done. Call me later."

"Alright, will do."

I hang up as I grip the truck handle for a second before climbing in. The interior smells faintly of leather and pine, the dashboard dusty but well-kept. The door creaks slightly as it shuts.

Maybe Isaac's right. I need to start believing this is my fresh start and not be hung up on the past.

But fresh starts don't change what's happened. And some shit has a way of catching up with you.

I glance around, noticing the number of trucks in the parking lot and along the streets as we pull away. Back in New York, it's all busy, fast, and loud with sedans and honking taxis. Here, it's quieter and slower. A different kind of energy altogether.

"Seems like everyone drives a truck around here," I say, buckling my seatbelt.

Keith chuckles, shifting gears smoothly. "Yeah, it's just more practical. Hauling wood for the fireplace, dealing with rougher roads... It fits the lifestyle. Back in the city, your car made sense, but out here, it's a different story. Plus, when you get your own place, having a truck might come in handy. No rush, though."

Keith owns a few vehicles: his sturdy truck, Sage's sleek sedan, and an old convertible with a soft top that looks like it's seen a few summers but still holds its charm. I'd rather have one car, so I'm willing to give up the Mercedes.

"All right, let's go." His voice carries a note of excitement that's contagious. "Did your dad ever tell you how I came about getting the practice?"

I shake my head as part of me stiffens. Talking about my dad still feels hard. But I'm curious about the stories Keith might have. "No."

He flicks his gaze to me for a moment before turning his focus back to the road. His hands grip the steering wheel. "I met Sage here, and she couldn't move to the city, so I was moping around, trying to figure out what to do with myself. The practice was up for sale because the doctor was retiring. Your dad gave me the money to buy it. I paid him back as soon as I could, but I wouldn't be where I am without him. I miss him."

Tightness fills my chest, and I stare out the window, watching the scenery blur by. I try to swallow down the lump in my throat, but it's heavy. "So do I."

The drive takes a few minutes, but it feels longer, the scenery shifting from residential streets to a more open stretch lined with trees.

Keith pulls into a gravel lot beside a building partially covered in scaffolding. Construction materials are neatly stacked nearby. It's unfinished but full of potential... like everything about this new start.

I realize I don't know much about the doctor side of Keith. As we step out of the truck, I ask a question that's been on my mind. "So, did you always want to be a doctor?"

Keith locks the truck with a quick beep. "My dad and grandfather were doctors. Being a doctor is kind of in the family."

We walk up a brick pathway to a building that feels more like a large house than a practice, with its pitched roof and wide front porch. Keith unlocks the door, and we step inside. The polished wooden floors shine under the bright light filtering through large windows. Light-colored timber blends with cream walls, accented by indoor plants and wrought-iron chandeliers. The scent of something citrus lingers in the air.

The reception area is spacious, dominated by a white, high-front desk with wooden countertops. Two monitors sit behind it, and everything looks fresh and modern.

"This is incredible," I mutter, still taking it all in.

"We started with renovating the front," Keith explains. "Expanded the reception, added new furniture. The goal is to create more space for more doctors, chiropractic care, holistic treatments, naturopathy. This town needs it, and we're making it happen."

He gives me a quick tour of the reception area, a couple of treatment rooms with sleek equipment, and a cozy break room with a small kitchenette. "Right now, it's just me and a few allied health professionals who hire space. But once the extension's done, we'll have room for more."

The space feels different from what I'm used to… quieter, less clinical, and more inviting.

He opens a door to a room still under construction. One wall is missing entirely, framing the rough timber and scaffolding beyond.

Keith steps inside. "This will be your office-slash-treatment space. It'll have a private exit out back. I'm still figuring out the finishes."

I glance around the shell of the room, and somehow, it feels more real than the glossy reception. Maybe because this is the part that still has questions, just like me.

"I know it's hard to picture now," Keith says, rubbing the back of his neck. "But we're building something good here. The town's growing. Families are staying. And we need more hands."

I nod, knowing he's talking about me. Like if this place can come together piece by piece, then maybe I can too.

"How do you think you'll like working here?" Keith asks.

I pause, considering. The usual tension I carry isn't here; the absence of city noise and chaos giving me room to breathe. "I think this is the right step. It feels good."

Keith grins and grabs me on the shoulder with a friendly squeeze. "I'm glad. I really think this town will grow on you. The people here will love you. It's a joy working here, and having you on board makes it even better."

I return his smile, feeling a flicker of something unfamiliar but welcome... hope.

"Want to grab some food in town?" he asks. "Figure it's good to get you familiar with the spots. Plus, if you go alone later, you won't get bombarded."

I frown. That sounds bad. "Bombarded?"

Keith just laughs, unlocking the truck again. "You'll see."

We hop back into Keith's truck, and he drives a couple of minutes down the road before pulling into a small parking lot. A large sign reading *The Cozy Point* catches my eye, with people heading out, to go coffee cups in hand, pausing to linger outside, chatting. I climb out, watching them, wondering how long it will take me to become one of them.

Inside, the diner buzzes with life. The walls are lined with vintage signs and framed photos; a mix of old-town charm and coziness. Mouthwatering scents of sugar, salt, and coffee hit me. My stomach growls in protest.

An older woman with silver-streaked hair, a blue sweater, and rosy cheeks spots Keith and beams. "Morning, Keith!" She wipes her hands on her white apron as she approaches.

"Good morning, Genevieve."

Her eyes shift to me, widening with curiosity. "And who's this?" When she glances at Keith, her expression practically shouts, *You didn't tell me.*

"This is Adrian. He just moved here," Keith introduces casually.

"Well, of course you are. I've been hearing all about you. Welcome, sweetheart." She extends her hand but surprises me by pulling me into a hug. I stiffen, and by the time I awkwardly pat her back, she's already pulled away.

"Let me get you two a table." She arches an eyebrow at Keith like she's silently asking if we're expecting anyone else. Keith shakes his head, and she leads us to a booth tucked in the back corner. It's perfect. I can see the entire diner from here. I've always felt more comfortable with my back to the wall, a habit from years of needing to anticipate what's next.

"Can I get you started with some drinks?" she asks, handing us menus.

"Sure. I'll have an Americano, no sugar or cream," I say.

"And your usual, Keith?" she asks.

"Yes, thank you."

She saunters off, adjusting her apron as she goes. Flipping open the menu, I pretend to read while sneaking glances around.

The diner is filled with the comforting sounds of conversation, the hiss of the espresso machine, and the occasional clink of silverware hitting plates. I'm reminded of a familiar Sunday morning spot my dad used to take me to: the smell, the sounds, even the regulars in their usual seats, it's all coming back.

"So, what's good here?" I ask, hoping to save myself the effort of choosing.

"The big breakfast is a good choice if you're hungry. If not, the frittatas and baked goods are amazing. Honestly, everything here is great. That's why I brought you. Figured you needed to taste the best of what Pulse Point offers."

"You're really trying to sell me on a place I already agreed to live in."

He grins. "There's still time for you to run."

Run to where? I swallow the thought, staring at the menu.

Genevieve returns with our drinks. "Have you decided what you're having?"

"I'll take the big breakfast, please. Poached eggs with a side of avocado."

"And for you, Keith?"

"Fried eggs on toast and crispy bacon, thanks."

She writes it down and disappears into the bustling kitchen. I glance around again, noting a table stacked with newspapers and used books. Keith already gets the paper delivered daily, though I've initially avoided reading it since the last headline wasn't exactly flattering. But curiosity got the better of me. I dug it out of the trash when Keith wasn't looking and read the article that's now etched into the town's memory, thanks to a woman by the name of Amelia.

Keith's voice pulls me back. "They're quick with the food here. Morning rush, you know?"

"Yeah, makes sense," I mumble.

A server swings by with two steaming plates balanced expertly on her arm. "Big breakfast, with poached eggs and avocado for you," she says, sliding the plate in front of me. "Fried eggs on toast with crispy bacon for the doctor."

Keith grins. "Actually, Kallie, he's a doctor too."

She winks at me. "Welcome."

I mumble a quiet "Thanks," and for a few moments, we eat in comfortable silence. The food is greasy in the best way.

Keith wipes at his mouth with a napkin, then leans back. "So... what do you think of the food?"

I finish chewing, wash it down with a sip of coffee, then nod. "It's delicious."

He doesn't push, just nods back, like he knows I'm not just talking about the meal. But the combination of the food, the quiet, and the back corner is all something I needed. That's what I am realizing about Keith. He doesn't need to say much. He reads people in a way that we doctors do. Or maybe it's just him, still looking after me because I'm his best friend's kid.

After we eat, heading outside feels like stepping into a different world. People are stringing up lights between trees, setting tables along the blocked-off main street.

"You wait till tonight. The setup is unreal."

"I don't get the fuss about a welcome party. I don't need one."

"I know, but this town likes to welcome newcomers. It's a good way to meet everyone. When I lost Sage, these people were there for me. They helped me get back on my feet."

Guilt clenches in my chest. I wish I could've done more. Been there for Keith, maybe if I had, I wouldn't be in the mess I am right now. "You should've called me. I would've come earlier."

"No need. That's what I'm saying; this town is like family. You didn't need to drop your life because mine fell apart. They helped me rebuild."

His words feel foreign. Family? I never thought of the city or the hospital that way.

Maybe showing up tonight isn't just about me. Maybe it's a way to thank them for looking after Keith when I wasn't there.

"I'll come," I say quietly. "Maybe have a drink. I won't stay long."

Even with the article and my picture out there, everyone I've met in this town so far has been kind to me. So maybe the party won't be such a bad idea.

CHAPTER 4

AMELIA

WHERE THE HELL IS my other shoe?

I stomp into the hallway, yelling for my sister, Hazel, who has a chronic condition called 'borrowing without asking'. She's eleven years younger and somehow still the biggest pain in my ass. All I want is for her to ask before taking my stuff. Is that too much?

Our house is a war zone. Not just a little messy, it's a full-blown bombsite. The kind of place where you have to step over sofa cushions, dodge sneakers, and pray you don't step on a Lego piece. The hallway walls, once a nice shade of cream, are now covered in everything from sticky fingerprints to random scribbles, thanks to Felix. The living room? A battlefield of laundry, snack crumbs, and half-finished homework is scattered across the coffee table.

I would've moved out ages ago, like Aurora, but Mom needs me. So, I'm stuck here, playing referee in a house that has zero respect for personal space. Privacy? What's that?

Alone time? I wish. Everything I own magically becomes family property.

"Hazel!" I yell. "Where are my black shoes?"

"Which ones?" she shouts back from somewhere in the house.

I blow out a breath and march toward her room. The second I reach her door, I know I've made a mistake. The smell alone—a mix of sweet perfume, dirty clothes, and what I swear is nail polish remover—makes my eyes burn. Clothes are everywhere. A towel hangs off the dresser. The bed? Unmade, of course, with at least three dirty plates stacked on the nightstand.

She's sitting in the middle of it all, headphones in, totally unaware that she's about to get a rude awakening. I yank one out. "This shoe. Where's the other one? And for the final time, start asking before you take my stuff."

Like I just interrupted her peace, she blinks up at me. "I don't know where it is."

Of course.

Frustration simmers beneath my skin, but I inhale sharply. I'm not going to let her get to me. "Fine. Then help me find it." *I need these shoes with my outfit, and we're already running late.*

The shoes are perfect... a tiny heel, just enough to be dressy without killing my feet. And since I'm covering today's event for an article, I must look polished. Black tailored pants, a tucked-in blue blouse, hair straightened, makeup done. Ready to be professional, or at least I would be if I weren't being trapped here by my sister's mess.

I scan her room, my fingers twitching. "We don't have time for this, and you're not even ready. I bet no one else in this house is either. We need to go."

She rolls her eyes. "Calm down."

"Hazel, I'm working today. I can't be late."

"You need to relax. You need a life. Or a boyfriend."

"I need neither. I love work," I lie, ignoring the tiny pang in my chest. There's something about this assignment that gives me a flicker of excitement that I can't explain. The guest of honor, the one I wrote about, is kind of intriguing. I doubt he's looking forward to officially meeting me, considering I dug into his past. But hey, journalism isn't about making friends.

I start tossing clothes onto the bed, searching for my shoe. "I swear, if it's buried under this mess—"

She huffs, but joins in, half-heartedly sifting through the piles. We're at it for what feels like forever before I check under the bed. Big mistake.

"Oh, my God. That's disgusting." I scrunch up my nose at what I see. "Are those moldy sandwiches? What's wrong with you? How do you live like this?"

She shrugs. "I'm sixteen."

"When I was sixteen, I was nothing like this. This is... This is disgusting."

"Found it," she announces loudly as she holds up my shoe triumphantly.

I snatch it from her hand, muttering, "Get ready. You have five minutes."

With the shoe crisis averted, I charge into the kitchen, where my little brother, Felix, is currently standing on a chair, trying to reach the top shelf of the pantry.

Mom's in the living room, perched on the edge of the sofa, looking exhausted but determined. The dining table is still covered in breakfast dishes, despite my telling the kids to clean up three times.

Ten minutes later, I'm chasing Felix around the house with a pair of navy pants while he cackles in his underwear.

"You're getting dressed if it's the last thing I do!"

I finally get him into the pants, while Mom rounds up the others and gets everyone into the minivan.

Counting heads, I take a deep breath. "Everyone's in the car? Do you all have everything you need? Does anyone need to go to the bathroom?"

Silence.

Then, predictably, "I forgot my water bottle," says Jasper.

I groan and sprint back inside, grab it, and return. "Anything else?"

"I didn't bring a toy," Felix cries.

"I don't want to go," Atlas moans.

"I need to pee," Sofia says, unbuckling.

I blow out a slow breath. "I asked if anyone needed to go."

"Well, I didn't need to go then," Sofia says.

Once everyone's buckled back in, I speak. "Everyone. Behave. We won't stay long. I have work, and you all need to listen to Mom."

I turn up the music as I pull out of the driveway. They're still somehow louder than the radio, but at least we're moving.

"If you want to stay later, someone else can drop us home," Mom says.

Family's my priority, but I can't jeopardize the promotion. I'll decide what to do based on how tonight goes.

I keep my eyes on the road as I answer, "I just need to get my pictures and take my notes for an article."

Mom, sitting up front, gives me a tired but excited smile. "Don't worry about me. I can't wait to see everyone. I hate being cooped up. And with all the fall decorations? It's going to look so pretty."

I have to agree that the town festivities in fall are one of the best times of the year.

"Well, let me know if you need to leave early," I add, concerned that pushing herself too hard could lead to something bad happening.

She nods. "Will do."

And with that, we head toward the chaos, because apparently, I didn't get enough at home.

Once we arrive in town, before I can even shift the car into park, the door is opened, and my siblings rush out. My family is absolutely doing my head in, but at least I can trust the townspeople to keep an eye on them.

The soft glow of fairy lights covers the town square, hanging from building to tree to gazebo, illuminating the crisp evening. The air carries the scent of cinnamon and roasted nuts, mixing with the woodsy tang of a bonfire crackling in the distance. The long communal table stretches down the street, dressed in white linen and decorated with delicate, colorful flowers and neatly arranged glassware.

A small folk band plays near the town hall, the sound of a fiddle blending with the murmurs of conversation. It's spectacular. Almost enough to make me forget the sheer craziness of my life. *Almost.*

I lift my camera and snap a few pictures, not sure where to start; there's so much to take in. Wine barrels set up for games, a town hall ready for dancing, hay bale sofas draped with crisp white sheets, and makeshift coffee tables made from overturned barrels.

Turning slowly, I try to fit it all into the frame, but part of me just wants to stand still and soak it in. It's the kind of effort that makes me love this town. It's also the kind of effort I wish wasn't being wasted on a man with a reputation for breaking rules... medical ones, no less. A doctor, of all things.

I back up a few steps, angling my camera to get the perfect shot. A photo that would make my whole article pop. The light hits just right, framing the town hall doors and the glow of string lights above the hay bale sofas. I hold my breath, finger hovering over the shutter—

"Oof—"

A firm grip steadies me, large hands wrapping around my arms. The warmth of his touch seeps through my sleeves, holding me before I can stumble. I peer up into familiar piercing blue eyes, a chiseled jaw, and the shadow of stubble that makes him look frustratingly good. His scent is a mix of deep wood and velvety black cocoa. My stomach drops.

It's Adrian. As in, *that* Adrian. The one I wrote about and stopped to help with the flock of turkeys.

"Sorry," he says, voice deep enough to vibrate right through me as he lets go of me. He's dressed in jeans and a top, with a worn leather jacket, like he didn't even try and still somehow nailed the fall festival look. I noticed the first time we met, that for a guy, he knows how to dress. Plus, they're designer. I spot the fabrics and logos immediately.

His gaze holds mine for a second too long, and recognition flickers in his expression.

I cock my head when I finish my inspection. "You're missing something."

His eyebrows knit together, his eyes darting around. "What am I missing?"

"Your turkeys."

He exhales a laugh, shaking his head. "I never want to see them again."

"Well, you might not have much of a choice."

"Why's that?" he asks, one eyebrow lifting slightly.

"Thanksgiving's next weekend."

He groans. "Great. What does the town do? Dance with them?"

I snort. "No, we keep them as town mascots. Cooking them is off-limits."

His expression darkens. "Those turkeys are gonna haunt me forever, aren't they?"

"Yep. But you haven't met the goats yet."

"Goats? Jesus. I need to hide."

I grin, taking in his broad frame, the way he towers just enough to make me lift my chin. He's entirely too good-looking to fade into the background. "You're not gonna stay hidden here, you know. The single people are going to eat you alive."

"Not you, though?" His voice dips, the challenge unmistakable.

I lift a shoulder. "I have priorities. Work, family. Before I even think about anything else, I need to know your story."

His gaze flickers with something unreadable, the amusement in his eyes shifting.

Just as he opens his mouth, Keith approaches, clapping a hand on the man's shoulder. "I see you've met Adrian."

I barely have time to hide my expression before Keith turns to introduce me. "This is Amelia. She writes for the newspaper."

My stomach drops as I've been outed. I ignore my insides and keep my expression neutral as I wait for him to smirk and make some comment about the turkeys, or worse, pretend not to know me at all.

But Adrian's gaze sharpens, the humor draining from his face. His jaw tightens. "You wrote that article about me?"

There's no point pretending I don't know what he means. The entire town read it... probably at least twice. And here he is, standing in the middle of a street party thrown in his honor, with townsfolk acting like he's their new favorite person. I square my shoulders, meeting his stare. "Yeah. The town deserved to know the truth."

Okay, so there's a disconnect. A big one.

I wrote a piece that I thought was giving the people a heads-up. But from the looks of things, the smiling faces, and the chatter, either they didn't care, or they read it and still decided to roll out the red carpet. Am I the only one not rooting for him?

Did the article do nothing... or just make me look bitter?

My throat tightens. "I stand by what I wrote."

His jaw works, like he's holding something back. Then he lets it slip. "Funny. You didn't even talk to me. But sure, publish your assumptions and call it truth."

That's not the reaction I was expecting. Where's the defensiveness or sarcasm? Not disappointment lacing his words. Guilt prickles beneath my skin, and I struggle to find my voice.

"If you're going to tear someone apart," he adds, "at least get the whole story next time."

The air between us grows heavy. Keith clears his throat, patting Adrian on the back. "Let's not get into that tonight. We're here to welcome you."

I force a tight smile, but my pulse pounds in my ears.

Adrian doesn't respond. He just walks away, his broad shoulders stiff, and Keith gives me a look that's part disappointment, part warning, before following Adrian.

My stomach twists, but I push it down. He'll get over it. He's a grown man. A smart one, *supposedly*. If he can't handle a little accountability, that's not my problem.

Still, the guilt eats at me. Because, damn it... I told myself not to care, but Adrian's words don't sit right in my chest. *Should I have added his side of the story to the article?*

I shake it off and head toward the table. If I'm going to deal with this mess, I need fuel. Something heavy enough to silence my thoughts.

Luna stops me before I can get there. "I think your mom needs to go home. She's looking a little tired. Do you want me to take her?"

I smile. "That would be great, but let me get her something to eat first."

"How's it going tonight?" she asks, falling into step beside me. "Did you get any good shots? Talk to Adrian?"

I swallow hard, my eyes flicking to where he stands with Keith, looking like he's ready to bolt. "Oh, we talked."

"Did you get an interview?"

Working on another piece about him was what Luna asked for. Swallowing hard, I tuck a stray strand of hair behind my ear. "Not exactly."

She hums. "Well, there's still time."

Glancing at Adrian again, I watch the way his jaw tics, his hands clenching at his sides. *I wouldn't count on it.*

But even as I say it, I know deep down... I need to hear his side of the story.

CHAPTER 5

ADRIAN

"Are you okay?" Keith's voice is low beside me.

"Yeah," I say, but my mind betrays me, and my gaze drifts back to Amelia.

She's standing near the end of the table, her camera in hand as she scrolls through photos. She smiles at something a dark-haired woman says, but it's the same unguarded one she gave me earlier. One that made her seem real.

It's a shame. When I first met her, she seemed easy to talk to... funny and warm. Someone I could've liked, maybe even trusted. But now, knowing she wrote the article, I see her differently. She's a reminder that my past isn't something I can outrun. She could make things worse. Make it impossible to forget.

"Come on, let's sit," Keith says.

I follow him because I have no idea where I belong in all this, and I'm tempted to leave.

As we weave through the crowd, I feel them... whispers that carry through the air, eyes assessing me. They think they're subtle, but they're not. A prickle runs down my spine, my appetite fading fast. I remind myself that it'll pass. The staring and the murmurs will eventually die down. I just have to keep my head up.

I take my assigned seat, and of course, Amelia's right in front of me.

My mouth tightens, but I force my attention to the woman next to Amelia. She looks very similar, though older, with pale skin and bluish shadows beneath her eyes. Her hair is Amelia's natural brown, but with no blonde streaks, unlike Amelia's, and there's something weary about her. Amelia is fussing over her, filling her plate, and making sure she eats.

"Are you alright?" Keith's voice pulls me from my thoughts.

I hesitate, watching as Amelia rises and moves toward a group of kids. For a split second, I wonder if they're hers. I glance around, half-expecting to see a guy in the mix... someone hovering close. But there's no one.

"Yeah." I clear my throat. "I think I'll grab some food."

I fill my plate, ignoring my lack of appetite. Roast chicken, mashed potatoes with gravy, buttery cornbread, and mac and cheese. When I sit back down, Keith is caught up in conversation with someone, and I expect to eat in silence.

The woman beside me leans in slightly, smelling of lavender and something powdery. Her deep brown eyes study me, and I brace myself for the familiar sting of judgment.

A trace of red lipstick lingers on the rim of her wineglass. She swirls the liquid slowly.

"How are you settling in?" She's in her mid-forties, with a face that carries kindness. At least she's not whispering, not giving me that judgy look.

I swallow my bite, forcing it down. "Good. Only been here a week, so... we'll see."

She smiles, her eyes meeting mine. "I'm Diane. I work at the pharmacy."

"Nice to meet you," I say, meaning it.

"I'm actually starting at the hospital tomorrow," I tell her, if only to fill the space.

"I thought you were living with Keith and working for him?"

I take a sip of water. "He'll bring me on when the practice expansion is finished. For now, I'll work at the hospital. It'll be interesting to see how it compares to the city."

Diane nods. "That's right... You're from New York. I went once, when I was little."

"How did you like it?"

A loud crash startles me, my gaze snapping toward the commotion on my right. A child...one near Amelia has knocked over a plate.

Amelia's already moving, crouching down to clean up the mess. But she's not alone. A woman beside her grabs napkins and rushes over. Then a man in a plaid shirt, I vaguely recognize from earlier, kneels beside her with a broom. Another teen passes a stack of fresh plates like it's all rehearsed.

No one scolds the kid. No one makes a big deal out of it. They just move in quietly, like they've done this before.

I watch Amelia in the middle of it, calm, steady, and still somehow making it all look easy.

Her eyes flick to mine, catching me staring. Heat rushes up my neck, and I quickly look away. I don't want her to get the wrong idea. We have nothing to say to each other.

Plus, she'll only twist it.

"So," Diane continues, rescuing me from the moment. "After the speeches, the dancing starts. That's pretty much it. Everyone just talks, drinks, and has a good time."

"I don't dance." I haven't danced since seventh grade, and for good reason. It was a middle school dance in the gym. I'd psyched myself up for days, convinced myself I was going to dance with the prettiest girl in school. I walked across the gym toward her, but just as I reached her, I tripped over a backpack, right at her feet. She laughed. Fuck, everyone laughed. Even the DJ made a joke into the mic about me breakdancing. I stood up, red-faced, and walked straight out the door.

So yeah. I don't dance.

This would be a good time to leave.

But Diane leans in like she's about to share a secret. "Sorry to tell you, but that won't fly here. Good or bad, you get up there and try. You'll be dragged up if you don't."

I huff a quiet laugh. "Thanks for the warning. I'll be sure to leave before that happens."

"Not happening," she says, amused. "They won't allow it."

Out of the corner of my eye, I see movement. Amelia's gathering the kids, and the two older women join her. It looks like they're leaving, all of them, moving together like a well-practiced unit. I'm relieved because she won't be able to write a story about my bad dancing.

"What's her story?" I ask Diane before I can stop myself.

Keith interjects, finishing talking with the person beside him. "Their dad left before Felix was born. And recently, their mom's atrial fibrillation has been unstable."

Atrial fibrillation. It's when the heart beats out of rhythm... fast, chaotic, like it's panicking. Blood doesn't flow the way it should, which means clots can form, strokes can happen. Sometimes medication helps. Sometimes people need surgery. Sometimes... it gets worse.

I glance over at the kids. My stomach knots. "And those kids—"

"Her siblings."

They're loud, messy, and bickering over dinner. And all of them live with a mom whose heart might give out without warning. Whose next dizzy spell could land her in the hospital, or worse...

"How many?" I whisper.

"Seven kids in total."

A breath escapes me. *Seven.*

The sight of them disappearing down the street makes me think of the Brady Bunch. There are so many of them. Did they come here on a bus? A truck? A car? What kind of car even fits that many?

Once they leave, the night carries on. The plates are cleared. Dessert is served.

And Amelia is gone.

I can finally relax.

A chair scrapes back somewhere near the end of the table, and someone stands. I don't recognize him. He's tall, well-dressed, a little too polished for this. He clears his throat, not loudly, but somehow, it cuts through the noise, making conversations stop. Even the kids go still, like they can sense the change in the air.

"Good evening, everyone. Thank you all for being here. It's always a pleasure to bring the community together, and tonight, we have a special reason to celebrate. As many of you know, we take great pride in our town, its history, its people, and the way we look out for one another. And part of that means making sure we have the best medical care possible. That's why we're grateful to welcome Dr. Adrian Pierce to Pulse Point.

"Adrian comes to us with years of experience and a dedication to medicine that will serve this town well. I know some of you may have already met him, and I hope the rest of you will take the time to do so. Now, I won't stand here and pretend that change is always easy. But I will say this... Every new beginning is an opportunity. And having another skilled doctor in our community is something we should all appreciate. So, let's show Dr. Pierce the kindness and hospitality this town is known for. Welcome to Pulse Point, Adrian. We're glad to have you."

It hits me... This must be the mayor.

I nod, then keep my head down so I don't have to see their reactions. Not everyone agrees or wants me here. The tension coils in my stomach, twisting tighter with every polite word masking unspoken judgment.

At least he doesn't mention the article, doesn't touch on the controversy swirling around me. At least he has the sense to avoid that. Then the mayor turns, smiling. "All right, if Adrian could come up and say a few words."

Fucking hell.

Keith's hand clamps onto my shoulder. "You got this."

I don't.

Everything in me screams to stay seated, but I won't let them win. Not tonight. I rise, walk toward the front, feeling every stare prickling against my skin. I shake the mayor's hand, grip the microphone, and focus on Keith.

"Thank you." I smile, ignoring the way my pulse is rapidly beating hard against my ribs. "I appreciate the warm welcome. I'm grateful to be here, and I hope you're all having a great night." I pause to take a breath. "This is more than I expected, more than I've ever had, actually. I appreciate you opening your doors to me. And hopefully, I'll see you all around. Just... not in the hospital."

A few chuckles ripple through the crowd, exactly as I intended. My shoulders finally relax. I actually pulled it off without completely embarrassing myself. I hand the mic back and return to my seat. Keith leans in. "Good one, man. You did great." A firm pat on my back, and then he turns back to his dessert. I stare at my plate, grateful for his support.

I don't get a chance to pick up my fork when a tap on my shoulder startles me.

I turn to find a woman in her seventies standing there, her eyes twinkling with mischief. "It's tradition, dear."

"Sorry, what?" My mind races. Please don't ask what I think you're asking.

"The first dance," she explains, extending a delicate but firm hand. "Goes to me."

I hesitate. "And... who are you?"

She winks. "Floral. I'm as old as the town itself."

"Nice to meet you, Floral. I'm Adrian."

She hums in approval. "Very handsome, Adrian." Then, without warning, she tugs at my arm. "Now, come on. We have a dance to start."

"I don't really dance." I try one last time, but there's no graceful way out of this without looking like a complete jerk to a sweet old lady.

"Nonsense," she says as she pulls me to my feet. "I'll teach you."

I don't get a choice when Keith encourages her. She holds on to my arm as she guides me to the town hall, where overhead strands of twinkling lights weave through the beams. The space is both cozy and yet suffocating, a contradiction I can't shake, much like this entire night.

The band strikes up a song, one I vaguely recognize, and before I know it, I'm following Floral's confident lead. Her hands are small in mine, her frame light as she guides me with surprising strength.

"So," she says. "I have a granddaughter."

Here we go.

"She's single. A hairdresser. Very pretty. You're single, right?"

"I am."

But before I can tell her I'm not interested in being set up, her eyes light up, and she speaks. "Wonderful! You two would look great together."

"I'm not interested, sorry."

"What do you think about cougars then?" She winks.

Fuck me... I gotta get out of here.

The song ends, but before I can make a break for it, another woman steps in, taking my hand.

"I'm up next," she says cheerfully.

Jesus Christ.

Over her shoulder, I catch a glimpse of Amelia, and I freeze. I thought she left. The sight of her startles me. She's watching, and I can't tell what she's thinking, but I'm sure it's nothing good. My stomach churns. Is she taking photos or notes? Filing away every interaction to twist into another piece?

I force myself to ignore her, to focus on the next dance, but it's impossible to shake the intensity of her stare.

By the time the third woman approaches, I'm done. But to avoid offending someone or starting more rumors, I mutter about needing a drink and break away, finding Keith near the hay bale seating.

"You ready to go?" I ask.

A smirk crosses his face. "Why? I thought you were having fun."

"Yeah, well, why don't you go out there?" I nod toward the dance floor. "They'd love you."

"Because I know exactly what they're up to," he says, amused. "They're trying to set you up."

"Nailed it."

Keith chuckles. "Welcome to town life." Then his tone shifts. "Be careful, though. If you break someone's heart in this town, it won't end well. People hold grudges. Just… don't get serious unless you're absolutely sure."

"I'm not planning on it." I only just moved here, and dating someone is the last thing on my mind right now.

As we leave, I say goodbye to a few people. They seem surprised I'm leaving early, but understand when I mention having to work tomorrow. I've noticed the whispers have died down now, and the looks are more subtle. Maybe it was just the initial shock of my arrival, or maybe it's only just begun. Either way, tomorrow, I plan to start fixing my reputation. I have to. I need a fresh start. I need to put the past behind me.

Chapter 6

Adrian

I PULL INTO A spot for staff at the hospital. I don't have a permit, no special pass allowing me to be here, but I park anyway.

Stepping out of the car, I inhale sharply, trying to steady the knots twisting in my gut. Keith isn't here. I don't have the comfort of his presence beside me, his easy confidence to lean on. It's just me today, and that thought weighs heavily on me.

This hospital isn't the towering skyscraper I'm used to. No glass windows reflecting the city skyline. Instead, it's a long, single-story brown brick building, stretching wide rather than high. It's different. And yet, as I glance toward the entrance, I know that behind those walls, everything will be the same: sterile hallways, scent of antiseptic, the sound of machines.

And the people? Will they be the same too? *Will they whisper? Will they care?*

I shove a hand into my pocket, and my fingers graze the cool metal of my keys before clenching into a fist. My other hand grips the handle of my briefcase, damp from my sweaty palm. It used to be my dad's when he was a doctor, so the leather is scuffed, edges worn, and the latch sticks if you don't press it just right. I didn't know what to bring, so I packed my laptop, a stethoscope... things that make me feel like I have some control over the unknown.

Being the new guy again sucks. But there's no turning back now.

I've spent years working in the same hospital, surrounded by familiar faces, routines that I could navigate in my sleep. But here? I'm starting over. The feeling is foreign and unsettling, stirring up old memories I'd rather leave buried.

As I push through the entrance decorated with autumn wreaths and paper turkeys, heat greets me, a huge difference to the cool morning outside. The front desk is manned by a receptionist, a woman in her forties with short blonde hair and blue framed glasses perched on the bridge of her nose. She glances up as I approach, scanning me... probably taking in my suit, the briefcase, the slight pause in my step.

Straightening my shoulders, I clear my throat.

"Hi, I'm here to see Anita Smith. I'm Dr. Pierce."

Despite her name on her badge, she introduces herself, offering a polite nod. "Good morning. I'm Nina. Do you have an appointment?"

"Yes."

"Alright." She smiles and gestures down the hallway to the right. "Follow this corridor straight down. There are plenty of signs."

I hesitate for half a second, waiting to see if she's going to call ahead to warn Anita that I'm coming. But she doesn't reach for the phone, so I just nod. "Thanks."

As I walk away, my grip tightens around my briefcase, my fingers slick. The material threatens to slip from my grasp, and I adjust my hold. The suit feels too stiff, too formal. I don't belong here yet.

My appointment isn't until nine, and I'm a little early. I slow my steps, taking in the space around me. The hospital is small, almost cozy, compared to what I'm used to. The waiting room, visible through an open doorway, has worn but comfortable blue chairs, a coffee machine humming in the corner. It's strangely reassuring.

Everything feels familiar. And yet, I'm the only thing out of place.

Finally, I reach her office, the nameplate confirming it. I take a big breath, pressing my lips together. I know she's aware of my dismissal, but I wonder if she'll treat me differently because of it? I raise my hand and knock; my pulse thrums in my ears, matching the beat of my hand against the wood.

"Come in," a voice calls from inside.

Here goes nothing.

I twist the handle and push the door open. The office is compact but cluttered, bookshelves lining the walls, filled with medical textbooks, binders, and what looks like a few personal trinkets. A large desk sits at the center, and behind it, Anita rises to her feet.

She's dressed in a deep purple blouse, her hair pulled back in a neat bun. There's a warmth in her expression as she steps around the desk, hand extended.

"Dr. Pierce, it's lovely to meet you."

I shift my briefcase to my other hand, wiping my palm against my pants, hoping she doesn't notice. Then I reach out and shake hers. Her handshake is firm and confident without an ounce of stiff formality. She smiles, genuinely. I'm not sure what to do with that.

"Take a seat, Dr. Pierce."

"Please, call me Adrian." The title feels heavy, dragging up memories I'm trying to leave behind. "Dr. Pierce is... Just Adrian is fine."

"Fair enough." She settles back into her chair, still smiling. "I'm really happy you're here. Keith's been excited about your arrival, and we're lucky to have you for the year."

Unsure how to respond to that, I nod.

"Obviously, if Keith's practice is up and running before the year's up, you're not locked in. We'd be happy to let you out of the contract."

"Really?" I'm relieved. I hadn't considered that possibility. I'm so used to contracts, so this kind of flexibility feels almost too good to be true.

She nods. "Keith needs the help, and we're a close community. We look out for each other. If things wrap up early and you want to move on, we'll work something out."

I exhale, tension easing just a little. "I appreciate that."

Keith's practice didn't make me feel... this anxious. Even just touring the building, it felt welcoming, a place where I might find some footing. But being here, with familiar hospital sounds and smells, has my past pressing in from all angles. But I can do this. *I can make it through a year.*

Redeem myself. Set myself up for a fresh start, a different future.

Anita rises, grabbing a sheet of paper. "Before we start the tour, I just need to give you your work email address. It's linked to the hospital's bulletin system, a kind of hospital pulse point. Keeps you in the loop."

She chuckles to herself at the reference to Pulse Point, the town, and I find myself smiling.

Maybe this won't be so bad.

I take the paper, glancing over the printed details of passwords, logins, basic information. It's routine, but it feels like the first real step into this new life.

"Alright," she says, standing. "Let's get started."

I follow her out the door, preparing myself for the moment I meet my colleagues.

"I don't think you'll get too lost, but everyone here will help you." We turn left, and she gestures toward a section of the ward. "This is the trauma unit."

That's where I first entered the hospital from... the emergency waiting room. The receptionist doesn't notice us, too busy talking to a family that's just entered.

There are only two things that are different from the city. It's a much smaller scale, with no research center but they've got most of the same equipment for basic emergencies, which relieves me.

She walks me through the hospital, pointing out the pediatric wing, trauma, orthopedics, and other wards before we finally arrive at the medical floor... my new home base.

At the central desk, a few nurses are huddled together, whispering. Their gazes flick toward me, probably gossiping. I hate it. I just want to settle in, to stop being the center of attention. I bet they've all seen the article. My name in bold. The piece Miss Amelia wrote about me haunting me even here.

"Okay, let me show you a room on the ward. This is where you'll mainly be."

She leads me down a hallway lined with doors, some open and some closed. "These are the patient rooms. Some have two beds, some have four. That one is for infectious diseases or for VIP patients."

"VIP patients?" I ask, raising an eyebrow. In this town, who gets special treatment?

"The receptionist will sort that out. You won't need to worry about it."

Sure. Except for the number of beds, the rooms all look the same... hospital beds, bedside tables, chairs, oxygen masks, dull white walls. But the view from the windows is different. Instead of city buildings looming outside, there's greenery. That's something, at least. A better view for patients to recover with.

I meet a couple of nurses, Jaclyn and Matty, who greet me politely as they walk by, and another doctor, Rowan. He barely acknowledges me, just a curt nod before hurrying off. He seems busy, and that's fine by me. The less attention, the better.

"All right, let me show you your office."

I'm excited to be finished with the tour.

"Lockers are in the break room where you can keep your clothes. You're welcome to wear scrubs every day; you don't have to wear a suit. There are fresh scrubs outside the bathroom, so you can shower, change, whatever works for you."

I nod, appreciating her effort to make things easier. As she shows me the room, I tuck my briefcase away under the desk, which makes it feel more permanent. She smiles. "Go familiarize yourself with the medical ward, and I'll check in with you in a few hours. You're not expected to do much today, but if you want to get started, the option's there. Tomorrow's your first real shift. Seven a.m."

When she leaves, my nerves spike. She grew on me... her easy personality. And now, I'm alone again.

I step out, heading to the reception desk on the medical floor. A woman behind the counter hands me a lanyard with a hospital ID badge holder.

"This will get you into all the secured areas, med rooms, ORs, your office, staff lounges, all of it," she says. "I just need to take your photo for the badge."

I nod and follow her instructions. Once the photo's done and she clips it into the holder, I ask, "Is there anything else I should know?"

"Well, I work mornings here, and another woman, Adelaide, covers the afternoons."

"Got it."

"The head nurse will help you with notes if you need it. She'll follow you, update you on patients, and answer questions."

That's new. In the city, you handled everything alone. No one checked in. Which now, looking back, was a bad thing.

"Thanks. Who's the head nurse?"

A light voice answers before the receptionist can. "That would be me."

I turn. She's in her thirties, blonde, navy scrubs, pink sneakers, bright smile.

"I'm Jess, the head nurse on this floor," she says, offering her hand. "If you're ready, I'll take you around to meet the patients."

I smile and shake her hand.

She gives me a rundown on my first patient, Mr. Grant, who's recovering from pneumonia. He's filling in a crossword as I enter. He lowers his pen and settles back into the bed. "You're new."

I nod. "Dr. Pierce. Just moved here."

I start by going over his chart, but the conversation quickly turns to stories about his wife, grandkids, and then his love of golf. The passion bubbles through my veins as I work out the best plan to help him. In this town, people expect you to know them, not just treat them. I shake Mr. Grant's hand before I leave with Jess, and this interaction reminds me exactly why I love being a doctor.

She shows me another patient. It's a rhythm I know, but something about it is different. More efficient. More personal. The town feel is stronger than I expected, and oddly enough, I like it.

I like it a lot.

After a few more patients, she pauses. "Dr. Pierce, I have to say something."

I tilt my head. "Go on."

She hesitates before looking up with a wince. "The article made you out to be some kind of devil."

I exhale sharply through my nose, but there's a sting behind it. "I was torn to shreds, wasn't I?"

"Yeah." She pauses. "But... was it true?"

"No," I say simply. Appreciating her directness, even though it brings back my anxiety.

She nods, smiling. "Figured. Come on, let's finish up. It's only your first day. We can't scare you off yet."

Even with the hushed voices, the lingering looks, and my reputation trailing behind me, I feel comfortable here. Like maybe I can breathe.

I step into the next patient's room and pause. The man in the bed is in his late fifties, lying on his side, arms wrapped tightly around his stomach. Coming closer, I notice his skin is a faint gray color, and when he tries to move to his back, he winces.

"It's okay, don't move."

"I've never been in this much pain, Doc," he whispers. "It started this morning... but now it's worse."

I scan his chart, fingers tightening around the board. Low-grade fever and elevated heart rate.

"Has he had imaging?"

"No," Jess replies.

"Then I want a CT scan."

"That's... kind of broken at the moment."

I freeze. "What?"

She shrugs. "We're trying to raise money for repairs, but it's a lot."

That's not good enough. I can't believe I assumed they'd have all the same equipment as the city. I'm angry at myself for misjudging that so badly. "We need it. It's essential."

"I know," she says simply. "But it's out of our hands. We send patients to Prescott Valley for scans."

We exit the room, and I immediately get on the phone to order an urgent CT scan at the hospital in the next town. While that's being arranged, I put in orders for IV fluids, lab work, and pain management. I also make him nothing by mouth in case surgery becomes necessary and ensure he's being monitored closely. If my suspicions about an abdominal bleed are confirmed, he'll need a surgical consult.

After talking to Jess and taking notes, I head back to Anita's office.

"How did it go?" she asks the moment I appear, her hands clasped tightly on her desk in front of her.

I take a seat, thinking about it before replying. "It was really great. Thanks."

She smiles. "We pride ourselves on being welcoming. Of course, not everyone will be a fan."

I already know that. I felt their glares and heard their words. But whatever. I'll prove myself.

I shift in my seat, crossing one ankle over the other, knowing I have to bring up an issue on my first day. I don't know how Anita will take it, but I can't leave without mentioning it. "I wanted to ask about the CT scanner."

She sighs. "We're doing our best to raise funds, but it's expensive."

"We need two, ideally," I say, already planning how I can help.

She chuckles. "That would be nice, but getting even one is a stretch."

I inherited money from Dad. Maybe it's time to actually use some of it. "Let me handle it."

She shakes her head immediately. "Doctors of the hospital aren't allowed to fund hospital equipment."

Damn. She saw that coming.

The rejection hurts, but pushing the issue won't help anyone.

Her smile softens. "Listen, I'll give you the numbers for the repair and a replacement. Think about it. We're open to ideas."

I nod, already trying to figure out another way I can help. "I'll work on it."

"Have a good afternoon, and I'll see you tomorrow."

"Thanks. See you tomorrow."

My first real shift. Today was just a warm-up, and I'm already exhausted, but it's the good kind of tired. I'd forgotten what it felt like to be drained for the right reasons.

I leave her office and walk back to the break room to collect my case. Checking my phone to see an email. I open it and immediately regret it.

The Pulse Bulletin.

The headline grabs my attention first: *New Doctor Joins the Fun at Welcome Party.*

Great. I officially can't escape gossip.

I scroll through the photos.

There's one of people stomping grapes with their bare feet. *Disgusting.* I'm definitely not drinking that wine.

Another photo captures the dinner table, glowing under soft lights, everyone gathered and chatting. I don't even remember when that was taken, but there I am, mid-conversation with Diane, who was actually quite welcoming.

Then, more pictures, including one of me giving the speech and also dancing. Surprisingly, I don't look terrible. The article itself isn't bad either. It's welcoming, almost kind.

But then, the twist.

Can he go against orders here as well?

A little jab. A subtle dig. And there, at the bottom, the name.

Amelia.

I stare at it, confused. I was expecting the sign-off to be Dr. Whisperer. *So does that mean she's both?*

The rest of the bulletin is filled with a mix of news and gossip, some pieces signed, others anonymous. It feels like the town's version of social media, where people spill everything. At least Russell, the turkey, seems to have moved on and found someone else to target. That article makes me chuckle.

Chapter 7

Amelia

THE SCENT OF VANILLA and jasmine reaches me before I hear the soft click of heels against the floor.

"Good morning," Violet chirps, stepping into view.

I glance up and smile. "Oh, look at us," I say, gesturing between us. "Matching outfits."

She laughs, her dark eyes flicking down at her outfit. "Oh, we did! Cheers to unintentional coordination."

She's wearing tailored black pants, the straight-leg cut giving her an effortlessly chic look, paired with heeled ankle boots that click with every step. My pants are more fitted, hugging my hips and tapering at the ankle, comfortable, but not quite as polished. I've stuck with my classic black loafers: clean, practical, and a little predictable.

We're both in shades of green, hers a deep forest, mine closer to olive, which leaves our hair as the only real difference. Hers is twisted into a messy bun, a few artful strands framing her face. Mine's sleek and straight, tucked neatly behind my ears. Less romantic, more... controlled.

I wonder if I could pull off her look... if I let things be a little more undone. Next time I feel like my wardrobe's in a rut, I'll try something less precise. Or maybe I'm just imagining all this because she makes it look so easy.

"How was the welcome party?" she asks as she props herself against my desk.

"Actually, not bad."

Which is true. I think about the fun my family had, and I'm grateful to Luna for taking them home. She texted me to let me know everything was fine, which helped me focus on getting pictures and notes. I saw a side of Adrian I wasn't expecting; his speech and dancing were surprisingly good.

"Mad I missed it." She pauses, then tilts her head. "Did you write something about it?"

I hesitate for a beat. "Yeah, I did."

"Well, send it over. I'm curious," she adds with a grin, clearly meaning it as a compliment, though something about it tightens my chest.

I tap at my keyboard and fire it off before I can second-guess myself. Since the offer of promotion, everything I write feels like it's under a microscope. Luna's watching my every move. Even though I bet no one else applied for this job, and it's technically mine already, I can't afford to screw up.

A whistle pulls me from my thoughts.

I glance up. "What?"

Violet smirks, scrolling through the photos on her computer screen. "Damn. He's a good-looking guy."

"Who?" I ask, even though I know exactly who she's talking about.

She moves the screen and taps it, her finger landing squarely on Adrian's face.

I make a dismissive huff. "I guess. If you're into that kind of thing."

"What? Hot men?" she shoots back, arching an eyebrow. "Did he say if he was single?"

"No, we didn't talk about that."

She grins, mischief sparking in her eyes. "Oh, so you've talked."

"Yeah, but only for the article."

A mischievous glint flashes in her eyes. "Are you gonna—"

"Not a chance." I shake my head. "Good-looking or not, he's a walking red flag."

Violet's lips twitch. "Did I say he wasn't a red flag? I'm just saying... he's pretty."

"Too pretty to do what he did?" I arch an eyebrow right back. "Don't let his face fool you. Guys like that charm their way through life; think the rules don't apply to them. A guy getting dismissed from work? That's not just a bad day. He probably thinks accountability's for everyone else."

She shrugs. "I don't know. Maybe there's more to the story."

"There always is. But I don't care. It's a dealbreaker for me."

Violet hums, but I can tell she's not entirely convinced.

I steer us back on track. "Anyway, read the article. Tell me what you think."

A minute passes as she skims through, then she nods. "It's great. You did a really good job."

Pride swells in my chest. "Thanks."

She stretches, then glances at me. "How was your weekend? Besides the party?"

I shrug. "The usual. Clean the house, buy groceries, get the kids ready for school. How was the engagement party you went to?"

"It was nice. We had a good time."

"Do you think Nell will propose soon?"

She laughs lightly. "Ever? Yeah. Soon? Hell no. We're still figuring things out."

"I just thought, it's been a couple of years..."

She shrugs nonchalantly. "Yeah, but we're young. No rush. I think good things take time."

"That's true."

Violet grins. "What about you?"

I snort. "This town doesn't exactly have a great selection."

The town's matchmaking attempts failed, so they gave up.

"Yeah," she says. "And the only new option has a giant red flag plastered on his forehead."

"Exactly." I sigh. "If I ever move to the city, maybe I'll actually find someone worth dating. But for now?" I gesture around us. "Slim pickings."

"Tragic."

I chuckle. "Yeah, well, I should take this article to Luna."

Violet nods. "It's really good. She's gonna love it. No question."

I hesitate. "You sure?"

She gives me a flat, unimpressed stare, lips twitching at the corners. "When am I ever wrong?"

I smile, but my stomach knots. For some reason, this part makes me nervous. I'm not usually the anxious type, but something about Luna's reaction to this article sets me on edge. Her approval matters more because of the promotion.

Bracing myself, I grab my laptop and stand.

The glass door to Luna's office looms ahead. I take a breath, square my shoulders, and knock.

She calls out, "Come in."

I step inside, where Luna sits behind her desk, the large window behind her spilling afternoon light across the office.

"Hi, I just wanted to show you my article from the welcome party."

She looks up, a small smile tugging at her lips. "It was a great event, wasn't it?"

"It was. The town always knows how to show up. I had a great time."

Luna nods, gesturing toward the chair across from her. "Send it to me."

I take a seat and email it to her. As she reads, I pick at my nails. The silence stretches, broken only by the occasional flick of her eyes across the screen.

Finally, she leans back, exhaling. "Great photos. And the article is solid. You did a great job."

Relief washes over me. "Thanks."

She pauses, tapping a finger against the desk. "But... I think we're missing something."

I stiffen. "We are?"

"Seeing him at the event.... Adrian. It just didn't seem like he was the villain we made him out to be."

The thought of this jeopardizing my chances fills me with dread. "You didn't like the article?"

"No, I loved it. It was sharp, scathing... everything it needed to be. But I think we need his side of the story. It would add balance and depth."

I can't even imagine asking him. "You want me to interview him?"

"Yes. If you can get his perspective and write a new article with his photo, it'll be even better. Honestly, your last few articles—including this one—are phenomenal. You've really stepped it up."

For a second, I just sit there, stunned. A flicker of pride swells in my chest. Relief floods in behind it, chasing away the knot that had been lodged in my stomach since I walked in. But the glow doesn't last long. I need to do a follow-up interview where I get up close and personal.

I inhale deeply, knowing there's no other answer unless I want to kiss goodbye to my promotion. "Okay. I can do an article on Adrian."

Luna nods, seeming satisfied. "Good. We'll put this one online and straight to print, and you can get working on the next."

I should be grateful. She's trusting me with more than just the dull town announcements and simple local updates. For once, I'm getting real stories. Poor Violet, though. She's the one stuck covering all the boring assignments. Not that she seems too mad about it.

I carry my laptop back to my desk, dropping into my chair with a sigh. Violet leans over, eyes curious. "How'd it go?"

"Yeah, good."

She raises an eyebrow. "What does that mean?"

"This can go online and print, but she wants me to interview Adrian."

Violet's eyes widen. "Oh?"

I nod. "I need to get his side of the story."

Her lips press together, and then she chuckles. She tries to hide it, but she fails, and soon, I'm laughing too.

"Just my luck." I shake my head.

Violet grins. "Gotta hang out with him more. Come on, it's not that bad. There are worse things to look at."

She wiggles her eyebrows at me, knowing we both admitted that Adrian's attractive.

"Listen, I'm not saying it's going to be the worst thing in the world," I say. "Just that I don't necessarily want to do it."

She shrugs. "Well, you've got no choice now."

I sigh. "Yeah, I think he started today at the hospital. So now I just have to figure out... do I visit him there, or do I go to his place?"

Violet laughs. "You're probably better off catching him at work."

I groan. "Great. Looks like I'm heading to the hospital this afternoon."

Violet grins, sing-songing, "Can't wait for the stories."

I groan again, but secretly, I wonder what exactly I'm walking into. What if he refuses? What if he brushes me off or turns it into a fight? I need this interview to land. Luna's watching, and if I can't handle one doctor—especially *this* one—what does that say about me? About the promotion?

Hours later, I arrive at the town hospital, my nerves bundled tight. I push through the cold air, my hands stuffed into my pockets, regretting not bringing a jacket. The cold cuts at my skin as I step inside, the fluorescent lights harsh against the sterile white walls.

I make my way to the emergency reception desk, glancing around. Patients wait in plastic hospital chairs, staff move with urgency, the smell of antiseptic fills my nose. I've never liked hospitals. Too many recent memories with Mom. The familiar woman behind the desk doesn't look up, her fingers tapping away on her keyboard. "Hey, Nina, do you know when Dr. Pierce is finishing up?"

"Amelia. Nice to see you. Looking to check him out?" Nina eyes me curiously, the corner of her lips lifting, as if she knows something I don't.

I scoff, shaking my head. "Hardly. I just need an interview. I'm writing an article."

Her knowing smile remains, but she doesn't give me the information I need. As I step outside, the cold air wraps around me again. With my phone in hand, I start jotting down notes. This article must be good. One more strong piece, and the promotion is as good as mine.

The automatic doors slide open, and my head snaps up.

It's not him.

I exhale, glancing back down at my notes, but anticipation tightens in my chest. My fingers numb as I scroll through my notes, trying to distract myself.

Then, finally, the doors part, and my breath catches.

Adrian steps out, suit pants hugging his frame, shirt slightly wrinkled, tie loosened just enough to make him look effortlessly undone. His dark hair is slightly tousled... end-of-the-day hair. His strong jaw is tight, blue eyes sharp as they land on me.

I swallow hard.

"Hi. Have a good day?" I say, forcing a casual smile despite the ridiculous flutter in my chest. It's nothing. Just nerves about the article. The promotion. The pressure to make this interview count.

At least, that's what I tell myself.

He barely reacts. "What do you want, Amelia? Or should I say, Dr. Whisperer?"

"I'm not—"

"Sure about that?" He crosses his arms, his stance firm. "Seems like people in that little gossip column love to ruin reputations."

"No one knows who's behind it. They're anonymous. If I find out, I'll let you know."

Rumor has it the gossip column came from some long-time freelancer the paper paid forty bucks an article. Nobody in the office had ever met them. They handed in their stories through a generic inbox like a phantom.

Adrian scoffs. "What kind of reporter can't figure out who Dr. Whisperer is? Unless, of course, they are Dr. Whisperer."

I stare at him, momentarily thrown. This accusation isn't new, but coming from him, it stings.

"Good call, Dr. Pierce, but I'm pretty damn good at my job," I counter.

His lips curl, but it doesn't reach his eyes. "I'd beg to differ. A scathing article about me? Ruining my reputation further? And now, not being able to figure out who's running that? Doesn't scream 'good reporter' to me."

I grit my teeth. I can't believe Violet thinks I'd be interested in this guy. He despises me.

But I'm here for a reason. "So you won't give me an interview?"

"What interview?"

I straighten my shoulders, hating having to ask him like this. "I just want to get your side of the story."

His eyes darken as the pulse in his jaw tics. "So you can twist it? No thanks."

He turns to leave, and in a moment of desperation, I reach out, catching his arm. My fingers meet solid muscle, and my brain short-circuits. His bicep flexes under my touch. I wasn't expecting this level of muscle from a doctor, let alone noticing how good he feels, but I do.

Adrian stills, his gaze dropping to where my hand lingers. My pulse spikes. I drop my hand like I've been burned.

"Please," I try again, my voice softer now.

His nostrils flare. "No. I also read your recent article about the welcome party."

I pretend I don't know exactly which part he's referring to. "That was nice, right?"

His eyes narrow. "You keep finding little ways to dig at me. If I agreed to an interview, you'd do it again. I'm not giving you the chance. Not at my expense."

He turns and walks away, his long strides eating up the pavement.

I stand there, watching him disappear into the night, trying to ignore the fact that, despite everything, I can't stop looking at him.

CHAPTER 8

ADRIAN

I YANK OPEN THE car door and slide into the driver's seat, gripping the wheel tightly, refusing to look back.

Every article she writes about me is full of bullshit, twisting the truth to fit whatever story she's after. And now she wants my side? Yeah, right. She doesn't actually care... This is just another opportunity for her to build her name, to add another dramatic piece to her collection.

I rub my temples as exhaustion settles deep in my bones. It's been a long day, and I don't have the patience for this. What I do need to figure out is how the hell I'm going to get the hospital the money for the CT.

Starting the engine, I pull out of the parking lot, driving slow. But as I pass the hospital entrance, a flicker of movement catches my eye.

She's still there.

Standing beneath the streetlamp, arms crossed, shifting on her feet. She's watching me. Waiting.

I snap my gaze back to the road. *Not my problem.*

The town is quiet at this time of day, the roads mostly empty except for the occasional car pulling into a driveway. I take the familiar route to Keith's; the tires rolling over the asphalt, my mind already drifting to the article I read earlier. Another piece from Dr. Whisperer.

A missing jewelry scandal.

Ridiculous.

But then there was another one about me.

It was my first damn day back, and the fact that I'm under a microscope pisses me off more than it should. I don't need anyone waiting for me to screw up. I already have enough pressure on me not to mess up and get dismissed from this hospital. If I don't succeed in Pulse Point, my career as a doctor is over.

By the time I pull into the driveway, my shoulders are tight, my head pounding.

Keith's car is here. And he's not alone.

Through the back window, I catch a glimpse of him on the porch, talking to an older guy, both dressed in polos and caps. Golf, I'm guessing. Keith had an early shift, so he must've wrapped up before me and gone straight to the course.

I'm not in the mood to face anyone else right now. I was hoping to shower, eat, and relax.

I turn off the engine and step out, stretching my stiff muscles before heading inside. As I walk up the steps, I hear their low laughter, the clinking of beer bottles. I could join them, but honestly, I don't have it in me.

I drop my briefcase inside the door and go straight to my room, peeling off my shirt as I go. A quick shower, dinner, then sleep. I need to be up early for another run before my seven a.m. shift. Maybe I'll find the gym this weekend so I can hit the weights again. It's been too long.

By the time I emerge from the shower, dressed in sweats and feeling somewhat human again, I head toward the kitchen, hoping Keith's friend is gone. But as soon as I round the corner, I spot him standing next to Keith, nursing a drink.

Keith looks up from his beer, grinning. "Didn't even hear you come in."

He gestures toward the guy beside him, an older man with short graying hair and deep lines around his eyes that speak of years of laughter and hard work. "This is my buddy, Adam. We squeezed in a round of golf; first time catching up in months."

Adam tips his beer toward me. "Man, I don't know how you do it. The hospital's got to be brutal. At least on the course, we only suffer from Keith's bad swings."

"Harsh." Keith grins. "But fair."

I shake my head, beginning to fill up a pot with water to put on the stove. I need something quick, something easy. "You guys eaten yet?"

Keith stretches. "Nah, we got carried away. I can help if you want."

"You don't have to," I say, already opening the pasta.

Adam laughs. "Listen to you two. You sound like an old married couple."

Keith shoots him a playful look. "Don't be jealous just because you have no one keeping you company."

Adam raises his hands in surrender. "Fine, fine. Speaking of company, what's the plan for Thanksgiving?"

Thanksgiving.

The reminder tightens my chest.

I haven't given it much thought after my encounter with Russell. Sure, I've seen the ridiculous turkey decorations around the hospital, but I haven't really felt the holiday coming. Thanksgiving's on Thursday, and I'm off that day. And honestly? I don't have a plan.

I glance at Keith. "What are your plans?"

He shrugs, sipping his beer. "Haven't decided yet. Could be fun to do something, though."

I nod absentmindedly, stirring the pasta, but my thoughts drift elsewhere.

To the hospital.

To the eyes watching me.

To *her*, still standing in the cold, waiting.

"I think we'll probably just have dinner to ourselves, right?" I glance at Keith, waiting for confirmation.

He shrugs. "Sounds like it." Then he turns to Adam. "You want to join us?"

Adam shakes his head and offers a half-smile. "I'd love to, but I can't. Plan to see my mom."

"Oh, that's right." Keith leans back in his chair. "How's she doing?"

A hint of amusement plays on Adam's lips. "Well, you know those women in the retirement village? They gossip more than the damn bulletin."

I chuckle, resting my forearms on the counter. "Yeah, Keith gave me the grand tour of the town the other day. We drove past the retirement home, but I haven't been inside yet. I'm guessing that Keith, you'd see a lot of patients that live there?"

Keith nods. "Well, my clinic does, so you'll probably get to know them soon enough."

I glance back at Adam. "Are they doing anything special for Thanksgiving?"

"Yeah, they try to make a big thing of it. Decorations, music, even a bit of dancing if they can get them to. Of course, there are always a couple of grumps who complain about the noise, but isn't that just life?"

Keith smiles. "True."

"You sure you don't want to stay for dinner?" I ask, checking the pasta boiling on the stove, making sure there's enough for all three of us.

Adam stretches his arms over his head, then nods. "Why not? Another hour won't kill me. Besides, it's nice having someone cook for me."

I grab some sauce and stir it absentmindedly as my thoughts drift back to Thanksgiving. If it's just going to be me and Keith, maybe I should pick up a turkey. It's not something I ever really did much before because I worked. Thanksgiving wasn't a big deal to me, but here, with Keith, it might be nice.

A quiet tradition.

A new tradition.

I could pick up groceries on Tuesday and hope the stores aren't cleaned out. I'll have to run it by Keith, but ultimately, I think we'll do a turkey dinner. Maybe watch some football, have a decent meal, just...relax.

By the time we've eaten and Adam heads out, Keith joins me in cleaning up. He's unusually quiet as he dries a dish, then sets it aside.

I still, gripping the edge of the sink as the memory of Amelia showing up at work plays on my mind. "What else do you know about Amelia?"

"She's a nice young lady." Keith continues before I can answer. "Big family. Her mom was doing well until recently, and now Amelia's just trying to get back on her feet."

I snort, shaking my head. "She might be a 'nice young lady' to you, but to me? Not so much."

Keith's eyebrows shoot up, the corner of his mouth twitching. "And why's that?"

"She cornered me at the hospital earlier. Wanted my side of the story."

He chuckles and shakes his head. "Amelia's the sweetest thing. I don't agree with the article she wrote, but I still believe she's not out to get you."

I give him a deadpan stare. "You're kidding me, right? Amelia's been nothing but difficult." Aside from the time involving Russell, but I'm not telling him about that.

"She's doing her job," Keith says, unfazed. "She works her ass off to support her family. Always has. She's got a hell of a work ethic. Kinda like someone else I know." He winks.

I roll my eyes. "If she really wanted my side, I might consider it... if I trusted her not to twist my words. But I don't. People already whisper about me. I don't need them talking about me any more than they already do."

Keith sighs, setting down the towel. "Fair enough. But sometimes, getting your side out there isn't the worst idea."

It's tempting... clearing the air, setting the record straight. But what would that change? She's already made up her mind.

"If I could trust her, sure," I admit. "But I don't. I just want to move on from it."

Keith studies me for a moment, then nods. "I get it."

There's a beat of silence before he changes the subject. "So, how was your first day?"

It's a simple question, but it catches me off guard.

No one's really asked me that before... except Amelia today.

It feels weird. But also kind of nice. Especially coming from someone who understands the industry.

I lean against the counter, rubbing a hand over my jaw. "Surprisingly good."

Keith nods slowly.

"I mean, I was nervous, obviously, but people seemed decent, for the most part. A few whispers and looks, but overall, it was alright. Met lots of new people. The place looks different but smells the same. Even though it feels familiar, it's not like the city, you know? We don't have everything at our fingertips."

Keith nods. "Glad it wasn't terrible. What's your schedule looking like this week?"

"Mornings." Which is a nice way to start a new job. But I am on a mix of days, afternoons, and nights over the first six weeks.

"Perfect. I'll be around, so if you need a sounding board, I can help."

I nod in appreciation, but my mind is already shifting to something else. "There's an issue, though."

"What's that?"

"They need to fix the CT scanner. Ideally, they need a new one too. But apparently, I can't buy one for the hospital."

"Yeah, they won't let you. I haven't looked at the contract myself, but I've heard it's not allowed."

I shake my head. "I should double-check. Maybe there's a way around it."

Keith shrugs. "Maybe. But if they've been managing without one, they'll survive a little longer while they save up."

I grip the counter, my jaw tightening. "That's not the point, Keith. There's no CT scanner in town. That could cost someone their life."

His expression sobers.

I drag a hand through my hair at the memories. Flashes of that day with my dad slam into me. "I want to have the right tools to save as many lives as possible."

Keith doesn't say anything for a moment. Then he sighs, voice quieter. "I know."

The exhaustion of the day presses down on me again, but this time, it's heavier.

Keith watches me carefully, then nods. After a moment, he clears his throat and says, "Well, if you do find a way to buy them one, maybe hold off until after Thanksgiving. Otherwise, you'll end up the guy who donated the scanner and getting stuck with turkey duty."

I snort and shake my head. "Right. Because that's the real tragedy here."

"Hey, dry turkey is no joke. I had to suffer through it once, and I still have nightmares."

I laugh. "I'll make sure to brine ours properly, then."

Keith grins. "Good. I don't want to choke to death before we figure out how to get that scanner."

CHAPTER 9

AMELIA

"I'M STUCK," I SAY, slumping into the chair across from Violet.

She looks up from her laptop. "What do you mean?"

I let out a slow breath and drag a hand through my hair. The smell of fresh coffee fills the air, completely different from the frustration churning in my belly. "I went to the hospital yesterday to see Adrian. Tried to get the interview. He refused."

Violet frowns, stirring her latte absentmindedly. "Why?"

"He thinks I'm going to twist his words or something," I explain. "I thought the last article wasn't bad."

"It was great," she says firmly.

I sigh. "Yeah. But he doesn't like it. And I need to figure out how to get him to talk, because Luna asked for this interview, and if I don't deliver, I can forget about that promotion."

Violet taps her chin, considering. "I'd be that pestering person if I were you. Keep annoying him until he gives in. Show him you're more than a person trying to get a story, that you're a person trying to do the town right, and that includes its people."

"You really think that'll work?"

She grins. "Absolutely. You can't back down on this. Luna asked for it. You want the promotion. That means you need the interview. Just keep showing up, asking again, and eventually, he'll crack."

I let out a dry laugh, shaking my head. "This isn't like your boyfriend, where you bat your eyes and get away with things. Adrian's different. He's stubborn. The few glimpses I've had of him, he doesn't seem like the type to budge."

If I can't get this interview, I don't get the promotion, and that means no raise. Without that, I can't keep covering Mom's medical bills and my family's expenses.

Violet leans back in her chair, smirking. "You won't know unless you try."

"True." I take a sip of my now lukewarm coffee, then glance at her screen. "Anyway, what are you working on? I feel bad always dumping my problems on you."

With a grin, she flips the laptop toward me. "Oh, you know, riveting journalism. Genevieve from the diner is about to start making her famous pies, and I'm tracking how fast they sell out for Thanksgiving."

I sit up straighter. "Oh, that reminds me, I need to get one of those for Thanksgiving." I tap my fingers on the table, an idea forming. "Maybe... and get one as a peace offering."

Violet gasps as her eyes light up. "Yes! Bring one to Adrian. He must give you the interview then."

I tap my lips, considering. "Bribery does have a long and successful history."

"Not a bad idea, right?" she says smugly.

I smile. "Not bad at all."

She shifts her laptop back toward her.

"So, what else are you working on?"

"Just the bakery piece?"

"Yeah, mostly. I went down there earlier, took some photos." She pulls up one on her camera and hands it to me. "Look how proud she is."

The image is warm and inviting, Genevieve standing in front of the bakery, arms crossed, a crisp white apron tied around her waist, beaming. The pies behind the glass case look too good, golden-brown crusts glistening under the light.

"They're honestly so good," I say. "How haven't you managed to snag one before they sell out?"

Her grin stretches wider. "Who says I haven't?"

I narrow my eyes. "Listen, if I don't manage to score one, you better share some of that with me."

Violet laughs. "We'll see."

I glance back at the photo. "There's something different about those pies. It's not just one flavor. She makes multiple, and somehow, they all disappear instantly."

"Exactly." She takes her camera back with a satisfied sigh. "Well, good luck getting one."

"Thanks, I'll need it." I stretch, glancing at my watch. "So where are you going for Thanksgiving?"

She tucks a strand of hair behind her ear. "Nell's parents."

I grin knowingly. "Ah. So, the pie is a good kind of—"

"Exactly." She points at me, eyes gleaming. "Gotta seem like the perfect daughter-in-law, and nothing says, *I belong in this family* like bringing the best pie in town."

"You've got it all figured out."

"Damn right."

I push back from the table, finishing the last sip of my coffee. "Alright. After work today, I'll head to Keith's house. Try to catch Adrian there." I'm not sure if I'm walking into a chance or a total waste of time. Still, I have to try.

"Good idea." Violet gives me a thumbs-up. "And don't forget the pie, Thursday. That might just be your golden ticket."

I roll my eyes but can't hide my grin. If Adrian's as stubborn as I think he is, I'll need all the help I can get.

Later that evening, after a long shift, I make my way over to Keith's house.

The neighborhood is quiet, and there's a faint scent of wood smoke from Keith's place. I don't see Adrian's car out front, but that doesn't mean he isn't here. He could've parked around the back or maybe gotten a ride from someone at the hospital. Either way, I'm not turning around.

I hesitate for only a second before stepping onto the porch and knocking on the door.

A moment later, the door swings open, and Keith stands there, his warm smile as familiar as ever. He wears a checkered shirt and navy pants, just in from work. His practice badge still dangles from his pocket. In all the years I've known him, he's had the same clothes. I'd love to give him a makeover, but I asked once, and he said no.

"Amelia. How are you?"

"I'm good, thanks. How are you?"

"Can't complain." His gaze flickers with curiosity. "What can I do for you?"

I nervously shift on my feet. "I was actually wondering if Dr. Pierce was around."

Keith's lips twitch, like he already knows the answer will disappoint me. "He's still at work. Sorry, Amelia."

I try not to let my disappointment show. "Oh. Do you know when he'll be back?"

He shakes his head. "No idea. But you could always wait here. Have a cup of tea with me? I wouldn't mind the company."

I glance at my phone, seeing a text from Mom. I let her know earlier that I'd be late home. The thought of not being there makes me unsettled. My family relies on me, and I hate letting her down by not being there to help. But I need this interview. More money means I can stop juggling overdue notices. It also means filling her prescriptions without checking my bank balance twice.

I force a smile. "Sure. I'd love a cup of tea."

Keith nods, stepping aside to let me in. His house is warm from the fire burning. As I follow him to the kitchen, I recognize the jazz tune. It's something old and soothing.

He moves with ease, grabbing cups and turning on the kettle. "How's your mom doing?"

I hesitate, fingers brushing the edge of the counter. "She's... okay." It's not exactly a lie. Just the best version of reality that I can give.

Keith gives me a sad smile. "You're a good daughter, you know that?"

Emotion clogs my throat. I'm not used to hearing things like that from anyone other than my mother. "Looking after her is just… what I do," I say softly. "She's always been there for me and my siblings. It's the least I can do."

He nods as he hands me my tea, then leads me out onto the back deck. The night air is cool but not cold, the light fading around us.

"So," he says, settling into his chair. "What are you here to see Adrian for?"

I take a seat and blow on my tea, watching the steam rise into the air. "I need an interview. Which he'll probably say no to again, but Luna's insisting."

Keith's a doctor, so he might understand the pressure, or he might think I'm just another journalist chasing a story. Part of me hopes he'll see past that because he's known me my whole life.

We sit in silence. My mind travels to the moment Adrian made it clear he wasn't interested in an interview. He barely gave it a thought before shutting me down. Sipping my tea, I look out at Keith's backyard. It's peaceful here. No siblings fighting over the last piece of toast, no one stealing my shoes, no yelling. Just stillness.

Wouldn't it be nice to come home to this?

Keith sighs, which pulls my gaze to him. "Listen, Adrian had a rough time back in the city. He's a good kid, but the bulletin hasn't been kind."

I shift uncomfortably, knowing that was half my fault, already feeling a kind lecture coming on.

"You know, Amelia, you could have left that last line out of your last article," he says gently. "But you didn't."

A pit forms in my stomach. He's calling me out, and I can't even deny it.

Keith takes a sip of his drink, clearly thinking.

I don't know if he's disappointed, angry, or both. So I wait, expecting him to say I went too far, or that I blew my chance with Adrian completely.

Finally, he says, "There's one thing I know he cares about."

I sit up straighter. "What is it?"

Keith watches me for a moment, then leans back. "Some medical equipment at the hospital, called a CT scanner, is broken, and he's been trying to get it replaced. But he can't use his own money to fix it."

I listen carefully.

He stares into the distance before meeting my eyes. "I think if you helped him run a fundraiser to get the money, he might trade you for the interview."

"Why does he care so much about that particular equipment?"

Keith gives me a look, as if he knows, but doesn't say it out loud. "That's not my story to tell. If he wants you to know, he'll tell you."

I press my lips together, mulling it over as I sip my tea. The idea isn't terrible. It might actually work.

A fundraiser. That's something I could do. I know people, restaurant owners, small businesses who could sponsor, even the local radio owes me a favor. If I asked the right people, got some traction, it could gain momentum fast. And if Adrian sees I'm actually trying to help, not just chasing a headline, he might be willing to talk. This could work, and maybe it would mean more than Genevieve's pie.

There's something about the way Keith said it, there's a deeper reason Adrian wants that equipment. I suspect it's something personal.

I glance at Keith again, but he doesn't offer more.

If I'm going to make this work, I need to treat it like any other story, so I set my empty cup down, already planning to call Ezra, Milton the community co-ordinator, and the mayor and pitch to them first. Adrian still hasn't shown up, so I decide it's time to leave.

"I should get going. I need to get home to Mom." I stand and straighten my top.

Keith stands with me, nodding. "Tell her I'm thinking of her."

"I will."

As I step onto the porch, I glance back. "Thanks, Keith."

He waves with a smile as I get in my car.

I don't have my interview. Yet. But now, I have a plan.

I'm about to take off when Adrian's car pulls up. My fingers tighten around the steering wheel, my heart kicking up a notch. I should leave. But instead, I shove the door open and step out, watching as he parks.

He gets out, his expression already set in a scowl.

"Why are you here?"

I swallow down the heat rising in my throat. He's a mess. His white dress shirt is wrinkled, his tie loosened, black suit pants slightly creased. As if he's been running his hands through it all day, his brown hair is ruffled, and a shadow of stubble darkens his jaw. When my gaze lifts to his, blue eyes pierce through me.

I cross my arms. "I need to talk to you."

"I said no."

The words sting, but I push through. "Adrian, please."

He breathes heavily and moves closer. "What is it?"

I square my shoulders. "I have an offer. One that I think would benefit both of us."

His eyebrows lift, the corners of his mouth twitching with something close to amusement. "Yeah? And what's that?" His tone is mocking, like he already knows I have nothing worth his time.

I force myself to keep my chin up. "A fundraiser."

He blinks rapidly. "A fundraiser?"

"For the hospital equipment you need," I say.

His jaw tightens, his gaze flicking toward the house. "He told you, didn't he?"

I smile. "Maybe."

Adrian rolls his eyes, shaking his head. "Yeah, the hospital needs the money. I need the money. What does that have to do with the article?"

"What if I help you run the best fundraiser this town has ever seen? Enough money to get the equipment needed," I say, letting the words settle before adding, "in exchange for your side of the story."

He drops his gaze to the ground. The silence stretches. I can almost see the battle playing out in his mind.

"I don't know. I don't know if I can trust you. How do I know you'll follow through?"

The accusation stuns me. My trust has never been questioned before. I've built my reputation on reliability. Heat rises in my cheeks. *Is this how he sees me?*

"You don't," I admit, uncrossing my arms. "But you could always give me the interview after the fundraiser. Would that be better?" I pause, trying to read his expression. "And the article will be fair. And the photo... must be good."

His nostrils flare slightly as he takes a deep breath. I think I have him. If I do, I'll have to email Luna tonight and let her know the plan.

"Fine," he says at last. "But do you even know how to run a fundraiser big enough to raise that kind of money?"

"Don't you worry about that. I've covered enough of them to know what works. I'll figure something out.

Nothing like an exciting challenge to keep me on my toes." The ideas are already coming together in my head.

"I'm glad I'm not the subject this time."

For a moment, we share a smile, the tension between us easing. But then it shifts, the air thickening again, something unspoken hanging between us. The sudden awareness of it sends a shiver down my spine. Adrian clears his throat, as if shaking it off.

"I better go." I pull myself back. "Gotta get home to my mom."

His gaze softens, a rare gentleness in his eyes. "Yeah, of course," he murmurs.

We both nod, then I turn away. He stands on Keith's porch, watching as I reverse out of the driveway and onto the street.

It's only when I can no longer see him that I feel like I can breathe again.

And yet, I'm still on edge.

Still feeling something I don't know how to name.

Chapter 10

Amelia

Thursday morning in our town is usually bustling, but today, it's downright chaotic. Dr. Whisperer has wasted no time putting out a headline about Thanksgiving, stirring up the town's excitement.

Thanksgiving Morning Chaos: Missing Turkeys
The town's entire flock of turkeys has vanished overnight, including our beloved Russell. Did someone steal them? And where could dozens of turkeys hide?

Dr. Whisperer

We stand in line outside the diner, the crisp autumn air biting at my cheeks, my breath visible in small puffs. The line snakes around the corner, people chatting, shifting on their feet, wrapped in coats and scarves, all here for one thing... Genevieve's famous pies.

I don't care what flavor I get. I just need two. One for my family and, more importantly, one for Adrian. He agreed to the fundraiser, sure, but I need this article to be damn good. It can't be half-assed. It must be perfect. If that means eating literal humble pie, so be it.

My younger sister, Hazel, is with me. I wasn't about to stand in this line alone, and I sure as hell didn't want to add more to Violet's plate today. She's working a few hours to cover this story before heading to her boyfriend's parents' place.

Inside, I'm bouncing on the balls of my feet, nerves eating at me as the line inches forward. It takes a full hour before we finally step inside, and when we do, the smell nearly knocks me off my feet. Warm sugar, melted butter, nutmeg, cinnamon, pastry. It's heaven.

My eyes snap to the glass cases, scanning the selection, and my stomach clenches. There aren't many left.

Heart pounding, I step up to the counter. "Genevieve, I need one pecan pie and a sweet potato pie."

She smiles, her hands dusted with flour, her apron slightly askew. "Lucky you, love. I've got pecan." Relief washes over me, even as she follows up with. "Sweet potato's gone, though."

Damn. That one was for the kids, but anything will do.

"Can we get the chocolate cream one?" Hazel asks.

"Of course."

She boxes them, whistling.

"You're doing amazing, Genevieve," I tell her, handing over the cash as Hazel grabs a pie.

She grins. "Only once a year. Gotta make it count."

Pies in hand, we leave the diner, clutching them like someone might snatch them away. The line outside has only grown, winding farther down the street. There's no way there are enough pies left for all these people.

Spotting Violet through the crowd taking photos, I wave goodbye before heading straight home.

Back at the house, the mess is already in full swing. Felix is running through the halls, screeching in his little Thanksgiving sugar rush from this morning's Lucky Charms. The kitchen is warm, rich with the scent of roasted turkey, buttery mashed potatoes, and freshly baked bread.

Mom sits on the recliner, looking exhausted but content. "That took a while," she notes, her voice light with amusement.

"The line was insane," I say as we settle the pies safely on the counter. "But we got them. Oh, and I'm heading over to drop one off at Keith's."

She nods. "All right, love. I'll be here, resting up. Need my energy for the game tonight."

The annual Thanksgiving game. Scrabble. It's loud, competitive, and full of laughter. One of the last things my mom held on to after Dad left. No prizes, just bragging rights. Last year, I won.

This year? Not so sure.

I check the time, then rush to shower. I throw on a pair of high-waisted flare jeans, sneakers, white sweater, and a coat. Comfortable but nice. Blow-drying my hair, I let it fall naturally, and add a touch of makeup. Nothing dramatic, but just enough to look put together.

When I come back downstairs, I scan the house one last time. Everything looks good, minus the kids causing havoc. My brother, Atlas, is glued to the Nintendo Switch, Jasper on his phone, both completely oblivious, while Felix is tearing through the living room like a tiny tornado.

I sigh. Not my problem right now. Hazel is on babysitting duties until I get back.

Grabbing the pecan pie, I head for the door.

I have a delivery to make.

I take the familiar drive to Keith's, my hands gripping the wheel tightly as I navigate each turn with extra care. The pie rests on the passenger seat like it's fragile. Because it is. The pie that I had to wait in line for an hour to get. The best pecan pie in town. The pie that could very well be my peace offering.

Keith's house comes into view, his porch decorated with a simple fall wreath. I park, hold my breath as I unbuckle, and carefully lift the pie. My steps are measured, as if any sudden movement might ruin my entrance.

I ring the doorbell, and a few moments later, Keith swings the door open.

"Oh, hi, Amelia. Happy Thanksgiving," he greets, eyes dropping to the pie in my hands.

"Happy Thanksgiving." I thrust it toward him like an offering, watching as his face lights up.

He inclines his head inside, and I step through the doorway, the house surprisingly quiet, the faint scent of something savory lingering in the air. My eyes scan the dining table, and my heart clenches when I see only two sets of silverware neatly placed on either side.

Just the two of them.

Adrian is at the table, lowering the last fork into place with quiet efficiency. He doesn't notice me, giving me a chance to take in his fitted black pants and red and black shirt. I swear I saw this style on the 'look of the season for men' in blogs this week.

"Look what Amelia brought us." Keith's voice grabs his attention.

Adrian straightens and walks over. His gaze meets mine, and something inside me flutters. It's nerves mixed with hope, wanting this to go well.

He drops his gaze to the pie. "What is it?"

I lift my chin slightly. "Genevieve's pecan pie."

"The best one." Keith grins.

I beam with pride, waiting for Adrian's response.

"I don't like pie." His face flattens.

My heart drops.

But before I can fully process the sting, his lips curl. "Kidding. You think that low of me that I wouldn't even like pecan pie? Everyone likes pecan pie. "

I force a laugh, but it's weak. "Yeah. Keith could've had it all, though." I try to sound nonchalant, brushing it off like it didn't get to me. But it did.

Something about the way they're just sitting here, alone on Thanksgiving, tugs at me. My family is chaotic, but it's never lonely.

This?

This is lonely.

And even though Adrian is as closed off as ever, Keith is such a sweetheart. He shouldn't be spending Thanksgiving like this. Neither should Adrian.

"Thanks," Adrian says finally. "For the pie."

I shift on my feet. "Well, later, if you're free, we play Scrabble as a family." My voice is casual, but I'm holding my breath, hoping. I need Adrian to see the good side of me, to let his walls down just a little. Maybe over dessert, we can talk about the fundraiser, start bouncing around some ideas.

"You don't have to come for dinner, but maybe come for dessert?"

Adrian crosses his arms. "Didn't you get a pie for yourself?"

"I did," I admit. "Chocolate cream. But I didn't get another pecan."

Keith looks at me, surprised. "You didn't want to get too many?"

I shrug. "You know how it is."

He nods. "Honestly, I'm surprised you secured one at all."

"Me and my sister got there early." I glance at Adrian again. "I wanted to get one for you guys."

Adrian rubs a hand over his jaw, and for the first time tonight, his posture softens.

Keith grins. "Well, you know what? We'd love to come after dinner and share the pecan pie."

Relief washes over me, and I smile, genuinely this time.

"So, I'll see you later for Scrabble?" I say, hopeful.

"No," Adrian replies at the same time Keith says, "Yes."

Keith flashes me a quick wink behind Adrian's back. He's got me. He'll make sure Adrian's there.

Adrian doesn't want to spend time with me. I get it. I'm the enemy.

But enemy or not, no one should be alone on Thanksgiving.

I clear my throat. "All right, I better get going. I need to get dinner on the table. I'll see you soon."

"Don't count on it," Adrian mutters.

"Can't wait," Keith counters with a grin.

I shake my head, smiling as I step out and drive home.

Getting back, the house is as noisy as ever when I walk through the door.

"Mom," I call out, hanging my coat on the rack, "we've got two coming over for Scrabble later."

"Who?" Mom asks from the recliner.

"Wait. Two?" Hazel calls from beside her.

"Keith and Adrian," I reply.

My siblings immediately start plotting how to crush our guests in the game.

I head to the living room to set up another table with extra space for drinks and snacks, then scan the house. The usual mess isn't terrible, but I make sure everything is at least presentable... The bathrooms clean, the furniture straightened, the kitchen counters wiped down.

Mom joins me in the kitchen, helping put the final touches on dinner. The food is spread across the table, steaming and ready, and when I call everyone over, they come rushing in like a stampede.

We sit together, passing bowls of mashed potatoes, sharing what we're grateful for, talking about ways to be better versions of ourselves. Unfortunately, Aurora wasn't able to make it because she came down with the flu and didn't want to get Mom sick.

Felix drops food on the floor. Sophia and Jasper start bickering, and I can see the makings of an all-out food fight brewing.

I narrow my eyes. "Everyone, eat your dinner, or there'll be no pie."

That gets their attention.

"Yeah, and we got the chocolate cream pie this time," Hazel announces.

Suddenly, they're all enthusiastic about finishing their plates.

Mom squeezes my hand under the table. "Thanks, love," she whispers.

Dinner winds down, and as expected, half the kids scatter, leaving me with the mess.

Before I can even think about tackling it, the doorbell rings.

I check the time. Damn. That went by fast.

Wiping my hands on a kitchen towel, I head for the door.

Sophia beats me to it, throwing it open, and there stands Adrian.

He hasn't changed, still in the same clothes as earlier. Like he had no intention of trying for this.

I smile. "Happy Thanksgiving."

"You already said that," Adrian replies dryly.

Keith steps up beside him, nudging him lightly. "Be nice."

"Yeah, be nice," I echo, smiling.

Adrian grunts, but his lips twitch like he's the tiniest bit amused.

I'll take that as a win.

CHAPTER 11

ADRIAN

THE HOUSE IS STILL busy with activity. Felix plays with toys, Jasper and Atlas are glued to their games, Hazel and Sophia stay in the living room. Amelia's mom remains curled up on the recliner, eyes fluttering closed every few seconds like she's fighting a losing battle with exhaustion.

The pie's long gone, just a few slices left. Everyone had seconds, and I can see why. I've never tasted anything quite like it. Now I understand the hype about them.

Keith's off in a corner, talking to one of Amelia's brothers about fixing something. And then there's Amelia.

She's cleaning up. Alone.

I watch her as she moves through the kitchen, her shoulders slightly tense, her hands working efficiently. There's something about it that doesn't sit right with me. It's not that she looks upset... She just looks like someone who must always do things on her own. And I know what that's like.

Without saying a word, I rise and grab a stack of plates. The big table is still a mess from dinner, and if she's planning on tackling that solo, it'll take all night.

I carry the plates into the kitchen, moving loudly, but she still doesn't notice me. She's standing at the sink, rinsing off dishes, completely focused.

Then she turns.

We're toe to toe.

She gasps. "Oh, my God! You scared me."

I shift the plates in my hands, holding them up slightly. "Didn't mean to." Our eyes lock, and for a second, neither of us say anything.

I clear my throat. "I just... didn't want you to clean up alone. You've done enough today, and I bet you're exhausted."

She gives a small shrug, like she's trying to downplay it. "I mean, I get some help. It's not too bad."

But I can see the truth: she does this more often than she should. What must it be like to take care of this many people, to have so many people rely on you? I've only ever had to take care of Dad and now myself.

"It'll be quicker if we do it together."

She hesitates, but then nods and takes the plates from my hands. As our fingers brush, I feel it... a weird little thump in my chest. Her eyes widen slightly, and I know she felt it too. The air between us crackles with unspoken words.

"You're staring, Dr. Pierce."

I turn away, pretending it didn't happen, and grab more plates.

We fall into a rhythm. Stacking dishes, wiping counters, moving around each other like we've done this before. It's quiet, but not awkward. Not really. Just... different. I'd dare say it was comfortable.

Her shoulder brushes mine as we both reach for the same cloth, and neither of us pulls away immediately. But I find myself whispering, "Sorry, I keep getting in your way."

She smiles but doesn't say anything, just resumes cleaning up.

Once the dishwasher is loaded and the kitchen is mostly back in order, I lean against the counter, glancing over at her.

She tucks a strand of hair behind her ear, sleeves still rolled up, hands damp from the sink.

Something strange swirls in the air between us, like there's more to say, but neither of us knows how to say it. She didn't have to bring that pie, or clean up, and make being around her this easy.

I spot one last plate and pick it up, bringing it over to her. When she reaches for it, I don't let go right away, so we're both holding it. She looks up, but doesn't step back for a second. Her eyes brim with something soft that wasn't there before.

"Amelia." Felix, the youngest kid, runs into the kitchen, clutching his stomach. "Mom said I can't have any more pie, but I just want a little more."

Amelia jumps, startled, and the plate slips from my hands, shattering against the floor.

"Shit," she mutters.

"It's my fault. I've got it." I crouch to start picking up the larger pieces, but she shakes her head.

"No, you're the guest. Let me do it." She glances at the kid. "Go grab me the dustpan."

He gives up asking for pie and takes off before she can even finish her sentence. He's back, and Amelia makes quick work of cleaning up the mess while I grab the bigger shards.

"You really don't have to help," she says, glancing up at me from under her dark lashes.

"I don't mind."

I stand, throwing the pieces in the trash, pausing for a second to admire her. My mouth moving on its own, I blurt, "Are you free tomorrow?"

She looks at me, rising. Her eyes do that thing again, making me lose my train of thought for a second. And it makes me wonder what it would be like to trace along her jawline with my thumb.

"For the fundraiser," she says, like she's reminding herself.

"Right. Yeah." I nod, shocked I said that. What was I expecting her to say? What was the plan if she didn't have a rational thought as to why we should spend time together... I refocus. "We need to start planning."

She empties the dustpan and wipes her hands on a towel. "Where would be a good spot?"

I run a hand through my hair, thinking. "Well, you know what? I don't think I've seen all of Pulse Point yet."

Her lips twitch. "Have you seen the bridge? The spot that's the reason why it's called Pulse Point?"

"No," I say, my curiosity piqued.

"There's a nice spot there. We could brainstorm in peace."

My pulse kicks up a little. Not because of the bridge, but because we'll be alone.

"Sounds good." But I'm wondering if we're just talking about brainstorming.

"What time works for you?" she asks. "I know you probably have plans—"

I shake my head, holding her eyes firmly. "No, I don't."

She smiles. "Ten?"

"Ten works." I pause and try to sound casual. "I'll bring coffee. What do you drink?"

"Oh, just whatever's easiest for you to grab."

"Come on, surely, you have a favorite."

"Okay... fine. Iced honey latte with white chocolate cold foam with a little drizzle of caramel."

"Consider it done."

We share a small smile before I step back, turning toward the living room where Keith is.

"You ready to go?" I ask him.

"Sure am."

We say our goodbyes and head out, and as I step outside, I can't stop thinking about Amelia. About this house, this family, this whole night. It's taken me by surprise how much I didn't mind the noise and chaos when I'm so used to the quiet and solitude.

Mostly, how much she does for everyone else.

CHAPTER 12

AMELIA

THE NEXT MORNING, MOM'S sitting in a chair by the window, a blanket draped over her lap, even though it's not that cold. She looks tired but peaceful, her fingers lightly tapping against the armrest as she stares outside.

I stay in the doorway, keys already in my hand, but my feet refuse to move. I need to meet Adrian, but looking at Mom like this makes a lump form in the back of my throat. *What if something happens to her when I'm gone? What if she needs me and I'm not there? Hazel and Jasper would use their phones to call me, right?*

Putting aside my negative thoughts, I focus on the positives, such as Adrian agreeing to let me interview him, and how today will be a quick meeting.

I step closer. "Mom, I'm heading off. You gonna be alright?"

She turns to me with a slow nod. "Yes, sweetheart."

I hesitate, searching her face for any sign that she's just saying that for my benefit. "I won't be long," I promise. "Just gotta get this meeting done."

She gives me a small smile. "What's it about?"

"A fundraiser. We're trying to raise money for some medical equipment."

"Oh, that's great," she manages, fighting a yawn and giving me an encouraging smile despite the exhaustion in her eyes.

"Yeah." I linger for another second more. "It's just the first meeting, so we'll be throwing ideas around."

She hums in approval. "Honey, I'm sure it'll be great."

"Call me if you need me." I kiss her on the forehead before heading out.

The drive is quiet, passing houses that still have autumn wreaths hanging on their doors, mini pumpkins, and fall garlands draped along the porch railings.

When I pull into the lot, I spot his Mercedes-Benz parked at the edge, right where the gravel meets the trees. And there he is, leaning against it, like he was made to be part of the scenery.

The sight of him makes me smile before I even realize it.

He's in black jeans today, paired with a blue sweater that brings out the color of his eyes. Freshly shaved, his jawline sharp, his eyebrows slightly pinched like he's assessing something—*probably me.*

I step out of the car with my camera, and my gaze immediately catches on the two coffee cups in his hands… One noticeably bigger than the other.

He lifts them slightly. "Here's your caffeine hit."

I cross the lot toward him. "You got it from Genevieve's Diner."

"You doubted me?"

I take the bigger cup, feeling the coolness seep into my fingertips. "Did you tell her how awesome the pies were?"

"I did," he says, taking a sip of his own coffee. "Told her next year, I'll need to put an order in."

I laugh, shaking my head. "Good luck with that. People have been begging her to take orders for years. She won't cave."

"She likes the line, huh?" he asks with a mischievous grin.

"She likes the buzz," I correct. "The thrill of selling out. It's a power move."

"Hm." He cocks his head, studying me. "I can be persuasive."

I arch an eyebrow. "Can you now?"

His eyes glint with something unreadable, and for a moment, we just stand there, the air crackling between us.

He pushes off the car and nods toward the trail. "So, where's this famous bridge?"

I gesture for him to follow. "Come with me."

The fundraiser stuff is still running through my head as we make our way along the flat path. I'm at ease as we walk, but when I look over, he seems wound up, shoulders tight, a firm hold on his cup. Maybe I should start easy... ask about normal stuff like his job.

Girl, get yourself together. This is just for the article. We've done dozens of interviews, and this is no different.

The bridge comes into view ahead, stone pillars rising above the riverbank, weathered by time.

"You need to see it from underneath first, then from the top." I nod, sipping my coffee.

"Thanks for last night," he says, glancing at me. "It was nice. Keith had a great time too."

I nod. "It's good to see Keith looked after. He's done a lot for us."

Adrian hesitates. "He's done a lot for me too."

His gaze flickers to me, but he doesn't say anything.

"Just with Mom's diagnosis, you know..." I add softly.

Understanding, he nods again.

We reach the base of the bridge. The small river flows beneath it, the water rushing over rocks. The sight of it is breathtaking in a quiet, understated way. I haven't come here in a while. I've been preoccupied, but every time I do it feels like this, and I remember why I love it so much.

"Wow," he murmurs, tilting his head back.

I snap a couple of pictures with my camera, then glance at him. "Maybe I should be taking your photo for the article."

He shakes his head and holds his hand in front of the lens. "Not yet."

I lower my camera. "Well, you need to think about where I'm getting this picture from because it has to be good."

"Don't worry, I haven't forgotten."

We make our way to the top of the bridge. From here, the view stretches out in every direction; the river flowing below and the forest stretching out beyond it. The kind of view that makes you want to stop and just take it all in.

"It's pretty, isn't it?" I ask.

"I didn't know what to expect, but wow, this surpasses anything I could've imagined," Adrian agrees as I take another step forward, and suddenly, my foot slips.

I flail my arms, but before I can even think about falling, Adrian grabs my wrist and pulls me against him.

"Gotcha."

My breath catches, and my hands press against his hard chest, his sweater soft beneath my fingers. He smells like a dessert... dangerous in its own way.

I swallow hard and step back. "Thanks," I mumble, my fingers twisting the camera strap.

His hand falls away, and I shiver, but not from the cold.

I shouldn't be thinking about this. But he's strong and handsome, and it's been a long time since I've even thought about a guy. Life has been in the way; my job has been my focus. And romance? Not even on the radar.

Not that it should be now.

Definitely not with him.

I clear my throat, steering myself back to why I'm here. "Let's just sit down."

We take a seat on one of the wooden benches, and I pull out my notepad and pen.

"Of course, that's been in your pocket the whole time."

My cheeks heat. "Adrian."

A trace of a smile crosses his face. "Mm-hmm?"

"Do you like your job?"

His expression shifts as he thinks about it. "Most days."

I smile, but it fades as I think about my own answer. My honesty might earn his trust, so I decide to admit my true feelings. "I love my job." I pause, my fingers tightening around my pen.

He waits as I take a breath, watching me with a patient look.

"I wish I could be reporting on more," I say. "Fashion. Lifestyle. High-end subjects. I love my community, but it's just..." I shake my head. "A little boring."

He tilts his head to the side. "Is it just this town, or?"

"It's the town," I say. "I've thought about moving to New York with my sister, Aurora, but my family needs me." I'm disappointed to give up that dream, but it's not what matters most.

Adrian watches me closely, no judgment in his face, just genuine curiosity. His soft gaze makes it so easy to continue opening up.

"I couldn't leave my mom now since she's unstable. And my siblings... they're too young to deal with that." I lift my chin, forcing a smile. "Anyway, I'm supposed to be asking you the questions."

He smirks. "You won't get much out of me yet. We've got a fundraiser to organize first. After that, I'll give you all the answers and the photo you want."

"Alright." I open my notebook, and he watches me, amused.

"So," I say, flipping to a new page, "I've already spoken to Ezra, Milton, and the mayor and received approval. I said we want to host it in the town square in a months' time. How does that sound?"

"Sounds good to me."

"I think a themed event would work best."

"Christmas, then?"

I nod. "The winter celebration. We need to plan the food, the activities... probably test a few games. There must be prizes. We need the whole community involved."

I've been writing down names since he agreed to do the fundraiser, even contacting a few because we don't have much time, and there's a lot of people in this community. And I don't want to leave anyone out.

"Sure. How do you want to do this?"

"A Saturday works best," I say, tapping my pen against my notepad. "People have Sunday to recover, we have time to clean up, and then Monday, hopefully, we have enough money for the equipment."

Adrian leans back on the bench, his arm draped lazily over the backrest, fingers tapping against the wood. The faintest grin tugs at his lips. "That sounds like a plan. Could really work to get at least one fixed."

"Fixing will be less money to raise."

"I'll put the money up to host the event. And the goal will be to raise one hundred thousand dollars."

I nod. "Then let's do this."

The feeling between us changes, shifting with a new sense of determination. I flip to the next page in my notebook, the paper crinkling under my touch. As I shift my grip, my fingertip catches the sharp edge. I'm not normally this accident prone, but something's different today, and I don't understand why I'm so nervous.

"Ah." I shake my hand as a sting shoots through my skin.

"Paper cut. Let me see."

I giggle, shaking my head. "I don't need a doctor."

He ignores me completely, taking my hand in his before I can protest. His grip is firm yet gentle, and I don't bother pulling away. He brings my finger close to his lips. I think he's going to kiss it, but he stops short, his warm breath brushing over my skin. This is dangerous, and I know it, yet my heart does this little skip that I haven't felt in years.

I suck in a breath, startled by the gentle warmth of his mouth on my skin.

"Better?" he asks, leaning back.

I curl my fingers, slipping them from his grip. "Is that what you do with all your patients?"

His lips pull into a wolfish grin. "No. You're the first."

I roll my eyes, refusing to let his charm get to me. Shaking off the moment, I tighten my grip on my notebook and refocus. "Okay, I'll put an article in the bulletin and do social media posts to create a buzz, but we need things for people to spend money on."

"What about gift wrapping?"

"Good idea."

Adrian nods, his gaze sharpening. "And have volunteers dressed as elves. Make it fun."

I jot it down. "Christmas photos, too. Some with Santa, obviously, but maybe family portraits as well? Something people can keep. I'll ask Violet if she wants to do it."

"That's a good idea."

I scribble furiously, my fingers smudging the ink. "A gingerbread house competition? We charge for the base, then extra for decorations."

"That's perfect." Adrian's grin widens. "You love Christmas, don't you?"

"Yes, I do. There's something about everyone being together."

The ideas come faster now, tumbling over each other as we build on them. For a moment, I forget about everything else... the article, my mom, the expectations pressing down on me. Right now, it's just this. A plan coming together.

I sip my coffee, and the thought of Genevieve sparks a new, exciting idea. "What about a bake sale?"

"Yeah. Christmas cookies, hot cocoa, gingerbread, candy canes." He ticks them off on his fingers.

I tap my pen against the page. "We could sell sugar cookies kits for families to make at home. I could get Genevieve to help with them."

His gaze flickers with interest. "Craft stations, too. Kids could make Christmas cards."

"Yes," I say, practically buzzing now. "What about a Christmas basket raffle? Different themes... one for toys, another for food, one with decorations."

Adrian nods, a rare softness in his expression. "I could take one to the hospital. For the kids."

The thought makes my throat tighten, but I push past it, continuing to write notes. "We could see if some local business owners would be interested in adding gift cards too."

The list grows once I pull up Pinterest. The options seem endless: Pin the Nose on Rudolph, Christmas karaoke, a snowball toss with white pom-poms. The usual games, but given a holiday spin. Duck pond, bean bag toss, balloon pop, face painting, spin the wheel.

By the time we finish, my fingers hurt from writing, but the satisfaction settling in my chest is clear.

I glance at Adrian, who looks just as caught up in the moment as I am.

"I think we've got something really good here," I say with a big grin.

He nods. "We'll have to start working on asking who can help with this so we don't have to take it all on ourselves."

"Agreed." I chew on my lip, an idea forming. "We should meet up this weekend to start organizing the schedule, volunteers, the games and prizes, and coordinating the resources."

"Sounds like a plan."

For a moment, we just sit there, the forest wrapping around us, and his scent wafting over me when the breeze picks up. Eventually, I shift, glancing over at him. "How's it going at Keith's?"

"It's nice," he says. "I mean, don't get me wrong, I'd like my own space. But it's nice having company while I settle in." He pauses. "I've started looking at properties online."

He's really staying. I shouldn't care this much about his plans, but here I am, wanting to know more. "Where are you thinking?"

"Out of town a bit. With a big piece of land. Somewhere peaceful." His eyes go distant, as if he's already picturing it.

I look over the landscape. "That's why I like coming here. My house, as you saw, is chaotic."

He chuckles softly. "Just a bit."

"But it's nice, you know?" I say. "Having siblings."

His gaze drifts to the ground.

"Do you have any brothers or sisters?" I know this is personal, and usually, he shuts me down.

He shakes his head. "No."

A lump forms in my throat. I nod slowly, his answer settling into my chest. I can't imagine growing up without family, no one who has your back, who annoy you but love you fiercely all the same. The thought makes my heart ache for him in a way I don't expect.

His phone rings, breaking the silence between us. He pulls it from his pocket, glancing at the screen with a deep frown. "It's the hospital."

I close my notebook and straighten. "We should get going anyway."

As he answers the phone, we start walking back. His voice is calm, but I can hear the undercurrent of concern in the way he listens, the way his fingers tighten around the phone.

They need him to come in.

He agrees, his jaw flexing slightly before he tucks his phone away. For all the confidence and strength he projects, there's a vulnerability beneath it, one I don't think he lets many people see, and I don't think he meant for me to catch it. I'm starting to realize that he's beginning to trust me with a glimpse of who he really is. He could've stepped away for the phone call or even lowered his voice, but he didn't. The familiar flutter of anticipation mixed with nervousness returns as we stop beside our cars, neither of us moving, the air between us thick with possibility. *Please don't let this end awkwardly.* I'm expecting him to put his wall back up and walk away.

"I'd better head off," he says, running a hand through his hair.

Nodding, I grip my notebook a little tighter. "Thanks for meeting me. I'll get started on announcing the fundraiser. Do you think a month is enough time?"

"Yeah, plenty of time to get it sorted."

I hesitate, not quite ready to leave yet, but I know he needs to. "I'll see you next week? Same time?"

"Sounds good."

He slips into his car, and once I get to mine, I sink into the driver's seat. The cool fabric is a welcome relief against my overheated skin. I grip the steering wheel for a moment before finally pulling away, heading back home with too many thoughts running through my head.

CHAPTER 13

ADRIAN

A WEEK LATER

I'm supposed to meet Amelia now, but I'm still stuck at the hospital after a night shift, finishing up paperwork after a new admission. I can't just walk away mid-shift. My patients come first. That's the reality of this job.

But the delay eats at me. We're supposed to be a team on this. She's counting on me. And worse, I don't even have her number to let her know I'm running late. *Stupid.* Neither of us thought to exchange that one major piece of information.

My shift was meant to end at eight a.m., but by the time I finally get out, mid-morning light has settled over the town. I drive straight to Pulse Point Bridge, hoping she's still there. But as I pull into the lot, my chest tightens. Her car is nowhere in sight.

I still check our meeting spot, clinging to the foolish hope that maybe she's waiting. But the bench is empty, the space silent except for the distant rustle of trees and the occasional chatter of birds.

Fuck. I've let her down.

Guilt rolls in my stomach as I turn back toward my car. I can't leave it like this. I need to make it right. Even if that means showing up at her home, I'm going to try.

As I pull up to her house, her car is in the driveway.

Thank God she's home.

At least I can explain what happened instead of leaving her wondering if I just didn't show up.

I take the steps two at a time and knock, my pulse kicking up as I hear the distant sound of kids laughing inside. The door swings open, and there she is... Amelia.

Her eyebrows lift in surprise, mouth parting slightly before she runs a hand down the front of her top. She's in sweatpants and a white hoodie, her hair in a messy bun, minimal make-up, looking more relaxed than I've ever seen her.

"I'm really sorry." I rub the back of my neck. "I got stuck at work. I couldn't contact you."

She crosses her arms. "I wasn't expecting you."

"I figured I owed you an apology in person." I glance down at my suit, suddenly feeling overdressed. "I'm a bit out of place here."

Amelia smiles. "At least one of us is comfortable."

That small bit of humor eases the tension, and I let out a breath.

"Well, I've got a few things started for the fundraiser from donations already." She steps back. "Do you want to come in and go over things? I probably can't head out again."

"If you don't mind. I feel bad about standing you up earlier."

"Come in, then. Ignore the mess."

That's it? No lecture?

I was prepared for pushback, and her forgiveness makes me feel both relieved and slightly unworthy of it.

She leads me inside. Felix darts through the hallway, his giggles filling the space. I spot her mom on the sofa, flipping through a magazine.

"Hi, Ms. Richards." I wave.

She looks up and gives me a small smile. "Adrian, lovely to see you again. I heard all about the fundraiser. Sounds like a great thing you're doing."

"It is. Hopefully we can pull it off."

We settle in the dining room, pushing aside a few scattered papers and half-finished crafts. Amelia already has supplies laid out—games that need tweaking, signs that need painting.

Did she do this at home because I didn't show up?

Guilt fills me as I feel like I'm another person relying on her. I need to help more so she realizes she doesn't have to do everything herself.

We dive into the work, transforming ordinary activities into Christmas-themed fun.

As we go, we make a list of bigger prizes we still need. I plan to visit Genevieve to talk to her about pies and sugar cookies. Then head to Derek to get haircut vouchers. As we go through the list of people, including who the volunteers are and who we still need to ask. I remember my conversation before work yesterday. "I talked with Dores from the grocery store. She said she can donate a gift basket and a few other things. They should be ready at the end of the week."

"Good idea." Amelia nods. "So maybe next week, we can meet back up, and we'll finish them up together."

"Alright." I pause, then add with a slight smile, "I should probably get your number now, huh?"

She laughs. "Yeah, that'd be smart."

We exchange numbers, and for some reason, it feels bigger than it should. Like another step toward... something.

As we wrap up, she leans back against the chair. "So... did you read Dr. Whisperer yet?"

"Yeah, I did. I knew Russell would be fine. He's a menace."

She grins. "He is. But he's also kind of funny."

"I'm honestly surprised no one's caught him and cooked him yet."

She gasps in mock horror. "No one would dare! Russell's practically a town mascot."

I shake my head, laughing. "Well, he did manage to free the rest of the turkeys. That was unexpected."

"Oh, I don't know." Amelia leans against the dining table, amusement dancing in her eyes. "I think Russell's smarter than he looks."

I study her for a moment, and I find myself smiling. There's something so magnetic about her leaning back, more comfortable, with her hair a little messy and faint paint smudges on her fingers from working on the signs. Which is exactly why I should leave right now.

CHAPTER 14

AMELIA

A WEEK LATER, I pull at the hem of my dress, nerves fluttering in my stomach just like last week. It's from Adrian; knowing I'm about to see him.

Balancing the few things I picked up to finish the other baskets and games, I take a steadying breath to calm my nerves and knock on the door. Adrian wants to take one to work tomorrow, and since I grew up with younger siblings, I knew to go and ask Walter from the toy shop for donations. He was so generous when he found out it was to fix the CT scanner, as he's used it before. The door swings open almost immediately, like Adrian's been waiting for me. He leans against the frame.

"Geez, watch out. I might think you're dying to see me." I ignore my stomach flipping. "People might get the wrong idea."

"I knew it would be you. Wasn't expecting anyone else to knock this afternoon."

"True."

"Here, let me take that." He reaches for the bags.

I let him. It's nice to have someone help.

He takes everything from my hands, and I shake my head, trying to ignore the brushing of his fingers on my arm.

"I didn't mean for you to take all of it."

"That's what I offered. I want to help you. Happy to do it."

I follow him inside. But instead of heading to the dining table, Adrian leads me to the living room, where a low coffee table is already covered in supplies.

"Figured we could sit here, put something on the TV, and be comfortable while we get everything ready," he says, setting the bags down.

"Sounds good."

He nods at the bags. "So, what did you bring?"

"Oh, just some extra donated toys for the baskets. Thought they might make them more appealing."

"Nice." He settles on the couch beside me, close enough that I catch his cologne and the cushions dip under his weight. My pulse quickens at the proximity. Is he sitting closer than necessary, or am I just hyperaware of every inch between us?

"Do you want a drink or something?"

I try to keep my voice even at the casual offer, to hide how his nearness is affecting me.

"I'm okay for now, thanks."

We start arranging small toys, treats, and raffle items into the baskets. As we work, Adrian grabs a couple of extra gifts from the side of him. "Some of the doctors at work pitched in too."

He's only just started, and I can't imagine what it would be like to be new to the hospital and a doctor. The pressure, the learning curve, trying to prove yourself while people's lives are in your hands. "How's that?"

He snorts. "You mean, how's work in general, or how are the doctors? Because that's a loaded question."

I grin. "Everything."

"Well, you remember being the new kid at school? That's me. Except now, I'm the awkward new doctor trying to fit in. And on top of that, people assume I suck, so I have to dig my reputation out of the trenches."

Did I contribute to this?

I wince as I realize what I've done. "That sounds rough."

"Eh, it's okay. Eventually, you'll know my side of the story, right?" He winks.

"Exactly."

He sighs heavily. "For now, I'm just taking it day by day, working hard, hoping people let me in eventually."

"Does it help that Dr. Whisperer still follows you around?" I tease. "They seem to be making you their latest project."

"Honestly, it's a daily thing now," he groans. "They can take the most boring thing and turn it into gossip. Like earlier this week, Dr. Whisperer made a whole article about my choice in black coffee and what that says about me. But I'm starting to tell the difference between your stories and theirs."

I bite my lip as a tiny thrill fills me that he's been paying such close attention to my work that he can identify it.

"Oh, yeah?" I desperately want to know what he's figured out about me through my writing.

"Yours have depth. You try to tell a full story."

"That's a nicer way of saying Dr. Whisperer is trash."

He shrugs. "Pretty much."

"So, aside from being the new guy on the block, how's life? What's it like compared to the city?"

He leans back, considering. "Honestly? I like it. People here are more humble. They listen. They don't always like the change, but at least I feel like I'm making a difference." He shakes his head. "I don't know. Maybe I'm rambling."

I give him a small smile. "I get what you mean, even though I've never lived in the city. That's why I love this town. Even when people give you a hard time, they eventually come around."

He huffs a laugh. "Still waiting on that part."

"Have you made any new friends at work yet?"

"Well, I see the same doctors every day, so I get the occasional 'hello' now instead of just a grunt. That's progress, right?"

"Definitely."

"I've got work next weekend, so if we need to do more, we'll have to do it Friday night. If you're free, of course."

"I don't have much of a life." I tuck my hair behind my ear. "Usually, just hang out with my family, work, sleep. When I get any extra time, I'll watch TV. Nothing exciting, really."

He looks at me, his eyes softening just a little, like he's trying to understand rather than just make polite conversation. "That doesn't sound too bad. Sometimes it's nice to have a routine."

It's a relief that he's not dismissing my life as boring. But I'm not sure how to explain it. "Yeah, I suppose. It's just... the same chaos, different day. Do you ever get bored of the same old thing?"

He hums, thinking. "I used to, but I've learned to appreciate the calm sometimes."

There's a pause between us, so I shuffle some papers, allowing me to think about how he mentioned wanting to fit in, and an idea forms. "Have you been to the bar yet?"

"No, but Derek from the barbershop invited me to go with him."

"Derek's great. He's always up for something fun. The bar's got a cool vibe. You should check it out sometime. Maybe we could go celebrate setting up the fundraiser?"

He raises his eyebrows as a small smile tugs at his lips. "Celebrate, huh? You're making it sound like we've already pulled it off."

"Well, setting it up is a win in itself, right?" I give him a teasing look, but deep down, I'm putting on a brave face, trying to convince myself as much as him. "It's a big deal, and we've got it handled so far."

Nodding, he laughs softly. "Alright. You're right, we're on the right track."

I'm excited about his agreement, but panic washes over me as I worry I just asked him on a date unintentionally.

We finish up the last basket, wrapping it with cellophane and tying a neat ribbon on top. It looks good.

"I think it's time for a drink before we keep going. All that made me thirsty."

"Just water for now, please."

As he gets up, I glance around the space, letting the moment settle in. It's easy, working with him. *Too damn easy.*

He gives me a bottle, and I immediately take a sip of water, settling back down as we finish organizing the last of the festival games. I read the list, noting we have the gingerbread kits ready, the duck pond items secured, and the face painting arranged. And then work on the roster for the day, assigning volunteers to jobs.

Next, we grab the list of people we still need to reach out to for donations and help. I call up for set up help from the local club and lawyer, and he rings the last few businesses we haven't called. Everyone has pitched in, leaving only a few final touches.

I'm satisfied and proud of what we've accomplished, but I'm still shaky from our closeness.

We sit on the floor, leaning back against the sofa, legs crossed. Our arms brush against each other, goosebumps scatter over my skin, but neither of us moves away.

Adrian turns on a TV show, and we fall into casual conversation, laughing at the ridiculous plot, making fun of the characters—just mindless chatter. It feels effortless in a way I'm not used to. At home, I never get to just sit, relax, and exist in the moment. And even crazier, I don't have to have the subtitles on to hear what is happening. But here, with him, it's different. It's... nice, but suddenly, I need to know more about him. "How old are you?"

Adrian glances at me. "Thirty-two. What about you?"

"Twenty-seven."

The silence stretches, and I realize how close we are now we're both slumped with exhaustion, our faces only inches apart. My heart races as I worry about the fallout if we act on this.

"I should get going." I shift slightly, though I don't really want to.

Adrian whispers. "Better get home for dinner."

He leans in. My pulse pounds. I close my eyes, tilting toward him—

Keys jingle in the doorway, which makes us both jerk away. My stomach drops as I scramble to my feet.

What the hell was I thinking?

Keith steps inside, looking between us. "Oh, hey, guys." His gaze falls on the baskets. "Wow, really making progress with the festival stuff."

I clear my throat, glancing at Adrian to see if he looks as flustered as I feel. "Yeah, just about done."

"You guys have dinner yet?" he asks.

I shake my head. "I was actually just about to leave."

Keith waves a dismissive hand. "Why don't you stay and eat with us? Just an hour."

Adrian subtly nods, and I'm totally torn about what to do. I should probably get away from him, but I don't want to go, now that I know Adrian wants me here. "I should check in with my mom first."

"Of course. I'll put in an order, just in case. If you don't stay, there'll be leftovers for Adrian to take to work tomorrow."

I nod and step onto the porch to call home. Mom reassures me the kids can heat up leftovers or cup noodles, telling me to take my time. She sounds the same, still breathless and weak. So, I know I can't stay too long.

When I walk back inside, both Adrian and Keith are watching me. Adrian searches my face, which causes me to fidget, while Keith seems oblivious to the tension swirling between us. "I'll stay," I say.

Keith grins. "Fantastic."

While waiting for dinner, we fill Keith in on the fundraiser. When dinner arrives, we gather around, eating and talking. Keith tells us about his day—how someone stuck a Q-tip in their ear and ended up in the ER to get it removed because Keith couldn't get it out.

"That's the most disgusting thing I've ever heard." I grimace. "Also, I'm never using Q-tips again."

Laughter fills the room, but I avoid Adrian's gaze. The almost-kiss lingers in my mind, rattling me more than I want to admit. Every now and then, I see him out of the corner of my eye staring at me, but I pretend not to notice because I feel conflicted about it.

Before I can overthink it anymore, I stand. "I should get going."

Adrian nods. "I'll see you next Friday." He says it so casually, completely unaware of the internal panic spiraling through me.

Dr. Whisperer would eat this up if they found out. A reporter cozying up to the controversial doctor she's been writing about? That would be the talk of the town. And I refuse to be that kind of headline, because then, I can kiss the chance of my promotion goodbye.

Adrian hasn't even redeemed himself yet. He hasn't addressed the issues that damaged his reputation in the first place from his time in the city. The last thing I need is for people to think I'm biased and undermine my credibility as a journalist. Going to the bar with him is helping him trust me, so I can get his side of the story, nothing more. It's simply like a business dinner.

I get into my car and roll down the windows, letting the cool air wash over me. My pulse is still beating too fast, my thoughts too scattered. I need to get my shit together before Friday.

CHAPTER 15

ADRIAN

AMELIA LEAVES, HER FACE flushed, and something like
relief or disappointment coils in my chest.

What the fuck was that?

Keith walks in as I follow, he's completely oblivious to
the earlier electricity in the room. I force myself to walk
to the sofa and sit, casually leaning back, trying to catch
my breath and give my heart a chance to stop hammering
against my ribs. As if I wasn't close to kissing the woman
who's been writing about me in the community paper.

"You guys have made really great progress with the
fundraiser stuff." Keith's gaze sweeps over the supplies
piled on the table.

I nod, trying to look calm, but my mind is spinning. She
was going to let me kiss her. Her eyes closed, and she leaned
in too, with lips slightly parted.

Fuck. Stop. Don't think about that.

But I can't stop. As much as I tell myself the memory of
her face so close to mine, the way her breath caught when

I whispered about dinner, the warmth of her arm against mine all evening, it's stuck on repeat.

Even on the porch moments ago, I wanted to reach for her again.

You're an idiot, Adrian.

She's a journalist. She writes about me. Whatever she's playing, getting involved with her is the last thing I need right now. I'm already trying to prove myself to this town while my past haunts me. I can't afford to give people more ammunition. Especially not when I'm finally starting to feel like I might belong somewhere.

But when she glanced at me, there was something vulnerable in her expression that made my chest tighten. Like she's as confused about what almost happened as I am.

"She's sweet, right? Good to see you making friends."

Friends. Right. That's what we're calling it.

I run a hand through my hair, trying to shake off the lingering awareness of how she felt beside me right here tonight. This is complicated in ways I didn't expect when I agreed to help with the fundraiser.

Now I worry what that means when we next meet up at the bar. Will I feel that same magnetic draw that had me leaning toward her? What if I was reading the signs wrong? *Does she just see me as a story? Am I just a chase to her because she wants to publish a new page-turning article?*

Keep your shit together. It's just a bar with a friend.

But even as I think about it, I know I'm lying to myself.

I review Mrs. Wynter's chart outside Room 101. Seventy-two years old, admitted with chest pain and shortness of breath. Her EKG shows some irregularities, but nothing immediately life-threatening. What concerns me more is the confusion she's been having. The classic signs of delirium that could indicate a UTI or medication interaction.

"Dr. Pierce." Dr. Young's voice cuts through the quiet ward. He's been the chief of medicine here for twenty years, and he's clearly used to being obeyed without question.

I peer up from the chart. "Yes, sir?"

"Mrs. Wynter in 101. I want you to discharge her by this afternoon. She's stable, taking up a bed we need for the accident victims coming in from the highway."

I stare at him with my mouth hanging open, certain I've misheard. "Sir, I think she needs further investigation. She's showing signs of cognitive impairment that weren't present on admission. Her family is concerned. I'd like to run a few more tests—"

"She's seventy-two, Dr. Pierce. Confusion comes with the territory." He's already walking away, our conversation clearly over.

"Dr. Young, wait." I follow him down the hallway, keeping my voice low. "With respect, sir, this isn't normal aging. Her son says she was completely fine yesterday. Something's changed."

He stops walking and turns, his expression hardening. "Dr. Pierce, are you questioning my judgment?"

The question hangs in the air like a challenge. I'm aware of the nurses at the station pretending not to listen, of the way the hallway seems to have gone quieter. This is exactly the kind of moment I've been dreading since I arrived here. Where I must choose between keeping my head down or doing what's right.

"I'm questioning the discharge order, yes. I think Mrs. Wynter needs at least another twenty-four hours of observation."

Dr. Young's jaw tightens. "Dr. Pierce, let me be clear. In this hospital, senior physicians make the decisions. You're not here to override twenty-one years of experience with your big city ideas."

Big city ideas.

The reminder that I'm the outsider, and I don't fit in here. *Maybe never will.*

"This isn't about where I trained, sir. It's about patient care. Her mental status change could indicate—"

"Nothing more than an old woman being in an unfamiliar environment. Discharge her. That's the order."

He walks away, leaving me standing in the hallway with Mrs. Wynter's chart firmly in my arms. Through the window of Room 101, I can see her son holding her hand. It reminds me of doing the same with my dad's.

I take a deep breath and walk back to the nurses' station. "Can you prep Mrs. Wynter for a urinalysis and complete metabolic panel? I want to rule out infection or electrolyte imbalances before discharge."

Jess looks uncertain. "Dr. Young said—"

"I'll take responsibility for the orders."

I sign the chart, knowing I won't be able to live with myself if I do otherwise.

Two hours later, the lab results are in, and I'm reviewing the numbers when my pager buzzes. Mrs. Wynter's room, urgent.

I hurry down the hall with Jess to find her son standing beside the bed, looking panicked.

"She just collapsed trying to get up for the bathroom."

Mrs. Wynter is trying to speak, but her speech is slurred and her eyes are unfocused.

I start her on IV antibiotics and fluids immediately, then page Dr. Young.

He arrives ten minutes later, his expression thunderous. "I thought I made myself clear—"

"Mrs. Wynter has a severe UTI with early sepsis," I interrupt, handing him the lab results. "Her confusion wasn't age-related. It was infection-induced."

His jaw working, he scans the numbers. The wait for him to speak is uncomfortably long.

He hands the results back to me. "How long have you been giving her antibiotics?"

"About five minutes. I also started her on IV fluids to address the dehydration."

"Dr. Pierce, walk with me."

We step into the hallway, away from the patient's room. Dr. Young stops near the nurses' station, running a hand through his dark hair. *Is my career over? Am I about to be dismissed again?*

"You were right. I should've listened to your concerns. Not based assumptions about your assessments on your history. That was wrong of me. What you did could've saved her life."

I nod, surprised by his apology. "Thank you."

We shake hands, and I watch him disappear around the corner, happy Mrs. Wynter is going to be okay.

Chapter 16

Amelia

"Amelia, can I see you in my office for a minute?"

Luna's voice cuts through the room as she stands by her door, and something about her tone makes my stomach clench. I save the draft of my piece about the school's new reading program and follow her into her office.

She closes the door behind me, which only adds to my uneasy feeling.

"Please sit," she says, settling behind her desk with a tight expression.

I take a seat, hands clasped in my lap, back straight. "Is everything okay?"

Luna rests her arms on her desk, leaning forward. "I wanted to give you a heads-up before you hear it through gossip. We've had another application for the position."

The words hit like a smack to my face. My carefully thought-out plan suddenly feels like it's tipping.

"Another application?"

Luna's watching my face carefully. "Tannis Wenzel. She's got ten years of experience with The Boston Times. Her portfolio is impressive."

The Boston Times. The name replays in my head as I try to process.

"I see." My voice sounds fragile and hollow even to my own ears.

"Look, you're still very much in the running," Luna continues. "Your community connections are valuable, and you know this town better than anyone. Tannis brings a different skill to the table."

A sense of dread fills me. "When do you expect to make a decision?"

"After my vacation. I'll be interviewing her next Friday morning." She leans back slightly. "Amelia, if you have a story that shows your journalism the best, now would be the time."

I nod, unable to speak through the tightness in my throat. The Adrian interview suddenly feels like my last chance.

I clear my throat, trying to remain professional. "Thanks for letting me know." Standing on shaky legs, I head back to my desk, where I stare at the computer screen. Ten years of experience at The Boston Times.

I can't compete with that.

"Hello." Violet waves her hand in front of my screen.

I blink, trying to focus. Turning to her, I let the words tumble from my heart. "There's competition for the promotion."

"What kind?" Violet's eyebrows knit together.

"I need a miracle story if I want to stand a chance."

"Shit." Violet drops into the chair beside me. "What are you going to do?"

All I keep thinking about is the interview Adrian promised. It could be my one shot to prove I'm the right choice.

"I have something in mind. The interview with Adrian. His side."

"Amelia, get the story. Show them that you're the one for the job."

Her words echo my inner thoughts, ones I've been too scared to voice.

The extra money that comes from the promotion will stop me from struggling.

Tannis Wenzel doesn't know it yet, but she's not competing for a job. She's threatening my ability to take care of the people I love most.

Later that day, I step out of the car, ready to celebrate the hard work of setting up the fundraiser. Tomorrow is the big day.

The street buzzes with conversation and bursts of laughter from passing groups. Pulse Point Tavern's neon sign glows, its light flickering against the windows.

I pull my beige trench coat tighter around me, suddenly questioning my outfit choice. The boots add a few inches to my height, making me feel more put-together, more confident. Dark jeans hug my legs, and the soft sweater skims my curves just right. It's casual, but deliberate. Just enough to look like I put in effort without making it obvious. My hair falls sleek and straight over my shoulders, and I only did the bare minimum with my makeup with a little mascara, a hint of color on my cheeks and lips. Anything more, and he might think I dressed up for him. Which, in fact, I secretly did.

Stepping inside, warmth rushes over me, carrying the scents of beer, fried food, and smoke. A loud cheer from a group gathered around the TV watching the latest football game pulls me in. The bar is packed, a mix of post-work drinkers, friends catching up, and people like me, meeting someone.

Leon, the bartender, spots me instantly.

"Hey, Amelia. How's your mom?" he asks, coming over to wipe down the bar in front of me.

I force a polite smile. "She's good."

It's always about her. No one ever asks how I am. I swallow down the familiar frustration and look around, scanning the crowd.

"What about you?" Leon leans against the counter. "What brings you in tonight?"

I smile. "Meeting a friend."

"Anyone in particular?"

Before I can answer, my gaze lands on Adrian.

He's seated at a table, already watching me. His lips curve into something subtle, something unreadable, then his eyes flick down, taking me in from head to toe. Heat rushes up my neck, and I have to fight the instinct to shift from foot to foot under his intense scrutiny. I swallow hard, suddenly too warm beneath my coat.

"Want me to bring a drink over?" Leon asks.

"Has he ordered?"

"No, he was waiting for you."

That shouldn't make my body tremble, but it does.

I shake my head. "No, but thank you, we'll order together."

Leon nods. "I'll come over and take your order in just a moment."

I move toward Adrian. He's chosen a table away from the main crowd, far enough from the sports fanatics that we won't have to yell to be heard, but not secluded enough to draw attention. It's a good spot.

"Hi." My voice comes out a little breathless. I hate that.

Adrian rises from his seat, giving me a full view of him. He's changed out of his usual work attire. No suit and tie. Just dark blue jeans and a fitted charcoal shirt, the sleeves rolled up his forearms. Relaxed but still devastatingly good-looking.

"You look beautiful," he says with a warm smile.

"Thanks." I unbutton my coat, draping it over the back of the chair. He pulls it out for me—a simple gesture, but one that sends a strange tug through my chest. I sit, and he pushes the chair in slightly before taking his own seat.

"Leon said he'll come over to take our orders soon."

"Okay." Adrian's smiling, but there's something in his eyes... something tired and distant.

"Rough day?"

He sighs, leaning forward slightly. The table between us is small, leaving little space. My arms rest against the wood, and his aren't far from mine.

"Interesting," he says finally.

"Interesting good or interesting bad?"

He doesn't get a chance to answer before Leon arrives with a small bowl of complimentary nuts. We place our drink orders—Beer for him, white wine for me. Adrian orders us an appetizer. I add to it, because somehow, I already know we'll be here for a while.

Once Leon leaves, Adrian runs a hand over his jaw. I notice the stubble there, darker now under the tavern's light, and for a second, I wonder how it would feel against my skin.

I shove that thought aside when he speaks.

"So, there was a problem at work," he starts. "An elderly patient came in with pain, but showing signs of confusion. My gut said something else was going on, but my superior ordered me to discharge her." He pauses, eyes dropping to his hands, which are tapping the table. "He said that confusion comes with being old."

Leon brings the drinks over and then quickly leaves again. Adrian immediately takes a long pull from his drink as if he needs it to steady himself. I stay quiet, eating nuts and just listening as I try to process this new information. This isn't the doctor I've been writing about. The man sitting across from me is talking about gut instincts and patient care.

"I couldn't do it. So I ordered more tests anyway." His jaw tightens. "Turned out, she had a severe UTI that was causing early signs of sepsis. If I'd discharged her like he wanted..." He shakes his head. "She could've died at home."

His words settle heavy in my chest. This Adrian genuinely cares about his patients and isn't the controversial doctor I thought he was.

The weight of holding that type of responsibility, having to choose between following orders and potentially letting someone die, I can't even imagine. "But you saved her."

"This time. But it gets me in my own head, you know? Makes me doubt myself. After my past mistake, I sometimes wonder if I'm just stubborn or if I actually know what I'm doing." He meets my eyes briefly. "I don't like following orders when they feel wrong. That's what got me in trouble before."

That earns a small smirk from me. "Yeah, I kind of gathered that."

He huffs a quiet laugh.

Holding his gaze, I feel exposed under his attention, those blue eyes seeing right through me. I was wrong and force myself to say what I've been thinking. "There's one person I trust when it comes to judging character, and that's Keith. If he believes in you, then I do too. If he wants you at his practice—the most important thing to him—then I trust that you're not some reckless doctor who doesn't care. And in the time I've spent with you, I see it too. You care. You've been kind to me and to my family. If you were truly an ass, you would've been an asshole to all of us. But you haven't been. That tells me something."

The words hang between us, my cheeks heat from the possibility of saying too much.

Adrian watches me, like he's searching for the right words but can't quite find them. Something flickers across his face, surprise, maybe? Before he looks down at his hands.

I take a slow sip of my wine, letting the rich, sweet taste settle on my tongue before setting the glass down. Across from me, Adrian leans back slightly, rolling his beer bottle between his fingers. His eyes lock on mine as he takes another swig, setting the bottle down with a quiet thump.

The silence stretches, thick with unspoken thoughts. Finally, he clears his throat, as if shaking himself from whatever internal debate he's having. "I keep thinking about what you said about whether I belong here. Moments like today remind me of why I became a doctor in the first place. The patients here are just so humble, and it makes going to work easy." Adrian takes another swig of his beer before setting it down. "Anyway, how was your day?"

I let out a breath, tracing the rim of my glass with my fingertip. "Not as bad as yours, by the sounds of it."

His eyebrows lift slightly. "What do you mean?"

"Well," I start. "You know how mundane and repetitive my work is. Lots of talk about the animals, local businesses, or who's moved into town." We exchange a knowing smile at that. "But today, I found out there's competition for the promotion I've been going for."

Adrian's expression stills. He stays silent, waiting for me to continue.

"It's someone from out of town," I say, my voice quieter now. "From The Boston Times. They're a much better fit on paper."

The words taste bitter. I think about what this means. Bills are piling up faster than I can keep track.

Adrian reaches across the table, his fingers covering mine in a firm touch. A jolt rushes through me as our eyes connect.

"I promise my interview will give you an advantage," he assures me. "I'll tell you everything. I'll give you a good photo. I'll make sure it's better than anything they could possibly submit." His fingers tighten slightly in a comforting way. "I bet you'll get the promotion."

My breath catches from his touch. The intensity in his gaze makes it impossible to look away. I want to believe him. *I need to believe him.* "I hope you're right."

"Everything will be fine. It'll all work out." His hand still rests over mine.

A flicker of unease twists in my chest. I glance down at our hands, suddenly aware of how it must look. *The gossip column. The town's eyes. The whispers.*

With reluctance, I reach for my glass, forcing him to let go. He does, his hand retracting, but not before his fingers skim lightly over mine in a way that sends a shiver down my spine.

Leon arrives with our snacks, setting the plates between us, breaking the moment. Adrian shifts, grabbing his beer again, and I focus on a handful of chips, suddenly grateful for something else to do with my hands.

"I honestly don't know what I'll do if I don't get the promotion," I admit once Leon is gone. It's like I'm acknowledging defeat before the fight is even over. I can't say I haven't thought about finding another job that pays better. But I love what I do, and the thought of giving that up makes me sad. "I'm ready to move up, especially because I need it for the sake of my family, but I don't have any options outside of the promotion. It's not like there's another newspaper to apply to if I want to stay in Pulse Point, and I do want to stay here. I don't know. Maybe something else will become available soon. A full-time position."

Adrian frowns. "Oh, so it's not a full-time role?"

I shake my head. "No. Luna wants to do fewer days, so she's looking for someone to share her position."

"You deserve a full-time promotion," he says, voice firm. "It'd be tough bouncing between the two roles."

"I know," I sigh. "But I'll take anything right now just for a little extra money."

"If you need help, I have a friend, Evan, in New York who owns a media company."

As lovely an offer as that is, I couldn't move to New York.

"I appreciate the offer, but I'll see how I go with Luna first."

We share a look, one that shifts something between us.

I'm about to spark up a new conversation... something lighter, like the upcoming fundraiser, because I can't believe that I just shared so much with him. I never do that.

Out of the corner of my eye, I spot Peri and Candyce from high school, weaving through the crowd toward our table, their eyes already zeroed in on Adrian with obvious interest. My heart plummets. I know that look. Candyce especially has a reputation for being bold with attractive men, and Peri always follows her lead. They're acquaintances more than friends. The kind of people who are friendly enough, but will step over you for what they want.

"Oh my God, is this the infamous doctor?" Candyce says, not even glancing at me as she slides up to our table. "I'm Candyce, and this is Peri. We've heard so much about you."

I don't understand the nausea in my stomach or the way my hands clench under the table. He's not mine, but still, I don't like this.

They openly flirt. Adrian remains polite, offering small smiles, answering their questions with just enough effort to be kind but not enough to encourage. His eyes flick to me between responses, as if checking to see how I'm handling it. His body remains turned toward me, his posture relaxed but away from them. I can tell he's uninterested, even if they don't see it.

"Are you single, Adrian?" Candyce asks in a sultry voice, completely ignoring my presence.

"We were actually just finishing up," Adrian says, gesturing toward me. "Having a work conversation."

Candyce finally acknowledges me with a dismissive glance. "Oh, right. The journalist." The way she says it makes it sound like a hobby rather than a profession.

My blood begins to boil. Once they finally leave, Candyce slips Adrian her number despite his clear disinterest.

I check the time, suddenly feeling drained. "I better get home."

His face pinches with concern. "You sure? You don't want to stay for another drink?"

"No, I can't drive after another." I wave him off, grabbing my jacket.

Understanding, he nods. "Fair enough. It was nice being here. Thanks for introducing me to the bar."

"It's got a cool vibe, right? A nice place to talk."

"I'm glad I got out of the house."

I laugh. "I bet Keith's waiting up for you."

"A hundred percent." He stands with me and gathers his things, then pays the bill before we step outside together.

The air carries the faint scent of rain. I keep walking, heading straight for my car, not wanting to linger. Not wanting to risk a moment of hesitation where he might lean in. Because if he did, I don't think I'd stop him.

"Thanks, and goodnight." I wave.

He waves back. "Night."

I reach for my car door, but before I open it, I turn back, hollering across the parking lot. "Oh, and hey?"

Adrian stops walking, looking over his shoulder. "Yeah?"

I swallow, meeting his gaze. "You deserve to be at the hospital."

His expression softens. "Thanks. And you deserve your promotion." He winks.

I smile, holding on to his words, believing them. Trusting that next week's interview might just change everything.

CHAPTER 17

AMELIA

I BARELY SLEPT LAST night. Excitement for the festival kept me up long past midnight. Now, the early morning light comes through my window, and I'm already moving.

I organize everything. Breakfast is ready, and I've prepped sandwiches for lunch in the fridge. Once I get Mom's things together, I need to get myself ready. Luna's bringing the family to the festival today, giving me the chance to throw myself into it completely. I need to be hands on, helping set up, making sure everything runs smoothly. I can't just leave it all to Adrian, and I definitely can't spend the day distracted, worrying about Mom.

With everything packed and ready, I pull open my closet, scanning for something festive. My hand lands on a red thrifted dress I plan to pair with a white cardigan, stockings, and boots. Perfect for the Christmas theme.

By eight, I'm out the door, picking up fresh pies from Genevieve's bakery before heading to the town square, which is already bustling. The banner is up, vendors are setting up their booths, and the food trucks are arriving.

Our setup moves along surprisingly well. Everyone chips in, lifting tables, arranging decorations, checking sound equipment.

Adrian and I both volunteered to work a few stations, freeing up more people to just enjoy the day. My first stop is the gift-wrapping booth. I lay everything out, wrapping paper in every color and pattern, ribbons curling at the ends, rolls of tape, stacks of gift bags. An empty money tin sits on the table, waiting to be filled. I take a step back, scanning the station, making sure it's ready to go.

"Hey." The familiar deep voice comes from behind me. I turn, grinning as Adrian walks over, his broad shoulders parting the crowd effortlessly. His short dark hair is neatly styled, not a strand out of place. His blue eyes meet mine, and there is a flutter in my chest. There's something confident about the way he looks, like he's not trying to impress anyone but still somehow does. He's wearing a well-fitted black jacket, and his jeans are worn but perfectly suited for today. His hands are tucked into his pockets, but he stands tall, relaxed, yet commanding in his presence. I can feel the warmth in his smile, and it pulls me in even more. There's just something about him that makes it hard to look away.

"Hey, yourself."

He glances around at the nearly finished setup, nodding. "This looks great."

"And it's not even done yet." I flash him a grin. "I picked up Genevieve's pies and stashed them behind that stand. People need to donate for the raffle to get their hands on one of those."

"Nice. Pecan?" He raises an eyebrow, a smirk tugging at his lips.

I nod. "Of course."

His eyes darken with amusement. "You're making my mouth water."

"Good. Hopefully, it does the same for everyone else."

He runs a hand through his hair. "I brought all the gift baskets and raffle items. Figured I'd bring them out now."

"I'll give you a hand." I glance over at Ingrid from Pulse Boutique, who's already manning the wrapping station. "Ingrid, I'm going to help Adrian unload his car, then I'll be back."

She waves us off. "Take your time, honey."

We walk side by side toward his car. The air between us feels charged. My pulse quickens every time his arm brushes mine, and I find myself stealing glances at his profile.

"I barely slept last night," I admit, breaking the silence.

Adrian glances at me, then back at the ground. "Yeah, me neither." He chuckles, shaking his head. "Kind of nervous, which is weird. It's just a fundraiser, but... I don't know. The pressure to raise enough money for the CT scanners is weighing on me. If we can even get one scanner, it means patients won't have to drive for diagnostics. We could catch things early, like cancer and heart conditions."

I pause for a second, taking in his words, then bump my shoulder playfully against his. "We've got this in the bag."

His lips quirk up slightly, and I can tell he wants to believe it.

"Oh," he adds, "I also have all the money from the tickets sold at work for the gift basket raffle. That'll add a nice chunk to the total."

"Perfect."

We reach his car, popping the trunk to grab baskets filled with neatly arranged goodies... Bottles of wine, handmade crafts, gourmet chocolates.

"Where are we keeping all this?"

"There's a safe spot near the main tent," he says. "Let's keep everything together."

"Good idea."

We barely make it back before people start pulling us in different directions.

Milton, the community coordinator, calls my name, asking if there's anything left to be done. I take a slow scan of the square. Booths are set, decorations are up, the scent of fresh coffee and pastries fills the air. The festival is ready.

I shake my head. "I think we're good to go."

Checking the time and my clipboard, it looks like the fundraiser isn't only ready to start, but it's also about time for my first shift at the gift-wrapping booth, because later,

I'm face painting. I nod to Adrian, signaling I'm ready, and head over to the booth.

For a while, I just stand there, proud, snapping pictures that I hope capture the vibrant energy of the crowd, and the way the town comes alive when we do something like this.

The fundraiser has officially begun. Today's going to change everything.

I'm wrapping gifts as fast as I can, my hands moving on autopilot, when Adrian strolls up to my booth.

"I see you're busy," he says, his deep voice laced with playfulness. "Figured I'd make you even busier by having you wrap something for me."

I glance up, giving him a dry look. "Really thoughtful of you."

"I try."

"Sorry, I'm flat out here." I finish tying off a ribbon before pushing the wrapped gift toward the waiting customer. "But I guess I can spare a minute. What do you need?"

He reaches into his pocket and pulls out a sleek, engraved pen, placing it gently on the counter in front of me. "Can you wrap this for me?"

I pick it up, turning it over in my fingers. The polished silver, the way the letters "make your mark" are carefully etched along the side, it's beautiful. "Who's it for?" I ask lightly, trying to ignore the ridiculous hope swelling in my chest.

Adrian only raises an eyebrow. "That would be spoiling it, wouldn't it?"

"I don't know. Would it?" I smirk.

He doesn't answer, just watches me as I put it in a box before I start wrapping, my hands suddenly not as steady as they should be. The thought sneaks in before I can stop it... What if it's for me? But no, that's stupid. It's probably for Keith. It makes sense. It's the perfect kind of gift for him, something for his office.

Still, my fingers tremble slightly as I fold the wrapping paper around it. I know Adrian notices. He leans in just a little, his presence hot, his eyes tracking my movements.

"You're making me nervous," I say, forcing a playful tone.

That earns a soft chuckle. "You'd make a terrible surgeon."

"Yeah, well, surgeons have eyes on them all the time. Not really my thing." I finish the last fold, secure the tape, and tie a small ribbon around it before sliding it back to him. "There. Wrapped with care. Don't forget that donations are accepted."

"Appreciate it." He hands over some cash before picking up the gift, and tucking a lock of hair behind my ear, just a small touch, he walks off into the crowd.

I shiver as I watch him go, swallowing against the strange lump in my throat. Shaking it off, I focus on my booth for a few more hours before my stomach starts making its own demands.

By lunchtime, I'm starving, so I step away to find food. Passing the choir that is singing Christmas carols in the main square.

I wander toward one of the food stands, scanning the options, when I catch sight of Adrian again. This time, he's behind the counter, wearing an apron, his dark hair slightly tousled, his sleeves rolled up to his elbows.

I grin. "Now it's my turn to put you to work."

He glances up, grinning. "Yeah, looks like it."

I step closer, pretending to consider my choices while my eyes flick over the menu. "Hmm." Plucking a candy cane from a small display, I unwrap it slowly. My hands shake as I bring it to my lips, suddenly aware that Adrian's watching. I take a small taste, the peppermint strong on my tongue, and when I glance up and catch his eyes tracking the movement, heat fills my cheeks.

His Adam's apple bobs.

Feeling flustered by the intensity of his gaze, I pull the candy away quickly. "This is a good candy cane." I try to sound casual, but my voice comes out a little breathless.

"Didn't realize there were bad ones," he says, still focused on my mouth.

I twirl the stripped candy between my fingers. "There are."

He shakes his head like he's trying to clear it. I don't know what I'm doing or how far I should push this, but something in his expression makes my stomach fill with butterflies.

Eventually, I settle on tacos. After I pay for my meal, Adrian hands me a steaming hot plate with the scents of seasoned meat and fresh cilantro filling the air around me. "See you around, Chef Adrian."

His lips twitch. "Enjoy your meal, Trouble."

The nickname sends warmth through my chest. There's something about the way he says it, like it's meant just for me.

I walk off, finding my sister, Hazel, sitting at one of the wooden picnic tables, already halfway through her lunch. I slide into the seat across from her, picking up a taco and taking a careful bite. It's delicious, so warm, flavorful, and comforting, I finish it in only a few bites.

"You guys really pulled this off," Hazel says, looking around.

I nod, taking it all in. "It's kind of surreal," I admit. "I think a lot of out-of-towners came, too. Which is great for the hospital fundraiser."

Hazel hums in agreement. "Genevieve's food is next level."

I nod. "She's amazing. I know she has chefs, but when she makes something herself? It's magic."

I grin but check the time, sighing. "I gotta go. Face painting duty."

"Lucky you."

"Yeah, lucky me," I deadpan. "Hopefully, they don't ask for anything too hard. My skills are... limited."

"Just stick to snowflakes and reindeers. You'll be fine."

I stand. "Keep an eye on Mom for me, okay?"

"Relax. Luna's got her."

"I know." I give her a grateful look. "Just still... watch her."

"Will do," she promises.

With that, I head toward the face painting stall.

I'm cleaning my brush, waiting for the next person, when I catch the familiar scent before I even look up.

You've got to be kidding me.

Adrian smirks as he leans down slightly. "What can you do for me?"

"What do you want? A full Santa beard? A little reindeer nose?" I smile back.

"Actually," he says, voice laced with amusement, "I was thinking Spiderman."

"You're joking, right?" I deadpan.

"Not at all."

I squint. "You want me to paint you as Spiderman?"

He shrugs. "What can I say? Childhood dream. Today feels like the day."

I let out a laugh. "Dr. Whisperer will have a field day with this."

"Good. Let them." He flashes me a warm smile.

"Alright then." I dip my brush into the paint. As I lean forward, he closes his eyes, and for a second, I just study his face. Long, sloped nose, thin lips, chiseled jaw, a hint of stubble, thick dark lashes resting against his cheeks, strong eyebrows. His skin is smooth, and I'm so close, I can hear his breathing, feel it even. My heart thuds hard in my chest, my hand trembling slightly as I move.

One of my hands finds its way into his hair, tilting his head just slightly, and God help me, his hair is soft. This is doing something to my body. It's suddenly so hard to concentrate.

Just as I finish the first stroke, a small voice pipes up. "Cool. Is that Spiderman?"

Adrian cracks an eye open. "Does it look like Spiderman?"

My little brother, Felix, beams at him. "Yeah. Can I be Spiderman too?"

"Are you sure? What about Batman?"

"No, Spiderman." He crosses his arms.

"Alright, you'll have to wait your turn."

He surprises me by standing right beside Adrian, like it's the most natural thing in the world. Adrian stiffens slightly, eyes going wide in shock, but he doesn't push him away. I watch him closely, expecting some discomfort, but instead, he just lets out a breath and adjusts to Felix's closeness.

I go back to work, my fingers finding their way back to his face, tilting him slightly again to finish the details. His eyes flutter shut, and I swear I see his jaw tic, like he's struggling with something.

God, he's handsome. I just want to tip his chin up and kiss him.

Thankfully, I finish before that thought can fully take over. Felix bounces on his toes. "My turn, my turn."

Adrian rises to his full height. "So? How do I look?"

I tip my head back, examining my work. "Very heroic."

He grins, hands me a lot of cash for donations, and before walking away, murmurs, "Thanks, Trouble."

My body tingles, and I have to bite back a smile as I watch him go.

I move on to painting Felix's face. "Are you behaving here?"

"Yes."

"What about your brothers and sisters?"

"Yes."

"Are you just saying yes?"

He giggles. "Yes."

I shake my head with a smile. The thing that surprises me more is how comfortable he was with Adrian. I know Adrian would have some experience with kids, but I didn't expect him to be so at ease with Felix. But he was. And that? That makes me... happy.

By four o'clock, the day is winding down. The auction baskets are sold, and the mayor stands up to talk. Thanking Adrian and me for the successful fundraiser.

I listen to the applause, wanting to hold on to this moment forever.

Adrian comes to stand beside me, our elbows brushing, his warmth close but untouchable. My fingers twitch with the urge to reach for him, but I know better. So, I keep my hands to myself.

After the speech, everyone starts packing up. The rental company is coming for the tables and chairs, but the smaller things need to be put away. Luckily, most of the items were bought and taken home, which makes cleanup easier. I'm so thankful for a town that not only shows up to help with these events but also participates in supporting our own.

As we walk around picking up trash, I shake my head at him. "I can't believe you let me paint Spiderman on you or that you wore it all day."

"Hey, today was supposed to be about fun." He slips his arm around me briefly before letting go.

"It was, wasn't it? It turned out really well."

"You're just jealous because you didn't get something painted on your face."

I giggle. "Totally. That's it."

"I could fix that for you."

I narrow my eyes. "Not a chance. It'd be a disaster."

"Nah, I think I'd do alright." He winks. "I do have steady surgeon hands, after all."

I shove him lightly. "You just want to make a mess on my face."

He gives me a devilish grin. "I'd only mess you up a little."

I laugh, but the swell in my chest is unmistakable.

We both reach for the same piece of trash at the same time. Our hands touch. Neither of us moves for a second. My heart stutters as our eyes meet. I pull back first, but Adrian picks up the piece of trash, his fingers trailing mine just slightly before he lets go. I swallow hard.

"You hungry?" he asks casually. "The food truck's still there if you want some."

"You know what? I might take you up on that. As soon as I get home, I'm gonna crash."

"Same. As great as today was, it's wiped me out."

We sit down, too tired to talk much. "I don't even want to check the final fundraising numbers. I'm scared we'll come up short. But if we don't raise enough for the CT scanner, I'm thinking I'll find a donor to raise more money."

Adrian nudges my foot under the table. "We'll be fine. And hey, if there happens to be an extra bit of money needed..."

I gasp dramatically. "Are you suggesting we fib the system?"

"Would I do such a thing?" A slight smirk pulls at the corner of his mouth.

I laugh.

His expression softens. "Just having decent medical equipment could save lives, you know."

"It's important to you, isn't it?"

He nods but doesn't say anything.

I can see it in his eyes. Something personal that's driving this need. I want to push to ask what makes him care so much, but the vulnerable look on his face stops me.

"Tomorrow," I say, my pulse picking up. "Do you want to meet at Pulse Point?"

"At our spot?"

"Say ten?"

He grins. "Sounds good. But I was thinking... maybe I should keep this Spiderman look."

"Don't you dare."

He chuckles. "Alright, alright."

He walks me to my car, staying just long enough for the moment to stretch between us. Then he waves goodbye, and I watch him go, something giddy swirling in my stomach.

I don't know when my family left because I was too busy all day, but I can't wait to see the article that my colleagues write up about the festival tomorrow. Because today was a huge success.

CHAPTER 18

ADRIAN

Is there more than just holiday cheer in the air?
If you were at the fundraiser yesterday, you might have noticed the undeniable chemistry between Dr. Adrian Pierce and our very own Amelia Richards. Sources say they were practically inseparable, sharing inside jokes and even getting a little hands-on. Purely accidental, of course. But the real question is: will their "just friends" act hold up much longer? The way he looked at her. Well, let's just say, if looks could kiss...

Dr. Whisperer

I PUSH OPEN THE door to the diner, the scent of fresh coffee and buttery pastries overwhelming my senses. Conversations quieten as I step inside, followed by hushed whispers. I catch a few glances thrown my way, the kind that hold just a second too long. My jaw tightens. It's been weeks since I arrived, but apparently, the town still has nothing better to discuss than my personal life. Even Genevieve, who's usually too busy running the place to care about town gossip, gives me a look, that familiar raised eyebrow I've seen her use on customers who've had one too many cups of coffee, her lips twitching like she's deciding whether to say something.

I frown. "What?"

She shakes her head, smiling knowingly. "Nothing."

That's a lie. But I'm not about to play into whatever rumor is making the rounds this morning. I focus on the reason I came: coffee. A large iced honey latte with white chocolate cold foam with a little drizzle of caramel for her and an Americano for me.

With coffees in hand, I make my way to Pulse Point. The drive should be quiet, but my mind won't settle. Today's interview feels different. I want this to go well for her, for the article to be exactly what she envisions. The fundraiser was a success, but the story behind it, the real reason we did it, is just as important. What I'm not sure about is whether we can sit across from each other and pretend that almost-kiss didn't happen, pretend there isn't the tension that seems to bubble whenever we're in the same room.

I pull into the parking lot and scan the area. Her car isn't here yet. The disappointment that hits is deeper than I expected. I've been looking forward to seeing her, even if things between us feel complicated now.

I settle at one of the picnic tables.

Glancing down at myself, I smooth out the crisp white shirt I chose for today. It's nothing fancy, just clean, fitted, paired with dark jeans. A suit would've been overkill, but I still wanted to look... decent. Professional but presentable.

Who am I kidding? I just didn't want to look like an idiot in her article photo.

A familiar car pulls in, and before she even steps out, I'm already smiling. I shouldn't be this happy to see her, not when we're supposed to be keeping things professional, but it's impossible not to.

Amelia climbs out with her camera, a leather notebook and pen in hand, radiating confidence. She's dressed in fitted black pants and a soft blue sweater that hugs her figure just right, the color making her eyes stand out. Her long brown hair with blonde tips is loose today, catching in the breeze as she walks toward me, and for a second, I just take her in, effortlessly put together and just as beautiful.

"Hey." I hold out her coffee. "Thought you might need this."

"You remembered. Thank you." She accepts it with a small smile. Then walks toward the table and sits down, flipping open her notebook with slightly less urgency than usual. "Let's get started," she says, her voice softer than yesterday but still focused. "We'll do the interview first, and then I'll grab your picture."

Something feels off today. As if something's bothering her.

I lean forward slightly, covering her hand with mine. "Everything okay?"

She glances up. "Yeah, just... trying to stay professional."

I nod, understanding exactly what she means, so I pull my hand away, and her grip on her pen shifts.

I watch as she pulls out her phone and sets it between us. "Mind if I record this?" Her finger hovers over the screen.

"Go ahead," I say, waving to the phone.

The red dot appears, and suddenly, my story settles on me like stone, but I push through. "All right then." I settle in. "Ask away."

She nods, her expression unreadable, though I swear I catch the flicker of something... concern, maybe?

"Let's start with the fundraiser."

I glance down at my fingers, tapping against the coffee cup. My throat tightens. "I guess I should tell you why it meant so much to me." The words feel heavier than they should. "My mom left when I was twelve. It was just me and my dad after that."

Shifting in my chair, my grip tightens around the cup. The familiar ache spreads through my chest; it never gets easier talking about him. "He was my rock. The kind of man who worked hard, never complained, and always put me first. And then, a year ago, he passed away."

Amelia doesn't move, but I can feel her attention on me like a steady pulse. I clear my throat. "He had a massive heart attack. We were at home. I remember performing CPR, my hands pressing down on his chest, counting in my head, yelling at him to wake up. I don't even remember calling the ambulance... just the feeling of helplessness."

I can feel myself pulling inward, like I'm trying to protect myself from the memory as I'm sharing it. "It was like an out-of-body experience. When it's someone you love, when you're trained to save lives, and you still can't do a damn thing... it destroys you. I had no medical equipment at home, and by the time the paramedics arrived, they told me to stop. But I couldn't. I just... couldn't. I kept going, even when they pulled me back. Even when I knew it was too late."

The forest around us rustles, birds chirp, and branches sway in the breeze, but all I hear is the sound of my father's last breaths. My throat tightens, and I have to force myself to breathe normally.

I close my eyes, trying to pull myself together, before I reopen them and speak. "From that moment on, I made it my mission to make sure no one else died in my hands. I know it's stupid to think that way... I mean, death is inevitable, but I swore I'd do everything I could to stop it when I had the chance."

Amelia's focus is intense, but in the caught-off-guard kind of way. Like she's truly taking in everything I have to say. I drag a hand through my hair, not caring that I'm messing it up for the photo.

"That's why, when I was at my last job, I couldn't accept the dismissal of a patient. They were deteriorating, and I wanted to try something... anything... but the orders from my senior said no. I wasn't supposed to intervene. But I couldn't just stand there and let them die. So I did something." I can still see that patient's face, still remember the way the monitors looked, the moment when I made the decision that would change everything.

A beat of silence. Then her soft voice asks, "What happened?"

The combination of my dad's death, the patient, the lawsuit, everything crashes over me, and for a minute, I'm not sure I can get the words out. My throat feels raw. "I ordered extra tests, imaging, even tried new medication, but sadly, he died anyway."

Her lips part slightly, but she doesn't say anything.

"The board didn't like that I went against orders. Six years of my life at that hospital meant nothing. The patient's family called it negligence. They didn't know... didn't care that I was trying to give them a chance. They only saw a doctor who didn't follow protocol. And I get it, but all I could think about was what that family must have felt, losing someone they loved just like I did." I've never told anyone this, well, not the whole story, not like this. It doesn't feel as terrifying as I thought it would.

I rub my jaw, staring down at the table. The frustration that's been building for months finally spills over. "Nobody gets to tell me how to feel. Not when they still have their brothers, sisters, or parents. I have no one. So all my care goes into my patients."

Amelia sits quietly, the conversation hanging between us.

"And do you think you've changed?" she asks softly. "Now that you've moved here?"

I think about it for a moment. Images flash through my mind—the fundraiser, the community coming together, the way people here actually seem to care about each other. It's different from the isolation I felt at my last job, but the drive is still there. "Not in terms of wanting to help people. That will never change. But I've learned that this path isn't easy. And it never will be."

My fingers tighten around my coffee cup. "The CT scanner project bothers me because I know what a difference it could make. I became a doctor to save lives. And I'll do everything in my power to help. That's why I'm grateful to everyone who donated their time, their hard work, and their money to this. It will change lives."

She looks at me... really looks at me. And in her brown eyes, I see something that I've been longing for. *Understanding.*

It's not pity. Not judgment. Just pure understanding.

I swallow hard, letting the silence stretch.

Finally, she gives me a soft smile. "I didn't realize your mom left when you were young."

"Yeah," I say quietly. "I don't blame her. Mentally, she just couldn't cope being a parent, and it was the best thing for her." The words come out automatically; it's what I've told myself for years, but I'm not sure I believe them anymore. Maybe it's easier than admitting she abandoned me.

She doesn't say anything, just watches me.

"She died only a couple of years later."

There's a flicker of something in her expression—genuine sympathy that she doesn't try to hide this time.

She grabs her phone and stops the recording, her voice gentler now. "Adrian, I'm sorry your mother left you. I can relate to that because my dad left. He moved across the country and started a new family."

"Fuck. I'm sorry."

She waves it off like it's not a big deal, but I wonder if, deep down, it hurts like mine does. It's the reason I don't trust easily, and my circle of people is so small. *Is that how it is for her too?*

"That's all the questions," she says, smiling softly.

"Let's get the money shot." I wink, standing.

She giggles as she rises, and the sound is the brightness we need right now.

I follow her to the bridge, grateful for the shift in focus.

"The light through the trees is casting these beautiful soft shadows across the cobblestones." She glances back at me with something warmer in her expression.

"I think here will be perfect." She nods to the spot where the pillar meets the bridge's archway.

I lean against the bricks, one knee bent, hands tucked into my pockets. The rough texture of the wall presses against the back of my head as I give her a natural smile.

She lifts her camera, takes a few shots, then lowers it slightly. "You know, you make this look effortless. Most people get all stiff in front of a camera."

"Maybe I just have the right photographer."

With a roll of her eyes, she bites back a grin, ignoring me to take a few more shots. But when she lowers the camera, the air charges, like it did yesterday.

She's not packing up. Instead, she's just looking at me, and I can see the conflict in her eyes—professional duty mixed with something deeper.

I push off the wall, closing the distance between us slowly. "Amelia…"

She doesn't step back. "Adrian, we shouldn't—"

But her voice lacks conviction, and when I reach up to brush a strand of hair from her face, she doesn't pull away.

The urge to kiss her pulses in my veins. It's probably a bad idea, but looking at her now, seeing the way her brown eyes look up at me… Fuck it.

I dip my head, closing the space between us, and press my lips to hers before she can talk me out of it. She stills, just for a second. Then, she melts into me.

My hands roam over her back, memorizing every curve, every shiver under my touch. Her lips are soft, warm, intoxicating. I part my mouth, tracing the seam of hers with my tongue, and she responds instantly, opening up to me, her tongue meeting mine. Electricity shoots through me, and I deepen the kiss, pressing her tighter against me, her camera wedged between us.

I turn her around as her fingers tangle in my hair, tugging slightly, and I groan against her lips, walking her backward under the bridge until her back meets the wall. I cage her in, one hand braced beside her head, the other gripping her waist.

We kiss like we've been dying for this moment, because we've been dancing around it for too long. And it's perfect. *She's perfect.*

Her body presses against mine, a fire of desire burning inside me, and I don't want to stop. I don't want to let this moment slip away.

When we finally pull apart, gasping for air, I rest my forehead on hers, my hands still holding her like she might disappear.

Her voice is breathless when she finally speaks. "What are we going to do now?"

CHAPTER 19

AMELIA

His arms tighten around my waist, pulling me close until there's no room between us. Resting his forehead against mine, he exhales slowly, his breath hot against my lips.

"I won't get the promotion if anyone finds out I'm with you." My voice is rough with something that isn't quite regret but isn't exactly peace either. "Even the appearance could kill my chances. Luna needs to trust that I can maintain professional boundaries." I tilt my head back, meeting his gaze, and it's impossible to ignore the way his blue eyes darken under the daylight. He kisses the tip of my nose, a touch so soft it sends a shiver through me.

I can see him wrestling with something as his grip tightens slightly.

"Maybe…" he starts, his thumb tracing along my hip. "Maybe we could keep this between us. You know, just see where it goes without everyone watching."

Something coils in my chest at his words. "So, we're a secret?"

"Not a secret. Private. There's a difference. I just want to figure out what this is without the whole town having opinions about it. I'd like it to stay out of the bulletin. And I don't want you to face repercussions at work when we don't know what this is yet."

I study his face, seeing the conflict there. I completely understand the idea of exploring whatever this is without judgment. It sounds appealing.

"It's not something I've ever done before."

He lets out a soft chuckle, shaking his head. "Me neither."

His mouth finds mine, claiming me like I'm something he's been waiting for. My hands slide over his arms, up his neck, threading into his hair, pulling him closer. Every inch of him is solid, heat and muscle beneath my fingers, a presence I could lose myself in so easily.

We part, and he presses his lips against my temple, his breath a little uneven. "You're too good to be true."

"I could say the same about you." I don't want to distance myself from him.

It's going to be hard to keep this casual.

"At least we have a place to meet," I whisper.

His eyes flick to the bridge above us. "No one really comes down here?"

"No, hardly ever. Maybe some boys who are trying to fish on occasion."

"Come on, let's get out of here before we do something that'll make this whole self-control thing harder than it already is." A low rumble leaves his chest. "Don't tempt me, *Trouble*."

I grin as my stomach flips. "Thanks for the interview. Can't wait to show Luna tomorrow."

We're still standing close, his arms loosely around my waist. Our fingers brush as I pull away, tangling just enough to share heat. It's crazy how something so small can make my skin tingle.

"You're different than I expected." I'm not even sure if I mean the words to come out.

"Different?"

"Opposite of me, but exactly what I needed."

He studies me for a second before his expression softens. "I'm alone, and you come from a big family, and somehow, you're letting me in." His fingers trail lightly over mine. "I mean, I know it's just been one dinner, but the way your family welcomed me, it's not something I'm used to."

I nod as we head to our cars. "I know how much that means to you."

He smiles, but there's something vulnerable in it. "Not gonna lie, I was surprised at first. But the fact that everyone's so welcoming and kind, it makes this so fucking hard." He looks away for a second before locking eyes with me again. "Because I want you. I want this. But we both deserve the things we've worked for. You need this promotion. I finally have a chance for a fresh start. People accepting me."

"I know," I whisper, hating how small my voice sounds. Hating even more that he's right.

His hand cups my jaw, his thumb rubbing over my cheek. The tenderness of the gesture makes it worse... makes me want to lean into his palm and forget about promotions and fresh starts and all the very logical reasons this can't work.

My throat stings as I glance at the time. "All right, well, we better go, or my mom will start asking questions."

He nods, but he still loosely holds my hand. "And Keith will get suspicious if I'm late. I told him I'd go golfing with him when I got back."

A small smile plays at the corner of my lips. "That's a bit cute." I turn my head, studying him in the daylight as we walk back toward the parking lot. "But you don't strike me as a golf guy."

"I'm not." He shrugs, running a hand through his hair. "Never really played before. It's not something I did, not even with my dad. But maybe it'll be nice. Something to do with Keith. A bonding thing."

I stop beside my car, arms crossed. "What did you and your dad do together?"

His expression shifts slightly. "Watched sports, mostly. He was really into them, so we'd go to games. Nothing much beyond that."

I nod, letting his words settle between us before I say, "Mom and I used to walk. The kids would go on their bike rides, before, you know, she got too tired." The flashbacks hit me hard—how she would point out different flowers and trees, and always pack extra snacks. Now she gets exhausted after doing something as simple as showering.

"She'll get better," he says gently. "Lots of people live perfectly healthy lives with atrial fibrillation. It's just the initial diagnosis and adjustment that's tough."

"Yeah," I murmur. "Medication, testing, all of that." I want to believe him, but the cardiologist's words about lifestyle changes and monitoring keep playing in my mind. And I can see the worry in Mom's eyes, even when she's trying to be optimistic.

A quiet moment passes, and our fingers brush once more. The separation feels wrong, like snapping something I desperately want to hold on to.

When I straighten, I hesitate, glancing at him.

His hands are in his pockets, shoulders slightly tense. "I don't want this to end. I only just kissed you."

A lump forms in my throat, and I force out a wry smile. "Worried you'll need me more than I'll need you?"

He huffs a quiet laugh. "Come on, don't make me sound sappy. I know you like that hard-ass side of me."

"Oh, I know it's there," I tease, leaning against the car. "Just... not with me."

He watches me with that sharp gaze of his. "Nothing like the reporter I thought you were."

"So, you don't think I'm Dr. Whisperer now?"

He shakes his head, the corner of his mouth quirking up. "Hell no. Deep down, that heart of yours is too big to be malicious." His gaze softens slightly. "Sure, you added a few twists, made me sound bad without my full story, but... I still don't love how you painted me in that first article. I get why you did it, though."

I swallow. "My thoughts on you have changed. I would never write about you like that now. And I'm going to spend tomorrow making sure this article reflects who you really are. Hopefully, the town will see you differently."

He brushes his hand tenderly against my cheek. "I hope so."

I smile. "Go have fun at golf. Can't wait to hear all about it. Text me later."

"And you... go hang out with your family. Can't wait to read my article."

"Oh, you'll love it."

"Not too nice. Don't want to shock the town too much."

I shake my head. "No, I just want them to see what I see."

I glance around the lot, noting it's still empty, but we're completely exposed out here. Anyone could drive by. His gaze holds mine before he steps closer, stopping me before I can get into my car. "We shouldn't—" I start, but he's already moving.

His hand finds my waist, and then his lips are on mine, sending my stomach somersaulting.

I giggle against him, breathless. "God, I feel like a teenager." But even as I say it, I'm pulling back slightly, my eyes darting toward the road. "Someone could see us."

He grins. "But it feels good, doesn't it?"

I nod, fingers grazing his wrist. "Yeah. Feels great."

"I'll see you soon?"

I swallow, nodding. "See you soon."

The next day, I walk into work with a lightness in my step, something I haven't felt in a long time. Excitement bubbles under my skin as I settle at my desk, ready to tackle the day.

"Hey," Violet calls from across the office, looking up from her screen. "Great event Saturday."

"Thanks." I can't help but grin.

"I sent you the pictures. Did you get the interview for the article?"

"Yeah, I did." I pause, trying to find the words. "His story makes sense, you know? It all fits together."

She nods. "Did you get a photo of him?"

I groan dramatically. "Ugh, he's so damn annoying."

She leans in. "What do you mean?"

"Just so photogenic. Like, it took one shot. One. And it was perfect." I recall yesterday, the way the light caught his features, how he looked so effortlessly handsome even after sharing something so personal and painful. And then there was that moment when he looked at me with such raw vulnerability, like he was trusting me with pieces of himself he'd never shown anyone else.

Violet laughs. "Some people are just like that. So unfair."

"How was the wedding you went to yesterday?" I ask, changing the subject.

"Oh, it was beautiful." She sighs. "Honestly, so nice. But also, kind of daunting. You know, that many people all at once."

"You'll make a beautiful bride."

She beams. "Aw, thanks. So would you."

I glance down quickly, avoiding her gaze. My heart stutters for a second, and I almost say something about Adrian. But I don't. *Not yet.*

The stakes are too high right now. I can't risk anyone thinking I'm unprofessional, not when I'm up for this promotion. Once I get it and can finally pay off the bills that keep threatening to go to collections, then maybe I can be more open about whatever this is between us.

I shake off the thought and get back to work, pulling up my notes and typing the article. I'll edit it after I get the first draft down, then add a photo.

By the time I finish, I'm happy with how it sounds. I attach the image, review it one more time, and then call Violet over. "Come, take a look at this."

She leans over my desk as I show the article to her. Her eyes scan the screen, and then she grins. "This is great. And... wow. He does look hot."

"He was easy to work with."

"You did a really good job."

Smiling, I email the article to Luna and head to her office. "Hey, I sent you the interview with Adrian Pierce." I sit in the chair across from her desk.

Luna starts reading, nodding along. "Oh, great pho-to." She scans the article further, her expression shifting. "Wow. His story is... heartbreaking."

"Yeah," I respond. "When he told me, I felt awful. His dad, everything he went through... and now he's here, trying to start fresh." I have to keep my voice neutral, even though his story makes my chest ache. I can't let it show.

She exhales, looking up at me. "It makes a lot of sense now."

I nod. "It does."

"Well," she says, tapping her fingernails against her desk. "I'm glad he's here. And this is a great article. Your best work yet."

A warmth spreads through me. "Thanks, Luna."

"Get it scheduled for print."

I hold back a grin. "Will do."

Back at my desk, I pull out my phone, staring at his number. I shouldn't text him. But I want to. We agreed to keep things a secret. But after sharing something so intimate yesterday, the distance almost feels cruel.

> **Me:** *The article was a huge hit with my boss. Thank you. I feel the promotion coming.*

A response comes almost immediately.

> **Adrian:** *I never doubted you.*

CHAPTER 20

ADRIAN

"Hey, Dr. Pierce."

Sitting at the nurses' station, I hear Dr. Lowell approach. I look away from the patient's chart to find him standing next to me. He's about my age, with dark hair and sharp eyes that rarely miss anything.

"Hey," I reply, adjusting the tablet in my hands.

"How's it going today?" His tone is casual, but the fact that he's even asking surprises me. Most of the staff here are polite enough, but there's still certain people who are not quite sure what to make of me yet. But Lowell's question feels genuine, like he wants to know.

"Good," I answer, keeping my expression neutral. "Just catching up on patient notes. You?"

"Same." His gaze flicks over my notes before meeting mine again. "How are you settling in?"

"It's been good," I admit, tapping the edge of the tablet with my thumb. "The work's decent. I'm enjoying it." I hesitate for a minute before adding, "Had a tough case this week. A teenager came in with a severe asthma attack that spiraled into respiratory failure. We weren't sure she'd pull through, but this afternoon…" I sigh heavily. "She opened her eyes, breathing on her own. We finally turned a corner. It's been a win."

"Nice work." He nods in approval as he grabs a stethoscope from the desk and loops it around his neck.

I shift in the chair. "You just started your shift?"

"Yeah, nights this week." He rolls his shoulders, like he's shaking off the last bit of his day before settling in.

"I've had all shifts," I say before I can stop myself.

"You're still the new guy. So they throw you into the deep end." He chuckles.

I nod, tucking that thought away. There's something reassuring about the way he says it, like being the new kid is only temporary, and I'll earn my place here eventually. It's not something I expected to matter to me, but it does. "I'm used to it. Did nights all the time in the city."

"Right, city life," he says, watching me like he wants to say more but doesn't.

It's silent between us before he straightens. "I'd better get moving. Got rounds to do. You probably have things you're trying to tie up before heading out."

"Yeah, alright."

"See you around, Pierce."

"See you."

As soon as he walks off, I return to my notes, but I can still feel a stare on me.

"Well, that was interesting," a voice mutters.

I glance to my side. Dr. Patel, one of the ER docs, leans against the desk, arms crossed, a knowing look in his eyes.

"What was?" I ask.

He nudges his chin to the now vacant area beside me. "Lowell doesn't usually talk to anyone like that."

"He spoke just fine."

"Yeah." Patel smirks. "To you. He tends to be a short individual, not saying much to the majority of people. I think the most that's gotten out of him are acknowledgements that he's heard you."

I refocus on my notes, but my mind continues thinking about the interaction longer than it should. The way Lowell looked at me when I talked about the patient, like he understood exactly what that victory meant. And the casual way he called me Pierce, like we'd been working together for months instead of just crossing paths. There was something different about the whole exchange, something that felt less like colleague small talk and more like something else entirely.

A few hours later, I throw my bag into my locker, stretching out the tension in my shoulders. Keith's out tonight, catching up with Adam and someone from out of town, so the house is mine.

I pull out my phone and stare at the blank message screen. We've only kissed, so are we at the point where I can just invite her over? What if she already has plans? What if this is moving too fast? I type out a message before I can second-guess myself any further.

> **Me:** *Guess who's got the house to himself tonight?*

This feels like something a teenager would do, sneaking around when the parents aren't home. But I hit send anyway.

Amelia's reply comes almost immediately.

> **Amelia:** *Is this you asking me to come over? ;)*

I chuckle to myself at her fast response.

> **Me:** *Need time to shower and wash off the hospital. Come over after 8?*

> **Amelia:** *Done.*

Another text comes through before I can set the phone down.

> **Amelia:** *Also, did you see the article went live? Let me know what you think.*

Me: *Haven't seen it yet. I'm at the hospital. Will read it.*

Amelia: *No pressure. Just wanted you to know it's out there.*

I stare at her message for a moment. Out there. My story. My truth. Now the whole town can read it. And the anticipation settles in my chest, making me finish my notes faster.

By the time I walk into my house, I'm already peeling off my scrubs, triple-checking that Keith isn't home. The moment the hot water hits my skin, I close my eyes, letting the day wash away.

Because tonight, I'm not thinking about work.

I'm thinking about Amelia. About what it'll be like to have her here, in my space, without having to worry about who might see us. About whether she'll be as nervous as I am, and if this will feel as intense behind closed doors as it does everywhere else.

I'm getting dressed when I hear the car pull into the driveway, followed by the knock.

When I open the door, Amelia moves toward me with a bright smile lighting up her face. The glow from the porch light catches in her brown and blonde highlighted hair, and there's something effortless about the way she moves towards me... like she belongs here, like she's always belonged here.

"I read it," I say, before she can even speak. "The article."

Her eyes fill with cautious hope. "And?"

"It's perfect." My voice catches. "You... you got it right. All of it. Even the parts I didn't know how to explain properly."

She smiles as she takes the first step up. "I'm glad. I wanted to do your story justice."

"You did more than that," I say, and kiss her.

My hands find her waist, pulling her flush against me, and I feel the soft gasp she breathes against my lips. I don't let her go, walking her backward into the house without breaking contact, my foot kicking the door shut behind us. Then I remember Keith. What if his plans change and he comes home early? The last thing we need is him walking in on us. My hand fumbles for the lock, twisting it into place. It won't keep him out if he really wants in, but at least it'll give us a warning.

I pin her against the door without breaking the kiss. She makes sexy, breathy sounds that go straight to my dick. I swallow every one of them, loving the way they vibrate against my lips. When I finally pull back for air, I rest my forehead against hers, my chest rising and falling with each breath.

"God, I fucking missed you," I murmur.

"I missed you too," she says, a little breathless. "I didn't think I'd be able to get this for days."

"What are you doing to me? I've never needed someone like I need you." The admission feels dangerous, like I'm giving her something I can't take back. I've never been the guy who gets attached this fast. But with her, all my usual walls seem pointless.

A hint of color spreads across her cheeks, and fuck, she's so beautiful when she blushes. I can't stop myself from brushing my thumb over her cheek, from soaking in the heat beneath her skin.

She lets out a shaky breath.

"Do you want a drink or something?" I ask, remembering my manners.

She shakes her head as her teeth graze her bottom lip. "No. I want you."

The words hit me hard. She's not holding back, and that does something to me. Something reckless.

I kiss her again, drinking in every bit of her need, her want, her urgency. She fits against me so perfectly that when I lift her, her legs naturally wrap around my waist.

I carry her to the bedroom, barely aware of anything but the way her fingers curl into my hair, the way her breath catches.

By the time I lower her onto the bed, I'm desperate to feel her, to see her. My hands slip under her sweater, tracing the softness of her stomach.

Her hands are already at the hem of my shirt, fingers dragging across my skin like she can't get enough. The way she's looking at me—her eyes darkened, breath uneven, hands needy—has my chest tightening.

I yank my shirt off, tossing it aside.

"You're beautiful," she whispers.

I huff out a laugh. "Isn't that my line?"

"Guys can be beautiful too."

The way she says it—so sure, so sincere—makes my heart fucking swell.

"Thanks," I murmur before capturing her lips again, my hands pushing up her sweater. I need to see her, all of her. She lifts her arms, letting me pull it over her head, and then her hands are already at the button of my jeans, undoing them with ease. There's no question about what's happening between us. The certainty of it, the way she wants this as much as I do, sends a rush of heat through me that's almost overwhelming.

I let her strip me down, just like I did to her, peeling away everything until there's only skin, and the sound of our breathing.

She's in a baby blue set. Lace that hugs her body just right. My fingers brush along the edge of her bra, my gaze dragging over every inch of her. She's so fucking beautiful, and for a second, I can't quite believe she's here, that she's mine, even if it's just for tonight.

"Chose it for you," she admits, almost shyly.

Fuck, I love when she's shy. She's being vulnerable with me, and I know that she doesn't share that with anyone else. She usually only shows her strong side.

I tip her chin up with a finger. "Why do I fucking love that?"

That gets her snapping back, her lips on mine again, all hesitation gone.

"You're the most beautiful thing I've ever seen," I tell her.

Her breath hitches when my fingers glide over the lace of her bra, tracing the delicate fabric where it meets her skin. I watch the way her chest rises and falls, the way her lips part just slightly, like she's waiting, like she's daring me to do more.

I take my time, kissing my way down her throat, along her collarbone, tasting the warm, soft skin beneath my lips. She tilts her head back, giving me more, her hands fisting in my hair like she needs something to hold on to.

"Adrian," she breathes.

My name on her lips is my undoing.

I flick open the clasp of her bra, letting the straps slide down her shoulders before I ease it away. My palms skim over bare skin, soaking in her heat, the way her body responds to my touch. Her nails drag down my back, leaving a sting in their wake, and I groan against her throat.

I want her so badly.

"You're driving me crazy," I murmur, my lips brushing her ear.

She lets out a breathless laugh. "Good."

I press a teasing kiss to the corner of her mouth before heading lower, my hands smoothing over her hips as I push down her blue lacey thong. She shifts beneath me, helping me, and soon, there's nothing left. Just us completely bare to each other. The way she's looking at me, like she wants me just as badly, makes me feral.

I drop my gaze over her, memorizing every sexy curve. Her fingers graze along my shoulders like she's doing the same.

"I need you. Please don't make me wait anymore," she whispers, her voice raw.

A rush of heat floods my chest, and my pulse quickens.

I press my forehead against hers, steadying myself, soaking in the moment because I know this isn't just need. It's so much more.

Kissing her slowly, I pour everything into it. She matches me, fingers gripping my face, her body arching into mine like she was made for this. Fuck, made for me.

"I've got you," I promise against her lips.

And then, I ease her back down onto the bed. Her fingers hold on to me like I'm something she can't bear to let go of, and I don't want her to.

Not now.

Not ever.

Chapter 21

Adrian

THE SOFT LIGHT FROM the bedside lamp touches her skin, highlighting every curve, every dip, every place I want to touch. She's breathtaking, waiting for me like this. My fingers brush the length of her thighs, tracing lazy patterns over her warm skin, feeling the way she shivers beneath me.

"Spread your legs, baby," I murmur, rough with need.

Her gaze locks with mine, dark and hazy, filled with trust and hunger. Slowly, she parts her thighs, and my pulse drums, the heat between us turning electric.

I drag my fingers over her wet pussy. "Is this all for me?"

"Yes." She arches into my touch, her body asking for more before she even speaks the words.

I glance up, taking in the flush spreading up her neck, the way her lips part as she struggles to breathe. She's lost in this moment, lost in me, and there's something about that... about knowing I'm the one making her crazy.

I slide my fingers over her thighs, slow, teasing, watching her face as I do. Her eyebrows pull together, her lips tremble, her body fights to stay still. I want to memorize this. Every expression, every sound, every little way she responds to my hands.

"You're beautiful," I murmur, kissing just below her belly button, feeling the way her stomach quivers beneath my lips.

She reaches for me, fingers digging into my shoulders, trying to pull me closer, but I hold still, letting the anticipation build between us. I want her desperate, aching, needing me the way I need her.

I move up, capturing her mouth in a slow kiss. She tastes like everything I've ever wanted but never thought I could have. The need to see her face, to watch her react to what I'm about to do, tugs me back. When I pull away, her eyes are heavy-lidded, her chest rising and falling fast.

Her hands slide to the back of my neck, tugging me back to her lips. "You're killing me," she whispers against my mouth.

I grin, dragging my lips down the side of her throat, savoring the way she gasps when I nip at the sensitive spot just below her ear.

"You can handle it," I tease.

She shudders, her body soft and ready for whatever I give her.

And I plan to give her everything.

I drag my fingers through her wetness again, and her head tips back, exposing her delicate neck. When I push one finger inside her, she feels so soft, warm, and perfect.

Her pussy clamps on my finger as a moan slips from her parted lips. I move slowly, not wanting to rush any of this. I want to take every second in, memorize everything. When I slip in a second finger, her legs try to close.

"Keep your legs open," I command.

She tries to keep her eyes locked on mine, but the more I move my fingers in and out, the more she fails. Her body softens, opening up to me completely.

"Fuck, Amelia, you're so beautiful."

I lean forward, kissing the side of her neck over her pulse as she breathes, "So good."

"I've barely gotten started," I say. "Don't know if I want you to come on my fingers or my mouth."

"Both." The way she says it, breathless and demanding, makes my dick throb. Fuck, she's going to be the death of me.

My thumb moves to circle her clit in hard but slow circles. "So greedy."

Her breathing turns into sexy little pants when I increase my speed, her body following whatever I give her.

"Oh, my God!" Her eyes roll back into her head.

I want both too, but I want to feel her come apart on my dick, and I need a taste, so I shuffle down.

"You made a mess of my fingers," I say, sucking each one clean before gently blowing on her clit, causing her to shiver once more. "I better clean you up."

"Yes," she replies huskily.

I lean forward. "But let me start with kissing your lips." My mouth meets hers, and she kisses me back ferociously.

God, I love kissing her. Her tongue plays with mine with the perfect pressure, her taste intoxicating, and our rhythm in sync. When she breaks for air, I drag my mouth along her jaw, behind her ear, nipping there again. She shivers, but I keep going, peppering soft kisses along her collarbone, down to one tightened pink nipple. I suck on it hard until her body is shaking beneath me. Lifting off that nipple, I kiss along to the other breast.

I want her so fucking needy by the time I get to her pussy. I do the same thing to her other nipple, but this time, she arches her back into me, loving every moment. Her hand slips into my hair, pulling it tight between her fingers. *She's ready.* Shuffling down, I kiss her soft stomach, down to the top of her pussy, where I inhale. She smells so fucking perfect.

"I can't wait to taste you."

"Adrian, please don't make me wait longer."

I lift off, looking at her. "Did you ask me to go slower?"

"No!"

But I drag this out a little more, intending to drive her insane. Bringing my lips from her inner knee, I kiss slowly up toward her pussy.

"Oh my God, you're killing me."

My hands grip her thighs, keeping them apart, feeling her muscles twitch. I don't waste another second. I bring my mouth down, her scent so much stronger now, her pussy glistening. My mouth waters, and I lick her with one long swipe.

"So fucking good," I mumble against her.

She rolls her hips against my face, and my fingers let go so she can grind hard on my mouth. As my tongue slips inside her, she moans my name so loudly my dick pulses. "Adrian."

God, the sound of my name coming from her sexy mouth makes me grunt, and I go feral, hands shifting to her ass, pushing her pussy on my face as my tongue moves faster in and out. Literally fucking her with my tongue before I shift to her clit. I roll my tongue firmly around it, peering up at her as I do.

Her chest rises and falls fast as she groans my name, her head flipping around everywhere, like she's trying not to come.

"You're so good," I moan as I continue rolling my tongue against her clit as she grinds on my face. She's trembling hard. I know what she wants.

My two fingers move to her opening, and I push them inside at the same time my mouth moves to her clit and sucks it hard between my teeth.

My fingers thrust inside her slowly, knowing exactly where her sweet spot is.

She moans loudly, and I murmur against her pussy. "Come on my face."

"Oh, fuck." And with that, I graze my teeth along her clit as I drag my fingers along her front wall. Her whole body shudders against me, and the feel of her in my hands, under my mouth, collapsing like this is making my heart beat wildly and my dick harder, if that's even possible. I'm so desperate to be inside her, my dick is leaking, but I won't come... only in her.

She goes still beneath me, her breathing changing, and her hands tighten in my hair as she rides out her orgasm.

"Are you okay?" I ask, lifting off her after she's come.

"More than okay."

It's an incredible thing, knowing I did this to her. That every shaky breath, every tremble still leaving her body, every drop of pleasure, it's all because of me.

She rolls her eyes playfully at my smug grin, but doesn't bother hiding the wicked curve of her lips.

I kiss my way back up her stomach. My hands press into the mattress on either side of her face, hovering above her, soaking in the sight of her spent and glowing.

"That was perfect," she murmurs. "Thank you. But look at your face." She lifts a hand to my jaw, tracing over the damp scruff on my upper lip and chin. "You're all covered in me."

"That's how I like it."

Her fingers grab my head and tug me down to her mouth. I groan into the kiss, deepening it when I feel her other hand move, sliding down my stomach, wrapping around my cock.

"Fuck." The strangled curse rips out of me.

Her fingers close around me, stroking me just enough to make me twitch in her grip. She watches me with dark, knowing eyes, glee flashing across her face as she feels just how fucking turned on I am.

A slow smile curls her lips. "I like this."

"Yeah?"

She nods, biting her lip. "I like knowing you want me this much."

There's something about the way she says it... something vulnerable beneath all that teasing confidence that makes my chest ache.

"Amelia, I always want you." I breathe hard, trying to get myself under control. "Let me grab a condom."

She watches as I get off the bed, heading for the nightstand. The rustle of the foil packet, the snap of latex against my skin should be nothing, just part of the routine, but her eyes stay locked on me, lips parted, her breath coming faster.

"You like this?" I stroke myself once, just to tease her.

"God, yes." Her voice is breathy. "It's so hot watching you do that."

I groan. "Fuck, Trouble, you're killing me."

She giggles, but it's soft, faint with need. "I'm also jealous of your hands," she says. "It was nice touching you."

I climb back onto the bed, settling between her parted thighs.

"Next time, you can touch me first," I promise, dragging my lips over hers in a kiss that's far too brief for either of us. "But right now, I need you."

Her legs hook around my waist, locking me in place.

"You ready?" My body is screaming at me to stop talking and take what we both need.

She nods frantically. "More than ready."

I press the head of my cock to her entrance, and then, fuck...

I groan as I push forward, sinking into the tight, wet heat of her. She gasps, her back arching off the bed, her nails biting into my arms.

"Jesus, you feel so good," I grind out, barely able to think past the way her body clings to me.

"Adrian," she moans, her hands sliding up my back, gripping me like she needs me closer, and deeper.

I brace myself above her, hips rolling in slow, steady strokes, letting her adjust, savoring the way she shakes beneath me. The perspiration slicking our skin as her walls pulse around me... it's all too much, and yet, not enough.

"Harder, please," she whispers, eyes heavy.

Jesus Christ.

Another groan escapes me, and I shift my hips forward, sinking deeper, drawing a cry from her lips. "You're so fucking perfect for me."

She tightens around me, her thighs clenching, her body pulling me in. Her hands are gripping my arms, her nails digging into my skin, grounding herself as I keep thrusting, harder now. The sounds of our bodies moving together fill the room.

"You take me so well," I murmur, watching her face, needing to see every second of this. "You're incredible."

Breath stuttering, her thighs tremble against my sides. She's close. I can feel it in the way her pussy clenches around me, the way her body starts to quiver.

"Gonna make you come again." I slam into her just right, angling my hips to hit that perfect spot inside of her.

She shatters with a cry, her whole body locking up, squeezing me so tight it's almost unbearable. Her head falls back, mouth open, a moan breaking free as she pulses around me. "Adrian."

The pleasure rips violently through my body.

"Amelia—" I bury myself inside her, shuddering through my orgasm.

For a long moment, neither of us moves, our bodies tangled, our hearts beating hard against each other. I can't think, can barely breathe. That was... Fuck, I've never felt anything like that. The way she felt around me, the sounds she made, it was like everything else just disappeared.

"You doing okay?"

She finally gives a blissed-out smile. "More than okay."

I gently bring my lips to her damp forehead. "Yeah?"

She puffs out a breathless laugh. "Yeah."

The only sounds in the room are our slowing breaths and the faint rustle of sheets as she shifts, curling further into me.

I pull the blanket over us, holding her against my side, my fingers tracing slow circles on her bare shoulder. Pressing a kiss to her temple, I inhale the faintly sweet scent of her. This is new to me, the whole wanting to hold a partner instead of finding an excuse to leave.

Her fingers trace mindlessly over my chest. She tilts her head up, meeting my gaze, her brown eyes still heavy, and her cheeks flushed. "That was... really good."

I grin. "I'll take 'really good.'"

She laughs, soft and genuine, and it hits me right in the chest.

A quiet moment settles between us. The kind I wouldn't normally let linger. But with her, it doesn't feel uncomfortable. It feels right.

Her fingers trail down my arm, slow and thoughtful. "You ever get scared?"

"Of what?"

"This." She swallows. "Feeling something like this."

I know what she means. It's the kind of fear that comes when something is too good, too real. Like if we acknowledge it, we might lose it. And the thought of that, or worse, losing her, sends a panic through me. I've already lost too much. My mom, my dad, my reputation. I can't imagine adding Amelia to that list. What scares me the most is how much I already need her, when I've spent so long convinced I was better off alone. The more time I spend with her, the more I want to spend my time with her.

I tighten my hold on her, smoothing a hand down her back. "Yeah," I admit. "But not enough to stop."

She searches my face, and whatever she sees there must be enough, because she nods, a small, satisfied smile tugging at her lips. "I feel the same."

I shift, rolling her beneath me just enough to steal another passionate kiss. One that says we're not done yet.

CHAPTER 22

ADRIAN

"You're doing what?" Isaac practically shouts through the phone.

I move from the middle of the sidewalk to lean against the brick wall of The Point Bakery while people pass by, arms full of shopping bags, the smell of fresh bread lingering in the air. I have the day off since I'm working the weekend, so I figured I'd spend it in town running errands.

"I'm buying a girl flowers," I say, keeping my voice casual, though my heart's beating a little harder than I'd like to admit.

It's been a few days since I last saw Amelia, and we've been texting, but it's not the same. The ache of missing her has stayed with me. I want her to know I'm thinking of her. Flowers seem like the right gesture. Something beautiful, and something thoughtful. But we're keeping things quiet. No one's supposed to know about us. So, I'll send them to her whole family with a note about welcoming me to town and hope she gets the message.

Isaac whistles low. "So, you're dating someone already? I figured you'd be the first one to settle down, but this soon?" He chuckles. "Shit, I might have to come down there and find a girl myself."

"That would mean you have to live here. Most people don't leave this place."

"What do you mean?"

"Families here? They stay their whole lives. They love it here, and honestly, I can see why." I glance around at the quiet town streets. It's different from the city: slower, warmer. "Even the hospital's good to work at."

"How so?"

I think about how to explain without sounding too sentimental.

"The patients, man. They're grateful. Kind. It's not better than the city. Just... different."

"Glad you're happy there. I just couldn't leave my life here."

I've been thinking about this for days now, weighing the pros and cons. I hesitate for a second, then say it. "I'm buying a house in the next few weeks."

"Shit, for real?" He laughs. "Well, now I'm definitely coming down for a housewarming party."

"Which means I'd actually have to organize one."

"Exactly!"

A woman's voice calls his name in the background. He sighs. "Alright, gotta get back to work. Talk to you later."

"Yeah, later."

I hang up and slip my phone into my pocket, then I push off the wall and head straight for The Flower Point.

Amelia's getting those damn flowers.

The shop is bigger than I expected, with an almost greenhouse-like feel: glass walls letting in sunlight, shelves overflowing with cascading vines, potted plants, and bursts of color. The air is filled with the scent of roses, eucalyptus, and something citrusy. It's not the kind of traditional florist I'm used to. Alongside the flowers, there are shelves of handmade soaps, candles, and tiny trinkets that catch the light.

A voice cuts through the quiet rush of the shop.

"Hi. How can I help you?"

I turn toward the sound, my body jerking slightly at the unexpected volume. A woman in her late twenties stands behind the counter, her brown curls pinned back in a messy updo, a warm but knowing smile on her face.

She studies me for a second, then her face lights up. "Oh, Adrian."

I hesitate, trying to place her, but she beats me to it.

"I saw you at the fundraiser," she says, her eyes intense with familiarity. "You know you're always going to be the talk of the town. The new doctor. Seems like you're making a good name for yourself. Keith speaks highly of you."

Keith. Of course.

I nod, offering a tight smile.

"He stops by every now and then, but you know how it is in this town. You see everyone, whether you want to or not." She laughs. "Speaking of which... I read Amelia's article about you."

"Yeah?"

"It was really something." Her voice softens. "I had no idea what you went through in New York. None of us did." She shakes her head. "Well, it wasn't right. I'm glad people know the truth now."

"Thanks," I manage, unsure what else to say.

"Genevieve was in here earlier. She said half the town's been talking about it. Most people feel awful about the gossip when you first arrived." Leila waves her hand dismissively. "You know how it is. Towns love their rumors until they get the real story."

"Perks of the town, I suppose." I smile.

"So, what can I do for you?"

I get the feeling that if I don't accept her help, she's going to keep talking just for the sake of it. So, I go with the easiest option.

"I'm looking for flowers... for a family." The lie slips out easily, even though every part of me wants to say, *They're for Amelia.*

The woman murmurs, crossing her arms. "What kind of flowers?"

"I don't really know," I admit. "Something... special. A thank-you."

She considers for a moment, then nods. "How about a mix of colors with pops of green? Maybe some red leaves for contrast? Something that really stands out."

"Sounds good." I sigh, relieved. "I trust you. Just... make it big. Like $200 worth."

I don't miss the way her eyebrows lift slightly.

"Generous," she murmurs. "Oh, sorry, I didn't even introduce myself properly. Leila." She waves her hand.

"Nice to meet you, Leila."

"Want these delivered, or are you taking them with you?"

"I'll take them now."

She beams, already moving toward the back. "You really made an impression on this town, you know. The fundraiser was a hit."

I nod, remembering that day, how the whole community came together, how much of a success it was, how it raised enough to fix the broken CT, and how Amelia had looked at me, smiling in a way that hit me hard. I know Amelia said they would show up to support their town, but it shocked me to see how this small town takes care of their own.

"I was hoping it would be," I say. "The hospital could really use the new equipment."

"Well, none of us actually know exactly what a CT's for," Leila teases, gathering stems with practiced ease. "But we trust that you do, because we know what you did for

Mrs. Wynter, and that means the world to us. That you took care of her because you knew something was wrong, so we're happy to help. That's what this town is about. Family."

I nod again, something warm moving through my chest. After everything that happened at my last job, having people trust my judgement means more than I expected. My fingers trail along the edge of the wooden counter. "Yeah. I've been enjoying that part of it."

"And the part where everyone knows your business?" She smiles, giving me a pointed look. "Not so lovely."

I huff out a laugh. "That part, not so much."

She winks before turning back to her work, moving around the shop, gathering flowers while explaining what they are. I try to listen, but the words blur together. Flowers aren't my thing.

Amelia is.

And if this makes her smile, then that's all that matters.

Once the arrangement is done, Leila wraps them in crisp brown paper, tying it with twine and ribbon. "Here you go. Sure to brighten someone's day."

I smile, grateful she doesn't ask who they're for. Pulling out my wallet, I hand her the cash.

As I take the bouquet, the scent rises between us, and I head for the door. But just as I step outside, I bump into someone.

"Whoa."

I take a step back, steadying myself, and then I recognize her.

Hazel.

She glances at the bouquet in my hands. "Those are nice. Who are they for?"

I force an easy smile, adjusting my grip on the flowers. "They're for your family," I say smoothly. "I was going to give them to Amelia to pass along to you guys."

Hazel narrows her eyes slightly, like she doesn't quite believe me. "I can take them if you want." For a second, I consider it. But then she adds, "I wasn't heading home right away."

Something tugs in my stomach.

"What are you up to?" I ask.

Hazel shifts her school bag higher on her shoulder, the strap digging into her uniform. Her fingers toy with the edges of a spiral notebook, the corners worn from fidgeting. She hesitates before speaking, eyes flicking down to the pages like she's trying to find the right words written there.

"Well, I've got this school project," she finally says, her voice softer than before. "I'm going to volunteer to co-ordinate a program at the retirement village. Help with yard work, groceries, that kind of thing. Something about giving back."

"That sounds great." And I mean it.

Her fingers tighten around the notebook. "Yeah, I guess. It's just... I'm not good at this kind of stuff, and everyone's too busy to help. And Mom—" Her voice wobbles for the first time. "She can't. I would ask Amelia, but she's been too busy with work and taking care of Mom. I don't want to add to her worries."

Guilt flashes across her face before she drops her gaze, staring hard at the ground. My shoulders tense. She's just a kid trying to handle everything on her own.

"I could help."

"You sure?" she asks suddenly, eyes darting back up.

"I don't have much to do today, honestly. That's why I got these flowers. Day off, no real plans. I don't have a little sister." I smile. "Might be nice to borrow one for the day."

That earns me a small smile.

"Sure," she says. "I was actually heading to the retirement village now."

"Mind if I tag along?"

She considers for a second before nodding. "Alright. You lead the way."

"Do we need my car?"

"Actually," she pauses, tucking a loose strand of hair behind her ear, "would you mind dropping me home afterward? Since you were coming with the flowers anyway?"

"Of course."

We cross the street toward my car, and as we settle inside, Hazel glances at the bouquet now resting on the backseat. "Those are really nice flowers," she says casually, but there's a gleam in her eye. "She's gonna like them."

I don't correct her.

She already knows. I should be relieved that I don't have to keep pretending, but another part worries about what Amelia will think when she finds out her little sister figured us out.

I start the car, letting the low rev of the engine fill the silence. "So, is this something you have to do all semester?"

Nodding, she stares out the window. "Yeah. We have to volunteer somewhere, and I picked the retirement village." She hesitates, her fingers tapping against her knee. "After seeing my mom sick—helpless—it made me think. There's probably a lot of other people in the same situation. Ones who can't take care of their yards or go grocery shopping and can't afford to hire someone to do it. I figured maybe it'd help to have someone looking out for them."

Her words hit me harder than I expect.

I grip the steering wheel, my mind drifting back to the hospital hallways and whispered updates. Back to the moment my father collapsed, helpless as his heart gave out right in front of me.

I know what she means.

Loss changes you.

It shifts your entire perspective, makes you see things you never noticed before. But I wasn't like Hazel. I was focused on grades, on med school, on getting everything right. I wasn't thinking about giving back. I was just trying to push forward.

Hazel, though. She already gets it.

I glance at her as she stares out the window, lost in thought.

She's already thinking about others in a way most people don't.

That's rare.

And damn, I envy it.

We pull into the parking lot of the retirement village, a quiet, well-kept space lined with trimmed hedges and a small garden by the entrance. A few older residents sit on the porch, chatting, enjoying the sun.

Hazel unbuckles her seatbelt. "Alright, we better check in."

"Lead the way."

Inside, the air smells of pine and lavender. A receptionist greets us with a warm smile, her eyes lighting up when she sees Hazel.

"We're so excited to have you," she says. "Honestly, this is such a lovely program. I'm sure you'll be missed once your time is up."

Hazel smiles. "I'm glad I can help."

The receptionist beams. "We're so happy to have you, Dr. Pierce."

"Please call me, Adrian," I offer, and she nods.

I've noticed lately, the whispers have stopped. No more sideways glances, no more hushed conversations when I pass. It's peaceful.

The receptionist hands Hazel a list and a small map with names circled. "These residents are struggling the most right now. Since there are two of you, you might get through more than one today, but it's entirely up to you."

Hazel studies the list, nodding. "We'll see what we can do."

We step out into the courtyard, and I let her take the lead.

"Any particular place you want to start?" I ask.

"Not really." She shrugs. "I figured we'd start with the closest and work our way around. See what they need help with."

"Good plan," I say.

"Maybe one of us could help with groceries, and the other could do something festive," I suggest.

She nods. "Good idea."

"How long do you have?"

"Only a couple of hours," she says. "Then I have to write a research paper for school."

"Fair enough." I glance down at the list. "Who's first?"

She scans the names. "Mr. Gideon."

I nod, tucking my hands into my pockets. "Alright. Let's go meet him."

The retirement village is a collection of single-story homes arranged in a square pattern around a central courtyard with benches and a small garden.

We head to Mr. Gideon's place first.

The moment he spots us through the screen door, a wide grin spreads across his face. He pushes it open and leans against the frame, eyes twinkling with mischief.

"Well, well, well, if it isn't the naughty doctor." He crosses his arms over his chest. "And Miss Hazel. Now, Hazel, I didn't know you kept such questionable company."

I can't help but grin. This guy's got personality.

"He's alright." She smiles. "Mom likes him."

Mr. Gideon lets out a dramatic sigh. "Ah, yes. Mothers always like the troublemakers." He gives me a once-over, then wags a finger. "You do look like a heartbreaker. Bet you've left a trail of crying women in your wake."

Hazel giggles while I shake my head.

"I think you're giving me way too much credit."

"I was a looker back in my day too, you know," he says, tapping his temple. "Had the ladies lined up, but I was a gentleman." He winks. "Mostly."

Hazel bites back another giggle. "We're here to help you, Mr. Gideon."

"Well, don't just stand there. Come in." He waves us inside. "Tell me what you're gonna do for me."

Hazel launches into her well-rehearsed explanation of the project. As I listen, I'm impressed. She's got a natural way of speaking. Clear, direct, thoughtful. She may be only sixteen, but she's already more put-together than most adults I know.

Mr. Gideon nods along, rubbing his chin. "Alright, alright, so you're basically my free labor?"

Hazel sighs. "We prefer to call it volunteering."

He snickers. "Same thing."

In the end, he decides he doesn't need help with groceries because he still enjoys flirting with the cashier too much. Instead, we tackle his Christmas decor together.

I glance down at Hazel's outfit: jeans and white sneakers. "Didn't exactly dress for pulling decorations out of storage, did you?"

She huffs, tugging at her sleeves. "I was just thinking the same thing."

Mr. Gideon plops down in a chair under the porch. "Don't worry, kid, real work builds character. You should see the kind of stuff I had to do at your age."

"Yeah?" I say. "What kind of stuff?"

"Oh, you know." He waves a hand vaguely. "Built a barn, chopped wood, walked uphill both ways to school. The usual."

"Uh-huh," I say, biting back a grin. "Sounds tough."

We spend the next couple of hours untangling strings of lights, carrying boxes of ornaments from the storage room, and setting up his elaborate Christmas display. By the time we finish, we're both dusty, slightly out of breath from climbing ladders, and a hundred percent over it.

Mr. Gideon claps his hands together. "Well! You both survived. That's good. Thought the doc might collapse halfway through."

I shake my head, wiping sweat from my eyebrow. "Not a chance."

Hazel snaps a quick photo of us with Mr. Gideon's fully decorated house in the background and sends it to her sister. I wonder what Amelia will think. My phone dings almost immediately.

Amelia: *Oh my God, THANK YOU.*

Another message follows a second later.

Amelia: *She asked me to help with that project, but I haven't had the chance. Been swamped with work and taking care of Mom. I've been thinking about you, though.* ⊠

I type back.

Me: *I've been thinking about you too.*

Hazel groans, reading over my shoulder. "Gross. Can you guys not flirt while I'm standing right here?"

Mr. Gideon barks out a laugh. "Get used to it, kid. Men like him? They never quit."

I shake my head, grinning despite myself.

As I'm dropping Hazel off at home, she steps out of the car, balancing the large bouquet in her arms. I start to get out to help her, but she waves me off with a look that tells me she doesn't want me coming to the door. "Thanks for helping today."

"Anytime." I nod toward the flowers. "Make sure those get to where they're supposed to go."

She smiles. "Oh, I will."

"If I'm free next time you go to the retirement center, I'll tag along again."

Hazel grins. "Alright. Just don't let Mr. Gideon mess with you."

"I think he's already got my number." *I may have given it to him before I left.*

She laughs, waves, and disappears inside.

Chapter 23

Amelia

I sink into the black leather chair beside Violet as we both get our hair done after going thrift shopping together. The salon is busy with blow dryers humming, scissors snipping, and stylists chatting with clients as they work on their hair, and in my case, my entire mood.

This is our time to relax and catch up, free from work stress. At the office, we're all business, but here? This is where the real gossip flows, and where secrets leak fast. And the bonus is that we always walk away with fresh material for an article and our own personal tea.

Violet flicks through a magazine, not really reading it, and turns to me. "Did you see the new person who came into town last night?"

I shake my head, knowing I was too busy being distracted by Adrian. "No. Who is it?"

She glances around before leaning close to me, whispering, "Well, she's already gone, but the rumor mill says it was Adrian's ex. Crazy stuff, though definitely not true. But you know how people talk."

My stomach tightens just a little, not with jealousy, but with curiosity. We haven't talked about exes, and honestly, what Adrian and I have is supposed to be private. No drama, no baggage, just something fun and easy. Something secret. But those flowers yesterday… the way he looked at me that night at his place…

I think about how the whole family reacted to the bouquet. Mom got teary-eyed, and Hazel just gave me this knowing look that made my cheeks burn. The card said it was for the whole family, but I knew better.

But I can't help the way my mind reels. What if it really was his ex? What if she came back for him? I hate the thought of him having unfinished business with someone else, but I do hope it's nothing because I'm starting to care more than I should.

Still, if I really want to know, I can just ask him. And I do.

I pull out my phone and send him a quick text.

Me: *Hey, rumor has it, your ex-girlfriend was in town last night.*

Adrian: *That would be interesting, considering I haven't had an ex in years. If she was here, it wasn't for me. Gotta love town gossip.*

I relax, but it isn't lost on me that I cared way more about his answer than I should've.

I show Violet the message, and she snorts. "Told you it wasn't her." Then her eyes narrow. "Wait. You texted him?"

I shake off the uneasy feeling as I lie to my best friend. "Why not? I already have his number from the festival, and if it was her, I'd want to write about it."

The lie tastes bitter, but that answer seems to satisfy her, as I'm biting my tongue, holding back the real reason I texted him. Because the truth is, if I tell Violet, I'll tell my family, and if I tell my family, it's no longer just a secret. And once it's out there, it becomes real in a way that feels too big, too fast. Right now, it's just ours.

But there's one thing I do want to share.

"But I did find out," I say casually. "He helped Hazel out yesterday."

Violet raises an eyebrow. "Oh?"

I nod. "Leila's been raving about how handsome he was, how polite, how he spent a ridiculous amount of money on a bouquet for our family."

Violet grins. "What a lucky family."

"Right? Hazel came home with these flowers that looked like something out of a wedding catalogue. Huge, every color imaginable. Definitely expensive."

Violet adjusts a foil on her head. "So, what's Hazel's project again?"

I glance up at the giant wall mirror in front of us, catching the reflection of other clients getting their hair done. "Her new semester project is all about volunteering, so she organized a program to help residents at the retirement village with yard work or groceries."

"And Adrian just happened to help out?"

"He ran into her after visiting the florist and decided to give her a hand." I smile. "She said he was really good—actually worked hard. But she also said old Mr. Gideon gave him a hell of a time."

Violet's eyes spark with interest. "Oh? What happened?"

I chuckle. "Apparently, Mr. Gideon was being his usual self, giving Adrian grief at first, then cracking jokes and somehow roping him into giving him dating advice."

Violet gasps, her face lighting up. "No way! How old is this guy? Eighty? And he's out here looking for love?"

"Yup." I shake my head, laughing. "And he thinks he's got a shot with the cashier, Dores."

Violet practically howls. "I love that. What a king."

"Right? Super cute."

She nods. "Hey, love is love, no matter the age."

I nod, but before I can say anything else, our stylist, Mia, walks over and checks one of my foils. I can only afford the front pieces framing my face, but it's enough to brighten it up again. It's been at least eight months since I was last here.

Mia sighs dramatically. "Ugh, I hope I find love soon. Bit of a drought over here. Last interesting guy to come into town was Adrian, and, well..." She waves a hand. "Not exactly my type."

"No?"

She shakes her head. "Too nice. Too quiet. I think I have a thing for bad boys."

I smile. "Don't we all?"

Violet eyes me playfully. "I wouldn't call your taste a bad boy."

I shrug. Thankfully, she's thinking about my past boyfriends and not Adrian. "No, I guess not."

"But..." She grins. "We work in news, and you do love a good story."

The timer dings, and Mia claps her hands together. "Alright, Amelia, it's time to wash these foils out."

As I make my way to the sink, I can't help but think maybe Violet's right. Maybe I do love a good story.

And Adrian? He's definitely becoming one.

The toner sits in my hair, the chemical scent strong, but we're almost done, so our conversation slows now partly because the stylists are cutting our hair, and partly because the roar of blow dryers drowns out any chance of talking.

I close my eyes, letting the warm air blow over me, my head tilting slightly as my stylist works. Thoughts drift to Adrian, wondering when I'll see him again. Maybe tonight? My stomach flutters with anticipation. I'm picturing his eyes on me, like nobody else exists.

"You know," Mia, my stylist, says conversationally, "I was thinking Adrian would be a great match for my sister."

My stomach twists so violently I feel like I might be sick. *Oh.*

I swallow, forcing a neutral smile. "Oh, yeah?" I keep my voice light, casual, and unaffected, but my insides are anything but.

I want to say no. I want to say he's already mine.

But is he?

We never laid out rules. Never said if we were seeing other people. But Adrian doesn't seem like that kind of guy. Still, the thought of someone else trying to set him up burns in a way I didn't expect.

"She's really sweet." Mia continues, oblivious to my internal panic. "Works at the bank, loves working out. I think they'd be perfect together."

"Mm-hmmm," I mumble through a clenched jaw.

I try to ignore the uneasy feeling, but it's still there, hanging on so much that before I can talk myself out of it, I grab my phone and type out a message while Mia isn't behind me.

> **Me:** *So, the hairdresser wants to set you up with her sister.*

I swear, sometimes, he's just waiting for me to text him, especially with how quickly he responds.

> **Adrian:** *Well, I'm not interested in anyone else. Only you.*

A warm rush of relief and satisfaction spreads across my face in the form of a smile.

"Okay, what was that?" Violet's loud voice cuts in, making me jump. "Why are you grinning like that? Who's texting you?"

Shit.

I flip my phone face down on my lap. "It's just Hazel." I hate how easily it's becoming to deceive my best friend. "Filling me in on more about her and Adrian at the retirement village."

Violet's eyes narrow. "Oh? Did something else funny happen?"

The way she zeroes in on me makes my heart race. I'm dodging way too many questions, spinning way too many lies.

"Yeah, I'll tell you later," I say quickly as the blow dryer roars to life again.

Thank God. I don't have to say anything else.

I step out of the salon, feeling good, loving my fresh blonde highlights.

Violet got sucked into some keratin treatment for her flyaways, but I'd budgeted for this appointment and nothing more. No extras. No indulgences. Just the basics.

I start heading toward my car when suddenly—a hand catches mine.

I gasp, my pulse spiking, but then I see him.

Adrian.

His blue eyes meet mine, filled with hunger. His short dark hair is a little messy, like he's just run his hand through it, and there's a tiny bit of stubble along his upper lip and chin, giving him a rough edge. He stands casually, like he's been waiting for me.

I don't bother asking how he found me. He knew I was here.

Before I can say anything, he tugs me into the alley. The space is narrow, dimly lit; the brick wall cool against my back as his body covers mine, hiding me from anyone who might pass by.

"I couldn't wait another minute to see you," he rasps.

My heart hammers. "Thank God," I breathe, before his lips crash into mine.

I inhale him, his scent deep with velvety cocoa. It's intoxicating as his hands press against my waist, pulling me flush against his hard body.

God, I want him.

Right here. Right now.

I've never done this, never had sex in a public place, but the way he's kissing me... the way my body melts into his, the way he grips my hips like he's seconds from losing control... I'd do anything.

"Do you have your car here?" I ask.

"Yeah." His lips brush against my jaw.

"Why?"

"I want you."

Adrian pulls back just slightly, his blue eyes flickering with something dangerous. His hand cups my face, his thumb dragging over my lower lip.

"You make it hard to say no when you say things like that."

I arch into him, a silent beg. "Then don't."

His hands tighten on me before forcing himself to step back.

"We shouldn't," he says, but his voice is strained, like he's fighting himself. His reaction to my text, the way he said he's not interested in anyone else, has given me a boldness I didn't have before.

"But you want to, don't you?" I challenge.

He searches my face. "Do you have somewhere to be?"

"Nope."

He brushes a finger through my hair. "By the way, I like your hair."

I grin, my pulse erratic as he twirls it with his finger. "Thanks."

"I'll try not to ruin it."

At this point, I don't care what he does to my hair as long as he's on me, in me, everywhere.

His hand finds mine again, and our fingers tangle together.

"Where's your car?" he asks, his voice husky.

"In the hairdresser's lot."

"Meet me at our spot?" He grins.

"Yeah." I know exactly why he's asking. We're a secret still. And if I leave my car here for too long, Violet and others will start asking questions.

We pull apart, our hands staying for just a second longer before we let go. I practically run to the car trying not to be too quick to draw attention to myself.

Then, I slip into my car, my breath coming fast, and drive.

Ten minutes.

That's all it takes to get to Pulse Point.

And the second I park and open the door, Adrian's already in the backseat of his car waiting, his expression dark and hungry.

His hands rest on my waist when I climb in next to him. "It's going to be a hell of a long week not seeing you. I have to work all weekend, which sucks."

I know the feeling. The thought of days without him leaves an ache in my chest I don't want to acknowledge.

But I don't want to waste time thinking about that.

He moves me on top of him, straddling his lap, and oh, God, I feel him.

He's hard. He's ready.

A small, needy sound slips from my throat as I rock against him.

"Fuck, Amelia," he grits out, his fingers tightening on my waist, holding me still.

I kiss him, swallowing the low groan that rumbles from his chest, feeling the heat of his body through our clothes.

He thrusts his hips, just once, just enough to send a spark all the way to my toes. But he doesn't rush. He lets me set the pace.

"I like this," he rasps. "I like you using me, doing what you want to me." His eyes burn into mine. "Take me as hard as you want."

A shiver runs through me.

I lean back slightly, my fingers fumbling with his belt, my heart pounding loudly in my ears. He watches me, his hands sliding down my thighs.

But I need to get out of these clothes first.

I shift beside him, quickly shimmying out of my jeans, my skin flushed and feverish. The car is hot, full of our ragged breaths and the scent of us.

I keep my top on. So does he.

His cock juts against his open fly, thick, hard, waiting, and there's something about it that makes me want to tease him first.

I slide down, dip my head, and take him into my mouth.

"Fuck, Amelia," he groans, his hand threading through my hair, holding but not forcing, like he just wants to feel me.

Grip tightening slightly, he gathers my hair carefully away from my face. I moan, my hand wrapping around his base, twisting, stroking, giving him the friction he's desperate for.

His hips jerk.

"Your mouth is perfection."

His encouraging sounds make me dizzy with power.

But then—

"Amelia... stop," he chokes out. "Get up here and fuck me. Now."

It's not just a request. It's a warning. A desperate, urgent plea.

I pull back, my lips swollen, tingling, my pulse racing.

Climbing over him, I reach down to guide him to my entrance, when—

"Wait... condom." His voice is rough, barely holding on.

He fumbles in his pocket, pulling one from his wallet.

"Let me." I take it from him, my fingers brushing his, my hands far steadier than I feel. I tear the foil with my teeth, roll it on, and once he's covered, I line him up and sink down.

Oh, God.

I freeze, my nails digging into him as my body stretches to take all of him.

It's so much.

So full yet I feel incredible.

I breathe through it, letting myself adjust.

His hands grip my waist firmly, waiting for me. There's something different in his touch this time, more possessive, more certain. Like he's claiming me in a way he didn't before.

And when I'm ready, I lift slowly, then sink back down, savoring every inch, every shuddering breath against my lips.

His eyes lock onto mine. Which are dark, intense, and all-consuming. It makes me breathless; I've never felt so special.

I start to move, my hands holding on to his shoulders, my hips finding a rhythm. He meets me, his hands guiding me, urging me harder.

Heat builds in my core.

I can feel myself climbing to orgasm.

So I move faster, chasing it, losing myself in the friction, in the way he feels inside me.

I hope he comes too, but I don't think I can stop—

"Fuck—"

He thrusts up just as my orgasm slams into me, the pleasure crashing through and tearing me apart.

His name spills from my lips. "Adrian."

He follows a second later, his arms locking around me, holding me tight as his body shudders, his release spilling into the condom.

For a moment, neither of us move.

We just breathe, holding each other, my head buried in the curve of his neck, my fingers still clutching his shoulders. My pulse is still racing, and there's this feeling of rightness, a connection so big, I can't ignore.

Finally, I exhale a shaky breath. "Well, that was unexpected."

Adrian chuckles, his hand smoothing down my back.

I pull back slightly, pressing a tender kiss to his lips. "So was you finding me outside the hair salon."

Then reality starts creeping back in. Our secret, the lies I've been telling to Violet, the carefully planned hook-ups to keep this hidden. I need to leave before someone notices I'm gone, but the thought of pulling away from him right now is breaking something inside me.

"I should clean up and head home," I murmur. "Mom's waiting for me."

Adrian nods, his hands gripping my waist before I finally force myself to slide off him.

We tidy up; the car fogged, still smelling like us.

I pull on my jeans. He tucks himself back in, adjusting his clothes.

"When will I see you again?" he asks, voice still a little rough.

I smile. "I don't know, but I'll definitely try to squeeze you in again."

He grabs me. "Funny."

I lean in one last time. He cups the back of my head, his lips claiming mine, like he doesn't want me to go just yet.

And neither do I. But I have to.

CHAPTER 24

ADRIAN

IT'S BEEN A WEEK and a half since I've seen her. Work has been hectic, and she's had family stuff going on after work. The texts help, but they're not enough… not even close. I need to see her face, hear her laugh, feel her next to me.

We agreed to meet at our spot, and since then, I've been thinking about her all the time, counting down the days, the hours, the damn minutes until I see her again.

I pull into town early, parking outside Genevieve's. The Cozy Point is warm and buzzing with people, and I swear each time I walk in here that the smell of coffee and butter take over my senses.

Heading straight for the counter, I order her favorite pie, two coffees, and a few extra things I know Amelia likes. Genevieve gives me a look as she hands me the cups. I pretend not to notice. She probably assumes the second coffee is for Keith. I try not to overthink it. But it's hard when every little detail feels like a secret I'm holding too tightly. If she gets this promotion, I want to stop hiding. I'd want her. Openly.

The drive to our spot is a blur. When I get there, I park near the bridge and take a deep breath, my pulse already picking up. The air is crisp, the kind that bites at my skin, but I barely feel it. If anything, I'm sweating.

I grab the small vase I borrowed from Keith's place, then search along the creek for wildflowers. It's not much, but it's something to show I care. I set up the food on the table near the bridge, out of full view, because I know we won't kiss if someone could see. I lay out a blanket, ready to cover her legs with, arrange the food, and place the vase in the center. Then I wait.

The time we fucked in the car has shifted something between us: the way she looked at me, and felt in my arms, was different. But I need to know where her head is at, need to understand what this is becoming. Because for me, it's not casual anymore. I'm starting to have strong feelings for her, and I'm hoping she feels the same.

I can't see the road from here, so I listen instead. The crunch of tires on gravel. A car door shutting. Light footsteps. My chest tightens. It's her.

I get up, brushing the dirt off my pants, adjusting my coat, running a hand through my hair.

She's wearing a cream cable-knit sweater and jeans today. A caramel coat wraps around her shoulders, her hair pinned half-up, two strands around her face slipping free in the wind. She looks breathtaking. Like something out of a dream.

She smiles when she sees me. I smile back.

"Hi."

"Hi, Trouble." I step forward, hands naturally finding her waist, pulling her in before she can react. I kiss her like I've been starving for it. Because I have. She melts against me, her fingers gripping my coat, her body fitting against mine like she belongs there.

I want more. But not today. Today is about something else.

I pull back, brushing my thumb against her cheek. "Come here."

She follows as I grab her hand, letting me guide her to the table. I take her handbag, setting it aside, watching as her eyes widen at the setup. Then I lay the blanket over her legs.

"Oh my gosh," she breathes. "This is gorgeous."

"Thanks for coming." I hesitate, searching her face. "I missed you."

A slow smile curves her lips. "I missed you too."

I take the seat across from her. She sips her coffee, eyes closing in appreciation.

"How's your week been?" I ask.

She shrugs, lowering the cup to the table. "Same old. Still covering trivial news. Luna's been out of town, so I haven't gotten any updates on the promotion."

I nod, my grip tightening around my cup. "That's actually what I wanted to talk to you about."

She watches me carefully. "What about it?"

This is it. The moment I've been dreading. My stomach churns because I know what I'm about to tell her could change everything between us. I hesitate. "Do you think she's already picked someone?"

Her expression falters. "I don't know. It's possible. But I've known Luna a long time, so she would've told me right away."

I nod, my thumb rubbing over her knuckles. "And if they pick someone else? Would you leave? Look for a new job somewhere else?"

"Why? Do you want me to leave?"

"No," I say quickly. "God, no. I just... I don't want you stuck in a job you hate. You're young, smart, and you could do so much more. I..." I let out a breath. "I don't want you to give up on something better and settle."

She presses her lips together, thinking. Then she sighs, long and slow. "I know," she murmurs. "I know, but I..." She stops. And I wait. Her shoulders rise and fall as she gathers her thoughts. "Can't leave my mom," she says finally, her voice quieter now. "I can't leave my family."

I nod, watching the way her other hand fidgets with the hem of her cardigan. Her loyalty to her family is something I admire, even if it complicates things. She's not running away from responsibility; she's choosing it. That takes strength.

"It's not just about what I do for Mom." She continues. "The specialist says once she's healthy, she'll be back to normal. And I believe that. I do." Hesitating, she bites her lip. "But it's more than that. I don't want to miss them growing up. I want to be here. I want to see it all."

A heavy knot forms in my throat. I get that. More than she probably realizes.

"I had a lot of fun hanging out with Hazel," I admit, shifting to face her better. "I told her that it felt like I was borrowing a little sister."

She laughs, and it eases something in my chest.

"Oh yeah, I heard about that," she says, eyes twinkling. "She also mentioned the flowers were for me."

Her gaze glances down to the table, where my fingers trace patterns on the back of her hand.

My heart beats loud in my ears, caught between embarrassment and satisfaction.

"Obviously, I couldn't tell Leila that it was for you," I add. "So I told her I needed a big enough bunch for the whole family."

She laughs again, shaking her head. "Hazel didn't buy it."

I pause, watching her expression closely. "Do you think she'll tell anyone?"

She shakes her head immediately. "No way. She knows how much this promotion means to me. I trust her."

A warmth spreads through me at her certainty. "I trust her too. Even spending just a little time with her, I've never met a sixteen-year-old like her."

She shifts, pulling her knees up and resting her chin on them. "She's a good kid."

"Your family is amazing, you know?"

She grins. "Amazingly chaotic."

I chuckle.

She studies me like she's seeing something new. "You fit into this town, Adrian. We're lucky to have you."

My chest tightens. It's one thing to feel like I have a place in this town, but hearing her say it? That hits differently.

I clear my throat, glancing away. "Well, Hazel made my day, too. Going to the retirement home, even getting a grilling from Mr. Gideon, it was... I don't know. It felt good. Giving back." I pause, running a hand through my hair. "I mean, yeah, I help Keith with his place, but this was different. Getting my hands dirty, actually doing something useful, felt good. It's not something I did much in the city."

She watches me closely. "You really like it here, don't you?"

"Yeah, I do. I didn't expect it, but I've realized how much I love being outside. Fresh air, even in winter. All of it. And I'd love to help Hazel again, if I can swing the days off work."

"She'd love that." Then, thoughtfully, she adds, "You know, she's going to make such an impact in this town, helping people who really need it."

I nod. "I agree. And even if Hazel wasn't there, I wouldn't mind helping out again. It's actually got me thinking—how much time do I really have? Maybe once a month, I could offer a couple of hours at the retirement home, help with small repairs, or whatever they need. Some of them don't have much help, but even a little effort means the world to them."

She bites her lip, smiling at me in that way that tightens my jaw. "That's what makes you, you," she says softly. "You care."

I shrug, a little embarrassed, but her words stick with me.

Then she hesitates, tucking a loose strand of hair behind her ear. "Actually, speaking of that. I wanted to ask you something."

"Go on."

She shifts and sits up straighter. "I had to check with you first, but... how would you feel about me writing an article about you and Hazel helping at the retirement village?"

"An article? I don't mind, I guess. At least the article would put me in a positive light. And maybe it would encourage others to volunteer as well."

She nods, pulling out her phone. "I've already drafted the start of it, but I wanted to run it by you before I do anything with it."

I glance at the phone in her hands, then back at her. She looks almost nervous, like she's unsure of my answer.

And suddenly, I realize, I like that she's asking. I like that she cares what I think.

I lean in. "Well, that depends. Does this article mention how good-looking I am?"

She laughs, shaking her head. "Oh, my God."

"Because I think that's important information," I add, winking.

She groans and playfully nudges me with her shoulder. "I take it back. You don't fit into this town."

"We'd have to do another photoshoot. I suppose I can find time to pose," I joke.

"You're insufferable," she says through a giggle.

"Honestly, I don't mind, but don't you think it's going to start looking a little suss if you keep writing articles about me?"

She laughs. "I don't think so. News has been slow lately. Other than you, the only interesting thing that's happened is that out-of-towner who was supposed to be your ex."

With a sigh, I shake my head. "I still have no idea where they got that from. The poor girl has nothing to do with me, yet somehow, she was tied to me. I don't know where Dr. Whisperer gets their gossip, but damn, they're creative." I still have no idea who this mystery woman even was or why anyone would think she was connected to me.

Amelia grins. "Hey, at least you're keeping the town entertained."

"Great," I say dryly, though I can't help but smile. "But I guess it's not a bad thing, since you're keeping the paper alive."

She hums in agreement. "Exactly. So, I don't think anyone will question it."

I watch her for a moment, then shift closer, my voice quieter now. "So, we're just waiting on your boss to give you that promotion. And then, what's our plan?" My heart pounds as I ask. I need to know if she's thinking about us the same way I am. If she wants something real, or if I'm getting ahead of myself.

"What do you mean?" She shifts in the seat.

I reach over, gently taking her hand in mine, our fingers threading together. We both watch the way they fit, like it's something worth holding on to.

"I mean, what do you want it to be?"

She looks up at me, her eyes soft. "I like you, Adrian." Her voice is barely above a whisper. "A lot."

A painful pressure builds behind my ribs. *What if she doesn't want the same thing? What if I'm about to scare her off?*

I smile, squeezing her hand in mine. "I like you too, Amelia. I want us to be together."

Her breath hitches, and for a second, she just looks at me. Then she smiles, small but sure. "I'd like that too."

I give her hand a light tug, pulling her a little closer.

"So after the promotion, could we date?" "Yes. Definitely."

Relief floods me, and I grin, capturing her lips in a kiss. She leans into it, and for a moment, it's just us.

Then, the sound of rustling nearby makes us pull apart.

Turning my head, I freeze. "What the hell?"

Russell is staring me down at the end of the table. *Russell*, the damn turkey. And he's not alone. He's brought an entire tribe—Turkeys, geese, swans, ducks—every damn bird imaginable is closing in around us.

"Amelia, what's going on?"

She stares wide-eyed at the growing army of feathers. "I don't know," she whispers. "But I'm slightly terrified. There are a lot of birds."

I nod slowly. "Okay. Don't move. Let's just see what Russell's up to."

Asshole.

Russell takes a bold step forward, his beady eyes locked onto me like he knows I just called him an asshole in my head. I press my lips together. "Uh, sorry."

He steps closer.

So do the rest of them.

"Shit," I mutter under my breath.

And then one of the birds lets out an ear-piercing squawk, and suddenly, they charge.

"Run!" Amelia shrieks.

We bolt, laughing, abandoning everything—blanket, vase, food, coffee—and sprint toward her car, birds flapping and screeching behind us.

The first raindrop lands on my cheek.

I glance up. More follow, light and steady. Of course. The perfect ending to our crazy afternoon.

Amelia wipes a drop from her forehead and starts giggling.

I laugh too, shaking my head. "This is not the date I had in mind."

She grins. "No, but it's us. And it's kind of perfect."

CHAPTER 25

AMELIA

THE NEXT DAY, I sit at my desk, fingers hovering over the keyboard, staring at the half-finished article about a burnout incident in town. The smell of my old coffee mixes with the faint scent of ink and paper. It's not the kind of story I want to be writing, but right now, it's all I have.

My foot taps restlessly against the wooden floor. Luna still isn't back. And until she is, I won't know if I got the promotion. Adrian's words aren't lost on me. What if she does give it to Tannis or someone else? The thought makes my stomach twist with anxiety because I don't know what I'll do.

Violet strolls over. "You ready for a break?"

I glance at the screen, sighing. "Give me a couple more minutes. I need to wrap this up, and I want to get new photos of the burnout."

Folding her arms, she leans against my desk. "Fair enough. Any guesses on who did it?"

I shrug, lowering my voice. "Honestly? I don't care."

"Not a cop, just a reporter."

"Exactly."

The office is busy around us, but my focus is slipping. My mind keeps drifting back to Luna's office, envisioning myself sitting behind her desk, assigning stories, editing pieces, bringing in something new, something different. Maybe even a new column with more worldly, compelling stories instead of mundane local incidents. It could happen. If I get the promotion.

Violet nudges me. "Come on. Coffee first, then to the scene."

We walk the couple of blocks to the diner. Inside, Genevieve shoots me a knowing look before shaking her head and turning away.

"What was that about?"

Violet shrugs. "No idea. Maybe you weren't smiling the right way."

"Not in the mood to fake one today."

We order our coffees, but as we wait, I can't shake the feeling of eyes on me. A couple of people whisper, glancing my way. My stomach knots.

Paranoia? Maybe.

"Any idea when Luna's announcing the promotion?"

I clear my throat, turning to Violet. "She said when she gets back from vacation."

I let myself drift into the fantasy of the new position again.

"Order up!" The words break through my thoughts, and I shake it off, grabbing my coffee.

As we step outside, Mia from the hair salon passes us. "You never told me you had a boyfriend." She playfully whacks my arm.

Heat creeps up my neck as confusion floods through me. "What?"

She winks and rushes off to answer her phone before I can ask anything else.

I turn to Violet. "Okay, what the hell is going on?"

"No clue, but people are acting weird toward you."

The unease follows me as we reach the scene of the burnout. I snap photos, interview a few shop owners. Each has a different version of the story: out-of-towner, a reckless new driver, someone who shouldn't even have a license. The usual mess of speculation. I write down their statements and start heading back.

The second we step into the newsroom, Olive calls out, "Oh my God, you little devil!"

I turn, whispering, "What is everyone talking about?"

Olive grins, waving her phone. "You. And the hot doc."

My stomach drops.

My heart follows.

No, no, no.

Violet steps in before I can even speak. "What? Where? What are you talking about?"

I swallow hard. She doesn't know. No one knows. Not about him. Not about us sneaking around the last few weeks. Not about any of it.

I reach for the phone, but I already know what I'm going to see. A headline. A picture.

The Naughty Doctor and the Scandalous Reporter Breaking News: Pulse Point Romance Sparks Controversy

A shocking photograph has taken both the medical and journalism worlds by storm, exposing the unexpected romance between Dr. Pierce, a physician recently dismissed from New York City Hospital, and journalist Amelia Richards. The two were caught in a passionate kiss at Pulse Point, igniting debates over professional boundaries and the risks of mixing business with pleasure.

Sources reveal that Amelia Richards, known for her hard-hitting stories, has been working toward a big promotion, a career milestone now overshadowed by the media firestorm. "The office was buzzing," an anonymous coworker disclosed.

Meanwhile, Dr. Pierce, already facing scrutiny over his controversial departure, now finds himself under an even harsher spotlight. With staff and patients whispering about his latest scandal, the question remains, will this romance survive the winter, or will it cost them both every-thing?

Dr. Whisperer.

A chill runs down my spine. The image is clear as day: me and him passionately kissing.

Violet turns to me, eyebrows raised, catching my hand, pulling me into the conference room, and closing the door.

"Girl, what the fuck?" She smiles playfully. "I can't be-lieve you didn't tell me. You naughty girl."

I open my mouth, but nothing comes out. I'm trying to process how this photo even exists, let alone how it's spreading around town.

"It's not like that," I finally manage, but it comes out wrong.

She crosses her arms with a *come on, I'm not stupid* look. "Amelia, it's okay. I'm happy for you."

"It kind of happened fast." My voice is weak.

She tilts her head, unconvinced. "That picture doesn't look like 'kind of.'"

I rub my temples. "We only just spoke about wanting to be together. We wanted to figure it out privately first. That's why I didn't tell you. I'm sorry."

She grabs my arms, rubbing them. "Don't be sorry. I'm happy for you. But now I expect a full debrief."

We don't have much time before someone finds us here, so I tell her everything quickly.

When I get back to my desk, I snatch my phone. My hands tremble as I stare at Adrian's contact. Should I warn him? Ask him what the hell is happening? The thought of calling him makes my stomach roll. What if he thinks I leaked the photo? Before I can decide, an email from Luna pops up about a meeting. The subject alone makes me feel like the ground has just shifted beneath me. ***Urgent: Need to Discuss.***

Chapter 26

Adrian

The moment I step into the hospital, I feel a shift in the air. Whispers trail in my wake, eyes darting toward me before quickly looking away. A muscle in my jaw tightens.

Nina's the first to pounce, her brow furrowed with concern as she leans in. "Is it true?" she asks, her voice laced with curiosity.

I already know what she's talking about. The article exposing me and Amelia.

I let out a slow breath, giving her a small, tight-lipped smile. "It's not like I can deny it. Not when there's a photo plastered all over the internet."

She nods, sympathy softening her features. "Sorry, Dr. Pierce. People just love gossip."

I force a shrug, mumbling, "Yeah, well, the beauty of mid-town living."

I leave before she can ask anything else, diving into my first few patient consults to escape the noise. But the unease stays with me. I pull out my phone to check in with

Amelia. She would've seen the article, and the thought of her dealing with this alone makes me sick with worry. She's been working so fucking hard for that promotion. Why did this have to blow up now?

I type out a quick text.

> **Me:** *Hey, saw the newspaper. Are you okay? Let me know if you want to talk.*

I hit send and lean back in my chair, running a hand over my face. This doesn't affect my career. My job is secure. But any chance at redemption? Shattered.

But for Amelia, it's a conflict of interest. I can't be the reason she loses everything she's worked so hard for.

My phone buzzes.

> **Keith:** *Adrian, what the hell? Call me.*

I ignore it, too focused on the fact that Amelia still hasn't replied. She's usually quick to respond. A pit forms in my stomach. The rest of the day drags. More stares, more whispers.

I can't just go home. Not yet. I need to see Amelia and make sure she's okay. We had agreed to keep this quiet until after her promotion, but now that it's out, I don't know if she blames me for ruining everything.

What if this leak means we're done?

I can't stop worrying, so I drive to her place.

The door swings open before I even knock, and my heart clenches the second I see her. Amelia's eyes are red-rimmed, her face pale and drawn. She's been crying. *A lot.*

Her hair is a mess, loose strands falling around her face, and she's wearing an oversized gray sweater that hangs off one shoulder.

She starts to fold her arms over her chest, as if trying to hold herself together, but I can't stand the distance between us.

"Amelia," I start, stepping forward and gently pulling her into my arms. She buries her face into my chest, hugging me tightly back.

"I'm really sorry," she whispers. "I don't know who or how they found us."

She pulls back just enough to look at me, staying in my arms. "Violet and the others were shocked. Everyone was. The office was talking. I couldn't even go into town because I knew people would be waiting to grill me."

"And here we thought Russell was the biggest problem that day." I try to lighten the mood.

She laughs, but it doesn't reach her eyes.

"I'm really sorry, Amelia," I say, cupping her face gently. "I hope this doesn't ruin things for you. You deserve that promotion more than anyone. What's between us has nothing to do with your career. You earned this on your own."

Hazel walks by and winks at me. "Knew it."

I swear I see Amelia's lips twitch upward for the briefest moment. It's such a small thing, but it eases the knot in my chest. We'll be okay.

I press a soft kiss to her head. Her hands still rest on my chest.

But just as I'm about to speak, there's a loud crash, followed by a raw, gut-wrenching sound that slices through the air, straight through my spine.

"Mom!" Amelia's voice is pure panic as she bolts. My stomach drops, a cold dread washing over me.

I hurry after her, stepping through the doorway into the room where my throat tightens. Her mother is on the floor, unmoving.

The world tilts. My heart slams against my ribs as I rush forward, but my feet falter for just a moment. One second. I'm frozen, because suddenly, I'm not here anymore.

I'm there. Back there.

Staring at my father's lifeless body.

No. Not now. Not again.

Amelia's sobs snap me out of it. "Call an ambulance!" I shout.

I drop to my knees beside her mom, checking she's breathing. It's there, but labored.

Her left arm lies slack against the floor, and her face droops on one side. "This isn't just her AFib. I think she's having a stroke."

Hazel appears in the doorway holding Felix, the other kids behind her, their faces pale with worry. "Stay back," she tells them gently, keeping them away from the scene. "Give them space."

"Can you squeeze my hand?" I ask her mother. Her right hand grips mine weakly, but her left hand doesn't move at all. Her speech is slurred when she tries to speak. The minutes stretch, and every second counts with a stroke. I keep checking her pupils and trying to keep her alert.

Finally, a siren sounds, and then heavy footsteps enter as paramedics rush in. I force myself to step back as they take over, my breath coming fast and shallow. Her mother remains conscious but confused, her left side clearly affected. They check her vital signs, do an ECG, and begin a stroke assessment, checking her face, arms, and speech while noting her irregular AFib rhythm. The kids still huddle in the hallway crying, while Hazel tries to keep them calm.

Amelia clutches my arm, fingers trembling. I squeeze her hand.

She looks up at me, eyes wide, voice barely a whisper. "Is she going to be okay?"

I swallow hard. "I think so. She's in good hands now."

Amelia nods, but she doesn't let go of me. And I don't let go of her.

Not this time.

"You go with your mom. I'll stay here and take care of everyone." My voice is steady, even though my insides are anything but.

Amelia hesitates, her grip tightening around her phone. "Are you sure?"

"Yes. Go. Keep me updated."

She nods, then grabs her purse and hurries after the paramedics, following her mother as they wheel her out on a stretcher. The door clicks shut behind her, and the silence that follows is deafening.

Beside me, Hazel lets out a choked sob. Her small shoulders tremble, her face streaked with tears. I open my arms, and she falls into me, burying her face in my chest. I hold her tight, rubbing slow circles on her back. "It's going to be alright," I whisper, even though I don't know if it's true. Fuck, I hope it is.

Her breathing evens out after a moment, though I can still feel the occasional shudder. I pull back slightly and rest my hand on top of Hazel's shoulder. "How about we play a board game with everyone? It'll keep our minds busy."

Hazel sniffles and wipes her eyes, and when she looks up at me, I see myself in her gaze. The same worry, the same helplessness.

My phone vibrates in my pocket.

Amelia: *They're taking her to another town. Stroke center.*

That's good. It means specialized care and interventions. But it also means the damage could be significant. I quickly type back.

Me: *Kids are fine. Felix is calm, and the rest are about to play Uno.*

I look around the living room, where Hazel has gathered everyone.

"Is Mom going to be okay?" Sofia asks.

Hazel shuffles toward her. "The doctors are taking really good care of her. She's in the best place right now." She glances at me, and I nod, needing to keep it simple until we know more.

A moment later, she replies.

Amelia: *Thank you.*

I let out a deep breath, but the tension in my chest doesn't ease. My phone vibrates in my hand: Keith.

Fuck! I completely forgot to update him.

"Hey, Keith," I answer.

"Are you still at work?" His voice is casual, but there's an edge of curiosity.

"No, I came to check on Amelia."

"Yeah, I figured."

I rub a hand over my face, lowering my voice as I step away from the living room. Hazel's at the coffee table, dealing out UNO cards for the kids. "Her mom collapsed. Paramedics took her to a stroke center."

Silence. Then a sharp inhale. "Damn it." He pauses. "What can I do to help?"

I glance at Hazel, her expression tired but focused on the game.

"Can you bring some dinner? I'm watching the kids, and I have no idea if they've eaten."

"Done. I'll be there soon."

I hang up and force a breath before sitting down on the floor with Hazel and the others. Within minutes, I'm getting my ass handed to me by a bunch of kids.

By the time Keith arrives, takeout bags in hand, the place turns into utter chaos. Kids arguing over food, trading bites, and laughing for the first time all night. It's a welcome distraction.

When things settle, and the kids start getting ready for bed, my phone buzzes again. Amelia.

I step into the hallway and answer immediately. "Hey."

"Hi." She sounds completely drained.

"What's happening?" My heart pounds as I brace myself for the worst.

"She had a stroke. But we got her here in time. They treated her fast, and the doctors think she's going to be okay."

The tightness in my chest finally loosens a little. Thank God. Her story isn't going to end like mine.

"That's great news."

"Yeah." She sighs. "I'll stay until they kick me out."

"Everything here is taken care of. Have you eaten?"

"No. I'm not hungry." She sounds exhausted.

I get it. When you're running on stress and adrenaline, food is the last thing on your mind. But she needs to take care of herself.

"I know you're not, but you need to eat something. Even just a sandwich."

"Maybe later," she says softly. "Adrian... thank you. For everything today. For being there for my family when—" Her voice cracks slightly.

"You don't need to thank me," I tell her. "I'm just glad your mom's okay."

"I should go. The doctor is due back soon."

"Call me if you need anything. Anything at all."

"I will."

CHAPTER 27

AMELIA

THREE DAYS LATER, I sit by Mom's hospital bed, reading a fashion magazine I found in the patient lounge with the steady beep of the monitors filling the room. Mom looks better today. Her color is returning to her cheeks, and when she squeezes my hand, her fingers are warmer than they've been. I've been staying all day, only leaving when the visiting hours end. Adrian texts me every morning and night, checking in on both of us, but I haven't had the energy to do more than send brief updates. I miss talking to him properly. At first, I think I can manage everything with the help of my sisters, Hazel and Aurora. Aurora drove down as soon as I call her.

Offers pour in from neighbors, from the people around town, from well-meaning friends, but I can't bring myself to accept them. I need to handle this myself. I need to know that I can handle everything without falling apart. If I can't manage this crisis, how can I prove I'm ready for bigger responsibilities? How can I show that I'm leadership material when I'm barely keeping my head above water?

But eventually, reality hits: I can't take care of the house and my siblings from here. And as difficult as it is at first, allowing more people in when I know this is my responsibility, I let them help.

Mom's getting stronger, though. Every day, she looks more like the woman I remember. I hold on to hope that when she finally walks through the front door, she'll be her old self again—healthy, happy, and whole.

A knock sounds, and a nurse walks in holding a care package. I close the magazine and rise to take it from her. As I bring it to Mom, she smiles.

"Luna said she was having something delivered," I say, looking over the items in the box, including chocolate, slippers, lip balm, hand cream, eye masks, a crossword book, gift cards, and herbal tea.

"It's not from Luna."

My eyebrows pinch together. "It's not?" I look up, meeting Mom's gaze.

"It's from Adrian and Keith the nurse said."

A fluttery sensation sweeps through my stomach, and I will my mouth to expel words, but I can't seem to form them. My mouth just opens and closes repeatedly. Mom doesn't seem to notice; she's too busy trying to open it, but she doesn't have the strength, so I help her.

She goes straight for the large-print crossword. I give her a pen and then sit back down, grabbing my phone from my pocket.

> **Me:** *Thanks for Mom's care package. She's already working on the crossword.* ⊠

> **Adrian:** *I'm glad she likes it. How are you?*

I swear, every time he asks how I am, a weightless feeling washes through me. I don't need to hesitate; the honesty just rolls out of me.

> **Me:** *I'm better today, feeling less stressed. Seeing Mom able to sit up independently today was a huge relief.*

> **Adrian:** *I'm glad she's getting better. I don't like seeing you sad and stressed out.*

I don't get a moment to reply before another message comes through.

> **Adrian:** *If you ever need someone to talk to, you know I'm always here for you.*

Later that week, I'm back at work while Aurora sits with Mom in the hospital, when Luna calls me into her office. I've been nervous for this moment. The promotion announcement was supposed to happen last week, but Mom's stroke pushed everything else out of my mind.

"Amelia, please sit." She glances down briefly, her tone and body language already tell me everything I need to know. My heart splinters as she continues. "I know this has been an incredibly difficult time for you with your mother's health scare. I was just at the hospital yesterday. She looks so much better."

"Yeah, she's getting stronger," I manage, touched that Luna has been visiting regularly, even though I haven't seen her there. I'm caring for the kids between visits to keep home as normal as possible.

Luna nods, her expression pained. "I'm so relieved. You know how much I love her." She takes a deep breath. "Amelia, this is one of the hardest conversations I've ever had to have. But feelings aside, I've decided to give the promotion to the other applicant."

The words disintegrate any part of my heart that's left. She's not from town, and doesn't have a family crisis taking her attention.

"I want you to know this wasn't about your mother's situation," Luna says quickly as if reading my mind. "The other applicant has more experience. I'm sorry, I really am."

"I understand," I whisper, nodding.

"Take the rest of the day if you need it," she offers.

I shake my head. "No, I'm fine. Thank you for letting me know."

I text Adrian the news as I walk out of her office feeling hollow, like everything I've worked for just crumbled in my hands. The worst part is knowing she probably made the right call, even if it breaks my heart.

Later that day, I go straight to Mom, like I always do.

"How was work?" she asks. A simple question. But a big one.

I glance away, staring at the bland hospital walls. Do I tell her the truth? That today wasn't great? That today was the day my hopes finally collapsed?

I shift in the stiff plastic chair, my back aching from sitting in it for hours every day. Mom's in a shared room, but her only roommate is a woman curled up under her blankets, asleep. At least I don't have to worry about her overhearing.

"I didn't get the promotion." The words taste bitter. I force myself to look at Mom, to hold her gaze as I say it. "Luna gave it to someone else."

Her expression softens as she grips my hand. "Oh, darling. I'm so sorry."

I shrug, pretending it doesn't hurt as much as it does. "It's not your fault. Luna had to do what was right for her business."

Mom studies me carefully, the way only a mother can. "I know it's hard. But you wouldn't have wanted the job just because you've known Luna forever, right? If she thought someone else was the right fit, you have to trust that decision."

I swallow the lump in my throat. "Yeah. I know. It just... sucks. And now, with more medical bills coming, I really needed that salary increase."

Mom squeezes my hand. "Sweetheart, you're not happy there."

The truth of it hits me harder than I expect. She's right. I'm not happy. The promotion was just a reason to stay, an excuse to keep pushing forward in a place that no longer fits me. Maybe this whole thing—the rejection—was just the final straw.

A nurse steps in, interrupting us. "I need to give her some medication before physical therapy."

I stand. "I'll step out for a bit. Be back soon, Mom."

Outside in the corridor, I lean against the wall, my heart pounding as I pull out my phone and scroll to Violet's name. My thumb hovers over the call button.

I hit dial.

Violet picks up after the first ring. "Hey, you. What's up?"

"I think I'm going to quit," I blurt.

A pause. "What? Why? I know people are talking, and I can see how uncomfortable it's getting for you. But quitting right now? Are you sure about this? Do you have something else lined up?"

"No, but I can't keep pretending everything's fine when it's not. I'll figure something out."

"What about the medical bills? You said money is tight. Look, I know it's awkward here right now, and I hate seeing you go through this. But don't let them push you out. Why don't you start looking for a new job, but stick it out while getting your paycheck? I can keep an ear out for opportunities, and we can grab lunch away from the office when you need to vent."

Her words sit like a rock in my stomach. She's right. She sees what I'm dealing with every day, which makes her advice comforting and frustrating. I just need to stick it out while looking for something new. But as I hang up and walk back toward Mom's room, I can't shake the feeling that I'm about to make a decision that'll change everything. Whether I'm ready or not.

CHAPTER 28

ADRIAN

> **Me:** *What trouble have you been causing today?*

> **Amelia:** *Only the good kind…*

> **Me:** *The best kind of trouble always is.*

I'm sinking into the sofa, the worn fabric familiar under my fingers, as Keith and I watch some sports replay on TV. The commentators' voices fill the space, but I'm barely paying attention. We've both been working hard, so there's been some movement in the practice. Keith mentioned some big changes at the clinic, and I promised to check them out.

The practice opening is still a while off, but I want to see it, to feel like I have a direction. But do I? Doubt has taken root in my chest from the way I momentarily froze with Amelia's mom. If it wasn't for Amelia's sobs, would I have moved? The way I saw my father in her. The way I failed. How can I keep being a doctor when I don't even trust myself anymore?

"Are you listening?" Keith's voice cuts through the noise in my head.

I turn to look at him. His face is lined with concern, his eyebrows drawn tightly together. "Sorry," I mutter, rubbing my temples. "What did you say?"

He leans forward. "I said, where are you? You've been a million miles away. What's going on?"

I hesitate, my stomach heavy with rocks. Admitting the words out loud will make them real. Keith's been nothing but supportive since I got here, believing in me when I barely believed in myself. What if telling him this changes everything? What if he realizes he made a mistake hiring me?

"I just... I don't know if I should keep being a doctor."

Keith's expression shifts immediately, his body turning fully toward me. The game is forgotten. "What do you mean? Why not?"

I swallow hard, my fingers gripping my thighs. "With Amelia's mom..." I shake my head as the memory hits me like a fist to the chest. "I froze. I saw my dad. It was like watching it happen all over again. Me, standing there for a second. Helpless."

Keith's jaw tightens. "That wasn't your fault."

"Maybe. But what happens when I'm at work and someone comes in thinking they're having a heart attack?

What if I freeze again? What if I can't move? How am I supposed to do this job when I don't even trust myself?" The confession burns my throat. "It's happened multiple times now. Every time, I just get stuck in my own head."

Keith leans closer, his voice steady. "First of all, you couldn't have saved your dad. He died instantly. There was nothing you could've done. You know that, deep down. But you won't let it go because it's you. If it were someone else, if it were a patient coming to you with this, you'd tell them to stop blaming themselves."

I look away, digesting Keith's words. I know he's right. I went to medical school, so I know how sudden cardiac arrest works. But there's still this voice asking why I didn't do more.

"And second," he continues, "with Amelia's mom, from what I heard, you saved her life."

"I didn't save her life. I freaked out. I checked her over, saw she was breathing faintly, and tried to keep her alert until the paramedics came. That's it. That's all I did. Anyone could have done the same thing."

"That's all you did?" Keith scoffs. "That's exactly what you were supposed to do in a home without access to equipment. And you did it. You helped her."

I shake my head, but Keith doesn't let up. "Listen to me. This town needs a doctor like you. Someone who actually gives a damn. You're sitting here, contemplating throwing away your whole career because of a moment of doubt. That alone shows how much you care," he says, raking a hand through his hair. "And let's be real, you're letting those big-city hospital guys get into your head. They didn't like the outcome, so they put the blame on you. But we both know that's not how medicine works. You can't save everyone. No one can."

My chest tightens from his words. The thing is, I want to believe him. I want to accept that doing my best is enough. But every time I close my eyes, I see my dad, Amelia's mom, patients who might need me to be better than my best. "But I should be able to."

Keith shakes his head. "That's not fair. Not to yourself. Not to the people who need you. You did everything you could. And you have the experience, the skills... hell, the heart for this job. You think I'd ask you to work for me if I thought you weren't good enough? Come on, give me some credit."

I look at him and feel a little better. Keith doesn't do empty reassurances. If he says something, he means it.

"And don't think you have to do this because of your dad, or because we've known each other forever. This practice? It's my life. I wouldn't bring you into it if I didn't believe in you."

The lump in my throat grows. I don't know what to say. Maybe there's nothing to say yet. But for the first time in a long time, the doubt inside me isn't quite as loud.

Keith's voice is low as he leans forward, his elbows resting on his knees. "I believe in you. You just need to believe in yourself and heal from the past. Remember, this town is your future."

His words land heavily, pressing against the doubts I've been wrestling with.

Keith shifts, a small smile tugging at the corner of his lips. "Also, there's a beautiful young lady who's taken quite a shine to you. That's another good reason to stay."

I glance at him, but he just stares as if I'm the one being ridiculous. "You know…" he continues, "that was something that drew me to this town. I came here with your dad because my car broke down. I met Sage. I fell in love. And now? I'm still here. This place became my home."

I watch his eyes soften, lost in memories, and for a moment, I see the love he still carries for her, even after all these years.

"I'm not saying you need to figure it all out right now," he adds. "But don't give up on your job, on love, on starting over. You're so young. You have so much ahead of you. Don't let what other people think weigh you down."

I let out a slow breath, rubbing a hand over my face. I know he's right. I shouldn't care what people think, but because I've run from one failure to the next, I can't help but feel maybe they're right to judge. "It's just… so hard. I feel like I always have to prove myself."

"No, you don't. The biggest hurdle's behind you: the hospital's dismissal. And as for Amelia. That had nothing to do with them. You and Amelia? It's nobody's business. You'll be old news soon enough. Just ignore it and live your lives."

"Yeah," I admit. "I miss her."

Keith nods knowingly. "She's with her family. She has to be. But that doesn't mean you can't be there for her too."

"I wish I could help, take some of the weight off her shoulders."

Keith leans back, studying me. "Then tell her that. Let her know she's not alone. Offer your help, your support. That's what she needs."

I stare down at my hands. "I hope that's enough."

"You two are alike, you know. Stubborn as hell. You both carry too much, convinced you have to do it all on your own. But having someone to lean on... that's exactly what she needs right now. And maybe, deep down, it's what you need too."

I rub the back of my neck, thinking. "She's dealing with so much—her mom being sick, not getting the promotion—I don't want to be just another person who needs her."

"You're not. You're offering her something she might not even realize she needs. Someone to be there for her," he says. "Just start there."

Keith had twenty-five years of a good, solid marriage. He knows what he's talking about. And if he's giving me advice, maybe I should be listening.

"Once my practice is finished," he says, "you won't be in that hospital much longer. So try to enjoy it while you can. Ignore the noise, take in the experience, and when it's time, you'll leave it behind. This town will love you, just wait."

I shake my head and get up to refill my drink. "I don't know what's in your drink tonight, but maybe you need something stronger."

"I'm just glad you're here. It's been nice not being in this space alone with my thoughts. Sometimes they're hard to sit with. Grief is a strange thing; it makes you want to hold on and let go at the same time. But having someone around, someone to cook with, talk to...it makes it easier. And I'll always appreciate that. When you do move out, I'll miss the company, but I'll be okay. Sage taught me that much."

I push past the tightness in my throat. "I was lonely too, before coming here. After losing my dad. Before realizing I had only a handful of real friends. You know, the doctor friends I thought I had? Only one checks in. The rest? Not even a text."

"It's different here. And you're not alone."

I nod. Maybe I really do have a place here. Maybe, I finally belong.

CHAPTER 29

AMELIA

I TUCK THE EDGES of Mom's blanket neatly around her legs before carefully placing the tray across her lap. The scent of warm soup and buttered bread fills the small hospital room, hiding the antiseptic smell in the air. The bright lights above feel cold, but she looks better today... more color in her cheeks. She's still weak, but at least she doesn't seem exhausted by just existing.

She adjusts her pillows with a small sigh, her movements slow. "So," she starts. "I saw the article about you and Adrian."

I freeze, fingers still resting on the edge of the tray. The words settle into my chest like stone. It's been a few weeks since the news about me and Adrian came out. I didn't want to bother her with it. I want her to focus on her recovery.

Slowly, I lift my gaze to hers. "How?" I pull my hands back, settling onto the chair beside her.

"One of the nurses brought me the paper to point you out." She continues, watching me carefully, "I've been waiting for you to talk to me about it. You used to talk to me about everything. I know me being in the hospital again is a lot to take on." She grabs my hand. "But I'm still here for you. I can still listen, even if I am still healing."

My stomach drops.

"So?" she presses, turning her head slightly, waiting for me to talk.

I swallow, suddenly hyper-aware of the quiet beeping from the machines monitoring her. "I don't know what we're doing, Mom." The words sound wrong, like I'm trying to convince myself, so it won't hurt when he decides to walk away.

Mom leans back into her pillows, her food untouched.

"Mom, eat," I urge, nudging the tray closer. "We can talk and eat."

She hums but doesn't make a move to pick up her spoon. "Alright, but have you talked to him about what's going on?"

I blink. "What?"

"Have you called?" she asks, arching an eyebrow.

I shake my head. "We've texted."

"Why not call him and ask to see him?"

"Because I haven't had time."

She shakes her head. "That's an excuse, Amelia. Come on. Even your brothers and sisters come up with better ones."

I huff out a laugh despite myself. All this time I've kept myself busy, focusing on Mom, my siblings, work, and looking for new jobs to protect myself, when really... "I guess I've been scared, if I'm honest. What if he really has pulled away?"

Mom just watches me. "Do you like him?"

"Yeah," I breathe. "I do. He's different... more caring. The way he was with you, with the family."

She smiles. "He's been good to our family."

I nod. Shame churns my insides. How wrong I was about him. How quick I was to form an opinion based on gossip and first impressions. "And nothing like I thought he was."

"No, he's not." She pauses. "So instead of making up worst-case scenarios, how about you give him a call?"

My fingers tighten around the edge of the chair.

"Just check in," she says gently. "See how he's doing. Maybe he's just giving you space. He's a doctor, Amelia. He knows people need time with their families. He's probably just being respectful."

I chew on my lip, knowing she's right. He has his own experience with a parent experiencing a medical emergency, but his ended very differently. I've been in my own world and forgot that piece of the story he revealed to me.

"Now go," she orders, finally picking up her spoon. "I expect an update when you come back."

I stand, my pulse picking up speed. As I walk down the hospital corridor, I picture him here, moving through the halls in his scrubs, that determined set to his jaw, the way his blue eyes soften when he speaks to you. *Me.* I imagine him with patients, families, offering comfort and hope.

I push through the heavy doors leading outside, wondering if it would be easier to have this conversation in person? No. He's at work, and I can't just show up at the hospital, demanding his attention, when he has patients.

I move toward the quietest corner I can find, away from nurses on break, away from curious eyes.

Taking a deep breath, I pull out my phone.

I hover over his name.

Come on, Amelia. You can do this.

I press the call button and bring the phone to my ear. Each ring stretches longer than it should until, finally, he picks up.

"Hey." My heart leaps. "You okay?"

The concern in his tone melts something inside me. "Yeah. Of course. Always checking in on me."

"Always," he says, the faint sound of the hospital in the background.

"You're at work. I should let you go. Call me when you're free."

"No, it's fine. I've missed hearing your voice."

His words are like a hug.

"I won't keep you long," I say quickly, moving my foot along the concrete cracks. "I just wanted to call. See how you're doing."

"I'm good." He hesitates. "How's your mom?"

"She's really good," I say, smiling. "Thanks to you."

"I didn't do much," he says, almost stumbling over the words. "It just happened at the right time. We got help fast. That was the main thing." This is the first time we have talked about that day.

"Still," I say softly. "You being there to not only make sure I got the right help but staying with my siblings until Aurora got there means more than I can ever explain."

"I wasn't going to leave them or you to deal with that alone."

My heart stutters as I breathe, "Thanks."

"Any news on when she's getting home?"

"Not yet," I admit. I want her home, to get back to normal again, but then I worry about what happens when she leaves the constant monitoring.

He's quiet for a beat. "Have you eaten?"

I let out a breathy laugh. "No. I'll probably just grab something on my way home. The kids—"

"I can bring you dinner."

I blink. "Really?"

"Yeah," he says, like it's the easiest thing in the world. "Your mom's been asking about me, hasn't she?"

I bite my lip. "Maybe."

"So it's not because you wanted to call." His voice is playful.

I squeeze my eyes shut and admit, "I miss you."

There's a pause, and then a soft and honest, "I miss you too."

Something tight in my chest loosens.

"Would you like to come in and see Mom?" I ask.

His answer is immediate. "Of course."

"She really wants to thank you." I exhale, pressing a hand to my racing heart.

"I finish up in a couple of hours. I'll come by then?"

"That'd be great."

Knowing I'll see him again gives me hope we'll find our way back to where we were.

"See you soon."

"I'll see you later." I can barely suppress the giddy feeling bubbling inside me.

As I hang up, hope spreads through me. My steps feel lighter as I head back to Mom's room.

When I step inside, she's mid-bite, chewing her soup-dipped-bread. The sight of her eating, really eating, without looking drained or sickly, fills me with gratitude.

She barely gives me time to sit before she asks, "Are you blushing? What did he say?"

I shake my head with a small laugh. "We didn't talk about any of the drama," I admit. "Just... checked in. And he did ask to bring us some dinner, though."

Mom lowers her bread onto the tray. "So you're starting to overthink the conversation?"

I groan, leaning back against the chair. "It's hard not to. I'm so used to doing it, but even thinking about it now, I don't know what else I could've said. Sure, I could've talked to him about all of this drama, but it felt better to do so in person. Truly, I was just happy to hear his voice."

"Well, you've had a lot of emotions these last couple of weeks. First, that article, then my stroke, and then the promotion news. Honey, it's okay that it's a lot, but you don't have to do this on your own."

I sit and think about what she's saying and realize that I've yet to really discuss the things that have gone on recently, and it's a lot. I don't know that I realized I was holding on to all these emotions until Mom highlighted them.

A few hours later, the room buzzes with quiet voices. Sophia sprawls across chairs, Atlas doing homework with me; Aurora is reading in the corner with Felix, Hazel, and Jasper scrolling on their phones, when a gentle knock sounds at Mom's hospital room door.

I turn, and my heart skips a beat.

Adrian steps inside, holding a bouquet smaller than the first extravagant bunch, but just as breathtaking. The deep reds and soft pinks contrast against the stark white of the hospital walls. He's also carrying a couple of pizza boxes, which the kids immediately grab from him.

"Hi, Mrs. Richards," he says warmly, as he steps closer. "How are you feeling?"

Mom's face brightens. "Oh, Adrian, thank you. I'm doing well, thanks to you."

He shakes his head. "Nonsense," he counters, handing over the flowers. She brings them to her nose, inhaling deeply, and I swear her cheeks go a little pinker.

A man buying my mother flowers... it's been a long time since she's had that. Since someone outside of the family has made her feel special.

It's a nice feeling.

And I love how much he cares not just about me, but about my family too.

After hugging Mom, Adrian turns to me. For a split second, he hesitates, his gaze flicking between my eyes and my lips. Then, as if making a decision, he leans in.

I don't stop him.

Our lips brush, just the lightest touch, but enough to send a rush through me. My fingers twitch with the urge to pull him back, to kiss him again, but I'm aware of everyone watching us, Aurora's shocked expression, Hazel's knowing smile, and Jasper's disgusted face. Adrian steps away, about to greet the rest of the room.

Adrian met Aurora briefly the night Mom had her stroke.

Aurora watches us approach.

"Hi, Aurora," Adrian says, extending his hand with a warm smile.

She takes it without hesitation, her own smile genuine. "Nice to see you again."

"You too," he says, letting go of her hand.

Aurora nods before Adrian turns his attention to my other siblings. "How's everyone else?"

Hazel grins up at him, adjusting her oversized beanie. "Hey, guess what? I've done a couple more places, tidying up and grocery runs." She wrinkles her nose. "Not gonna lie, groceries are the easiest."

He takes a seat, arms crossed, listening to her with a smile on his lips. The way he gives her his full attention, as if whatever she's saying is the most important thing in the world, makes my heart ache in the best way.

For so long, I felt like I had to keep my feelings for him hidden, had to downplay what was happening between us.

But not anymore.

CHAPTER 30

ADRIAN

"Where the hell have you been?" Isaac's familiar voice comes through the line.

I shift my phone to the other ear as I walk down the hospital hallway. The day's been long, and my brain feels like it's running on fumes.

"Sorry, man. Life's been hectic."

"Everything alright?" Concern is etched in his voice.

I think about Amelia's mom, the stroke, work, and the festival. How everything in my life has flipped upside down. How my relationship with Amelia isn't a secret anymore.

"Yeah," I say after a pause. "It's all good now. Just, a lot all at once."

Amelia's mom isn't my story to tell, and Isaac already knows I like Amelia. So I go with something I can share. Something he'll understand. "I managed to raise the funds to fix the CT scanner we had," I say, rubbing a hand over my face. "But we need a donor to buy a new one."

Isaac goes quiet for a second. "Wait. They've been without one?"

"Yeah. It broke down, so patients had to get sent to the next town over."

"Shit," he mutters. "We've got six here, and even that never feels like enough."

I nod, even though he can't see me. "I know." My mind flashes back to the city ward... overcrowded hallways, patients waiting hours for scans, doctors stretched too thin.

The contrast hits me harder now. How much we accomplish here with so little compared to the city, with all the resources that never seem enough.

"I'm heading out tonight. We all miss you. You gonna come back and hang out one day?" The thought of going back hasn't crossed my mind lately. It'd be like visiting a place I used to live but no longer call home.

"Not right now, but I will at some point." I glance toward the parking lot, thinking ahead. *I'll take Amelia with me. Make it a holiday.*

"Good."

Dr. Wilson's voice cuts through the hallway behind me. "Hey, I need you in my office."

"Boss man's calling," I tell Isaac. "I'll talk to you soon."

"Alright, later."

I hang up, pocketing my phone as I step into Dr. Wilson's office. The moment I do, I know something's wrong.

His face is tight as he gestures toward the chair in front of his desk. "Take a seat."

Lowering myself down, I try to steady the nervous energy filling me. My heart is beating so hard I can hear it in my ears. This doesn't seem good.

Dr. Wilson folds his hands on the desk. "So, you and Amelia raised enough to fix one of the CT scanners," he says. "Good work on that. But here's the thing, someone saw the fundraiser, saw what you and Amelia accomplished, and they want to help."

He pauses, and I can tell there's more coming.

"They were impressed at the way you rallied the town, got people on board; that got their attention. They reached out wanting to contribute." He leans back in his chair. "Then the article came out."

My stomach drops. Of course. Just when I thought I'd finally moved past all that.

"But," Dr. Wilson continues, "This person... they actually respect that you didn't let it stop you. Said they admire someone who doesn't let public opinion derail them from what they care about."

My mouth parts, and I shuffle forward in my chair. "Honestly? That's a relief to hear. So what happens next?"

"The donor wants to stay anonymous," Dr. Wilson says. "So I'll handle ordering it and working with them. But I wanted you to know. What you did mattered. It's making a real difference here. You've been a nice addition to this hospital."

I rise from my chair, shoving my hands into my pockets to keep from gripping the edge of his desk. "Thanks."

Leaving his office on a high, I walk out, shutting the door behind me. Back at my desk, I focus on finishing up paperwork, forcing myself to push the conversation aside. By the time I'm done, the hospital picks up with early morning activity; the day shift slipping in as I gather my things and head for the exit.

At the front desk, Nina looks up from her crossword puzzle, flashing me a warm, familiar smile. "Heading home?"

"Yeah," I say, adjusting my grip on my briefcase. "Might make a quick stop first, though."

"Get some rest, Dr. Pierce. You look like you've been put through the wringer."

"That obvious, huh?" I chuckle.

She tuts, shaking her head. "Only because I've been there. Go on, get out of here."

I thank her and step outside, the early morning air hitting my face. Instead of heading straight home, I drive to the barbershop needing a freshen up.

The familiar scent of shaving cream and aftershave greets me as I walk in.

Derek looks up and grins. "Hey. How's it going? Come sit, I'm just finishing up."

Nodding, I take a seat as he dusts loose hairs from the back of a customer's neck. The man pays, exchanging a few words before heading out, leaving just me and Derek.

"How's work?" He drapes the cape over me.

"Well, people around here love a good story."

He laughs, running a comb through my hair. "Town life. Everyone's got an opinion."

"Yeah," I mutter. "Sometimes feels like I'm under a microscope." I catch myself before saying more. Derek's a good guy, but news spreads fast in this place.

"Comes with the territory," he says, flicking on the clippers. "Doesn't help you're always hanging around Keith, either."

"That's true. Everyone loves Keith." I look down as he runs the clippers through my hair.

"Speaking of hanging out. Got any plans tonight? I'm meeting some buddies at the tavern to watch the game."

Even though I want to see Amelia, she said she was hanging out with Aurora before she leaves. I haven't spent any time with guys outside of work and Keith. I need to try now that I plan to stay, and this is the perfect chance.

"You know what, I should probably get some sleep first, as I just finished a night shift, but yeah, I'm in."

Derek grins. "Good. We'll grab some food while we're there."

I pull out my phone and send Keith a quick text, letting him know I won't be home tonight. The best part? I don't have work later, so I don't have to stress about keeping my head clear for a shift.

"Same cut as last time?" Derek asks.

"Yes, please."

We talk a little about sports, work, even Amelia. I try not to dwell too much on that last topic. She called me yesterday, but it was brief, just enough to remind me how much I miss her. Talking about her makes me miss her that much more, so I try to avoid it today.

By the time Derek finishes, I feel at least somewhat put together again. He dusts off my collar. "Well, at least you'll be looking fresh tonight."

"Yeah, thanks to you."

He laughs. "You need a ride tonight?"

"Nah, I'm good. If Keith's home, he can drop me off, or I'll drive. Not planning on having a big one."

"Loosening up wouldn't kill you, man," he says, patting my back. "You've been through a hell of a transition. Let yourself enjoy it."

I nod. "Maybe you're right."

When I wake from a nap, my phone screen glows with a notification. I rub the sleep from my eyes and open it. My heart lodges in my throat as I read the headline:

Dr. Pierce: A True Healer at Heart

My pulse spikes. I can already tell who wrote it.

Amelia.

She's trying to make me look good, to change the narrative. She didn't have to do this. But she did. *It's her way of owning our relationship and crossing a professional boundary to set me in a good light.*

I read through it, something raw twisting inside me.

In a world where medical professionals are often scrutinized, it's easy to overlook the ones who go above and beyond the call of duty. Dr. Pierce is one of those rare individuals. A doctor who not only saves lives within the hospital but also carries his dedication beyond his scheduled shifts.

Recently, at the home of Evangeline Richards, he showcased exactly what it means to be a doctor, not just in title, but in action. While others were enjoying dinner, Dr. Pierce was saving a life. When Ms. Richards suffered a sudden medical emergency, it was his quick thinking and expertise that prevented a tragedy. With steady hands, he assessed her condition and took immediate action, getting her the

*help she needed before it was too late. Without him, Ms.
Richards might not be here today.*

And this wasn't an isolated incident.

*Stories like these define true heroism. It's not about recog-
nition or reward; it's about instinct, compassion, and an
unshakable commitment to humanity.*

*Dr. Pierce doesn't just wear the title of doctor. He embodies
it.*

*While others may see him through the distorted lens of
controversy, I see the man who saves lives. I see a doctor who
sacrifices his own time and energy to protect others. I see
someone who deserves our respect, our gratitude, and above
all, our trust.*

*In the end, the truth speaks louder than any headline.
And the truth is, Dr. Pierce is the kind of doctor the world
desperately needs more of.*

Amelia

I read it a few times, each word sinking in deeper. My
throat tightens, but not in the way it usually does when I
see my name in an article. This time, it's different. There's
no judgment, no twisted angle, just the truth.

She calls me a hero.

I'm not. I was just doing my job. But it hits me hard
that she sees me that way, that she's willing to fight for me
when only a few people have. And fuck, when I haven't
even fought for myself.

I rub the back of my neck. It's been a long time since someone believed in me like this. Since someone looked past the noise and saw me for who I really am.

Keith just pulled into the driveway. I want to call Amelia, but this conversation needs more than a rushed few minutes before Keith barges in asking about dinner plans. This deserves a private conversation.

I pull out my phone and send her a quick text.

> **Me:** I read the article. Thank you.

I hesitate, my thumb hovering over the keyboard before I add another message.

> **Me:** Really. It means a lot.

No over-explaining. No overthinking. Just the truth.

I grab my keys and head out.

Tonight, I'll let myself breathe. I'll go out, have a drink, and for once, not overthink every damn thing.

Just for a little while.

The tavern is a mix of laughter, clinking glasses, and sports commentary spilling out onto the sidewalk. It reminds me of the time I came here with Amelia.

I roll my shoulders, adjusting my checkered shirt, the fabric sticking slightly to my back. My palms are damp, so

I wipe them against my jeans, scanning the room as I step inside.

I don't know what his friends look like, so I focus on finding one person: Derek. Lucky for me, he stands out with his height and the ink winding down his arms and up his neck. He catches sight of me first, lifting a hand and waving me over. Relief loosens some of the tension in my chest.

I make my way through the crowd, avoiding a waitress carrying a tray of beers. Derek stands as I reach the table, shaking my hand and giving me a firm slap on the back. "Hey, guys, this is Adrian, the guy I was telling you about."

The others stand, each one offering a handshake, their smiles open and genuine. "Hey, man, welcome."

"These are my buddies, Elliot, Levi, and Noah," Derek says, nodding toward them in turn. "You'll see them around town."

I take in the group, who look like they belong here, relaxed and comfortable, like they've been friends for years.

Elliot, the one closest to me, taps his fingers lightly on the table, deep in thought. He looks like someone who deals with numbers all day. Probably an accountant or something in finance. Levi, with his calloused hands and easy-going grin, gives off more of a hands-on, blue-collar vibe. Maybe a mechanic or carpenter. Noah has a steady, observant gaze. Something about him screams first responder. Firefighter, maybe.

"Good to meet you, man," Elliot says, tipping his beer toward me.

I nod, grabbing a seat. "Likewise."

"Derek's mentioned you," Levi adds. "Figured we'd run into you eventually."

It's a strange feeling, stepping into a group that already has years of history. But as the conversation flows, I realize something. I don't have to prove anything to them. They just accept me as I am. They're not asking anything of me, just wanting me to be a part of their group.

"Drinks?" I ask after a while.

"We were waiting on you," Elliot says.

"Yeah? Then the next round's on me," I say.

"Like him already," Levi says, grinning.

I wave them off and make my way to the bar. The bartender leans in, her eyes heavy with the weight of long hours, and she offers a tired smile. "What can I get you?"

I place the drink order, then ask, "What do they usually eat when they drink?"

She rattles off a few options. I nod. "Can you get that going? And an extra plate for me."

"Of course. I'll bring it over."

Heading back to the table, I slide into my seat just as the beers arrive.

The game starts, and the tavern shifts. Conversations quiet, heads turn to the mounted TVs. Flickering blue light floods the crowd, all eyes glued to the action.

"Benny boy's having a good start," Levi says to Derek.

The way Levi says it sounds like more than just being a fan.

"Wait, you know him personally?" I ask, frowning.

Derek nods. "Yeah. That one." He gestures at the screen, and I catch a glimpse of a familiar last name. Chase.

"You got a team?" Elliot asks.

"Nah," I reply.

"Well, now you do." Levi nudges my arm. "Eels. Gotta root for the blue."

"Fair enough." I laugh before taking a sip of my beer.

The night flies by with laughter, easy conversation, and the ups and downs of the football game. The beer goes down smooth, the food is better than expected, and I finally feel... settled. I never hung out with the guys at the bar like this. Never had the time. Back in the city, I worked nonstop. First with going to school and residency, then with trying to climb the ladder in the hospital. It only landed me in a place where I was not known, no sense of community, and forgotten in the blink of an eye.

But here, I've got headlines with my name in them, and no one's pushing me out. It's weird but in a damn good way.

We chat, eat, and before I know it, it's time to leave. Outside, the night air has cooled, a slight breeze sweeping through the streets. I get a ride home, and I step inside to find Keith still up, lounging on the sofa, watching the TV.

"Hey," he says, glancing up from the sofa. "You're home early."

I walk over to the kitchen and grab a bottle of water from the fridge. "I'm going to try to get back on a normal sleep schedule after my last few night shifts."

"Good idea." Keith watches me. "Realtor's set for tomorrow, to look at those houses you found."

I lean against the counter. "What time?"

"Ten. I figured that gives you time to sleep in?" Keith stretches, flicking off the TV.

"Yeah, that works for me."

As Keith heads to his room, I stay there for a minute, thinking about the house I see in my head. It has five bedrooms, a big backyard, and a big deck. I can imagine kids on a swing set out back, hear them laughing.

But they're not just any kids. They're Amelia's siblings. Hazel pushing Felix on the swing, Sofia and Atlas chasing each other across the grass, and Jasper playing on his phone in a hammock on the deck. Amelia's there too, watching them with her mom.

I run a hand through my hair. When the fuck did this happen? When did I start imagining her in the house I'm trying to buy? Her family in my backyard? In my future? It hits me then that this isn't just a silly little crush, this is serious. I see a real future with her.

I glance at my phone, wanting to call Amelia, but it's late, and she's probably in bed after being at the hospital.

Before I can decide what to do, my phone vibrates in my hand. I jump.

Isaac: *So, when are you doing this house hunt thing?*

Me: *I'm checking out some places tomorrow.*

Isaac: *I want the biggest room.*

I grin, replying.

Me: *You fucking wish.*

Isaac: *Fine, I'll take the sofa.*

Me: *No sofa. There'll be a spare room. Relax.*

I can practically hear his smug grin through the phone. Isaac's never needed an invitation to make himself at home.

Isaac: *Good, let me know when I need to put in for vacation time.*

CHAPTER 31

ADRIAN

THE NEXT MORNING, KEITH and I pull up next to the realtor at the first house, which is close to town, tucked among other homes with barely a stretch of greenery between them. Too little house, not enough space. As I step inside, the dated interior confirms what I already felt: I don't want to be this close to town. After living in the city, I need space to breathe. But also, the walls are a dull beige, the carpet worn in spots, and though the layout isn't bad, it feels cramped. *This isn't it.* And if I needed further confirmation, when I head out the back, I step in something squishy. I look down.

Fuck's sake.

I snap a photo and send it to Amelia.

Me: House one, fail.

"Yeah, not the one," I mutter, turning back toward the door before Keith can even ask.

Amelia: *A shitty one, literally. LOL!*

I clean up as the realtor locks up behind us, already pulling out her keys for the next property.

We move on to the second house, a little farther out. The drive here is better, less traffic, more open sky. The house itself is more modern, with clean lines and a fresh coat of paint. The yard is a good size—there's even a small outdoor living area with a covered patio that could be something special with a little work.

"This one has potential," I say, stepping onto the patio. I can actually picture myself here, having people over, grilling on weekends.

Keith leans against the doorframe, arms crossed. "What's missing?"

I exhale, taking in the space. "It doesn't have that feeling. You know, the one where you walk in and just... know."

Keith nods. "Like my place."

I laugh. "Exactly. Sitting on your back deck, looking out. This one could work too, but I'd have to build that outdoor space."

Keith doesn't argue. He knows as well as I do that buying a house isn't just about practicality. It's about feeling like you belong there. We head to the last house, the one farthest out. The drive is different this time—long, winding, the smooth feel of asphalt stretching out ahead, lined with trees. I can already picture it... trading in the Mercedes-Benz for a truck, rolling up this driveway, dust kicking up behind me.

As we pull up, the house comes into view. A brick structure with a pitched roof and double timber doors that look like they've weathered decades of seasons yet still stand strong. The property is wide and open, filled with greenery, bare branches from the winter, not overly landscaped with flower beds or trimmed bushes. Trees sway in the light breeze, and I suddenly feel something shift inside me.

This is the one.

I take the steps up to the front door with Keith, the wood solid beneath my feet. The realtor opens the door, and I marvel at the interior. Inside, the polished wooden floors gleam under the soft afternoon light. The walls are painted in warm tones, giving the place a lived-in feel without feeling outdated. It needs a few minor updates, but nothing major. Nothing that would make me hesitate, only things that would make this house feel more like a home.

"One more bedroom than the last one," Keith points out as we move through the space. "Something to think about."

I nod, running my fingers over the doorframe of one of the rooms. If I ever had kids, would this work? The thought flickers through my mind, unexpected but not unwelcome. I never really considered kids until Amelia. *But I want is this.* A home, not just a house.

"Four bedrooms is better," I say finally. "One for me, one could be an office, and then two for guests if they ever need to crash."

Keith hums in agreement. "Makes sense."

The living room is my favorite part. A big fireplace, the kind that makes winter something to look forward to. I can already see it: carrying wood in the back of my truck, stacking it neatly outside. The kitchen is simple and practical—nothing fancy—but I don't need luxury. And then there's the deck.

I step outside onto the wooden planks overlooking the backyard. In front of me, a view of greenery, endless trees, and distant mountains. No buildings crammed together, no city skyline peeking over the treetops. Just quiet, open space.

I can picture it perfectly: sitting here in the early morning, coffee in hand, the world waking up slowly around me. I can picture Amelia too, sitting beside me, her hair tucked behind one ear; that little content smile she gets when she thinks no one's looking. Shit, I want her to be part of whatever I'm building here.

"What do you think?" Keith asks.

I take one last slow look around before turning to him. "This is great. " I point to the yard. "The space, the land, the view. It's exactly what I wanted when I moved here. A different start."

Keith nods. "Yeah. I think this is the one too."

I turn to look at the realtor before saying, "I'm putting in an offer."

"Let's celebrate, then." Keith grins.

We drive to the tavern, grabbing a couple of drinks to mark the moment. The place is quiet, just the usual locals enjoying a slow Saturday afternoon. The conversation shifts as we settle in, Keith leaning back in his chair with a satisfied expression.

"Oh, I forgot to tell you," he says suddenly. "They've almost finished construction of your office."

"Oh, yeah?"

"Once they're done plastering, you'll have to come check it out. I haven't picked out desks or anything yet. I figured you'd want to choose what you like."

I nod. "Yeah, I'd love that."

The rest of the afternoon passes easily, the kind of rare, peaceful moment I don't take for granted anymore. When I finally get home, my phone buzzes just as I step inside.

Amelia: *Mom's getting out of the hospital in a couple days. Would you be interested in coming over for dinner on Friday night? Also, it's game night. As if you could say no.*

I chuckle to myself and text back.

Me: *I'd love to. And get ready to lose.*

The next morning, I step into the hospital and switch gears. Back to work.

My first patient is a high-profile client, someone Dr. Lowell was handling before I took over for this shift. A musician, apparently. I didn't recognize the name at first, but after looking him up, I had to admit, he's actually pretty good. Not that it matters right now. What matters is the chest pain he's experiencing.

I'm in the room with him, reviewing his EKG results and explaining the next steps. Aspirin, nitro-glycerine, but then I don't finish as his monitor starts alarming. His hands grip the bedrail; he's sweating, his face going pale. *Heart attack.*

I'm already moving, hitting the emergency call bell as his vitals plummet on the screen. The emergency alarm blares. Adrenaline spikes as I know exactly what that sound means.

A team rushes in with the crash cart, urgency in their voices.

I signal for meds while we stabilize him. There's no time to think about his file or the blockage I'd just read about; it's about acting. He's still breathing, which is something. We just need to keep him that way until the surgical team gets here.

Once we get him stabilized and the team takes over, my part is done. I watch them wheel him away, then it's back to the waiting game.

The surgery takes hours.

When it's completed, I finally exhale, rolling my shoulders as the tension leaves my body. The cardiologist confirms a full bypass was needed, but the prognosis looks good. He'll make it.

I pause in the middle of the room, looking around at the discarded trash from opening various medications and blankets, I replay the moments of catching his heart attack before it caused irrefutable damage. I suddenly realize, I didn't hesitate. Not for a second. No panic. No self-doubt. Just instinct.

When I step back into the hallway, I notice something else, too. This place feels starkly different from the city hospital. Things were quieter here, steadier paced compared to the chaos that was New York. Maybe that's what spoke to me—the settled feeling that this place has given me—the hospital, the town, Keith. Amelia. I've met people who have shown me that I don't have to walk on eggshells or strive to be something I'm not. I even feel that way now with Dr. Patel, Dr. Lowell, and Dr. Wilson as they've welcomed me onto their team.

Maybe Amelia's article helped. Maybe I just stopped letting the past define me. I'm convinced that I have moved past my past, no longer allowing it to dictate my life.

Either way, I know one thing for sure now: I don't want to leave this town. I don't want to stop being a doctor. But I owe this change to one person, and right now, I want to give her something back.

I pull out my phone, dialing an old friend.

Evan Lincoln, the owner of Lincoln Media in New York, picks up after two rings. "Well, well, well. To what do I owe the pleasure?"

"I need a favor."

After the call, I hang up, wondering if I'll hear about the offer on the house soon. If not, I'll take house number two. Build the deck of my dreams, even if it doesn't have the view to match. But something tells me things are going to work out. Everything is falling into place.

Chapter 32

Amelia

"Drive safe," I call out one last time as Aurora rolls down her window.

"I'll text when I get back to the city." She waves before pulling out of the driveway.

An hour later, I stand outside Luna's office just before my break, my palms sweating as I grip the resignation letter in my hands. After talking to Mom last night, I knew I couldn't keep working here. She encouraged me to take the leap, her exact words echoing in my mind. *"If you quit, you'll be forced to try something different."* I've been half-heartedly browsing job listings since my talk with Violet over a week ago, but between juggling everything, I haven't given it my full attention. That stops now.

Through the glass, I can see Luna hunched over her keyboard, her dark hair falling in waves around her face as she types furiously.

I knock softly on the door. "Luna? Do you have a minute?"

She looks up, and her face immediately brightens. "Of course. Come in."

Gesturing to the chair across from her, she turns away from her computer. "Is everything okay?"

I shut the door and settle into the chair, the letter burning like a secret in my hands. "I wanted to tell you in person before I hand in the paperwork." Taking a deep breath, I meet her eyes. "I'm resigning."

Luna's expression shifts from confusion to something like panic.

"Are you sure?"

I give her a reassuring smile. "Yeah. I'll do the two weeks as per my contract, but after that, I'd like to leave."

She runs her hands through her hair, something I've only seen her do when she's stressed. "Look, I'm really sorry I couldn't give you the promotion, but you know I couldn't afford to lose—"

"Luna, it's fine." And I mean it. "You must do what's right for the business. I get it. But I also have to do what's right for me."

She leans back in her chair, reading my face. "I respect that. But if you don't mind me asking, what are you planning to do?"

As hard as it is, I respect Luna; she's still family to me. So, I want to be honest with her.

"To be transparent, my heart isn't in writing stories about day-to-day things in town. I've wanted more, but I held on because I thought that a promotion was coming eventually, and things would change with that. When you went with Tannis, it really opened my eyes to the fact that I've been sitting around. I need to chase after what I want, which is fashion and lifestyle."

Luna's expression softens with understanding as she reaches over to take my hand. "If you ever need help, you know I'm here."

"Thanks. I might take you up on that."

"Good. I'd love to be there for you." She reaches across the desk, taking the resignation letter. "This doesn't change anything between us, you know that, right?"

"I know. Thanks, Luna."

"Anytime." She sets the letter aside without reading it, her eyes never leaving mine. "I'm going to miss having you around here."

I stand up, feeling the decision settling in. It's scary, but it feels right. "I'll miss this place too. But I think it's time."

Luna rises from her chair and walks around the desk to face me. For a moment, we just stand there, the change hanging between us. Then she pulls me into a hug, brief but warm.

"You're going to be amazing with whatever comes next."

"Thank you, Luna. For everything. You were how I got started in this career, and you've taught me so much."

I leave the office on unsteady legs, my heart still beating fast against my ribs. Entering the breakroom, I find it empty. I collapse into one of the chairs and pull out my phone to tell Adrian.

> **Me:** *I just resigned from Pulse Bulletin.*

I stare at the screen, waiting for his response. A minute passes, and my phone vibrates. I've never read a message so fast.

> **Adrian:** *I know that couldn't have been easy. But I really believe in you. This feels like the start of something better.*

I find myself believing that, too.

Mom's out of hospital and trying to get back to her usual self, or at least close to it. Just over a week ago, she barely had the energy to sit up in a chair, and now she's chopping vegetables, getting involved with my siblings, smiling again. It's not perfect, but it's better.

I step into the grocery store, the automatic doors sliding open, letting in the cool evening air behind me. The aisles are quiet; just a handful of people moving around.

As I grab a bag of chips off the shelf, I catch Candyce from the bar watching me from the end of the aisle, her arms crossed over her chest. "Well, well. If it isn't the naughty journalist."

I breathe through my nose, forcing a smile. "Good to see you too, Candyce."

She laughs, flipping her ponytail over her shoulder before pushing past me. Typical. This town doesn't forget anything, but at least most people aren't making a big deal out of it anymore. *Except for one...*

I turn the corner and nearly run into Violet.

"Jesus," she huffs, hand over her chest. "You scared the crap out of me."

"Sorry, I didn't mean to."

She eyes the chips in my hand. "Stocking up for a solo binge, or?"

"Game night." I shift the bag under my arm. "Had to grab some food. Mom put me on snack duty."

"Ah." She taps her chin. "I needed a few things too, so I figured I'd stop in after work. Honestly, I'm still bummed you're leaving."

"I know. But I just wasn't happy there anymore. Of course, I loved working with you and Luna, but the job itself? I didn't enjoy it. I'm ready to do something that I love."

She nods slowly, studying me. Then, without warning, she reaches out and squeezes my arm before pulling me into a quick hug. "I know, and you're doing what's best for you. But damn it, I'm going to miss seeing you every day. Who else am I going to talk to about Nell?"

As I pull back from her embrace, I chuckle. "It's not like I'm leaving the country. We can still see each other and talk. What if we set up a monthly girls' date with coffee and thrifting to catch up?"

Violet smiles. "Honestly, that sounds so perfect. So what are you going to do while you look for your next position? You could work in retail, doesn't have to be full-time."

I hesitate. I've never considered retail before, but maybe she's onto something. "I don't know. I still want to keep writing. I don't want to let that skill go to waste."

"So do both," she suggests. "Work at the shop a couple of days a week, write the other days. Best of both worlds."

"That's actually... a really good idea."

"I have those sometimes."

I grin, feeling lighter. It would let me stay close to Mom, too. As much as she's improving, I don't want her pushing herself too hard.

Violet nudges my shoulder. "So, what are you really shopping for?"

I shrug, trying and failing to look casual. "Just snacks."

Her eyes narrow. "Uh-huh. Seems like something else is on your mind. Have you and a certain doctor talked?"

I try but fail at hiding my smile. "Adrian's coming to game night, if that's what you mean."

She grins like she's won something. "Ohhh. He's coming to game night? That's serious."

"He's come to it before," I say, remembering Thanksgiving Scrabble. "We just haven't had time to catch up. With Mom in the hospital, then getting her settled at home, and him working night shifts... we haven't really seen each other."

She folds her arms. "And house hunting?"

I pause, biting the inside of my cheek. "Yeah. He's been looking."

"So he's not leaving."

The warmth that spreads through me is impossible to ignore. "No," I admit, trying not to smile too much. "He's not."

Violet's grin widens as she leans against the shelf, arms crossed. "Well, I'm glad he's not going anywhere either. You deserve to be happy."

"Thanks." Heat creeps up my neck. "I really like him."

She nods. "So do I. And I'm glad people are finally seeing the side of him outside of the New York hospital fiasco. Everyone sees what a good doctor he is, especially to our town."

I smile, the words settling something deep inside me.

Violet's eyes suddenly light up with mischief. "Hey, and maybe we should double date."

I let out a short laugh. "I actually really like that idea. But, uh, we haven't even been on a real date yet. Just us."

"There's plenty of time for that," she assures me, waving a hand. Then, her smirk returns. "Unless, of course, you want to take him back to Pulse Point."

I groan, my face burning from the memory of that disaster floods back. "Yeah, because that worked out so well last time."

She snickers. "Chances of getting caught again are probably high. And, let's be real, you could probably use a break from the headlines."

"Yeah, you're right. We don't need another headline, but even if it happens, whatever. It's a small town after all. What do I expect?" But the truth is, I don't care anymore. Not like I used to. I'm done letting other people's opinions dictate my life.

Violet watches me for a beat, then says, "Like the article you wrote about him. It was beautiful."

Something tight and proud swells inside me. "He saved my mom's life. He deserved to be recognized for the hero he is and not the messed-up version of him that I made people believe when he first arrived." I shake my head. "He works harder than anyone I know. I wanted to make sure people saw that before I left."

"Go out with a bang, huh?"

"Yeah. Literally."

She winks, and I shake my head, but inside, my thoughts are spinning. It's ridiculous how much I miss him already. We've barely had time together, but the distance feels too much. It's not just the time apart; it's the way he's in my head constantly. How even something as simple as picking out snacks for game night has me thinking about him. The way I'm counting the hours until I see him again.

My family loves him. They're excited he's coming tonight. And, honestly? So am I.

Violet pushes off the shelf. "Alright, I'm out of here. See you Monday?"

I nod. "See you then."

She gives me a quick wave before disappearing down the aisle. Once I grab the last few things I need, I head to the register. I'm still floating a little, caught somewhere between nerves and excitement, so when I notice Candyce watching me again, her smug expression in place, I just smile. A real, genuine, unbothered smile. Let her think whatever she wants.

By the time I get home, the scent of slow-roasted beef and caramelized onions hits me the second I step inside. It's the kind of smell that belongs to old family recipes, ones I'll never be able to recreate, no matter how hard I try.

Hazel has set the table, plates and silverware neatly arranged, a small vase of flowers in the center.

I narrow my eyes. "Mom, what else do you need help with?"

Before she can answer, the doorbell rings.

I freeze, heartbeat skipping, and when I turn to look at her, she's already moving past me with a smile.

I swallow my nerves, opening the door.

Adrian stands there, looking effortlessly good despite the long shifts he's been pulling. Dark gray top under a black worn leather jacket, blue jeans, hair slightly messy. His blue eyes land on mine, and that familiar heat sparks low in my stomach.

His lips curve. "Hey, Trouble."

Before I can answer, he steps forward and presses a kiss to my lips. I kiss him back, not caring who's watching. He already has my family's approval, so I don't need to hide.

Inside, the energy shifts. The moment he steps in, conversations pick up. Mom moves around the kitchen, her voice light and full of something I haven't heard in a long time.

Adrian turns to her. "It's really good to see you feeling better, Ms. Richards."

She smiles, setting down a dish. "Thanks to you and the hospital team. I feel amazing."

He nods, settling back in his chair as his hand finds my thigh under the table. His fingers graze my skin before sliding down to grab my hand. We lace them together, hidden from view, and something about the quiet little touch between us makes me giddy.

For a while, it was nice being a secret. Having him all to myself. But this? Being open, being here, being his? It's even better.

Hazel immediately starts telling Adrian about Mr. Gideon, while Sofia glances at us. Felix was chatting about Spiderman with Jasper, who's ready to retreat to his room.

Mom moves back to the kitchen, and I sigh, squeezing his hand before standing. "I'll be right back."

"Where are you going?" he asks.

"Helping Mom," I say.

"I'll help too," he offers.

I shake my head. "No, you stay here and—" I nod toward the younger kids at the table. "Watch the kids."

"They seem fine to me," he says.

"That's exactly why you need to watch them," I say with a quirked eyebrow.

His smile is amused, and as I walk away, I feel the ghost of his touch lingering against my skin. Somehow, I already can't wait to get back to him.

I step into the kitchen, and Mom is whistling softly, the familiar sound tugging at something deep inside me.

"Tell me what needs doing." I roll up my sleeves.

She grins. "Grab the plates. Let's get this moving."

We fall into an easy rhythm, moving like we've done this a thousand times before. Before I even realize it, the food is served, and everyone is sitting down, eating.

For once, dinner is surprisingly civilized. Maybe it's because everyone is too excited for snacks and game night to waste time bickering. Plates are cleared faster than usual, conversation flowing between bites. Hazel throws in a sarcastic remark about being the car in Monopoly tonight, and Atlas fires back with he'll be the shoe to kick her butt, making the whole table burst into laughter.

Even Felix helps clean up, his tiny hands eagerly stacking plates and packing away leftovers. The house buzzes with energy, the kind that only comes from a full house, a warm meal, and something fun to look forward to.

By the time the last dish is put away, Hazel strides over to the coffee table, Monopoly board in hand. "Are you ready?"

Adrian leans back slightly, looking between her and the box. "Uh, for what, exactly?"

"Our family," I tell him, dead serious, "is very competitive about Monopoly."

"Really?" he says.

"You haven't seen us in full brawl mode," I say, leaning in, trying to keep a straight face.

He chuckles, but there's a wary edge to it. "I'm slightly scared."

I start unpacking the snacks I bought earlier, spreading them out across the table. Chips, popcorn, candy: all the game-night treats. I grab new drinks, passing them around, before sinking back into my spot next to Adrian.

Leaning in close, I whisper, "Now, I know we're together and all, but when it comes to game night, you're on your own."

He laughs at that, his breath warm against my ear.

"Amelia, don't scare our guest away," Mom scolds from across the room. "I'm sure you'll have beginner's luck, Adrian."

"Ah, yes, you'll need beginner's luck if you stand any chance of winning," I tease innocently.

She just shakes her head, taking her spot as the banker. I watch her for a moment, my heart squeezing as I take in the way she looks tonight. Sitting up, rosy cheeks, the exhaustion of the past weeks nowhere to be seen. Seeing her like this, truly happy and healthy, means the world to me.

The game starts off light-heartedly, but it doesn't take long before the competitive streak in everyone, especially Adrian, kicks in. He moves forward, eyes narrowing every time someone lands on his property. It's hilarious seeing him so into it, considering a few hours ago, he didn't even know what he was signing up for.

Mom disappears after a while, taking Felix to bed. When she's gone, I glance at Adrian, smiling. "Looks like you're officially part of the family now."

He leans in, and his lips brush my ear before kissing my temple softly. "I'm honored to be."

I shiver, biting back a grin.

As the night stretches on, more of my siblings drop off, tapping out of the game and heading to bed. Eventually, Adrian glances at the clock and sighs. "It's getting late. I should head out."

I try not to let my disappointment show, but I feel it in my stomach. "I don't want you to go. I missed being in the same room as you."

His gaze softens. "It's the weekend. Can I see you tomorrow?"

"I'd love that."

"Good. I want to take you on a real date."

A real date. The words send a thrill through me. My heart thumps wildly, my pulse loud in my ears.

"More than okay," I whisper.

He nods. "I'll let you know what time I'll pick you up."

I melt at the thought of him going to that much effort for me.

Anticipation bubbles in my stomach as I walk him to the door. When we reach the porch, he cups my face and kisses me.

I grab his head softly, pulling him closer. He groans as his hands slide around my waist, bringing me against him, and for a moment, it's just us lost in a moment. My body presses flush against his, our tongues tangling. I hold on to him tighter, and a whimper leaves my lips when his teeth drag over my bottom lip as we break apart. I'm breathless, and my heart races. It's more than a kiss; it's a promise of everything. He steps back, his eyes lingering on mine as he flashes a lopsided grin that makes butterflies swarm my stomach.

I lean against the doorway, watching him walk toward his car, jeans hanging just right, the dim porch light casting soft shadows across his face. He pauses before getting in, blowing me a kiss.

I catch it, grinning as I blow one back.

"I'll see you tomorrow," he calls.

I wave as he gets in, watching until his taillights disappear down the street.

With a sigh, I close the door, my cheeks aching from smiling so much. I move to start cleaning up, but before I can, Mom reappears.

"He's taking me on a date tomorrow night," I tell her, failing to contain my excitement.

Her smile widens. "I'm so happy for you, love. He's a good man."

He is, and it'll be nice to spend some more time with him. Because after all the secrets and uncertainty, this finally feels right.

Chapter 33

Amelia

I've changed outfits at least three times. A dress, then a skirt, then linen pants, but none of them are what I'm aiming for. I want to look effortless, not like I'm trying too hard. Elegant, but not over the top. Finally, Mom suggests dark jeans and black knee-high boots, and I slip into a pair with a sigh of relief. It's the perfect balance of casual and put-together.

I stand in front of the mirror, smoothing my hands down the material. My makeup is simple, just enough to enhance my features without screaming, *I spent an hour on this*. My hair is in a half updo, keeping my look sleek and polished, but not overly done. Black boots give me just the right amount of height without the discomfort of high heels.

I take a breath. This is happening. Our first real date. He wouldn't tell me where we're going, just said to dress comfortable, which left me second-guessing every outfit.

A firm knock on the front door sends my heart into overdrive. I press my palm to my chest as if I can steady it, but the butterflies inside me are relentless. My fingers tremble slightly as I reach for the handle.

When I open the door, he's standing there on time, of course.

Adrian's dark pants fit him perfectly, and his white shirt and jacket hug his broad shoulders in a way that makes my heart skip a beat. His hair is freshly cut, neat and styled, and I can smell his aftershave. A mix of deep velvety cocoa and entirely him.

He grins, running his gaze over me slowly. "Hi."

I smile back as my heart stutters. "Hi."

"You look beautiful." He leans in and kisses me.

"And you look very handsome yourself."

Mom steps forward, hands clasped. "Have a great time, you two."

"I will," I promise, though guilt tugs as I glance around the house. It's still unsettling, leaving her alone like this. But she looks more like herself than she has in months, and that helps ease some of the knot in my chest.

"Call me if you need me."

"I will."

She waves us off, and Adrian extends his hand. As I slide my fingers into his, he gives them a light squeeze before leading me toward his car. His palm is soft and warm, like he's silently telling me he's got me.

"This will probably be one of the only times you get to enjoy this car."

"Oh? Why's that?"

"I've been shopping around for trucks. Decided it's time to fully commit."

I turn to him with a teasing grin. "I can see you in a truck."

My mind flickers to an image of him with an elbow out the window, wind ruffling his hair, looking like a lumberjack, even though he's a doctor. His solid jaw, the way his strong hands grip the wheel. *Yeah, that suits him.*

As we reach the car, he opens the door for me like a gentleman, and I slide inside. Before I can even adjust my coat, he's already jogging around to the driver's side, slipping in with an easy confidence.

"So." I buckle my seatbelt. "Where are we going?"

"Not telling." He winks.

"There aren't that many places around here. I could just guess."

"You could," he says, pulling out of the driveway. "But where's the fun in that?"

"I'll figure it out soon enough."

His lips quirk in amusement.

A few minutes later, I do exactly that. My mouth parts as we pull up in front of the new town restaurant. Pulse & Co. "How'd you get a reservation here?" The waitlist is threemonths long.

He smirks. "I have my ways."

I shoot him a look. "You're not doing anything illegal, are you? Because I really don't need to end up in the headlines again."

He laughs. "No, I promise. Definitely not illegal."

"Good."

Before I can open my door, he's already there, pulling it open. His hand extends toward me, and I take it, enjoying the comfort of his fingers lacing through mine as we step onto the sidewalk.

"This is nice," I whisper. "No secrets. No hiding. No worrying about tomorrow's headlines."

He squeezes my hand. "I don't care what they say. Let them write whatever they want about us. We know the truth. That's all that matters."

I tilt my head up to look at him, my chest tightening at the sincerity in his gaze. "That's why I wrote that piece," I say softly. "I wanted people to see you the way I do. You deserve that."

"Thank you," he rasps as his blue eyes darken, and before I can say anything else, he pauses right there on the sidewalk, cupping my face and pressing his lips to mine.

It's brief, but God, it's everything. Heat floods through me, and for a second, I forget where we are, forget that people might be watching. It's just us.

"We should go inside before we skip dinner entirely," he says, the words ghosting over my lips.

"Probably a good idea," I say, still feeling the aftereffects of the pressure of his lips on mine.

We step inside the restaurant, where we're welcomed by soft conversations and the clinking of silverware. The smell of butter, garlic, and onions makes my stomach grumble. Warm lights shine over the wooden tables, and a fireplace in the corner adds a cozy atmosphere.

Our table is by the window, offering a view of the open field. Even though the deck outside has heaters, the chill in the air and the approaching threat of rain have kept everyone indoors. It works in our favor. No one can block our view.

We settle into our seats, ordering drinks first. The server gives us a few minutes to look over the menu, but my attention is already elsewhere.

The car ride was filled with easy conversation about Mom, work, but now, in the quiet space, I can finally ask what's been on my mind. "Have you heard anything about the house?"

Adrian sits up straighter, a spark of excitement in his eyes. "So, I want to start off this night with adding another reason to celebrate. They accepted my offer. Quick turnaround to close, too, so I'll be out of Keith's place at the end of the month."

I smile with genuine happiness for him. "That's amazing."

"I'll have to get the rest of my stuff delivered from storage. Probably order some new furniture, too. Honestly, my old taste doesn't really match who I am now." He plays with the condensation on his water glass. "I feel like I'm a different version of myself. So I want my home to reflect that."

I tilt my head, studying him. "That's a good way to look at it." The way he talks about reinventing himself, choosing to be different, makes me wonder about the life he left behind. Watching him get excited about staying here should make me feel secure, but it stirs up a questions that I've been mulling over for a while. "Can I ask you something?"

"Of course."

I lean in. "Would you ever consider going back?"

His brows draw together slightly. "Back where?"

"Home. To where you used to live. New York."

"No." His answer is immediate. Then, softer, "Are you asking because you think I'm staying here just because of you?"

I hesitate, feeling heat rise in my cheeks. "No, I'm just curious."

"I mean, you're one of the best things about being here." His lips curve. "You're blushing."

I cover my face with my hands.

He reaches across the table, his fingers brushing mine. "I'm not staying just for you," he says, his tone serious again. "But I'd be lying if I said you weren't a damn good reason to stay."

My heart swells. No one's ever made me feel this wanted or taken care of before.

I take a sip of water, trying to cool the warmth spreading through me. "I could never move away from my family," I admit. "Even though my mom's doing better, it still feels too risky. She's got a lot to handle, and I don't want to add to her stress."

"I get that," he says, nodding. "The kids, too. There's a lot of you."

I let out a small laugh. "Yeah, there is."

He pauses, his eyes searching mine. "But quitting your job... that was huge. Are you okay? How are you feeling about it now?"

I drop my gaze to my napkin. "I couldn't stay there any longer, writing the same mind-numbing articles day in and day out. I love Luna, but I was missing something. Something exciting, challenging." I glance up at him. "And since quitting? I actually feel happy. I should be scared, right?"

"Not necessarily. It was your choice. That makes a huge difference."

"What do you mean?"

He leans back, stretching his arm over the back of the chair. "Well, when I had to start over, it wasn't my choice. I was dismissed. It forced me into a whole new life. But you? You took control. You chose to change things. That's powerful."

I mull over his words, letting them sink in. Maybe he's right. Maybe I am in control of my own life more than I ever realized, and that feels liberating.

"I hope so," I murmur. "I have a couple of ideas floating around in my head about what's next."

I'm excited and terrified about my options. I expect him to ask for specific details, or offer advice, which I'd welcome.

Adrian's eyes spark with something unreadable. "Well, I can give you another option to throw in the mix."

I perk up. "Oh?"

He shifts forward, fingers tracing circles on the table. "I've been itching to tell you this, but I wanted to tell you in person."

Before I can ask, the server returns.

"Sorry to interrupt. Can I take your order?"

I glance at the menu, then at Adrian. "Honestly, just order whatever you think is good. I'll eat anything."

His mouth twitches in amusement. "Dangerous thing to say."

"I trust you."

Something flickers across his expression at that, but he doesn't comment. Instead, he rattles off a couple of items, and we agree to start there, with dessert to follow later.

Once the server leaves, he turns his attention back to me. "As I was saying, I have a friend who might have an opportunity for you."

My breath catches. "Wait, what?"

"I've mentioned him before. His name is Evan, and owns Lincoln Media in New York, and there's an opening for a remote position."

Eyes widening, I can barely grasp what he's saying. "You're kidding?"

He shakes his head. "Nope. It's in fashion, which I figured might be up your alley. It's city-based, but you can work from home."

"This sounds... way too good to be true."

He shrugs, smiling. "I mean, yeah, the job is real. Whether it's the right fit for you, that's up to you. But I figured you might be interested. He told me to pass his information to you so that you can reach out."

I stare at him, stunned. "You did that for me?"

His fingers brush over mine again; a soft, reassuring touch. "Of course."

Emotion wells in my throat, making it hard for me to breathe. "That's really kind of you," I say. "And if I can work from home and write about fashion? That would be amazing."

We sit back as the first round of food arrives: bruschetta with goat cheese and fig jam that's all locally produced.

We dig in, and I notice Adrian seems more relaxed here than I've seen him in a while. The light softens his features, and I forget about anyone else in the room. After a few bites, I ask, "So, how's work?"

He runs a hand through his hair. "Things are actually good. The people are decent... some keep to themselves, but there are a few who've been really welcoming."

"That's good," I say, genuinely happy for him. "Are you finally feeling settled?"

He hesitates, then nods. "Actually... yeah. And something big happened the other day."

I lean in. "Tell me."

He meets my eyes, something intense flickering there. "I had an emergency case... a heart attack. And I handled it. No hesitation. Just got in there, took control, and helped." His fingers tighten around his glass. "I haven't told you this, but your mom helped me a lot with moving forward after my dad passed. Because of her, I was able to confront my fear, let it go, and just focus on doing my job again. And it felt good. Really good."

I reach across the table, and he releases his glass, letting me hold his hand. "I had no idea it bothered you that much. You should've told me."

His thumb brushes over my skin, eyes locking on mine. "I didn't know how to. I barely wanted to admit it to myself."

And as we sit there, fingers intertwined, I realize something. I don't just like Adrian.

I'm falling in love with him.

CHAPTER 34

AMELIA

As we step out of the restaurant, the night air is crisp and laced with the scent of rain on pavement. I don't want the night to end. Not yet.

Adrian glances at me, and a broad smile crosses his face. "Wanna go somewhere else? Just us?"

"Definitely."

I let myself sink into the moment, into him. His hands find my lower back, pulling me close. I enjoy the heat radiating from his body, the steady rise and fall of his chest against mine. When he leans down toward my ear, he whispers, "I've missed being around you." His breath tickles my skin, sending a shiver down my spine.

And then, as we turn, reality comes crashing in.

Russell.

He and his crew are hanging out near the exit, gobbling loudly, their presence an unavoidable obstacle. Adrian exhales sharply. "You've gotta be fucking kidding me."

"Seriously? He really has it in for you."

"I don't know why."

But instead of puffing up and strutting like he owns the place, Russell simply bobs his head in acknowledgment. No fluffed-up feathers. No aggressive posture. I glance at Adrian. "Maybe he likes you now?"

Russell lets out a deep, throaty gobble, something between a chuckle and a warning.

"Wouldn't say that too loudly."

Still, as we move past, he doesn't block our way, charge, or flap his wings in protest. Instead, he steps aside, letting us pass without a fuss. A rare, almost unsettling moment of peace.

Once we're in the clear, Adrian slides his hand into mine, lacing our fingers together. "Let's go home."

A flicker of something dark and wanting passes over his face. "Keith's out tonight." He pulls me in closer. "I can't wait any longer to have you again. Please come home with me."

His words send an ache to my core. "Mm. I like the sound of that."

The drive to Keith's place is filled with anticipation. My pulse is erratic, my skin buzzing with awareness. Adrian keeps one hand on the wheel, the other resting on my thigh, his thumb tracing slow circles against the fabric of my jeans. Every glance he throws my way is thick with promise.

By the time we step inside, our restraint disappears.

The door barely clicks shut before I'm reaching for him, my hands fisting in his shirt, tugging him down to me. His lips crash into mine hungrily, and I lose myself in the kiss. Fingers tangling in my hair, he tilts my head back as he deepens it, stealing my breath, my thoughts. Everything.

"Fuck. I want you," he murmurs against my mouth.

I shiver, gripping his neck as he bends, scooping me up effortlessly. My legs wrap around his waist, my body pressing into his as he carries me.

I know exactly where this is heading.

And I don't want to stop.

Inside his room, he lowers me to my feet.

Only a second passes before our mouths fuse in a kiss so desperate it feels like we've been starving for this moment. I move instinctively, fumbling with the last of his buttons, yanking his shirt off, and letting it fall to the floor.

My fingers skim over his chest, tracing the hard planes of muscle, down the ridges of his stomach, a subtle tension building in my palms as I explore every inch of him.

A low, guttural sound rumbles from his throat when I drag my nails lightly across the waistband of his pants. The sound alone makes me needy.

I'm tugging at his belt, pulling at the fabric in my urgency.

"Fuck, yeah," he groans. His words send a fresh ache between my thighs.

His hands are on me, fingers curling around the fabric of my jeans, gripping tight as he tugs downward. Then I lift my arms, letting him peel the top off in one swift motion.

"Beautiful," he murmurs.

I stand before him in my black lace set, the one I picked with this exact moment in mind, hoping and praying this would happen tonight. His gaze roams over me, slow and deliberate, drinking me in like I'm something worth savoring. And God, I feel it. Even though he's not touching me, his stare alone is enough to send tingles scattering across my skin, as if his fingers are tracing the same path his eyes follow.

He stands before me in navy boxers; the fabric doing little to hide just how badly he wants this.

Stepping closer, his hand finds my hip, pulling me flush against him.

Our mouths collide again, and when we break apart, he slips my bra straps off my shoulders, his fingertips grazing my skin as he reaches behind me to unclasp it.

My bra hits the floor. I kick it aside, already reaching for him, my fingers dipping beneath his waistband, pushing the fabric down.

A bead of pre-cum glistens at the tip of his cock, and heat floods my body at the sight.

I drop to my knees, never breaking eye contact.

"Fuck," he rasps.

His fingers thread through my hair, watching my lips part and my hand grab around the thick base of him, feeling the heat, the weight, the way he twitches in my grasp. Slowly, I drag my tongue along the tip, tasting the saltiness of him, savoring the way his Adam's apple bobs as he swallows.

His hand tightens in my hair, a sharp tug that sends sparks of pleasure straight through me.

I open my mouth wider, taking him in, feeling his thick length glide along my tongue. I take as much as I can, and when I glance up through my lashes, I find his gaze locked on me, his jaw clenched, eyes dark and heavy-lidded.

"Jesus," he groans.

My lips curve around him as I hollow my cheeks and suck, my hand stroking in a steady rhythm. His grip in my hair tightens more, his other hand bracing against the back of my head, guiding me, urging me forward.

"Gonna let me come down your pretty throat, Trouble?"

I hum around him, feeling the way his thighs tense beneath my hands. I want that, but not yet. Not when there's something else I crave even more.

So I pull back at the last second, releasing him. Sitting back on my heels, I lick my lips as I watch him. His hands flex at his sides.

"I should've known you were a fucking tease."

I stare up at him.

He's hungry...

And I'm more than ready to be devoured.

"Come here. Now you'll pay."

He grabs my wrists as he helps me to my feet. His hands find the waistband of my thong, and he rips them clean off, the fabric snapping, falling to the floor in scraps.

A gasp escapes me, but he doesn't give me time to process. His hands are on my hips, lifting me effortlessly, laying me back on the bed. Before I can catch my breath, his mouth is on me, and he kisses his way down my body, worshipping every inch of me.

Until he reaches the place I need him most.

And when his lips brush the top of my pussy, I know I'm about to be ruined.

CHAPTER 35

ADRIAN

WHEN MY LIPS TOUCH her soft skin, I inhale deeply.

"Mm, you smell so fucking good."

She mumbles incoherently.

I lower my lips further down to lick her in a slow and teasing way. The one taste sends me feral, and I lick her repeatedly as I whisper, "You taste so good. I can't get enough of you."

She rolls her hips, rubbing her pretty pussy over my face. "Yesss, Adrian."

I love hearing my name in a breathy moan. My hands grip her thighs as I continue eating her.

"Don't stop," she calls out as I lift her legs up on my shoulders to spread her wider.

"Never." I bring my fingers up to her pussy and slowly enter two fingers inside. My mouth comes down on her clit, circling it with my tongue in hard circles, and I pump my fingers in and out, slowly at first, and then I go faster.

I'm dying to be inside her, but I want her to be just on the edge like I am, so we can come together.

Peering up at her to find her panting, I curl my fingers along her wall. She whimpers, and it makes my balls tighten as pleasure tingles through me.

"Are you close, baby?"

"Y-Yes," she groans, as my tongue and fingers continue moving.

"Good." I release my mouth and slip my fingers out.

Her eyes spring open, and she breathes heavily. "What are you doing?"

"I don't want that tight pussy coming on my hands tonight. I'm desperate for you to come apart on my dick."

She nods eagerly as I unhook her legs from my shoulders and put them on the bed. I quickly find my pants on the floor, pull a condom out of my wallet, rip it open, and slip it on.

When I turn back to her, she's up on her elbows, watching me, her teeth biting into her full bottom lip.

My eyebrow lifts as I pause in front of her. "Like what you see?"

She nods. "Yes, so much."

"Well, I could say the same about you, beautiful." I close the distance, climbing on top of her. Just the sight of her heated eyes makes my dick jerk.

She grips my arms, and I guide myself inside her slowly. My pulse quickens as I hold her gaze, wanting to be gentle at first, since this is only our third time together. I want to get to know her body and what she likes.

I move my hips back and forth slowly, before feeling her adjust, so I speed up, not too fast, because we're both on edge, and I want to enjoy this moment. I'm breathing hard to control myself. Fuck, she feels so perfect.

"You're incredible."

She gives me a small smile, but it fades as her eyes roll. "I'm going to come."

"That's okay, baby, come all over me. Let me feel it. I want to come at the same time."

I fuck her harder. And that's all she needs.

She closes her eyes, tips her head, her back arching as she comes beautifully on me. Her pussy clamps down, and I keep going, unable to last much longer. I'm too horny from her edging me that I pause to orgasm too, watching her eyes flutter open. She gives me a lazy smile as our eyes meet, and I lean over her to kiss her lips. "Don't move. I just need to clean up."

Once I've cleaned myself off, I head back out, and my mouth curves at seeing she's already in bed, curled up under my sheets, like she belongs there. The bedside lamp glows over her skin, making her look even more breathtaking. I smile as I step closer and slip in beside her.

She nestles against me, her warmth seeping into my skin as I wrap an arm around her, pulling her close. The scent of her hair, soft and floral, fills my senses.

"This is so nice," I whisper against her temple, pressing a soft kiss there. "Never thought I needed this... until you."

She tips her head back, her eyes locking onto mine. "What are you saying?"

I take a slow breath, my heart hammering in my chest. "I love you. I didn't think I could fall so fast, but you've been the biggest surprise of my life. Not only have I fallen in love with this town, but you... you are the most incredible thing it's given me. I've never felt lonely when I'm with you."

The three words hang between us, and suddenly, I'm terrified. What if I've misread everything? What if the way she looks at me doesn't mean what I thought it did? My chest tightens as I watch her, searching for any sign of what she's thinking. I'm about to backtrack, to laugh it off somehow, when a slow smile spreads across her lips, and she reaches up, brushing her fingers along my jaw.

"I love you too." She smiles. "I never thought I needed anyone. But then you showed up, and everything changed. I've never clicked with someone so effortlessly, never enjoyed someone's company the way I do with you. You helped me, even without realizing it. Just by being here, believing in me, you pulled me out of the rut I was stuck in. You made me see that life isn't just about responsibility. It's about actually living. I feel like my future is something to look forward to. Because I have you."

I hold her even tighter, my throat tightening with raw emotion. "So, what are we thinking for us?"

"Well, we're definitely a couple, that's for sure. I guess we take it day by day," she says softly, holding my gaze.

"My house will be ready soon, so that'll make things easier. And now that your mom's doing better, you could stay at my place more often."

Her eyes brighten as we stare into each other's eyes. "I'd like that."

"You know," I say, tracing her bottom lip with my finger. "When I first looked at that house, I pictured us sitting on the deck, having our morning coffee together. But honestly, I can picture you in the house with me."

"Really?"

I nod. "Yeah. I could just see us there, talking, laughing. It felt right." My chest softens as my heart swells, and I continue rambling. "It'll be nice. Just you and me."

I lean in and kiss her, pressing my lips to hers tenderly. Then whisper against her, "Are you able to stay the night?"

"Will Keith mind?"

I smile, brushing a strand of hair from her face. "We're two consenting adults, beautiful. We don't need permission, but I'm happy to text and ask him. But honestly? I don't want to let you go tonight."

She relaxes even further against me. "I don't want to go either."

I press another kiss to her temple, pulling her closer. "Then don't. Stay here with me."

She lets out a little laugh, the kind that makes my heart stutter. "So needy."

"I am," I admit without shame. "And I don't care anymore."

I wake the next morning to find her still in my arms. For the past half hour, I've just been lying here, listening to the steady rhythm of her breathing. I don't think I've ever woken up this content.

I'm scrolling on my phone when she stirs. Her lashes flutter open, and I smile down at her. "Morning, beautiful."

She stretches lazily, her lips curving up. "Morning. You're smiling pretty big."

"There's an article about us this morning," I tell her. "For once, it's actually a good one."

"Really?"

I show her the screen. There's a photo of us from last night holding hands, smiling. The picture mirrors exactly how I feel when I'm with her.

She scans the article, giggling when she sees a familiar name. "Russell even made it in?"

"Apparently, his silent approval was newsworthy."

"Well," she teases, nudging me. "Guess we won't be gossip material for much longer. We'll be too boring."

I kiss her forehead. "Doubtful."

I sit up reluctantly, already missing the warmth of her body against mine. I stretch before swinging my legs over the side of the bed. "Let me make you some coffee."

She hums with approval. "I might give my mom a quick call to check in on her."

"Good idea. Meet me in the kitchen?"

"Sure."

I kiss her before pulling on some clothes, walking through the house, and stepping out onto the deck. Keith's already sipping his coffee, the early morning sun seeping through the curtains. It's peaceful. But the thought of sharing mornings like this with her in my own place will be better.

"Need some more coffee?" I ask, knowing I fell asleep before I could text him about Amelia staying over.

He nods. "Sure."

As I move back inside, I hesitate before adding, "Amelia stayed the night."

Keith glances up, a grin tugging at his lips. "No problem. Am I in your way?"

I shake my head. "Not at all."

His smile widens. "I'm happy for you."

"Thanks." I move to pour two cups of coffee, waiting for Amelia to join me, and I realize something. Everything in my life feels just right.

Chapter 36

Amelia

I take a deep breath, my fingers hovering over the keyboard as I log onto the computer after working a full day at the Pulse Bulletin. My heart pounds, a tight knot forming in my chest, but I push through the nerves, trying to steady myself. This interview with Lincoln Media is a big opportunity, one that could change everything.

The name of the interviewer, Mya, flashes on the screen, but my excitement is already being overshadowed by doubt. What can I bring to the table? What do they see in me? But then I remind myself that Adrian wouldn't have recommended me if he didn't believe in my potential. And they wouldn't have agreed to interview me if they weren't open to the idea. I have to believe that I have something to offer, that I can do this. Plus, even Luna has agreed to be a reference for me, and I know that says a lot.

I glance around behind me, the space temporarily transformed into something cleaner and more professional. My mom and Hazel took the kids to the park to give me some silence, promising to keep them occupied for as long as necessary. It means the world to me.

Straightening in my chair, I tuck my hair behind my ears. I chose a black blazer over a simple blouse, pairing it with comfortable pants. Just in case they catch a glimpse of my full outfit.

This morning, Adrian had sent me a message wishing me luck.

> **Adrian:** *You'll do great. Call me when it's done. I love you.* x

His support calms me more than I expected as I reread the text. The monitor flickers, and then she's there. A woman with sleek brown hair, wearing a sophisticated long sleeve burgundy blouse. Her background is a pristine, modern office, the kind of place I imagined city offices looked like.

"Hi, Miss Richards. How are you today?" she asks, her voice warm.

I smile, though my fingers grip the armrest of my chair. "I'm good, thank you. How are you?"

"Good, good. I'm Mya, the HR recruiter for Lincoln Media. I'll be walking you through today's discussion regarding the full-time fashion and lifestyle editor position."

I nod, keeping my expression composed, even as my pulse quickens.

"I'd love to start by giving you some background on Lincoln Media, just to ensure you're comfortable with us as well."

"Of course."

As she speaks, I take in every detail. How the company was founded, their mission, their reach in the industry. It's everything I hoped for, but I listen carefully, making notes.

Then come the questions.

"Where do you see yourself in five years?" she asks, pen poised above her notepad.

I exhale slowly before answering. "Still in this town, hopefully working as a journalist on fashion and lifestyle. I'm really passionate about those topics. I think Lincoln Media has some things I align with, and if the fit is right for you, I'd love for Lincoln Media to be that position. I would love to take on more responsibility as the opportunities arise as well."

She nods approvingly, writing something down. "How do you handle tight deadlines and high-pressure situations?"

"My approach starts with prioritization. I assess what's most time sensitive and then work backward from that deadline. I track progress and I'm not afraid to ask for help or resources if needed."

She nods before briefly looking down and then back to meet my gaze. "How would you handle a situation where a designer is unhappy with the way their collection was featured in your publication?"

"First, I'd reach out to organize a direct conversation; either a call or in-person meeting. I'd listen to their concerns and explain our decision-making process. If there's a genuine error, I'd own it and discuss how we could correct it in a follow-up feature. And for future features, I'd want clearer communication, so having their input beforehand."

Her eyes twinkle with amusement. "That's a great answer."

The interview continues, flowing more easily now. Finally, she leans back slightly and offers a suggestion. "Would you be open to writing a trial piece? It would give both you and us a chance to see if this is the right fit before making it official."

I nod eagerly. "Of course, I could absolutely do that."

It's perfect, really. It gives me a chance to prove myself without the pressure of a full commitment just yet. If it doesn't work out, I won't have to feel like I let Adrian down.

The interview wraps up, and as soon as I log off, I grab my phone to text Mom to let them know I am done.

Next, I dial Adrian. He answers on the first ring.

"How'd it go?"

I laugh. "You've been waiting by the phone, haven't you?"

"Of course. Now tell me."

I pace the room. "It went really well. They want me to write a trial piece before making an official offer."

"That's amazing. I knew you'd impress them." There's the faint noise of the hospital in the background, machines beeping, muffled voices, speaker announcements. "I better let you get back to work. Just wanted to update you."

"When you get the job—and you will—now that I've got the keys, we'll celebrate."

"Definitely."

I hang up just as the front door swings open, and the kids come bursting in, their laughter echoing through the house.

Heading out of my room, Felix races past me, and my mom appears behind him, her eyes searching mine for an answer.

"Well?" she asks, her face lighting up with anticipation.

I smile. "It went great. I'm writing a trial piece for them today, just waiting on the email for the topic they want me to cover."

She pulls me into a hug. "I'm so proud of you."

I hug her tightly. I feel proud of myself too.

I spend the rest of the afternoon at my desk, the email open in front of me. My trial assignment...a feature on a new fashion line debuting at an upcoming runway show. My fingers hover over the keyboard for only a second before I start typing, the words flowing easily.

Summer Atelier Unveils a Bold New Collection.

Summer Atelier is known for pushing fashion boundaries, and their upcoming fashion show proves it again. The new collection blends tailoring with relaxed style.

Think of structured blazers over sheer slip dresses and bold color blocking that breaks the usual seasonal rules.

Textures take the center stage, with soft leather, airy silk, and metallic thread. Every piece feels purposeful, telling a story through fabric and shape.

But the heart of the show? A powerful collaboration with Karley Lincoln. Her floral artwork turns clothing into wearable art.

This isn't just a fashion show. It's a move toward something fresh, romantic, and deeply expressive.

I go on to explore standout pieces from the collection in detail, including a dark green trench coat with Karley's hand-painted peonies on the lining. I delve into Summer's background as an artist, tracing her journey from her days at school to this career-defining fashion collaboration, and then I bring everything together with a quote from Summer Atelier.

"Fashion should make you feel something beyond just looking good. Karley's work reminds us that beauty can be both bold and tender, and that's exactly what we want people to carry with them when they wear these pieces."

(Pictures here of the artists and a few of the pieces from the new collection.)

Before I hit send, I hesitate for only a second. I want them to get this article as soon as possible to show how serious I am, and how much I want this. But more than that, I want an answer. My fingers pause over the keyboard, my heart racing with the certainty that this is exactly what I want to do. I hold my breath and press send. The moment it's gone, a mix of relief and anxiety fills me. There's no taking it back now. I stare at the screen, then immediately reach for my phone to text Adrian. He deserves to know. He's been my biggest supporter through all this, and I want to share this moment with him, even if it's just the waiting part.

Later, I'm at the shops with Violet, wandering through the aisles of Pulse Boutique, a shop filled with home décor.

Something about the vanilla candles and the jazz playing overhead through the speakers just puts me in a shopping mood.

"What exactly are you looking for?" Violet asks as she scans a shelf filled with ceramic vases.

I run my fingers over a textured glass sculpture. "I don't know," I admit. "But when I see it, I'll know."

Violet raises a perfectly sculpted eyebrow. "That's very specific."

I laugh. "Adrian got the keys to his new place, so I wanted to get him something for the house. Something that represents us or him."

"Well, that's helpful." She laughs.

I sigh, shrugging. "Yeah, I know. And he's a guy, so that makes it even harder."

She gestures toward a section labeled *New Finds* in elegant gold script. "Well, Pulse Boutique is the place for unique stuff. I'm sure we'll leave with something."

As we wander deeper into the store, I find it. A piece that immediately calls to me. A framed quote that says, '*Gobble Gobble.*' I pick it up, and a slow smile spreads across my face. *This is the one.*

Violet leans in, peering at my choice. "That's... so weird."

I turn to her. "Why?"

She presses her lips together. "I mean, I just don't think it's a normal housewarming gift. But you know what? Who am I to say that it's not a good gift for Adrian?"

For a brief second, doubt flickers in my mind, but I push it away. No, I know him. He'll love this.

At the counter, Eloise, the shop owner, eyes my purchase. "What's this for?"

This is the problem with towns where everyone wants to know everything.

"A housewarming gift."

"You bought this as a housewarming gift?"

"Right? That's what I said," Violet chimes in.

Eloise shakes her head, amused. "Usually, people go for platters, candles, vases... something neutral."

I straighten, reinforcing my decision. "Trust me. He'll love it."

"Well, I'll wrap it up for you," she says with a warm smile. "Save you the trouble."

"Thank you," I say, relieved.

As we step away, Violet nudges me. "So, are you staying the night?"

I shoot her a sideways glance. "Why do you ask?"

"You know why."

"I'm staying for the weekend, actually."

Her eyes widen. "The whole weekend? You're leaving your mom."

"She insisted." I feel a flutter of guilt mixed with excitement.

Violet grabs my arm, grinning. "This is huge. When's the last time you took a whole weekend for yourself?"

I can't even remember.

"Well, it's about time you had some fun," she says, squeezing my hand.

I smile but don't respond. The thought of spending the weekend with Adrian, settling into his new space together, feels quietly perfect.

I grab a bottle of wine to go with the gift before heading back home to get ready. I dress in baggy blue jeans and a soft sweater. I don't want to dress up; I want to be comfortable. Sneakers on, hair in a ponytail, I throw my small bag over my shoulder, clutch the gifts, and head out.

"Mom, let me know if you need me," I say. Atlas is sprawled across the living room floor watching TV, but I catch Jasper's curious eyes. "I'm staying at Adrian's tonight," I add, and Hazel grins knowingly, while Sofia and Felix barely look up.

She gives me a motherly look and nods.

I drive to Adrian's, following the GPS through tree-lined streets I've never been down before. When I turn onto his block, I slow down, taking it in. His place is a brick house with the porch light on, showing off the double timber doors. After I park, I get out and walk up to the front door, which feels different now that I know he's staying permanently. But before I even reach it, my phone rings. Lowering the gifts to the step, I pull out my phone from my pocket. "Hello?"

"Hi, this is Mya from Lincoln Media."

I straighten, my heart pounding. "Oh, hi. How are you?"

"I'm great," she says warmly. "I just wanted to call and thank you for that article. It was incredibly well-detailed and impressive. I can't believe you put it together so fast."

Excitement fills my veins. "Oh, wow. Thank you."

"We would be honored to have you work with us."

I freeze. "Really?"

"Yes," she says. "When would you be able to start?"

My brain scrambles to catch up. "Uh, this week is my final week at my current job. After that, I'd be free to start."

"Perfect," she says. "I'll send over the contract, along with the list of equipment you'll need."

"The equipment?"

"Yes. We provide our remote employees with everything. A desk, chair, laptop, and stationary. The paperwork will lay it all out for you, but if you have any questions, you have my number and email."

Adrian's door opens, and he steps out, frowning. Silently picking up the wine and gift.

"That's..." My words catch, and I feel my knees go weak. "Amazing. Thank you."

The call ends, and I walk into Adrian's place, my whole body buzzing, barely able to contain my excitement.

"Who was that?" he asks, lowering the stuff on the island.

"I got the job."

Smiling brightly, he closes the distance between us and lifts me off my feet, spinning me around. "I knew it. I'm so proud of you." When he lowers me, his hands cup my cheeks.

"They're sending me all the stuff to work from home," I say, still processing. "But I don't know if that'll work long term. I might need to find a space."

Adrian's hands move to my hips. "Why don't you just work here?"

"What?"

"I have a spare room. We can set it up as your office. If they're sending everything, it makes sense. You'd be here during the day, and let's be honest, you're practically going to be living here anyway." The idea sends a thrill through me, but it's quickly replaced by uncertainty. What would that mean for my family? I've always been there to help Mom, but would working at his place, and then staying for dinner to sleeping over be too much?

I raise an eyebrow. "Oh? Is that so?"

A slow smirk tugs at his lips as he moves his face to my neck. "Yeah. Now that I've found you, I don't want to let you go." His breath is ticklish against my ear. "I want as much time with you as I can get."

My heart flutters, but I keep my tone even. "Well, in that case…" I reach over to grab his housewarming gift. "This is yours."

He grins, taking it. "Should I be worried?"

"Just open it."

As soon as he does, he bursts into laughter. "This is gold."

I laugh too. "I thought it was pretty funny."

"I love it." He sets it down on the console and pulls me close. "And I love that you get me."

I smile, resting my hands on his chest.

His eyes light up. "Let's sit out on the deck and share a glass to celebrate your new job."

We settle outside, a plate of snacks on hand, wineglasses resting on a new small wooden table between us. The December evening is cold but clear, and we've bundled up in coats. The sun is already set, and there's only the sound of distant birds and the occasional rustle of dry leaves.

I sit back, watching the view, sipping the wine.

"Let's grab a picture," he says softly, pulling out his phone, shifting closer. We snap a few selfies.

I glance at the screen, at the way we look together, at how right this moment feels.

"Perfect."

I meet his gaze. "It really is."

Then his expression darkens, intense flickering behind his eyes.

"Come here," he says.

The way he says it sends a shiver down my spine.

And I know I'm ready for what comes next.

CHAPTER 37

ADRIAN

I GRAB HER HAND and pull her onto my lap, bringing her body flush against mine. My hands grip her hips to keep her close.

She smiles. "What do you want?"

"I think you already know."

Her lips part slightly, teasing. "Then take me. Right here. Outside."

I love it when she's like this: bold and unapologetic. It's my kryptonite. Her hands slide up my shoulders as she straddles my thighs, shifting over the hard length of my cock beneath my jeans. Fuck. She knows exactly what she's doing to me.

"Take your top off. I want to see you," I grunt, trying to gain control.

"Demanding, aren't you?"

"Yes."

"Then make me."

She moans softly, dragging her fingers over my chest as she peels her top off. I watch, captivated, as her bare skin is revealed, her perfect breasts rising and falling with each breath she takes.

"You're incredible," I breathe, my hands already on her, palming her soft breasts, feeling her tight nipples in my hands.

I brush my thumbs over them, then lean in, taking one into my mouth. She gasps, arching her back, offering herself to me. I groan against her skin, tasting, sucking, savoring.

"Yes... feels so good," she breathes.

Her hips grind against me, and I can feel the heat of her even through my jeans. My self-control falls as she squirms, her whimpers filling the silent air. Moving to her other breast, I graze her nipple between my teeth, sucking gently until she moans. Her fingers thread through my hair, tugging, and I glance up and take her in my mouth again.

Her body rocks against me, desperate, needy. *So fucking needy.*

"Take your pants off. Now."

She slips off my lap, and her legs are shaky, but I steady her as she pushes her pants down. I reach for my belt, but she beats me to it, dropping to her knees.

"Let me," she whispers, undoing my belt and pulling my cock free. Her lips part as she strokes me, her touch soft, teasing. I suck in deep breaths through my nose, trying to restrain myself.

"You're going to be the death of me."

Her hand tightens around my cock, stroking slowly, making my breath hitch. But I don't let her tease me for long. Gripping her hips, I pull her back into my lap, my fingers sliding between her thighs, finding her wet. "Is this for me?"

"Always," she gasps, nails digging into my shoulders as I slide two fingers inside her.

"Fuck my hand, beautiful," I tell her. "Show me how much you want this."

She moans, rocking against my fingers, her breath coming faster. "Adrian, Oh, God." She tips her head back, exposing her neck. I lean forward to kiss her throat, tasting her, feeling every tremor as I push another finger inside her. She clamps down on me, but I don't stop as her thighs tremble.

"You're close, aren't you?" I rasp.

She nods, body tightening, but before she can fall over the edge, I pull my fingers out.

"What are you doing?" she whimpers, eyes wide.

"As much as I want to feel you come on my hand, I'd rather you come on my dick."

She shudders. "Both? Pleeease. Can I do both?"

"Fuck. With that begging, how can I say no?"

I slide my fingers back inside her, and the whimper she lets out nearly undoes me. Her hips rock to meet my hand, greedy and desperate, and my pulse hammers in response. She throws her head back, chasing the orgasm. My cock strains against my jeans painfully hard. Not when she's falling apart for me. "Adrian."

"You're so fucking beautiful when you come." I run my eyes all over every inch of her body, loving the way her skin flushes post orgasm. "But now I need you."

As the words leave my mouth, her hand grabs me.

"Fucking hell," I groan as she spreads my pre-cum over the tip.

I shift her to grab my wallet from my jeans, and she takes over, pulling out a condom, ripping it open with her teeth. The way she rolls it over my cock perfectly makes me lose control.

"Now," I growl. "Ride me."

She flashes me a wicked look as she straddles me again, positioning herself over my length. My gaze drops to where we become one as she slowly sinks down, taking me inch by inch. There's a softness in her that pulls tight in my chest. It's not just sex anymore. It's her choosing me, fully and completely.

"Fuck," I hiss. "So tight. So perfect."

When I'm all the way in, she starts to move, rocking her hips, and I grip her waist, guiding her. We find a rhythm, and each roll of her body sends pleasure rocketing through me. I hold back, wanting her to come with me, but she suddenly pulls away.

"Where the hell are you going?"

She doesn't answer, just turns around and settles back over me, guiding me inside her once more.

"Fuck," I groan, gripping her hips. "You look gorgeous like this."

As she moves, her breath shakes. I reach around, finding her clit, rubbing slow, hard circles until she cries out.

"I've never fucked like this," I admit. "Never outside. But with you... this is heaven."

Her body tightens, her moans turning desperate. I thrust up into her, deeper, harder.

"You gonna come for me?" I grunt against her back.

"Yes," she gasps.

"Good girl." I grip her hips, driving into her as her body clenches tight around me. The slap of our skin fills the air, the heat of her surrounding me, dragging me over the edge with her.

We come together, her name a growl on my lips as I orgasm. She collapses on top of me, breathing hard, her skin damp with sweat. Loving the way she feels on top of me, like she can lean on me, and she knows I've got her.

I kiss her shoulder. "You okay?"

She nods, shifting slightly.

I don't let her move away. Keeping her close, I gently adjust her so she's facing me, still wrapped in the afterglow.

I hold her tighter, grounding myself in her touch, then slowly rise, lifting her into my arms.

"I dreamed of having coffee here," I murmur. "But fucking you? That might be the best thing to ever happen."

She smiles, a little dazed, and I just want to hold on to this moment forever.

CHAPTER 38

AMELIA

AT SEVEN THIRTY A.M., I step onto Adrian's front porch. His house feels welcome in a way I didn't expect. I grip my bag a little tighter, nerves bubbling beneath my skin. Today isn't just another day; it's my first day at my new job.

Before I even knock, the door swings open.

"Good morning, beautiful." His gruff voice is still touched with sleep.

"Good morning." I grin. "Ready for me to take over your house?"

He leans against the doorframe, his gaze sweeping over me like he's memorizing every detail. "Beautiful, you've already completely won me over, and I wouldn't have it any other way. You can take anything you want."

As he steps aside, I walk in, the scent of his cologne wrapping around me. Sunlight spills through the kitchen windows, catching on the massive bouquet sitting on the counter.

"They're for you. I wanted you to have a great first day."

My heart stutters. "You didn't have to—"

"Oh, I did. It's your first day." He grins. "Leila's going to love me for keeping her in business with the most expensive flowers every time."

I laugh, shaking my head. "She's going to make you her favorite customer."

He shrugs. "I don't mind the title. I just want you to know how proud I am of you."

His hands slip around my waist, fingers firm as they rest against my lower back. The way he looks at me makes my stomach do a somersault.

"Thank you. What time are you meeting Hazel?"

"Soon. We moved it up. I wanted you to have time to settle in without me hovering." He nods toward the counter. "I grabbed you a coffee."

A to-go cup from The Cozy Point sits there, and a flutter stirs in my chest at the sweet, but thoughtful gesture. He thought of me before I even got here. He reaches out, brushing a loose strand of hair behind my ear. His gentle touch lingers for a second.

I smile, appreciating the thoughtfulness behind it.

Before I can say anything, he steps away and grabs something from the counter. One neatly wrapped gift. He turns back to me, his eyes flickering with something playful.

"I also got you this."

I glance at the gift, then back at him. "The flowers are more than enough." I'm already overwhelmed by how much effort he's put into making today feel special.

His grin widens, full of mischief. "No, no, no." He shakes his head, amusement dancing in his eyes. "That wasn't your actual gift."

He hands me a wrapped package, and as I peel back the paper, I burst into laughter. The engraved pen from the fundraiser.

"Oh my God, I thought this was for Keith."

"I made you think that. But it was always for you."

I run my thumb over the engraving, my heart bursting in the best way. "The fundraiser is what brought us closer. It's special to me," he admits. "So, when you're using this pen, just know I'm always with you."

I glance up at him, my throat tight. "Look at you, being all sweet."

He shrugs. "Well, it's you. You bring out this side of me."

I shake my head, still smiling. "I never thought I could feel like this. But I guess the right person brings out the right things."

His eyes soften. "So, you've got time before you start. Want to sit outside and drink coffee with me?"

"I'd love that."

We move to the deck, the morning sun stretching across the yard. I sink into the chair beside him, cradling my cup.

"I wonder what your first task will be?"

Excitement stirs in my stomach. "Not sure. Maybe another fashion piece, like my trial one. Or something completely different. I'm covering both fashion and lifestyle, so it could be anything."

He nods, sipping his coffee. "You'll be great either way."

"They mentioned potentially traveling," I add. "Short trips, events, Christmas parties. I'd be welcome, and they'd pay for my flights."

"That'd be good for you to meet everyone, to feel more like part of the team."

I nod slowly, turning the idea over in my mind. A few months ago, the thought of leaving for even a night would've sent me spiraling with guilt. But things have shifted. "My mom's really found her rhythm again," I say, almost like I'm convincing myself as much as him. "She's managing well, and Keith's always around to help."

Adrian watches me carefully. "You sound more comfortable with it than before."

"I am," I admit. "I think I needed to see her handle things without me hovering. She's stronger than I gave her credit for." I take a breath. "And maybe I needed to prove to myself that I could step away without everything falling apart."

He reaches over, squeezing my knee. "If you ever want to go, I'm happy to come with you."

I smile. "That means a lot."

His fingers drum lightly against my thigh. "Are you staying the night tonight?"

I hesitate, then sigh. "I'd love to, but I think my mom will want to hear about my first day."

His face brightens. "Then invite her and the kids here. We can have dinner."

"Really?"

"Why not?" He grins. "You're always welcome here, and I'd love to have them over."

The sincerity in his voice makes my heart swell. "Okay. I'll ask her."

He nods, satisfied. "I'll figure out dinner. When I get home, we'll have a big family meal."

I sip my coffee, unable to stop smiling. "I can't wait."

When I finish my cup, I stand, ready to get moving, but before I can step away, he pulls me onto his lap, wrapping his arms around me, holding me to him.

He presses his lips to my temple. "This. Us. Sitting here in the mornings with coffee. This is what I dreamed of."

My body warms all over at his sweetness.

"I feel so good here with you."

He tilts my chin down, our eyes locking. "You and me. This house. It was always meant to be."

I don't know if I believe in fate, but in this moment, wrapped in him, I know he's right.

We kiss and, eventually, I pull away, my lips tingling, and he smiles before grabbing his keys. With one last glance, he heads out the door, leaving me in his house.

I gather my presents and coffee, making my way to my new office. The space feels both unfamiliar and instantly mine, like stepping into a future I never dared to picture until now.

Sinking into my chair, my fingers curl around the engraved pen.

His house. His pen. His flowers. They surround me, wrapping me in security. A reminder that I'm not alone in this new adventure.

I blow out a breath, shaking off my nerves, and pick up my phone.

> **Me:** *Mom, bring the kids over to Adrian's for dinner tonight. Let's celebrate my first day.*

A second later, she responds.

> **Mom:** *Wouldn't miss it! Proud of you, sweetheart.*

I smile, set the phone down, and open my laptop. Taking a deep breath, I hit the power button. And then, my first official workday begins.

The first few hours are a whirlwind of onboarding. Digital paperwork to sign, training modules to complete, passwords setups, and introductory video calls with different department heads. I'm assigned a buddy who walks me through the company's editorial calendar and submission process. By mid-morning, I finally feel orientated enough to tackle actual work.

Emails flood in, the subject lines filled with possibility. Deadlines. Features. Research links. My first task sits at the top:

Spring Collection: A Fresh Start for Your Home & Wardrobe

Excitement fills my chest. It's a mix of home décor and wardrobe updates, blending two things I love—design and style. This is a total fresh start, inside and out.

Even though I don't live in the city, diving into research makes me feel like I'm right there. The energy of fashion week. The shine of new fabrics. The transformation of spaces as winter fades into a brighter, lighter aesthetic.

I sip my coffee, ready to begin. The company group chat pings in the corner of my screen, filled with other writers and editors bouncing ideas off of each other. It's reassuring, knowing I can reach out if I hit a roadblock. Which is kind, but I don't feel stuck. Not today. Because my trial article already proved I can do this. They loved my voice. My perspective. And now, I get to do it again.

I press my fingers against the keyboard. The nervous flutter in my stomach shifts into determination.

And then, I start writing.

EPILOGUE

ADRIAN

LATER THAT DAY, I slide into my new truck, the scent of fresh leather wrapping around me as I grip the wheel. I got a heavy-duty Chevy Silverado 2500HD. It's midnight blue, a color that looks almost black in the shade, but it gleams deep blue under the sun. Inside, it's all black leather and brushed metal, with a spacious crew cab that's perfect for hauling wood, groceries, or people. I've only had it for a few days, but already, it feels like an extension of me. A symbol of something new, something better. Maybe it's because I finally have my person—Amelia—back in my house. Not permanently, not yet, but I'll take what I can get.

The diesel engine roars under the hood as I rest my elbow against the frame of the open window. My other hand tightens around the wheel as the radio blares through the speakers. I'm heading toward the Richards' family home to pick up Hazel before making our way to the retirement village.

Just as I turn onto their street, my phone rings. I glance at the screen before pressing the button on my steering wheel. "Isaac. What's going on?"

"Not much." His voice makes me feel like I'm back in the city for a second. "Just figured I'd call, see what you're up to. It's been a while since we talked. How's life treating you?"

Slowing as I near the house, I nod even though he can't see me. "I'm really happy here. Things with Amelia are going really well. And I'm settling into the new place."

A low whistle comes through the speaker. "Damn, that's serious. Guess I'll have to come down, check out this place of yours, see how domesticated you've gotten."

"That'd be good."

"I've missed your ugly face."

Hazel steps onto the porch, waving to me. I pull up to the curb and shift into park. "Hey, I gotta go, man. Picking someone up to do some yard work."

"Yeah, yeah. Yard work, huh? You are getting your hands dirty?" He laughs like the idea is absurd.

"Calm down. It's for my girlfriend's sister and the retirement home. Feels good to give back, you know?"

"Look at you, all charitable. Must be that town air."

"Something like that," I say, watching Hazel jog down the steps. "Talk soon."

I hang up as Ms. Richards steps onto the porch. "I'll bring her back soon."

"That's fine, Adrian," she says, smiling. "Take your time. Thanks for picking her up."

"Anytime."

"Oh, and Amelia mentioned dinner. Do you need me to bring anything?" Ms. Richards asks.

"Nah, just yourselves."

"Looking forward to it," she says brightly. "Can't wait to see your new place."

"Thanks," I say. "And you're bringing Monopoly, right?"

"Of course."

"Mom, don't forget," Hazel calls over her shoulder as she comes to stand beside me.

Ms. Richards laughs. "I won't. Now go on, so you can get back in time."

Hazel hops into the truck, running her hand over the dashboard. "Nice ride."

"Figured it was time for an upgrade."

"The other one was a bit snobbish."

"Gee, thanks."

We laugh as I drive the short distance to the retirement home. When we step inside, the familiar scent of fresh linen and brewed coffee greets us. We check in at the front desk, then make our way down the hall to Mr. Gideon's place.

"Well, well, well," a warm voice calls out. "Look who's back."

"Thought I'd give her a hand today."

Mr. Gideon's eyes crinkle at the corners as he nods approvingly. "Good, son. Come on in."

Something about the way he says it—*son*—makes my chest tighten. It's been a long time since anyone called me that. It reminds me of my dad. I didn't garden with him, but we spent plenty of time together. And right now, standing here, I feel like he's around, watching over me. I miss him more than I usually let myself admit, but there's something peaceful about feeling his presence here, in this quiet moment with Mr. Gideon.

I shake it off and follow Hazel outside, whistling as I get to work. The maintenance isn't too bad today, just a few hours' worth of pruning and clearing, but it's enough to make me feel useful. Once we're done, we share a cup of coffee with Mr. Gideon before heading out.

I drop Hazel back home and head straight to the hospital, opting to change there rather than disturb Amelia. As I make my way inside, I nearly collide with Violet in the hallway.

"Hey," she greets.

"Are you doing the interview today?"

"Yeah, gonna get the photo and write it up," she says, then grins mischievously. "Hey, can I take a picture of you and send it to Amelia?"

She snaps the photo before I get a chance to answer, and her phone buzzes almost immediately. She smiles, showing me the message.

Amelia: *I'm jealous of you. But also, that's my favorite photo. Thanks.*

That makes me smile.

Soon, we gather to witness the hospital's brand-new CT scanner in action. Dr. Wilson greets me with a nod. "Come meet the patient."

I hesitate. "Oh, I'll just stand over here."

"No, no. You helped bring this here. They should meet you."

I shuffle forward, feeling slightly awkward but also proud. This second machine will save lives. And I had a part in that.

After talking with the patient, Violet pulls me aside for the interview. Once she's got what she needs, we pose for a group photo. She announces that the article will be up within the next twenty-four hours.

Before heading home, I text Keith, who's checking on the offices. In a few months, they'll be completed and I'll be finished at the hospital. I'm excited about. I'm ready for this new chapter.

Me: You busy tonight?

Keith: No, what's up?

3.Me: Come over for dinner. Ameila and her family are coming over. Join us.

A pause. Then a new message.

Keith: Yeah, okay. That actually sounds good.

Me: Good. See you soon.

Nothing beats a family dinner and game night. And I want this to be a thing. A real tradition. Maybe we can rotate houses. One week at Keith's, one at Ms. Richards's, one at ours… Mine and Amelia's. Because this is my home now. My town. My family. And I'm never looking back.

A few of us stick around to chat. Dr. Harrison mumbles something, and I barely catch it. "Sorry?"

He sighs. "There's a new resident starting. Dr. Thomas wants me to mentor them."

I frown. "Is that a problem?"

"I have a feeling it might be."

"Right. So, give her to someone else."

"Can't. He insists it has to be me."

I shake my head, amused. "Guess that makes you the old, wise one, huh?"

He groans, rubbing his face. "I'm not that old."

"If you say so."

I like the way he carries himself... calm, confident, like a man who's seen enough to know when to step in and when to step back. He gives off a solid, fatherly presence, the kind that makes people listen even when he's not raising his voice. And I guess if this new resident might be difficult, maybe Dr. Thomas figures they'll be easier to manage under Harrison's watch.

I pat his shoulder as I take a step back. "I've gotta get out of here."

"You're not working today?" he asks, glancing at the clock.

"No, I just came in to check out the CT scanner and, you know, get my picture for the front cover of the article. Not that it hasn't been there enough," I joke.

For the first time, he actually chuckles. "Fair point. I like you."

"Thanks." I grin. "I'll be thinking of you when I see you mentoring the new resident."

"Yeah, great for me," he mutters dryly.

I wave him off and head out.

As I drive to the store, it still hits me sometimes how different my life is now. The streets are quieter, the air cleaner. People wave when they see me, even if we've only met once or twice. I never got that in the city. Back there, it was all about moving fast, getting ahead. No one slowed down just to be nice.

But here? Here, I belong.

I grab a cart and move through the aisles, picking up everything I need for dinner. More silverware, since I don't have enough for this many people. I get a pie from Genevieve's instead of making it from scratch. I'm a solid cook, but baking has always been hit or miss for me. Why risk a disaster when Genevieve's pies are better than anything I could make anyway?

I pull into the driveway at 4:30. She's still at work in the office, so I let myself in and get started on dinner. The roast goes in first, then I chop the vegetables, setting everything up just right. The house smells incredible already... salty, buttery, and garlic.

Next, I set up a charcuterie board with all the favorites: cheese, dips, meat, and fruit.

It's stupid how much I love doing this. How much I love making a home for her.

A few minutes later, I hear footsteps. I turn just as she walks in, heading straight for me. She looks a little tired but beautifully happy, in the same clothes, and her hair messy from the day.

I open my arms, and she steps right into them, fitting against me like she was always meant to. My hands settle on her back, and hers glide over mine.

This here. This is everything.

I press a kiss on her forehead. "How was work, beautiful?"

She sighs against me. "Good. Day one done." Leaning back, her brown eyes meet mine. "And now I'm ready to eat and hang out with you and my family."

I smile, brushing my thumb over her jaw. "Keith's coming too, if that's all right."

"Of course. I assumed 'family' included him."

I pull her in again. "Thank you. I love you."

She lifts onto her toes, kissing me softly. "I love you too."

We stay like that for a moment, wrapped up in each other, before finally pulling away to set the table together.

For once, I don't feel like I'm making up for past mistakes.

I'm finally where I'm meant to be.

The End.

Bonus

Adrian

The last patient of the day finishes up, and I type out my final notes before logging out of the system. The general practice hums with the sounds of keyboards clicking and quiet chatter from the team finishing up their shifts. The faint scent of antiseptic lingers in the air, mixing with the comforting aroma of coffee that someone brewed earlier in the breakroom. My back aches from sitting for too long, my head foggy from the long shift, but a familiar sense of relief washes over me as I walk down the hall, knowing the day is finally done.

Keith's office door is slightly open, so I step in and drop into the chair across from him. His desk is cluttered with patient files, a half-empty coffee cup, and a stress ball he absentmindedly squeezes while scanning over notes.

"How was your day?"

He rubs his temples. "Good. Yours?"

"Same. But I'm beat."

Keith leans back in his chair. "Yeah, I'm tired too. We had that walk-in case this morning. Kid with the broken arm. Poor thing, but at least his mom kept it together, better than most."

I nod. "Yeah, that one was tough. Then I had a double-booked slot in the afternoon and ended up running behind. But we got through it."

"Clinic life," Keith says with a knowing grin. "Never a dull moment."

"Got any big plans for the weekend?" I ask, stretching my arms.

He shrugs. "Was gonna hit the golf course with the guys, but I don't know. Other than that, just cleaning the house, grabbing groceries. Super boring. What about you?"

I shift forward, feeling my own plans settle in my chest. "Well, it's mine and Amelia's one-year anniversary. But Amelia has to head to New York for work Monday, so she's flying out tomorrow. I booked us dinner for Saturday night at Pulse & Co because the Pulse Point Revival is playing. Other than that, I think we'll just spend tomorrow together, grab some lunch, but..."

Keith nods, then narrows his eyes. "You sound nervous. What's up?"

"I've been thinking about this for weeks, but I wanted to make sure everything was perfect before I said anything." I take a breath, gripping the arms of the chair. "I'm proposing to her tomorrow."

Keith sits upright. "You mean at Pulse & Co?"

I shake my head. "No way. I don't want to be in the headlines. I figured I'd do it somewhere more private, somewhere that feels like us. If I did it at Pulse & Co, it'd practically guarantee an article, and I have zero interest in that."

"Fair enough," he says, leaning forward. "Do you have the ring? Need any help?"

I nod. "Actually, yeah. I was thinking of setting up a picnic afterward with everyone there… her family, and you. I want her to think we're just going for coffee, a walk, something casual. Then, after I propose, you all come out, take photos, celebrate with us. I think that would mean the world to her."

Keith grins. "I'd love that. Just let me know the time. We'll figure out where to park so she doesn't suspect anything."

"Thanks, Keith. That'd be perfect."

I glance at the clock. "Speaking of which, I've got one more thing to do before tonight. Gotta go past Mrs. Richards's place and ask for her blessing."

Keith's eyebrows shoot up. "You haven't asked yet?"

"I've tried. But every time, something interrupts. And I don't want to do it over the phone. That feels impersonal and very disrespectful. Tonight's my last chance before the proposal." My stomach tightens just thinking about it. What if she says no? What if she thinks I'm not good enough for Amelia? I know Amelia would say yes regardless, but her mom's opinion matters to both of us. I need to do this right.

Keith nods. "You've got this. And for what it's worth, I think you two are perfect together."

I smile. "Thanks, Keith."

"Before you go, I wanted to ask how you're finding it here at the practice?"

"I'm settling in," I say, the words coming out smoother than I expect. The truth is, I wasn't sure how I would adjust, but the more I spend time here, the lighter I feel. "Honestly, the hospital had started to grow on me after a while, but here? It's like this place has its own energy. I feel so much happier than I ever did in the hospital setting. It's a different kind of practice, you know? In a hospital, everything's heavy. The air is thick with stress, with patients who are at their most vulnerable, along with all the paperwork and procedures. After a while, it weighs you down."

I pause, studying his face as he listens, his eyes thoughtful. He's always been calm, the one who never seems rattled, no matter what mess surrounds us. I wish I could be more like that, but I suppose that's why he's here to mentor me. To balance me out.

"I think a change and taking a new direction sometimes is what you need to make it easier. To make it all feel like less of a burden," Keith continues, leaning forward slightly. "And truthfully? In a couple of years, I won't be able to keep going. I'll need to drop my hours, step back from the managerial stuff. I need someone young, someone strong, and someone who loves this place the way I do. Someone who can carry it forward."

My heart beats a little faster, a mix of excitement and nervousness rising in my chest.

"And I think that someone is you, Adrian. I don't even need to look at anyone else. You've got the heart for it. You've always been family to me, more of a son. And that's why I know you'll take care of it when I'm not around as much. When the time comes, this place, this practice, it'll be yours."

My throat tightens slightly, the words catching for a moment as I fight back the lump forming there. He never had kids of his own. We're not family by blood, but in every other way, he's like a father. My heart swells with pride, and a smile stretches across my face.

"I've done the best I could," Keith adds, his voice a little softer now. "And I want to make sure you're taken care of. I've watched you grow, watched you push yourself. You've always had this spark, this drive. And I'm not worried. You'll take it all in your stride."

I stand up, clearing my throat, and reach out for a quick hug. This man stepped up when I needed someone most. Getting his backing on this matters. More than I expected it to. "Thanks, Keith."

"I couldn't leave this place to anyone else." He laughs lightly, and we both stand there for a moment, the unspoken understanding passing between us. It's always been like this. I don't have to explain myself to him, and he doesn't question my decisions.

I make my way out of the practice on shaky knees.

The drive to Ms. Richards's house is short but feels like a lifetime. I'm feeling the pressure, tightening my grip on the steering wheel. I park outside, inhaling deeply before knocking on the door. My heart races in my throat as I wait.

Hazel answers, her bright eyes widening. "Hey!" She swings the door open. "Come in."

Ms. Richards appears in the hallway, her face lighting up. "Adrian, love. How can I help you?"

"I wanted to talk to you about something."

Hazel crosses her arms. "Oh, come on. I want to know."

Ms. Richards gives her a pointed look. "Hazel."

I'd planned to do this properly, just me and her mom, but looking at Hazel's face, it hits me that Amelia would love to have her whole family part of this moment. Family is everything to her, and she's everything to me.

"No, it's fine," I say, stepping into the living room. "Everyone can know. This is a family question, after all."

I go inside and sit on the sofa, hands clasped, the throat thick with anticipation. "Ms. Richards," I say, looking her in the eyes, which are the same brown as Amelia's. "I wanted to ask for your blessing to marry Amelia."

She gasps, her hands flying to her mouth. "Oh, my God. Yes, of course!" Her eyes shimmer with tears. "Oh, Adrian, we've loved having you as part of this family."

Hazel claps, bouncing on the balls of her feet. "This is going to be so cool. When are you doing it?"

"Hazel!" Ms. Richards scolds, though she's smiling.

"Tomorrow. But I need your help. I want it to be special. After I propose, I'd love for you all to be there to celebrate. And Hazel, if you could take photos?"

"Absolutely." She claps. "I'm great at it."

"We just have to be careful where everyone parks," I add. "If Amelia sees a familiar car, she'll know something's up."

Ms. Richards wipes a tear. "Adrian, this is beautiful. We'd love to be a part of it."

A weight lifts from my chest, replaced by peace. "Thank you. This means everything."

Tomorrow, Amelia will say yes. I know she will. And after that, we'll step into the rest of our lives together.

The next morning, I wake to her warmth beside me, her body tucked against mine, my arm draped over her waist. She shifts slightly, and my eyes crack open, still heavy with sleep.

"Good morning, baby."

Truth is, I barely slept a wink, my mind running a million miles an hour, tangled in thoughts about what I'll say to her today, how I'll even start.

"Morning," she whispers, brushing her lips against mine in a soft, sleepy kiss that pulls me back into the moment.

I stretch, groaning slightly as I reach over her to grab my phone off the nightstand. I press a gentle kiss to her forehead, letting the moment settle into me, the warmth of her skin, the sound of her breathing. "Happy anniversary, baby."

She smiles, the corners of her eyes crinkling, her hair messy and wild from the night. It's the kind of smile that melts me, like I'm the luckiest person alive. "Happy anniversary."

"I'm just going to grab a couple things before we head out to celebrate."

She shifts in bed, the blanket falling from her shoulder, her eyes locking onto mine with that familiar, unwavering intensity. "Don't be long."

"I promise, it'll be quick," I reassure her, brushing a strand of hair away from her face. "And totally worth it." I give her a soft smile, hoping she believes me.

Reluctantly, I slip out of bed, tugging on a pair of jeans and a T-shirt. I make my way toward the door, but just before I step out, I glance back at her. The way she watches me, her quiet, knowing smile holds me in place for a second longer than I planned. She doesn't say anything more, but the look in her eyes makes it hard for me to leave. But I have to. I know soon I'll make it up to her. "I won't be long."

An hour later, I return, the car packed with everything for the surprise later. The scent of fresh coffee and warm pastries filling the air. She's still curled in bed, hair out, blankets tangled around her legs.

I hold out the cup, the croissant, and a large bouquet of flowers. The blooms are soft pink roses and white lilies, wrapped in delicate white paper and lace. "Figured I'd start the day right."

Her face lights up as she takes the flowers, her fingers brushing the soft petals as she inhales their sweet scent. I step closer. She looks up at me, her eyes still sleepy but sparkling. "You always do."

We linger there for a moment, sharing the quiet stillness of the morning, before we head to the kitchen. I grab the vase and set it on the counter as she arranges the flowers, careful with each stem. We sip our coffee, exchanging soft glances, the quiet connection between us growing with each passing second.

Once we sit down to breakfast, she hands me my gift first. I unwrap it slowly, revealing a sleek, engraved silver pen with our anniversary date etched into the side. It's simple, classic, and I know I'll carry it with me every day. "This is perfect," I say, running my thumb over the engraving, the heaviness of it feeling just right in my hand. "I'll take it to work with me."

She opens hers next, carefully peeling back the paper to reveal a mug covered in snapshots of us. Little glimpses of our past twelve months together. I watch as she runs her fingers over the glossy surface; her smile growing with each memory. "This is exactly what I needed," she says softly, as she looks up at me.

"You can have your morning coffee in this now," I tell her. "Every time we sit out on the deck together, just looking out at the world."

She sets the mug down and pulls me in for a kiss. "I love you."

"I love you too."

A little while later, coffee finished, I wrap an arm around her, drawing her close, and press my lips to her temple. I breathe her in, feeling the steady rhythm of her heartbeat, locking every second of this moment into memory.

"We need to get ready." My thumb brushes gently against her collarbone, the words tasting heavier than I mean for them to.

She tilts her head back, her eyes meeting mine with a glint of curiosity. "Where are we going?"

Her voice is soft, but there's a spark there, an eagerness, and I can't help but lean down again, my lips brushing lightly against hers before I pull back, keeping her close. My fingers trace along the edge of her jaw. I smirk, shaking my head. "Don't ask questions. Just come with me. I wanted to do something for us."

She gives me a side-eye but plays along. "What do I wear?"

"Doesn't matter. Nothing dressy."

Lately, we've been caught in routines, with me working long hours at Keith's practice, and her working from home.

"I just want one more day with you before you go." It's one night, but it still feels too long. I know she has to go. She's done it before, but that doesn't mean I want her to.

She touches my arm, grounding me. "I'm not going anywhere. It's just a night."

I nod, but I don't say what I'm thinking: that a night without her still feels like too much.

We hop into my truck, and the afternoon sun casts through the windshield, making her look even softer, even more beautiful.

The drive is quiet, comfortable. The kind of silence that only exists between two people who don't need to fill the space with words.

When we pull up, she recognizes Pulse Point instantly.

"Why didn't you just tell me we were coming here?" she asks, turning to me with mock annoyance, but her smile gives her away.

"Because I wanted it to be a surprise." I grip the wheel a little tighter. "If I told you, you might've suggested somewhere new. But I wanted to come here today. It's been a while since we were last here."

We haven't had a reason to come here with my house and us working. But today, I wanted to bring us full circle.

Her expression shifts, her eyes softening. "Oh."

I climb out first, grabbing the bags from the backseat before she can peek inside.

She laughs, her eyes shining. "You're not risking a picnic this time?"

"No chance." I chuckle. "Even though Russell and I are on decent terms now, I still don't trust him."

We make our way down to the river, the sound of water tumbling over smooth stones filling the air. My heart beats so loudly, I'm surprised she can't hear it. Every step feels like I'm walking toward the rest of my life.

The breeze carries the scent of pine and damp earth. She slips off her shoes, dipping her toes into the cool water, while I settle beside her, close enough that our arms brush.

This is perfect.

The world slows.

The river hums, birds chirp somewhere overhead, and trees rustle around us.

I look around to see if I can spot them—*our family* hidden somewhere—but I can't. I swallow the thought that they aren't here and just do what I want to do before the fear of rejection takes over. Deep down, I know she'll say yes, but there's still that tiny voice asking, 'what if?' which won't go away until I hear her answer.

After a few minutes, I clear my throat. "There's... another reason I wanted to come here today."

She pauses, looking at me fully now. I stand, brushing crumbs from my jeans before offering her a hand. She takes it, and I help her up.

Then I drop down on one knee on the rocks.

Her eyes widen, hands flying to her mouth as I pull a small box from my pocket.

"Amelia Richards," I say, my hands shaking. This is it. What I've been working towards. "Will you do me the honor of becoming my wife?"

Tears well in her eyes, her response instant. "Yes."

A smile breaks across my face as I stand.

She nods quickly, laughing through her tears. "Yes. Of course."

I slide the three-stone ring onto her finger, the center diamond cushioned by two smaller stones representing our past, present, and future. She throws her arms around me, nearly knocking me over. Our lips meet, sealing this moment forever.

Cheers erupt around us as our family and friends step out from their hiding spots, clapping, cheering, congratulating us.

Hazel snaps photos while Ms. Richards pulls Amelia into a tight hug. Keith slaps my back. Laughter, tears, joy all swirls around us in a beautiful blur.

We all spend time eating and drinking everything that I pre-packed. The kids are playing soccer and throwing balls, the others in the creek, tossing rocks, their laughter echoing through the trees. I glance over and spot Russell, standing off to the side, his pack gathered around him, watching quietly as the scene unfolds, a knowing look in his eyes. I feel a strange sense of gratitude toward him. For bringing us together, but for also not causing a scene right now and instead watching over us.

Later that day, an article appears on the front page of the community newspaper.

Doctor Pierce Makes a Bold Move: A Romantic Proposal That Has Everyone Swooning.

I shake my head. So much for avoiding the headlines. But then Amelia tugs me closer, beaming, and I realize I don't care; this is a headline I'm more than happy to be in.

I keep reading, my eyes landing on another headline that catches my attention.

Hospital CEO's Daughter is the New Resident in Town.

How much trouble can Miss Thomas, now, Dr. Thomas, get into? Always known for her intelligence and good looks, she's also known for being a bit of a rebel. So how will this next chapter in her life treat her now that she's back in town?

I hold up the paper, and Amelia lifts her head. "What's up?"

"One of the doctors mentioned the new resident, and I'm just reading about it," I say. "He has to mentor her, and it's gonna be funny because he doesn't want to. But he has no choice because her dad only wants him."

"Why?" Amelia asks, intrigued.

"Apparently, he thinks he can keep her in line. And clearly, based on this article, it's exactly what we thought... she's defiant."

"Oh, this will be interesting," Amelia muses.

"I wish I could see how it plays out. But I don't miss the hospital politics."

"But you like it at Keith's, don't you?"

I nod. "Oh, definitely. I wouldn't go back to the hospital. Actually..." I glance around at the scattered conversations and kids playing nearby, then lean closer to her. "I didn't get to tell you, because I was too busy asking everyone to come down today, but Keith asked me to take over his practice in a couple of years."

She grins, hugging me. "That's amazing. You're taking him up on it, right?"

"Of course. I love it there. As long as you're okay with it."

"Why wouldn't I be? We're a team now. What affects you affects me."

I kiss her forehead. "With you by my side, I'll be able to do anything."

She smiles, eyes shining. "I love you."

"I love you so much more."

www.ingramcontent.com/pod-product-compliance
Lightning Source LLC
Chambersburg PA
CBHW050958180726
48291CB00006B/1892